CW00405725

#tractor4gr

(May – June)

*A(nother) diary highlighting the plight of Mr H
and his desire to own a tractor*

Joanne 'New-Shoes' Hughes

Copyright © 2016

Disclaimer:

In parts, this book is based on actual events, persons and companies. Some names and identifying details have been changed to protect the privacy of individuals. Some of the characters, events and companies portrayed and the names used herein are fictitious. Any similarity of those fictitious characters, events, or companies to any actual person, living or dead, or to any actual event, or to any existing company, is entirely coincidental, and unintentional.

Book cover designed by: Nick White Writing

For my family and friends...

You can't buy love and you can't buy happiness. Seize the day and enjoy spending time with each other. Life is short and you never know what is around the corner.

(PS – still love you today Hugs)

xxx

Introduction

Greetings tractor-ites!

I am hoping that if you are reading this book then you have already read the first book *#tractor4graham*. It sets the scene as to who I am and more importantly who Mr H is.

If you haven't though and are frolicking and reading the books out of order (which is something that I would do, as I am a big frolicker) then I need to quickly run through some fundamentals.

I am 42 and live with Mr H in an old farmhouse in Staffordshire. We have been together for 25 years. Mr H wants a tractor to use on the four acres of land that we own and I have told him that if my book(s) sell(s) then he can use all the profits from it/them and have a tractor. The fact that we are on to a sequel is not boding well for him, as it means that we haven't raised enough money from the sale of the first book. We only recently bought the last two acres and are in the process of getting it fenced.

We have two Border Collies, Lucy who is 15.5 and Bonnie who is 11.5 years old. Lucy isn't sleeping well at the moment. Casper the black and white cat joined our family a few years ago and we are getting George, Chester and Cyril the Alpacas when the land is fenced and their shelter is sorted.

I have decided to name the sequel *#tractor4graham2*. I was going to name it 'tractor parts' as maybe I was aiming too high with the tractor itself. Hopefully, I will sell enough to get him a steering wheel, or maybe a big wheel so that he can play 'brum-brum' with them in the garden and pretend that he has a tractor. This book is a continuation of the tales in the first book and therefore you need to understand some of what has happened so far.

Mr H cannot ever let go of anything. I took his favourite pillow (because it had mould growing on it) and it went off to landfill heaven. I haven't told him this. 'Pillowgate' is referred to in this sequel.

I can't do Maths in my head and do not understand Physics. I hate politics and have zero general knowledge. I admit to being totally dim most of the time. I am not a morning person. I cannot make a good cup of tea. These are common themes that also crop up in my tales.

I am constantly dieting (well, I pretend to) and use the free APP 'My Fitness Pal' (or MFP) to log my calories. Unfortunately, I tend to log exercises when I need more calories (mostly to drink some alcohol), so it's no wonder that I never lose weight.

I'm pretty sure that Mr H is trying to kill me. First of all I thought that he was poisoning me, then it was shooting and now I think he has moved on to other means...

I reference everything to the cost of a Starbucks latte, to justify buying it.

I went to the hairdressers at the end of the first book. My natural mud coloured hair is now blonde.

I think you'll pick everything else up as you go along...

Something important is that these tales are 'fact-ion*'. They are based on true events but as they are how I perceive a situation or view it as a 'people watcher' then there is the element of poetic licence. Only Mr H and I are real. No one else in the book has their real names used (except for the pets) and a lot are made-up characters provided for your entertainment.

* One of my friends helpfully said, 'So it's all total made-up bo***cks then?' I have good friends...

Enjoy! And more importantly go and encourage your friends to buy the book! The kindle version nets Mr H more royalties, so buy a few of them instead of a paperback (of course if you are now reading the paperback then that doesn't really work... but then you can lend it* to your friends and hold it prominently while you're reading on the train so that others are encouraged to buy it too!)

* Mr H just read this and said, "Don't encourage people to lend it! That won't get me my tractor." He is a star...

Enjoy!

Sunday 1st May

Missions for today:

- *Remember to say 'White rabbits' as it's the first of a month (I don't know why I do this)*
- *Get rid of remnants of headache (and think about booking doctors to check out this brain tumour idea)*
- *Vacuum out the cars*

A few memories popped up on Facebook today. One was when I was down in smelly London eating curry. The waiter in the curry house obviously thought that I was totally dim (he had the measure of me quite quickly to his credit) as when he brought me the hot hand towel he told me not to eat it. Obviously I knew what it was and he didn't need to tell me that… I do have Google on my phone after all.

The second memory on Facebook was to do with the Anti-Capitalist march that takes place on May 1st each year in London. I was giving a seminar in London on 'How to manage people in the work place' a few years ago near to the place where the march was starting. It always makes me chuckle that people working in the City are told to 'dress down' for the day so that they won't become targets for any of the protestors. Some of the bankers' idea of dressing down for the day is to wear chinos (with creases), Thomas Pink shirts (with cuff links) whilst still carrying around their monogrammed briefcases with their double-barrelled surnames. I guess there are some things that public school can't teach you... Personally, I wanted to beat them up just for dressing like that.

It also made me chuckle that these 'Anti-Capitalist' protestors all had iPhones and were drinking venti lattes from Starbucks whilst waving their banners to moan about Capitalism. I don't do politics but even I spot the irony of this situation.

Being a bank holiday it's been pissing it down with rain all weekend (you really don't need weather reports on a bank holiday). My mission to vacuum out the cars has therefore been delayed again. Instead I have been doing my monthly invoicing and accounts, so that I can keep Mr H in the manner to which he has become accustomed.

He has been a star in return by putting on the fire to keep me warm (it is friggin' freezin') and he hasn't tried to eat any of the Revels that he bought for me. Literally, just as I wrote that he reached for the bag. Looking in it to see that there were only ten left he has decided to let me have them all. He might also have decided to let me have them all when I let out a low growl and curled my lip at him. It was one or the other...

Whilst we are on the subject of Revels... I am pretty sure that the 'family' size bags have been getting smaller and I'm thinking of contacting Trading Standards as they clearly offend trade description legislation. Given that I have just wolfed a 'family' bag down in 20 minutes flat, there is no way that they could possibly feed any family other than a single person. There's only two of us in our house, so we must be the smallest family that you can get - and they definitely didn't feed our family. I have just logged my calories onto MFP and unfortunately at 3:23pm I now have 18 calories left for the rest of the day. I might have to do some lunges to be able to have a latte for my dinner...

Mr H is currently siting on the other settee trying to order some masking tape. He does like to research products before ordering them but I think he's taken this one to the extreme. I would have clicked on 'Amazon', searched for 'masking tape', chosen 'lowest price first' and then clicked on the first one and bought it. Mr H has been reading the customer reviews. Personally, I think that anyone that took the time to review masking tape is probably a lump of coal short of a tonne. He just read one out to me that was for a 25 metre roll. The reviewer said, 'it worked as it should' (well d'uh!) but, 'I was disappointed that there was only 25 metres.' I shall just pause to let you take that in.

I'm now wondering why he needs some masking tape. I wonder whether it's part of his plan to do away with me. Maybe Mr H is going to tie me up and throw me in the moat. I might need to text Miranda to keep an eye out. Maybe this is why he is so interested in the sticking capabilities of the tape?

I must admit that the one time that I did read a lot of reviews on Amazon was for the 'Veet for men' product. You should go and have a look if you haven't read any of them. They are hysterical and they will definitely cheer you up if you're glum! There are reviews with titles like… 'took my frickin' eyebrows off' and underneath comments like:

'Like other reviewers I don't do instructions so I just slapped this stuff on like I was basting a turkey. In the minutes that followed, my ball bag felt like the sun on its hottest day and my john thomas was as red as Mr Tumble's fricking nose.'

Seriously – if you want to feel good in life just log in and read them. They are totes hilaires (in the words of the kidz)…

I think Mum is a little bored today as she sent me a message to say, 'Why haven't you poked me back on Facebook?' I'm now going to catch her out by doing it at midnight when she's bound to be asleep. This will annoy her when she gets up in the morning and sees it.*

* I forgot that Mum was reading my book as I wrote it and obviously she has now seen this. I think I get my lack of intelligence from her side of the family too... I can hear Mum reacting to this as she's reading it. That's me out of the will then...

Bank Holiday Monday 2nd May

Mission for today:

- *Give Mr H back the cold that he's now given me*

As predicted, being a bank holiday, it is pissing it down with rain. I have kept my missions simple today as I won't be able to vacuum out the cars (unless I want to get electrocuted, which I don't, unless it will get rid of this cold... I might Google 'does electrocution get rid of a cold?')

Mr H has had a cold for the last few days. You might notice that I haven't written about it until now. This is because I didn't want to fuel or promote his moaning about 'man flu'.

Obviously now that he has given it to me, then being a woman, I can legitimately moan about it. I reckon that he has been licking me in bed during the night in order to pass it on (either that or it was Casper, but I recognise Casper's tongue, it's really rough and his breath isn't too bad). I haven't been giving Mr H any sympathy and he doesn't like it if I don't make appropriate oo-ing or arr-ing noises to comfort him in his time of dying.

I messaged Mum to tell her about my cold as I knew she would be sympathetic. She has reminded me to gargle salt water. Being the genius that I am, I ate some pork scratchings that we had in the pantry and have just cooked sausage sandwiches for lunch. There's so much salt in both of those that they are sure to help my throat. Having the cold though has made me go a bit woolly headed. This means that I am even more dim than usual. This is another reason as to why I only have one mission for the day. I really shouldn't be let loose on anything (or anyone) that requires any amount of thought today.

This woolly headed-ness came out in my cooking of the sausages. I forgot to mark the ones that Casper had licked and in all likelihood I have now eaten them rather than Mr H, as I had planned. Next time Casper licks something, I will mark it in some way. I have some permanent markers which should do the trick. I just need to Google

'Can permanent markers on food make you ill?' I'll do that later...

I really do have a crap immune system. In the doctor's words it's because I have 'an underlying medical condition' (my underactive thyroid). Personally, I put it down to having to pick up Mr H's dirty pants and socks and having to poo pick both goose poo and dog poo from the gardens. I'm sure 'passive poo picking' is a bit like passive smoking and can make you ill, even if you don't have a 'fingernail through the poo bag' incident.

I'm starting to think that maybe Mr H and I need to do a role reversal in this area. This means that I need to watch some YouTube videos of 'How to make a decent cup of tea' and he will have to learn not to gag when picking up poo (to be clear, he won't need to learn not to gag when picking up my dirty undies from the floor, as I have a meticulous fru-fru daily cleaning regime.)

Mum sent me a message to see if I was feeling a bit better and I told her that I was feeling 'pants'. She proceeded to send me a GIF on Messenger of a woman's bottom in white leggings doing some sort of exercise, with a close up of her bum wiggling. I think it's safe to say where I get my warped sense of humour from.

This has got me thinking though – where does the phrase 'feeling pants' come from? Just in case it is a Midlands thing and you don't come from the Midlands, it means that you are feeling cronky. And if you don't understand cronky, it means that you're not feeling well.

I resorted to asking Siri. (I had sent her to Coventry* for a few days, given that she had been getting a little sarcastic with me lately but I was too tired to type the question into the browser, so I have temporarily forgiven her.)

* I suspect that this is a Midland's phrase. It means if you shut someone out or give them the silent treatment. Sending them to Coventry would mean that they would be on their own because no one really goes there by choice. Locally I think it would be 'sending someone to Tipton.'

Unfortunately, with my cold, Siri couldn't understand me and 'Where does the saying 'feeling pants' come from?' turned into 'Where does satan feel my pants comfy?' This sent me to a whole host of weird websites about Catholicism and modesty that I did not want to click on (I didn't want to... but I did...) and one entitled 'Do you think sanitary pads are the work of the devil?' which was a discussion on mumsnet. Boy! Are those mums bored in life, I thought. I definitely did not click on this. If ever I become a serial killer and the Police storm the house and take away my computer, I don't want this showing up in my browser history.

The third one down was 'A link between marijuana and the devil' at cannabis.com. I was surprised that the drug has its own website, but then again one of my friend's teddy bears has his own Facebook page, so maybe I shouldn't be so surprised. Again, I did not click on this in case it sent some immediate electronic alert to the drug squad and they came to storm the house. (I'll do it later when I have at least straightened my wet curly hair and put some make up on. If men in uniform are going to descend then I really want to look my best when they slap the handcuffs on me. That's also reminded me to make sure that I have one of my professional photoshoot pictures to hand when they arrest me. I don't want a picture of my no-make-up selfie for Cancer Research being splashed across the news. They'd have to issue a warning to parents that the next news report contains 'scenes of a distressing nature'.)

I have only just remembered that I was trying to find out where the phrase 'feeling pants' comes from. I do find that I get side-tracked quite easily…

Facebook 'on this day' popped up this morning to remind me that a year ago I superglued myself to Casper, with the status update 'Jo and superglue… never going to be a winning combination.' Unfortunately I must have wiped this memory from my mind as I can't remember what I was supergluing and how I managed to superglue myself to the cat, whilst doing it. I'm pretty sure that I wasn't supposed to be supergluing something to him… It's a good job the status actually used Casper's name. One of my (rude) friends said, 'It's a good job that you didn't use the word pussy'. If I had then I might have been a bit more concerned as to what I had been doing a year ago…

Mr H has been trying to do the P60s and wages round up for the year. Unfortunately, something went wrong and the system told him that I needed to pay some NIC (which I didn't). I told him to phone HMRC up. "It's a bank holiday. They won't be there on a bank holiday!" He said it with his usual tone reserved for me – the one dripping with sarcasm. Me being the genius that I am remembered a friend telling me that the helplines were open on a bank holiday as the staff got paid double time so were happy to earn more money when it was bound to rain anyway.

So Mr H got straight through to someone (I suspect everyone else thought they wouldn't be open on a bank holiday and therefore no one was going to try phoning) and gold star to the person on the other end as they sorted out his problem really quickly. I asked him what had gone wrong. Apparently it was 'operator error' – Mr H had accidentally ticked a box that he shouldn't have done. It was a good job that he got it sorted as it meant that he could pay us.

(And given that I have a cold, I tend to internet shop when I'm poorly as it makes me feel lots better, so I really needed to be paid.)

I was chatting with a friend on Facebook earlier who was feeling pants too. She was grateful for my virtual hug and said, 'Men are so rubbish at giving hugs and sympathy.' Funnily enough what then ensued was the discussion that I mentioned on Thursday. She said that if she had been given 'man lessons' in school then she would definitely have spent more time working on being gay. I know exactly where she is coming from... (I have just read this back and realised that it's a good double entendre. It was a happy accident as with this cold I really am dim...)

Tuesday 3rd May

Missions for today:

- *Get up at 7:45am (not being a morning person, this is a really hard thing for me to do)*
- *Get rid of this cold (preferably give it back to Mr H, as his seems to have totally done one)*
- *Check whether I have lost weight*

I had to get up early this morning. I set the alarm because it was bound to be the day that Lucy decided not to wake up at 6am. However, she did bark at 6am and I once again pretended to be fast asleep, so that Mr H could get up and let her out.

The stoopid cold was still there this morning. I was thinking of taking a photo of the green phlegm in my throat and putting it up on Facebook. 'Ewwww! How disgusting', I hear you say. But to be fair, my friends put pictures of their kids teeth up when they fall out and the great big hole in their mouth where it used to be, so I'm not sure that showing my gunky tonsils is much different to that. Although I'm not going to put it under my pillow for the tooth fairy, unlike their kids do... I'll put it under Mr H's instead.

The reason that I had to get up early this morning was to give Mr H a lift back after he dropped the minibus off that he had borrowed. Me and mornings are not destined to be together (unless I'm curled up fast asleep in 'morning's' lap that is). I did think about driving in my pyjamas. But then I remembered that I wasn't a hypocrite and had only just this week berated people that go out in their pyjamas. So I went with a coat over the top of them. I'm kidding! I didn't have the energy to get my coat, so I put a onesie on (not the one soaked in pig blood. Although I should have done for comedic effect...)

When I got back I noticed that call minder had left a message. It was Dad phoning to say that he was going to be coming over tomorrow to work on the spare rooms. He ended the message with,

"So when you get out of bed and get this message, call me back."

The cheek of it! As if I was in bed. To be clear, I would normally have been but I took this opportunity to take the high moral-offended-ground because I was actually awake. I phoned him back and told him that I was up and he said, "Oh! Well normally at this time you are curled up on the settee drinking a latte." I have concluded that he is more observant than I give him credit for. You really can't argue with the truth... and he spoke it...

Because I was up early, I started work early and by lunchtime I had done over half a day's work. By this time I would normally have only done an hour or so. Maybe I really should try and be a morning person, I pondered... then thought, 'Who am I kidding!' when reality kicked back in.

Mr H was back at lunchtime and now that it was the day after a bank holiday we felt that it was safe to venture out into the wide world again. I used to be a people person, but people kind of ruined that for me. OK - I admit it. I stole this from some e-card thing on Facebook. But it speaks the truth. I'm sure that God was having a laugh when he made us and that our tolerance gradually decreases the older that we get.

Mr H texted me before he left work to arrive back at lunchtime to ask if I wanted to go to the garden centre. It took me all of ten seconds to decide to ditch work for a bit. OK, I lie, it was one second (if that). I asked him if we were going to have lunch there and he said, "Well, maybe a coffee and a cake." A simple 'yes' would have sufficed. Jeez, men really do exaggerate things.

Mr H needed some seeds to begin planting tomorrow so that we (well the freezer) would be full of veg for the next year or so. We took a trip to 'Boobies' garden centre. Obviously this is not its real name. It's Dobbies. But once when me and my sister were driving past there with Dad, Dad mis-read the sign and said, "Boobies?! I wonder what they sell there?" The name has stuck since. I can't remember Dad looking happier than he did at that moment in time (until we told him that they sold plants and garden furniture).

We have a membership card which entitles us to a free coffee each month and we get 10% off all plants and seeds. Given that I am inherently tight, we save the £10 yearly fee in our first visit of the year. Places do make me chuckle though. You can have whatever free coffee you want and the girl behind the counter said, "Do you want a medium or a large latte each?" "Er.... well obviously if it's free, I want the biggest latte you do." Obviously I didn't say this, I just wrote it on their customer feedback form. Well, they gave you a free packet of seeds if you filled one in…

I felt really young sitting in their restaurant. The average age was about 75 and I felt out of place as out of all the couples sitting there at least one of them had a walking stick or Zimmer frame. This actually made me smile, not because of their disability obviously, that would be plain mean. (Although the stares we kept getting did make me feel a bit uncomfortable.) The reason why they made me smile was that I really hope that if ever I reach old age then I will be like these couples and still get out and about. To be clear though, I want to be the one without the walking stick and preferably sitting with a hot male carer, pretending that I need help getting to the toilet.

After we had scoffed the biggest scones with cream and jam, and taken about 40 minutes to drink the massive lattes, I spotted something on Mr H's nose. "Is that scone on your nose, or is it just a sun tan?" It turned out that it was a bit of scone. "Well, I've just had to brush off scone dust from my crotch, so it's no surprise," he said. 'Doreen' the 80-something sitting nearby nearly choked on her breakfast tea when she heard this. Funny how when her husband was trying to talk to her from the same table she kept telling him that she had forgotten her hearing aids and couldn't hear him, but she seemed to hear every word of our conversation.

As we were leaving we saw a sign up saying that scones were on offer 2-4-1. "We didn't get ours for that!" I said. But then I spotted that the offer was only for scones bought after 2pm. At the same time Mr H and I looked at our watches and noticed that it was 1:40pm. We both thought the same thing. We could buy our seeds and come back and buy two more scones. And I could give them to Mr H for his dinner, which would save me having to cook for him. We didn't. Obviously we're not that piggy. We also have rubbish memories and forgot.

We caught up with the 93 year old Farmer when we got back from Boobies. He said, "Do you want 19 geese?" I paused but couldn't make up a euphemism for that in the time available. I think he was disappointed. He loves a bit of innuendo. Instead I said, "I'll swap them for Mr H." I weighed up the pros and cons and this is what I toyed with in my head:

Mr H	19 geese
Costs a lot to feed with no return	Eats a bit of corn and can sell eggs
Likes toys – especially anything with a tyre	Likes toys – especially the tyre on the moat
Snores at 3am and wakes me up	Fights each other at 3am and wakes me up
Doesn't poo on the lawn (that I know of)	Poos on the lawn
Lucy doesn't eat his poo (that I know of)	Lucy eats their poo
Annoys me with incessant chatter	Annoys me with incessant honking

To be honest, it was a close call, I thought. The Farmer decided it for me though when he said, "Oh he's trouble, I think I'll stick with the geese." Apart from the poo-ing on the lawn and the cost of food there wasn't really much in it. Maybe I will send Mr H to poo on their lawn to see if they prefer it to goose poo.

My second mission was to see if I have lost weight from eating (relatively) well for the last two weeks (we won't count the family sized Revels on Saturday. Everyone knows that treats on a weekend don't count and we have already established that they weren't really 'family' sized). I don't actually weigh myself but I knew that I had lost weight as my head torch slipped down to my nose last night and my watch has gone baggy on my wrist this morning. Unfortunately, my jeans are still as tight as ever and my muffin top is turning into a full on soufflé. Once again I blame my genetics. I never lose weight from my double chin or stomach but my head and wrist get smaller quite easily. I'm sure my skinny head and wrists were exactly what attracted Mr H to me when we met.

I washed my hair again and thankfully the weird ginger has gone and the blonde has come back. I shall start putting the pink chalks back in my fringe to jazz it up a bit. Some people call this a mid-life crisis. It really can't be. I shall be doing this in my 70s and I doubt that I will live to 140. Not with Mr H trying to kill me anyway...

I really need to stop thinking this. We have been together for 25 years, I think he would have done it by now if he was going to. Let's face it, netball has been more successful than he has as it has nearly killed me twice… (this is covered in the first book – so if you haven't read it then go and buy it!)

Wednesday 4th May – Sunday 8th May

It's been a mad mad few days! Work has taken over my life this week, so I haven't had time to write my book and have had no missions.

Wednesday was an annoying day. The world and his brother on Facebook think it's funny to say 'May the fourth be with you.' It isn't. Everyone does it every year. Every year it isn't funny. I don't even like Star Trek, so I don't get the reference at all.

It was a really hot day on Wednesday. Because of this Casper decided to lie inside in the kitchen by the warm Rayburn. Cat logic is just as bad as man logic. I wonder if scientists were to cut open the brains of cats (obviously when they're dead) and compare them to the cut open brains of men (dead or alive, I'm not fussed....) then I'm pretty sure they would find some striking similarities. This has made me think of their weird ways...

1. Male cats will happily sit and wash their balls in public. (I know that men don't actually wash theirs in public, but I'm sure they would if they could reach them with their tongues.) But men will scratch away at them in public without any thought to anyone else around them.

2. Cats will harass you for food and won't leave you alone until they get it. Mr H likes his dinner to be prompt and he will sulk if it's not ready on time. "I've got to leave for badminton in 20 minutes, I'm going to have to go there hungry now," I've heard on too many occasions now.

3. If cats don't get their food on time then they will go and find their own prey, be it a mouse, a bird or in Casper's case, a squirrel. If Mr H leaves for badminton without his dinner he manages to find some prey (usually from McDonald's or the two billion takeaways in Wolverhampton) on the way.

4. Cats are totally fickle. One moment they adore you and you are their world. The next second they hate you and are plotting to kill you. I don't think I need to say any more about this similarity and Mr H...

Thursday was voting day. As Mr H and I only have one stab vest between us then we always opt to do a postal vote. We usually cancel each other out as well (well we would – but given that I do 'Home admin' in this house, posting is my responsibility. His envelope doesn't actually get to see the post box. It's not my fault if the doggy poo bin near to us on the A460 is the same colour as the post box...) Cancelling each other out with votes is a common theme with me and my sister. She cancels her husband's vote out as well (she doesn't have a dog but I wonder whether she also mysteriously forgets to post her husband's vote...)

We chatted to the Farmer today and I had tied my hair back and was wearing sunglasses. He didn't recognise me and the Farmer's wife came up to me later and asked if everything was alright as the Farmer had seen Mr H with another woman. "She was chubbier than you though, so I don't think you've got anything to worry about. And she wasn't as pretty as you either." I thanked her for her reassuring words. Old people are like men – it is important to praise them, even when they don't do things well. I never know when I might need her to set the dogs onto someone else after all...

Mr H's masking tape has finally arrived from Amazon. He asked me to put my arms out so he could test the 'tensile strength' (?) of it. I have no idea what he meant – or even if that's what he said, but I am getting suspicious as to why he's bought it...

Mr H forced me to watch *Question Time* tonight – well ok – it was a trade-off. We watched *The Mysteries of Laura* first and then I had to suffer this nonsense before he allowed me to watch *Silent Witness* afterwards. Tom Ward is on my laminated list and I like a bit of eye candy before dropping off to sleep. You're not going to get that from watching *Question Time*.

I think Mr H might think twice about making me watch QT again though. My constant, "Who is that then?" and, "Blimey! Nigel Lawson looks like he's had botox" and, "She's pretty – is she the token glamorous guest?" questions seemed to annoy him. He is a hypocrite though – whenever we're watching *Law & Order SVU** he will look up after playing with his phone for ten minutes and say, "So what have I missed?" "What's happened to Olivia?" "Where's Elliot these days?" This is just as annoying for me. But being a man he doesn't see his hypocrisy. Luckily I am there to point it out for him...

*I chuckled when autocrapet tried to change SVU to SUV.

I do think that I might need to go back to the doctors though as I'm not convinced that my hearing is great. I could have sworn at one point one of the members of the panel on QT said, "She's a true blue dyke Tory." I thought 'That's incredibly offensive – I'm surprised that David (or is it Richard?) Dimbleby has let that comment go. As I said this to Mr H, he said, "No. They said, 'True blue dyed in the wool Tory.'" Oh....

Friday was a lovely sunny day as well. I took the opportunity to find my shorts out during the afternoon. This involved a lot of swearing as I was balancing on one leg with my torch turned on, on my iPhone, leaning into the cupboard to find where I had shoved them to the back last year. I dusted off the dead spiders and mouse droppings and put them on (and noticed that they were a bit tight around the soufflé top).

At that point I realised that for the sake of mankind I shouldn't have my pasty white legs on show. So I got my fake tan out of the drawer and proceeded to spray that on them.

Unfortunately, I forgot that I had been wearing socks in the morning and the sock marks indented on my legs and fake tan made it look like I had tiger stripes on my legs. I also forgot that I had fake tan on my mitt and scratched my nose as I had an itch. When I got downstairs Mr H burst into laughter and said, "The phrase 'brown nose' has never been more relevant." I went back upstairs and tried to put some foundation on to cover the fake tan as it wouldn't wash off. It didn't work and I spent the rest of the day hiding from anyone and everyone. The Farmer's wife saw me at one point and said, "You're looking tanned on your nose."

I also realised that having put on weight over the winter months means that I look pregnant when I wear shorts and a vest top. To avoid people wondering whether I was or even worse asking when the baby was due I did consider buying one of those badges that says, 'baby on board!' and wearing it. I relayed this story to Mr H and he said, "It really should just say 'chicken kebab on board'". He then chuckled for a few minutes. 'At least he's happy', I thought... 'thoughtless, but happy'.

Thinking that with summer approaching I really should make more of a concerted effort to diet, I carefully considered my lunch choice today. Unfortunately, my evil inner fat twin won and I had a homemade pheasant korma instead. There wasn't much sauce in it so I decided to improvise and added half a jar of lasagne white sauce to it. I also added my usual accompaniment to the dish — a boat load of olives. Surprisingly it was extremely tasty. I really should have been a professional chef I thought. It's really easy – I don't know why we make such a fuss of Michelin Star restaurants and these chefs that have trained for years. In ten minutes I had created a genius dish. Maybe I will apply for *MasterChef* next year, I pondered...

Today was a sad day for Boaty McBoatface. The government minister in charge of the new name for the research ship (Boring McBoringface) decided that democracy was a load of hooey and called the ship after David Attenborough (or is it Richard?) instead. I can't help but think that poor Sir David is now going to have the nickname 'Boaty' though. This is where I sigh at the government. They have missed a great opportunity to engage young children in science, in my opinion. It's another of the reasons as to why I don't do politics. And Sir David is 90. He will probably be dead by the time the ship is ready (sorry Sir David), so no kids of the future will know who he is. I did feel a bit guilty when Mr H shared the BBC news story and I commented, 'I hope it sinks.' I don't really. I hope someone sets it on fire (note for thickies: it's a joke... (Or maybe it isn't?))

Saturday was also a lovely sunny day. Facebook reminded me of one of my memories on this day. Mr H and I had been watching Downton Abbey a year ago (we were on catch up and about five months later than everyone else) and Isis the dog died. I think they killed her off because of her secret links to terrorism*.

* That's reminded me that our package from Bobby still hasn't arrived... I must Messenger him.

When we were watching it, I remember turning round to Mr H and saying, "Oh no! Isis is dying." As I turned to look at him, he brushed a tear away from his cheek. Being the sensitive wife that I am I made sure that I didn't embarrass him. I put as my status on Facebook, 'Watching Downton Abbey and one of us is crying because Isis is dying.' I was so pleased with my sensitivity and the fact that I hadn't dropped him in it. I don't know why Mr H was mad. Apparently putting the tag line *#itwasntme* had something to do with it...

I spent three hours weeding today. Although I really need to think a bit more about things in advance. Not only did I still have weird streaks of fake tan on my legs (and my nose), putting sun cream on top of it only seemed to make it look worse. Also, when I was trimming the hedge and had to reach above me, a load of evergreen small branches descended on top of me and got stuck to the sun cream and fake tan combo.

At this point the Farmer and his wife had some visitors and they decided to introduce me. Goodness knows what they thought at the sight of this mad woman with brown blotches, covered in white sun cream with greenery on top. It reminded me of 'tarring and feathering' from years ago (although being crap at history I'm not really sure what this is to do with. My guess is it was some sort of primitive fancy dress outfit). My mumbling of, "I was just trimming the bush" didn't really help matters either. It took me half an hour to pick all of the branches out of my cleavage (I did not do this in public – although I refer you back to what men will happily do in public, so maybe I should have done? I bet the Farmer would have liked that...)

I also got attacked by one of our chickens today. I used to think that it was Brownie that attacked me but she died a few months ago and now I've realised that I have been blaming the wrong chicken. It is Brownie's evil twin that has been attacking me. I swear that Mr H has been teaching her to attack me. Normally it isn't so bad as I am usually wearing jeans and wellies but today I was in shorts and sandals. I now have two big bite marks on my leg where she jumped up and pecked me (and broke the skin and it bled) and now, thanks to Alexandra's caring advice, I am going to have to check whether my tetanus is up-to-date when the doctors opens tomorrow morning.

Like I say... it has been a mad few days.

Monday 9th May

Missions for today:

- *Try and work outside in the garden as it has been glorious sunshine for the last few days (and being Britain it won't last)*
- *Phone the doctors to check about tetanus from chickens (and try to not be humiliated when they laugh at me and write 'crazy lady' on my medical records)*

Now you would have thought that this first mission was an easy one. Unfortunately for me the gods were conspiring against me. I (rather optimistically in hindsight) decided to put shorts and a t-shirt on today. As soon as I did this the sun went behind the clouds and the wind got up. As I was wrestling with the free standing parasol, it decided to try and take off (with me hanging from it) and I nearly ended up in the moat. Thankfully my t-shirt got caught on the apple tree and I didn't have to explain to Mr H when he got back at lunchtime why I was soaking wet and covered in algae. (He laughs enough when Casper has fallen in the moat after being chased by the farm dogs.)

Unfortunately, at the time that I was attached to the apple tree, my paperwork decided to blow around the garden and some of it landed in the moat. The geese thought that it was some tasty treat and proceeded to attack it with their beaks. I thought it ironic as the presentation that I had been writing was entitled *'Ever feel like you're drowning at work?'* I was pondering the irony as I watched my soggy papers sink to the bottom of the moat. The geese, having decided that it was not a tasty treat, swam off in disgust.

I set up my laptop on the garden table and the Wi-Fi decided not to work to connect to my printer. On the plus side I must have burned off 300 calories walking backwards and forwards to my office with my laptop every time I have needed to print something out.

Just as I was settling down (with all my work safely weighted down with paperweights, rocks and anything else I could find to hand – Casper was one of them) Lucy decided to do a big poo right next to where I was sitting. Not wanting to sniff 'eau de faeces' all day long, I got a poo bag and cleaned it up.

Once again the gods were conspiring against me as I trod in one of her poos (the sneaky devil had not just done it in one place but had outfoxed me and moved around during her evacuation). Usually this wouldn't have been a massive problem but open-toed sandals and fresh dog poo do not make for a good combination. Again, on the plus side (I like to find positives in all situations), I can go shoe shopping. If Mr H does his usual look of, 'you have got plenty of shoes, why do you need to buy some more?' then I shall put the poo-ey sandal in his side of the bed. I'm sure that will stop his man moaning-nonsense.

Although I am still dieting, I felt that this was a two KitKat and latte moment. It was the only way to get over the morning's trauma. I have just checked the weather report and thunder and lightning is forecast in two hours. After faffing around setting up my garden office, I think I've lost two hours already and it will probably rain soon...

As luck would have it the gods decided that I had been teased enough today and the day got hotter and there was no thunder nor lightning. Mr H had his inspection from the gun licence people and I was extremely disappointed when a guy wearing chinos and a check shirt rocked up. I'm sure last time some young fittie policeman in uniform, including stab vest and baton (I don't know why I get so excited by this) who also had a gun in his car (I was even more excited by this) came to do the inspection. If I had known that there wasn't going to be some young uniformed fittie at the door then I wouldn't have bothered putting make-up on today.

After he left, me and Miranda (who had brought us a cake today) had a chuckle at how the system was going to pot if Mr H was classed as being of 'sound mind'. (I think Miranda came to bring me the cake because I'd told her a fit policeman was turning up today). She looked disappointed when she saw the chinos too... but I was pleased because I at least got a cake out of it.

Mr H has been a happy boy today. He's been preparing the land for the Alpacas. Today, Matt helped us get the greenhouse down so that we can move it in readiness for George, Chester and Cyril's arrivals. We weighted it down as Mr H said, "Remember what happened last time, when it blew away?" I didn't remind him that he was the reason last time that it blew away. I pick my battles and he was happy and out of my hair and I wanted it to stay that way.

As a good and helpful wife I put the washing out on the line. Remember that the washing is one of Mr H's jobs in this house because it's really easy and the machine does the hard work. I now have to retract that statement as he has put my white vest top in with all the coloureds and it now has a blue-ish hue to it. That reminds me of a journey on the bus into Wolves once where I single handedly prevented a big fight from breaking out (I might be exaggerating a bit).

I was on the bus listening to two older ladies chatting about their lives, which basically consisted of running around after their menfolk by cooking and cleaning for them, while the men went down the pub every night. I nearly went over to them to tell them to leave them and live their own lives but I was too busy ear wigging to other conversations to go over (and I had a prime spot on the bus which I didn't want to lose). They were chatting about washing their menfolk's white Y-fronts and one of them piped up (quite animated), 'It's crucial in life that we separate the whites from the coloureds'.

Unfortunately, the black guy sitting next to me had only just got on the bus and had caught the tail end of their conversation. He mis-interpreted their convo* and sighed and tutted really loudly and started muttering about old people and their old fashioned ways. I leant towards him and whispered, "They're on about their washing and having to do everything for their husbands. They're not being racist - although from their conversation their menfolk are sexist pigs, so they really should ditch them." He chuckled and said, "Well it's a good job you were sitting next to me today, or a fight might have broken out." "What? Between you and the old women?" "No!" He said. "I've just realised that the bus driver has over charged me. I only wanted a single and he's charged me for a return." *This is* why I love Wolverhampton. There's never a dull moment, it's totally random and things are never what they seem at first...

* I like to think that I am young and hip by using shortened versions of words like the kidz do.

I totally failed in my second mission and tomorrow I will have to listen to the doctor's receptionist laughing at my request to check whether my tetanus shots are up to date because of my encounter with Brownie's evil twin...

Tuesday 10th May

Missions for today:

- *Phone up the doctors about Brownie's evil twin biting me*
- *Pop to Essington Fruit Farm to buy some bacon and sausages (lean and skinny)*
- *Don't drop my iPhone on the floor*

I did actually manage to succeed in my first mission today.

After the receptionist had stopped laughing at my encounter with the chicken, she checked my records and said that there was nothing on my notes to show when I had last had a tetanus injection, so she would need to book me in for one. Our doctors, I have to say, are totally awesome. The receptionists are always friendly and they have always managed to squeeze me in with the nurse if ever I need an appointment. (I like to think this is partly to do with the thank you letter we sent them when we first went there after moving house. After our previous experience, we couldn't believe how normal these guys were.)

Our old doctors, before we moved to Wolverhampton, had Gestapo-type women on reception who made you feel that you had committed some war crime and should not be darkening their doors with your presence. They demanded to know the intimate details of your ailment before you would even be allowed to be considered for getting on the list to see the doctor. I used to make stuff up that I had Googled just to be sure that I would be seen.

I would Google things like *'colorectal carcinoma'* (obviously I didn't know this was a real ailment and my actual search was *'really bad illnesses that can kill you'*, of which this then popped up) and tell them that it affected King Jehoram and that I think he might have passed it onto me when I was sitting next to him in the cinema at the weekend. The doctor would then be really surprised when I was in front of him telling him that I was there because I had a rash on my bum.

Our current doctors have lovely receptionists and the doctors and nurses are all lovely too (and remember the new fittie doctor that I told you about in the first book, who has just joined the practice - bonus!) They don't care what your ailment is. They will get you in to see a doctor for the tiniest thing here. I think there are a lot of rashes in Wolverhampton...

I'm digressing though...

Apparently my chicken bite was the second one that she had encountered in her 19 years in the job and so my opening line on the phone of, 'OK. I'm going to be your random phone call of the day...' was totally unnecessary. The receptionist wants to see the chicken bites when I go in on Thursday to get my jab. I think it will be a novelty. Most of the patients coming to see the nurse there have chlamydia (and yes I needed autocrapet to spell that word because I obviously have never had it myself.) She must be bored with seeing chlamydia... I'm sure when you've seen one case of it, they all look the same...

My second mission was also a success today. The Fruit Farm* are making their tea room bigger and I got the added bonus of checking out the fit builders as I wandered in to get my sausages (lean and skinny). Olive and Donald weren't there today, so there was no witty banter about the size of sausages. There was a little boy, aged about two, in there though and he was playing with one of the members of staff's hat. I thought, 'Blimey! Maybe they are thinking that if Brexit happens then they will need to start getting their staff in at an early age.' Another customer in the queue behind me commented, "They start them early here!" I said, "Wait until he's 40 or 50, then he will be trouble." She said, "I know what you mean. My husband is trouble. But I shouldn't say too much as he's stood right behind me."

* Notice that I don't need to wear my stab vest for a visit to the Fruit Farm. It's generally full of lah-de-dah people and I've never felt threatened in there – well except the one time when a young couple were arguing over whether to buy the fillet steak or the steak loin (maybe it was us? I don't remember now...)

I don't think her husband was listening to her though (like Mr H with me really). He looked totally zoned out and a bit zombie-fied. If he hadn't have walked to the car, I actually would have thought that he was dead. I nearly thought of asking her how she managed to have trained her husband to be so quiet but I was running late to get Mr H his lunch, so I said goodbye. Her husband did not react at all. I did notice that she was buying a few bottles of mead though. I pondered that maybe she kept him permanently drunk on mead and that's why he was so quiet. Maybe this is where I have been going wrong with Mr H. He hardly drinks and is vocal and a pain in the ass. I might try spiking his tea with whisky and see what happens...

I made a lovely lunch for the two of us today but knew he would moan when he walked in. We had fish, salad and crusty bread and because of the big dinners we've been eating lately I've been trying to cut out excess calories (it allows me to consume more alcohol instead). So Mr H comes in and says, "Where's the mash? I'm out again until 10:30pm, I need a proper meal!" I did wonder at this point what would happen if I died.

Would he not manage to eat until someone reminded him to do so? How on earth do men rule the world?!

Luckily because he is out until 10:30pm, then I have had a lovely day. I've got my work done and put my music on really loud and had a good dance around the house. There is something to be said for the power of music. You just can't help joining in with Phil Collins with the drum bit of 'In the Air tonight' and Bon Jovi's 'Livin' on a prayer.' Although, I really should remember that if I'm on the train and listening to them through my headphones then not everyone else wants to listen to (or see) my drumming on the table (nor my accidental singing along of 'Tommy used to work on the docks'...)

Just as I have been writing this, my computer anti-virus says that my computer is running slowly and I have 11 unnecessary applications open. I'm quite sure that they are all totally necessary, especially if they are to do with shopping. I daren't click on it though, it might be some ruse to hack into my bank account (they would be disappointed to be fair and probably would put money in out of sympathy). I will wait for Mr H to come home and confirm what I can click on. He's good at IT.

Miranda has just texted me, as the Farmer has popped on holibobs for a few days, so between us we are looking after their pets. Apparently, their cat had been accidentally shut in the barn, so tomorrow I am on 'cat wee and poo' duty to check whether it has made a mess in there. Life is rock n roll down here... I did wonder why Casper was looking so fat. He obviously was the one eating the food that I had put down for the Farmer's cat. Oh well...

As Mr H is out for most of the night I have opened a bottle of wine and am enjoying some 'me' time (not of the disgusting rude variety that you are thinking). There was some cardboard wrapped around the top of the bottle that said, 'Do you want to win hundreds of bottles of wine?' 'Hell yes!' I thought as I read it.

Apparently, you have to complete the following sentence with something witty, in order to win. 'I deserve hundreds of bottles of wine because...'

I'm thinking maybe, 'I deserve hundreds of bottles of wine because I've just been sent down and they don't allow prisoners to buy wine.' Or maybe, I should just be honest and say, 'I deserve hundreds of bottles of wine because I've been with the same man for 25 years *#wineishowigetthroughlife'*. Or maybe, 'I deserve hundreds of bottles of wine because I'm thinking of trying lesbianism and I need to blot out 25 years of man nonsense.' I'll keep thinking… I just hope the judge is a woman, if so then she will totally empathise with my plight.

I totally failed in my final mission. It's a good job that I bought a £1.99 plastic cover for my iPhone. For two day's running I have dropped it on the floor. Today it landed with a massive bang on the kitchen tiles and I was rapidly trying to think of an excuse that I could give to Mr H as to why my phone had gone to electronic heaven. (I was thinking that it was going to have to be survival of the fittest and that poor Lucy was going to have to be the scape goat.) Luckily though my shelling out on an expensive case for it worked and I didn't have to pretend that Lucy had knocked it off the coffee table. I'm pretty sure that my warranty ran out when I dropped it in my curry in Poppadom Express in London, so it would only be Mr H that I had to lie to.

I'm sure it's just a coincidence that the numbers button on the bottom left now only works when the phone is upright and not flat. It was amusing writing a message to a friend and not being able to use punctuation marks. It made me think that this is Mr H in his daily life (he may be good at Physics but his English is appalling).

Wednesday 11th May

Missions for today:

- *Google some publishers for the original book and write my intro letter and cut and paste some extracts from the book into a document to email them*
- *Cook a nice chilli for dinner*
- *Go and inspect the barn for cat wee and poo*

I failed in my second mission before it even started but only because Mr H randomly decided to say, "I'll cook dinner tonight. Shall I make a chilli from the mince in the fridge?" My suspicions were aroused immediately. He hasn't cooked pretty much on any night out of the last three weeks. I'm going to have to sneak upstairs and see if he's been looking at tractor-porn on his computer again. I think I would be less concerned if he was watching nudey-rudey stuff of the female variety. I hope that I don't find that he has bid on one on eBay (just to clarify, I mean a tractor. If he has bid on a Thai Bride then she can help cook and clean and put up with his man nonsense. I won't be mad if he's bought one of them).

The only downside with letting Mr H cook is the devastation that befalls the kitchen. He has happily trotted off to badminton whilst I am left with hours of clearing up the four work top space savers that he used to cut mushrooms, onions and peppers on. There are at least five jars of different spices strewn across the kitchen and don't get me started on how many spoons he's used. But, as men are like little children it is important to praise them.

Although, I'm now thinking that maybe he has got to the age where he needs to learn the valuable life lesson, that life is cruel and you don't always get what you want. I'm just not going to do it tonight. He's out of my hair and if he goes off in a strop then I won't have a relaxing night. You have to pick your battles…

As he was leaving for badminton, he said, "I'll be back late." Now. This is what he said yesterday. He wasn't supposed to be back until 10:30pm but sneakily arrived back at 8:30pm. I don't like it when he comes back earlier than he says, as I need half an hour (at least) to psych myself up for his return. He has assured me tonight that he won't be back until around midnight. He did pull a face as he was leaving though and said, "Don't you like it when I'm back early then? Don't you like spending time with me?" Once again Tractor-ites, I gave him 'the look'. He really should know by now not to ask such stupid questions.

As I was clearing up the kitchen (and glugging my wine whilst doing it), I forgot, once again, that my knowledge of Physics isn't great. I was trying to balance my wine, whilst tipping the saucepan with the chilli in to fill up the plastic containers for the freezer. Yes that's right, the inevitable happened. The saucepan slipped from my grasp and a load of chilli slopped onto Lucy's head below. (Luckily I saved the wine.)

She was obviously hanging around the kitchen, knowing that my knowledge of Physics would be to my detriment but most definitely to her benefit. She was right. Of course, if she has bottie problems then I'm denying all knowledge. Let's face it, it's going to be months before this book is out, so I can pretend to Mr H that her bottie issues were nothing to do with me.

Her bottie issues are likely to be a lot worse than if she had only eaten a normal chilli con carne as well. Mr H mis-read one of the bottles of spices and accidentally put curry powder in the chilli. When he finally found the chilli, which was in the new chilli grinder* that I had bought him, he couldn't see it coming out and put a boat load of that in there as well. I said to him, "Look! It is coming out. Put it over my hand and grind it and see." He said, "Oh yes – you're right. It is coming out." I think maybe his gammy eye is back again...

* The chilli grinder unfortunately looks like a vibrator and for the first few months I hid it in the pantry out of sight in case Mr H's mum thought that it was one. It now lives in full view of everyone in the kitchen and I'm sure she constantly bites her lip when she comes here and sees it.

I really need to stop being dim. After Mr H had ground some chilli onto my hand, I got distracted (it was probably the wine) and I accidentally rubbed my eye with my hand. I can assure you that I will not be doing that again, ever. It once again reminded me of the Veet for Men reviews on Amazon.

At one point while he was cooking the chilli, Mr H was looking for some spice beginning with 'M' and was opening all the drawers in the spice cupboards trying to find it. I'm thinking it was 'Magic' – something but all that has made me think of is 'magic mushrooms' and I don't think that's right.

Being a man he doesn't bother to follow instructions. As we have so many herbs and spices in this house, we have two cupboards with them in. I have a nicely printed out sheet that lists them all in alphabetical order and states which cupboard and which drawer of the cupboard they are in. I pointed this out to him but he insisted on pulling out each drawer and cupboard to look through them all. What is it with men and not believing you? He totally and utterly pointlessly wasted two minutes of his life looking for something that I had told him wasn't there (and I was right). I didn't waste two minutes of my life watching him. Well, I was watching him, but I was drinking wine, so I at least used my time wisely.

Alexandra and I had a chat on Messenger earlier. We were talking about one of our usual topics of conversation, the one where we are thinking of converting to lesbianism. I think she felt my pain when I told her the story of Mr H and looking for the spice beginning with 'M'.

We also talked about the fact that whether you were gay or straight didn't matter as long as you were a nice person. Personally, I know a lot of straight people that are total A-holes. Although we did say that marrying an animal wasn't really right and that reminded me of an article I had read in the newspaper once that said how a man had married his wardrobe. Obviously, I'm joking - I don't read newspapers. I suspect it was a link that someone had posted on Facebook.

Whilst Mr H was cooking our chilli/curried bolognese, I was looking at how to approach a publisher, on Google. I have now written my letter and extracted some (hopefully) funny parts of the book and will be whipping it off to some in the next few days. Fingers crossed tractor-ites (although this will look stupid now if I do get one and they are publishing this book, which you are now reading). This is starting to become a bit like *Terminator* where at the end of the film Sarah Connor is recording her story and will John Connor still send his Dad back to save the day, knowing it is his Dad but then he doesn't know it is his Dad and if his Dad hadn't already come back then will he need to come back again in the future? OK. I'm getting confused now... where's the wine?

I was even more suspicious that Mr H had bought a tractor on eBay when he randomly texted me from badminton, 'Love you tonight xx'. Apparently my reply of, 'What have you done?' didn't go down well. Honestly, he does like to confuse me.

My poo and wee patrol mission was a success. I checked the barn and there was no poo or wee to be found – phew. The cat had been shut in for a day and a half. Mr H isn't that clean when he's not shut in. I'm wondering if the cat actually went down the toilet and then flushed it. And it managed not to sprinkle on the floor either. And I bet it washed its paws afterwards. Animals really are less work than husbands.

The Farmer's cat has been sitting on the top of their conservatory pretty much since it was let out of the barn. Casper and their cat do not get on. Casper is a fighter. I have therefore had to feed the Farmer's cat on top of the conservatory roof. I had to stand on an upside down bread tray (I have no idea where it came from) in order to reach the roof and the cat. I have a feeling that 'tales from A&E' will be coming at some point soon...

Tomorrow is tetanus time (the jab, not the actual disease, I hope). And I will have to put up lots of signs around the house reminding us not to feed Bonnie after 8pm as she is going in for her dental work on Friday. (I'm not looking forward to this – Bonnie being under anaesthetic. I'm not a baby when it comes to needles, not like Mr H...)

Thursday 12th May

Missions for today:

- *Don't come back from the doctors with Ebola*
- *Have witty banter in the nail salon*
- *Practise BSL (sign language)*

Mr H got a shock when he saw me up at 7:30am. Remember, I am not a morning person. He had (typically) forgotten that my tetanus jab was this morning and that's why I was up. Mum sent me a message telling me that she hoped that it went well and that when she wrote the word 'tetanus', autocrapet changed the spelling to 'tet anus'. Whoever wrote autocrapet does have a sense of humour at times.

I noticed that since the embarrassing Dentist's experience, Mum has not offered to come with me to the doctors. I like these doctors, I really don't want to have to move to a different practice. (I just had a 'grammar' moment when I couldn't remember whether 'practice' had a 'c' or an 's' in it. It's just reminded me of everyone moaning about their six year olds doing SATs this week and having to know what convovulated verbs are. I'm now thinking that I have remembered that wrong as autocrapet is insisting that convovulated isn't a real word and has underlined it in red... I'll Google it later and find out... Actually, scratch that - we all know that I won't. Life is too short for Googling boring random crap like that. Googling pictures of cats with their heads in toast though is well worth it.)

I forgot to take my face mask to the doctors (the new one that I had ordered from eBay, like they wear in the Far East to avoid dying from pollution), not my cucumber and mint one that supposedly will 'make you look ten year's younger' (it doesn't – unless you are 114 years old and then you could probably pass for 94). Luckily because I was in to see the nurse then I knew that I should only be in the waiting room for ten minutes max.

The receptionist remembered me from my phone call and came round the other side of the counter to look at Brownie's evil twin's bites on my leg. She was quite shocked at how bad they were. "Lucky chickens don't have teeth", she said. She then went pensive and said, "They don't do they?" "Well, I've never got that close to see, but no, I don't think that they do."

The rest of the patients in the waiting room had gone quiet while she was inspecting my leg and I swear I heard one of them say to her friend, "Can you get Chlamydia on your leg?" As predicted, the nurse was running to time and I was in and out like a shot (excuse the pun). When the nurse called my name, I scuttled down the corridor listening to a lot of the patient's tutting as to why I had only just arrived but was going in first.

On the way out I caught the tail end of a conversation where a guy was asking whether his wife's prescription was ready to be picked up. I swear that he said that her name was Joan Collins. When the receptionist asked for his name to confirm his identity, I thought that he said that his name was Jackie. Wolverhampton is always bonkers. Who knew that Joan and Jackie Collins lived here...

I was a big brave girl for my injection (Mr H would have cried) but still felt the need to reward myself, afterwards. I popped to Greggs and bought some chocolate cornflake cakes. The till in Greggs wasn't working properly and the server started bashing it really hard with her fist. She looked up at me and said, "It's useful if I've had a row with my husband in the morning, as it means that I can take my frustration out on this pretending that it's his head." I nodded in empathy. Another poor woman, dealing with man nonsense, I thought...

I also popped to Tesco as we were running low on milk. The Tesco is attached to a petrol station and as I was being served, the girl on the counter shouted to her colleague, "Dave! I think we've got a jumper. Is that a jumper on pump two?" 'Oo – how exciting' I thought. 'I wonder if they are going to make off without paying?' Sadly, that's not what she meant. The car had broken down and she thought that it was going to use jump leads from another one to get it started.

"Dave! Go and tell him that he can't jump from there. We might all blow up." 'Typical.' I thought.

That would have been ironic. To avoid being killed by tetanus, I instead get blown up in a petrol station. At least if I died from tetanus then I would probably have lived for a few more months. Luckily though, Dave had the situation under control and the car was safely towed out of the petrol station and we didn't blow up. I think the girl on the till was a little disappointed. I know that Mr H was, when I told him.

The nail salon was full of women moaning about their menfolk. Gemma wasn't in there but apparently her fears about the guy that she was meeting being gay came to fruition. He wasn't actually gay but it turned out that he was married. Unfortunately, having sat in the sun for all of 20 minutes I appeared to have gone red down the right hand side of my body. My neck was red, my right arm was red and my right leg was red. It looked like someone had thrown boiling water over me. Every time someone new came through the doors they exclaimed, "Blimey! What happened to you?" I pondered that I could tell the truth or I could lie and say that Mr H had thrown boiling water over me. Of course I didn't say that… I told them that he had tried to set me on fire.

When the gems were being applied to my nails, a text came through from Matt, down the farm. Apparently Mr H had got the Land Rover stuck in the field up to its arches. He assured me that the pictures would be on Facebook soon. This turned out to be a lie. He had to wait for Carrie to come down the farm and show him how to upload them. About two hours later (I'd lost interest by this point, mainly because I was relaxing with a beer in the garden) the pictures finally went up.

Miranda kindly put one of the pictures up in the 'tractor4graham' group saying: 'notractor4graham.'

Mr H was still chain sawing down the field so he said that I should go ahead and eat if I was hungry and he would grab something when he was done. Once again, being an adult, I decided, is ace. I ate exactly what I wanted for dinner. I had a can of beer, some crisps and a chunk of bloomer bread. I am now out of calories, so when we practise sign language in the pub later, I now need to be very expressive if I am going to be able to have another beer. MFP at the moment is telling me that I can't and that I need to exercise to have any more. It's such a party pooper at times...

Sign language practice tonight was, once again, totally hilarious. We were running a bit late so Jayne texted asking us what we wanted to drink. I said, 'Mr H will have a pint of diet coke and I'll have a Peroni, please.' When we arrived at the pub, Jayne said, "Is this what you wanted?" pointing to my pint? "Yes, that's right." "Oh — that's good then because when I ordered it, I thought it was a glass of wine and when the bar lady asked if you wanted a pint, I thought, I know she likes a drink, but I don't think she drinks wine by the pint."

Once we had started our practising, Jayne said, "I don't like men that are fast and limp and I feel like when I sign the word 'where' I'm juggling balls." Jayne is full of accidental double entendres - I do love her.

We have been thinking strategy for our forthcoming exam. You have to fingerspell at some point in the conversation and 'Wolverhampton' is far too long and I always forget half way through what letter I'm on. Because of this and our cunning ways, we have decided to pick town names that only have four-five letters max. I have baggsied* Bath and Derby and Jayne has baggsied York. Mr H was a bit miffed as he couldn't think of any other towns with short names so we resorted to asking Siri. I think Siri has started getting too big for her boots. Mr H was interrupting me every time I was trying to ask her about the towns, so my last request was, 'Siri – my arse of a husband wants to know which towns in the UK only have four letters in their name.' Siri answered, 'That's not nice.' But in my defence, Siri does not know Mr H and the nonsense that I put up with on a daily basis.

* I suspect that this is a local slang word. It means when you announce 'shotgun' to baggsy the passenger seat in the car. Oh? Wait... I've used the word 'baggsy' to define itself...

When we got back from the pub, Mr H went all boring again and put *Question Time* on. I was trying to get past level 1,658 on *Candy Crush*. I multi-tasked though and successfully said, "Oh yes. Absolutely. Uh-huh, you're so right"; as he threw questions or observations my way. I don't think that he noticed as he was too engrossed in the Brexit debate. I must admit though QT was at least comical at one point tonight. When David (or is it Richard?) Dimbleby asked a member of the audience about how he would deal with America, I don't think he expected, "I'd blow them up" as an answer. It was totally the best bit of the programme.

I left to go to bed early(ish) knowing that I needed to be up at 6am to take Bonnie to the vets. I put *Law & Order* on the bedroom telly but Mr H wandered up ten minutes later and immediately changed the channel back to QT. What is it with men thinking that they 'own' every remote in the house and can just turn over when they want? Never mind, I thought, I'll get my revenge somehow. Luckily I didn't need to as you'll see from tomorrow that Lucy woke him up at 2:30am. She had probably been having nightmares after being forced to watch QT...

Friday 13th May…. ooo spooky (I'm not superstitious really)

Missions for today:

- *Get up at 6am and don't repeatedly hit snooze and miss taking Bonnie to the vets*
- *Take Bonnie to the vets for 7:30am for her dental work (obviously related to first mission but is in itself a separate mission)*
- *Try and relax for the rest of the day before picking Bonnie up*

The day started off well. I didn't hear Lucy barking at 2:30am wanting to go out so Mr H was fast asleep on the settee when I got up at 6:10am. Presumably he had stayed there after letting Lucy out. I do have a confession though - I did hit 'snooze' more than once on the alarm (and I'd pretended to not hear Lucy barking at 2:30am. I should feel guilty about this. Let's be clear that I should, but I don't).

I didn't bother to put make-up on as the only people at the vets at that time of the morning are the nurses that book your pets in. None of them are hot and male, so I felt it unnecessary to set the alarm ten minutes earlier to do this task. (I call it a task because when you're 42, it's more like painting than 'touching up'.)

I think that Bonnie sensed that I was taking her somewhere that she didn't want to go as she wouldn't let me put her seat belt on and bit me. 'Ironic that she is going in for dental work', I thought. I'm hoping that we won't have the same palaver on the way back as her mouth will be numb from the anaesthetic and she will have fewer teeth to sink into my arm.

At 7am in the morning I was not in the mood to wrestle with a dog. I did ponder that maybe my mum-friends go through this on a daily basis. One of them has a three year old that bites her all the time. I think that I would bite her back. I didn't bite Bonnie back but then again she did smell of fox poo and I didn't really want to be phoning the doctors back to check whether there was some other injection I needed for what I might catch from ingesting that (and the receptionist had laughed enough at my chicken bite. Goodness knows how she would react if I told her that I had eaten fox poo).

Mr H crawled back into bed just before I left, so being the good wife that I am, I got dressed in the dark. Thankfully, I noticed that my cardigan was on inside out before I got to the vets. I had visions of Brandy and Precious the Shih Tzu being professionally made-up (both of them) and giving me sympathetic looks with my inside out clothes and Bonnie reeking of fox poo.

As I kissed Bonnie goodbye at the vets (I momentarily forgot about the fox poo), another girl was waving goodbye to her Labrador and was wiping away a tear. I decided to do a RAOK (random act of kindness) and provided some reassuring words. Her dog had a cancerous lump that needed removing and she wouldn't have put her through the anaesthetic if the vet hadn't insisted that it needed to be done. She said that normally her husband would drop the dog off but he couldn't so she had to do it. I empathised with her and thought of Mr H snoring back in bed at home.

After I got back, I nearly dropped back off to sleep on the settee but my tummy rumbling at 10am kept me awake. I ate a sausage sandwich (and gave Lucy some as she had gone into mourning with Bonnie not being around). I realised that although it was 10am, that was like lunchtime in my normal day. Given that I don't normally get up until around 9am and eat lunch by 1pm, then 6am until 10am would be around about the same time (coming from the girl that's rubbish at maths, I'm quite chuffed with this...)

I decided that I needed to keep busy or else I would stress about Bonnie, so decided to pop to the shops to buy a christening present and a 30th birthday present. I also thought a quick trip to Sainsbo's was needed as we were running low on CIF bathroom spray (and Mr H has been eating too much wheat, so I really need to not run out of it when his tummy explodes).

Whilst I was in Next choosing some baby clothes, a woman in her 50s (well, she might have been younger but quite clearly sunbeds and cigarettes had not treated her well) was talking loudly on her mobile phone. She said, "Well, I'm in Next at the moment because I'm trying to avoid children." I looked up and thought, 'You are standing in the children's clothes department. This really is not the best place to avoid children.' Just at that moment a woman with a twin buggy pushchair accidentally rammed the back of her legs trying to leave the department. I hurried to the homeware department to pay for my baby clothes, just in case a fight was going to break out. I was too stressed about Bonnie to deal with other people's dramas today. I also mentally chastised myself for not wearing my stab vest.

I headed off to Sainsbo's with my small shopping list. I really am dim though (you know this by now quite well, I suspect). After I had been successful in my baby purchase (to be clear, I didn't actually buy a baby. I only bought some clothes. I didn't have enough cash to actually buy a baby...) I tore off the top of my list so that only my Sainsbo's shopping was left on it. Unfortunately, when I did this, I had folded over the piece of paper before tearing it and had also torn off three of the items at the bottom of my shopping list. I then had to guess what they were. I only had the letter 'F' and what looked like a 'u' for one of the items. I really couldn't think of anything that began with 'Fu' except for a rude word that Mum says that I use too often. I happily remind her that my swearing also comes from her side of the family. (I know she will be outraged when she reads this bit.)

* When Mum was doing her read through she told me that this reminded her of something that had happened to my Grandad (her Dad). He had been moving the washing machine and dropped it on his bare foot and he screamed "F**k you!" Apparently my Grandma shouted back, "I'd like to see you."

Mum said that it was a really funny moment as she had never known my Grandma to be so quick witted. I told Mum that I get my swearing and sense of humour from her side of the family. This confirms it...

As I was wandering around Sainsbo's, I did not see the same old guy that had stalked me the last two times. Maybe he wasn't a security guard and was just some perv after all. I did get a shock as I was choosing my balsamic vinegar though. There was a bottle (and it wasn't even that big) that was £12.99. £12.99?!! For balsamic vinegar? At that price I would expect it to be 60% alcohol and I was really surprised not to see a security tag on it. But then again, I don't think the people of Wolverhampton are big into their balsamic vinegar.

The alcohol aisle, on the other hand, causes anything metal in your bag or on your person to magnetise to the shelves. I think it's because of the number of security tags on the bottles. I've often seen little kids attached to the top shelf, with their arms and legs dangling like a fly caught in a spider's web. I do wonder whether their parents have deliberately put them in the suit of armour just so they would be magnetised to all the tags. Quite clever really, as it was a cheap crèche whilst the parents did their shopping in peace.

I nearly thought about going through the self-service till but I'm still not confident that I can do it without a cashier being there to sort out the many problems that I seem to have. Mr H will take a whole trolley of stuff through the self-service till without any problems. I think it's Physics letting me down again.

The cashier on the till was really cheery but as soon as I had deposited all of my items on the conveyor belt, another member of staff put one of the 'This till is closing' signs on the end. No wonder she was so cheery, she was about to go home. She complimented me on my nice summery nails and also on my nice 'distribution and ordering of my goods on the conveyor belt'. What she actually said was, "Oh I do like a tidy conveyor belt". I couldn't think of a suitable reply that didn't have references to lady gardens or bushes so I kept my mouth shut and just smiled.

As I was leaving, the Round Table and Sycophants* were collecting money for charity but I didn't get chance to put any money in their bucket because a customer was having a go at them for giving money to the 'wrong good causes.' Not wearing my stab vest, I, again, sensibly decided not to get involved.

* Apparently, it is the Soroptimists. I did think that Sycophants was a weird name for a group of women fund raising for charity.

Just before leaving Sainsbo's, I texted Mr H to say that I was buying a hot chicken for us to have for lunch so that we only needed to have a snack before leaving for Sign Language in the evening. He texted back saying, 'Oh – I forgot to check whether I have my house keys.' He only had one thing to remember this morning and he hadn't even managed that.

He nearly didn't get his hot chicken. As I arrived home, I was merrily taking the bags out of the boot and depositing them by the front door and on my return second journey, I saw Casper with his head in the bag with the chicken, trying to claw his way into it. Luckily he had only just broken through the bag and I noted which bit he had touched, and decided that would be Mr H's.

Just to be on the safe side (unlike the sausage incident), I drew around it with green marker pen. To hide the colour green, when I put it on his plate, I covered some of Mr H's chicken with lettuce so that he wouldn't notice. As I have said before, I can be a frickin' genius at times. After we had eaten lunch I did notice that Mr H's tongue had gone a funny green colour but luckily he didn't look in the mirror, so my secret was safe.

Saturday 14th May

Missions for today:

- *Hope that Bonnie perks up properly after her visit to doggy hospital*
- *Finalise my extracts from the book and letter for the publishers*

We picked up Bonnie yesterday afternoon and she was apparently an angel in doggy hospital. The nurse had to wake her up to bring her out to us and, bless her paws, she was really groggy. I got (irrationally in Mr H's view) upset in the car on the way home as Bonnie didn't bark at all. She always barks in the car, the entire journey, no matter where you go.

Isn't it funny that when she is well and barks like a loon, it drives us insane but when she doesn't do it, I want her to do it because it's just not her. Even reading this back, I have decided that I'm coming across as a loon. Mr H said, "I wonder if the vet can give us some of what they gave her, for future use, so that she doesn't bark in the car again?" I think he was joking... (although it might be useful for those times that Mr H annoys me, so maybe I'll ask Henry when we're back next).

Bonnie has been really quiet since we've come back but she has gradually been getting back to normal. I knew this when she bared her teeth when I asked her if she was ok. 'Yay! My furry psycho is back', I thought.

Unfortunately today, I seem to have picked up a bug from somewhere, as I have had the trots. 'Why does it always happen immediately after I have just given the bathroom a thorough cleaning', I pondered. I wondered whether I got it from having to pick up the remains of a dead pigeon from the front garden this morning. Apparently, although 'outside jobs' are Mr H's domain, this doesn't extend to removing pigeon entrails from the grass (I think it comes within his 'I don't poo-pick' rule). There actually wasn't much to remove though as Lucy had been outside for the last hour and had devoured her way through most of the pigeon remains. I suspect that I won't be the only one with the trots in this house today...

The other possibility is that Mr H is back to poisoning me. He seems to be fine and he has returned the masking tape as apparently he said that it wasn't strong enough for his needs... hmmmmm.

We had a 'Neighbourhood Watch' newsletter come through the post this morning. Going to Neighbourhood Watch meetings is just like the programme, the *Vicar of Dibley*. Unfortunately, I am away when the AGM is on so I won't get to chuckle at the topics under discussion. Mr H will be there so he can relay the funny tales to me.

Although Bottie McTrottie had visited me this morning, I am very much an 'Eat your way through any illness' kind of a girl. I had some of the leftover chicken from yesterday on a sandwich. Unfortunately I had forgotten about Casper and whilst I was diving into the fridge for some salad cream he leapt onto the side after my sandwich. More unfortunately for him though, karma kicked in and he missed the side and slid down the front of the cupboard to the floor. He has been eating a lot of the food belonging to the cat next door and I think he had forgotten that he was carrying extra weight and needed to factor that into his leap. Of course it could just be that, like me, he is also crap at Physics.

After Mr H and I got in from sign language class last night, the news was reporting the story of the guy that had won in the High Court and didn't have to go to prison or have the death penalty* for taking his daughter out of school during term time.

* I'm not sure the sentence would have actually been that severe.

Mr H and I had a totally pointless conversation, for around 30 minutes, about the definition of the word 'regular'. Apparently, the legislation says that you can't take your child out of school unless they have 'regular' attendance.* Mr H and I obviously have a different definition to the word 'regular'. He will insist that he 'regularly' cleans his teeth or that he 'regularly' does housework. If you count 25% as regular than yes he is right (and I'm being generous with the 25%).

* Mr H has just come in and read this bit and said, "You need to change your book! It's factually incorrect."

(I think he has missed the point that most of it is made-up b****cks... but anyway I will indulge him.) Apparently, you can't take your child out of school at all and they must have regular attendance. In his view that means every day.

I'm now wondering why we even bothered to have this discussion. We don't have any children in school and happily take our holidays when it is cheap and the kids are all in school... Mr H says I have missed the point again. He doesn't want people being able to take their kids out of school, otherwise there will be loads of them around when we go on holiday and prices won't end up being cheap. Now if only he had said this at the start then our 30 minute discussion could have ended in 30 seconds with me agreeing with him. I don't often agree with him... but when it comes to money and a quiet life then I am most definitely in agreement.

I just took a break to go and sit in the garden and have a cup of tea. I am currently having a battle with an unknown animal with one of my 'fat ball' holders. Just to clarify, these are the wild bird balls made up of seeds and bound together with lard and come in yellow stringy packaging. For every week for the last three weeks I have put three of them in one of the holders that hangs from the apple tree and closed the holder at the top to hold them in. Consistently, for every week for the last three weeks, the three fat balls have mysteriously disappeared overnight after putting them in there with the top of the holder hanging loose at the side.

Yesterday, I cunningly thought that I had outfoxed the fat ball thief by sellotaping the top of the holder down. As I was drinking my tea I looked up and the sellotape was gone and so were the three fatballs. I am now going to replace them and tie string around the top of the holder and if that doesn't work then I think I will go for electric fence wire. If I see the Farmer's wife with frizzy stand up hair the day after using the electric wire then I will know that I have been blaming the wrong species...

Mr H is continuing to prepare the land for the Alpacas. He has been taking down the fence near the greenhouse so that the shed can go up for them. I took photos of him throwing the fence posts and it looked like he was tossing the caber. I put some pictures up on Facebook, with the caption 'Tossing the caber' and a few of my friends commented, 'What a tosser!', 'He really is a popular person with his friends,' I thought.

For the last few weekends there have been 'New Tricks' marathons on telly. Given my delicate tummy, I feel that I might be confined to the settee for the remainder of the day. In the episode that I just watched Brian gave Esther some red and white roses and she threw them back at him saying how thoughtless he was. I was intrigued by this and Googled 'Should you give a woman red and white roses?' A link to a website called *dumlittleman.com* came up with some 'tips for life' for men.

'Interesting...' I thought. Maybe I should leave it open on Mr H's computer, especially if it had anything useful to say. Sadly it didn't. The navigation button on the site wasn't working and I couldn't get to see anything else it had to offer – typical male site I thought, gets you all excited and doesn't follow through... On a positive note a Roxy advert popped up so I went to see if there was anything in their sale that I would like.

Apparently though, (coming back to the red and white roses) red and white roses together mean unity/togetherness. It turns out that Esther was mad because they were the flowers that were at her Dad's funeral.

Sunday 15th May

Missions for today:

- *Keep Bottie McTrottie at bay as important christening business is on today and I don't fancy having to ask Mr H to pull over on the M6 Toll because I have an urgent appointment with the toilet (which in this case would have to be a bush) and have some trucker pip his horn at me and make some rude gesture*

Today was the christening of one of my good friend's baby. Thankfully Bottie McTrottie had 'done one' although my stoopid headache was back. I really need to look into this brain tumour idea. (To be clear – I mean I need to check whether I have one and not go out and buy one. That would be a silly purchase, although if I were to buy one then I would try and get it through *Amazon Prime* same day delivery. I told you that my patience ran out aged 41 and this applies to my online purchases too.)

The christening took place in a Catholic Church and the priest looked about 103 years old. This is what he looked like but I suspect that he was older. He also, rather unfortunately, looked like the priest played by Ted Danson in *Three Men and a Little Lady*. He also had the ability of the priest played by Rowan Atkinson in *Four Weddings and a Funeral*. It made for an even more enjoyable service than normal.

First of all he couldn't get the microphone to work and then he totally frolicked with the order of service. I'm sure I said, 'We will' at the wrong time. Unfortunately, saying it after he has just done a bible reading that ended with 'sacrificing your child to evil' resulted in a few people turning to stare at me (funny that...)

I think that we all held our breath a bit when the priest held the babies being christened, although I noticed that he braced himself on the font while he did it. Thankfully, he did not have a case of the dropsies and all went well. Especially when one of the babies burped whilst being signed with the water.

We went down the toll road to get there and I have to say that Mr H has now mastered the art of parking closer to the pay machine, so that his trademark 'bouncing' manoeuvre is no more. I'm disappointed to be honest and now that it's gone, I kind of miss it. We had a conversation in the car about the Eurovision song contest that had been on last night. I think that I am the only person that doesn't like it. My Facebook feed was going berserk with references to it last night.

Someone had said, 'What about Eurovision? We can't Brexit as we won't be in Europe anymore.' I think they are confusing the EU with Europe. I said to Mr H, "Well of course we will still be in Europe – I mean – we aren't going to create a new consonant just because we aren't in the EU." After the sentence escaped my lips, I knew it wasn't quite right. Mr H said, "I think you mean continent." I blame Jimmy Carr. I had been watching *8 out of 10 cats does Countdown* before bed last night to keep up with my Maths and English practise and I must have had it on the brain.

Also, given that Australia now take part in Eurovision, then quite frankly, I don't think it matters where you are. I didn't do Geography GCSE but even I know that Australia isn't in Europe. We went there on honeymoon and it took us about 20 hours to get there. If it was in Europe it would have taken four hours max.

Although, Mr H is inherently tight so maybe he just booked the equivalent of London Midland to London instead of Virgin. A two hour Virgin trip to London seems to take about four hours with London Midland. Maybe that's why our flight to Australia was so long? We probably went via Northampton and took the scenic route.

Apparently, Australia did really well last night. The rest of Europe don't hate them, like they hate the UK. I don't know why they hate us so much, compared with the French we're quite loveable really. Obviously I'm joking, I meant the Germans. I did wonder whether maybe Kylie was performing for Australia. Ordinarily, in any other competition that would be a sure fire winner but if she performed in Eurovision she would need to come out as a bisexual S&M

donkey loving Muslim in order to succeed. And she would have to wear some outfit with flashing wings on it.

I've gone off track again (I think it's my age).

Back to the christening...

We got told off by a very old grumpy man when we were leaving the christening as apparently we had parked in a car park that we shouldn't have done. He happily told us that the car park was private and not for people using the church and that if everyone decided to park there then the cost of the upkeep would rise considerably.

Really he shouldn't have been parking there either by the looks of things as he accidentally put the car into reverse when he was driving off and backed into the hedge and brought some of the fence down. No wonder he was worried about the upkeep if this was how he and others that used the car park drove.

Tonight the Queen's 90th birthday celebration was on TV. I love the Queen and the Royal family and feel slightly guilty at the discussion we had in the hairdressers and nail salon about her 'needs' the other day. Although when she met Ant and Dec she did seem to linger holding onto Dec's hand for longer than necessary. (To be fair, so would I... He is still my phone screen saver and I can still feel the heat from his cheek against mine when we met him at BGT a few years ago.)

I put it up on Facebook that I was watching the birthday celebrations and one of my friends said that she had forgotten that it was on and that she would love to watch it but her husband probably wouldn't let her as he didn't like the Royal family. I asked her whether it was because of the time that the Queen had cut him up on the dual carriageway. I can't think of any other valid reason for not liking the Queen, except a bit of road rage.

Tomorrow my sister is going into hospital for a minor procedure but apparently she has to have a responsible adult with her and no recreational drugs for 24 hours afterwards. I said, 'We're screwed then...' I am the supposedly responsible adult that is going to look after her on Tuesday whilst her husband goes to work and I was thinking of taking her some Lucozade (it was what we were always given as kids when we were poorly – and a spoonful of glucose). I have a feeling that Lucozade is classed as a recreational drug. Whenever my cousin gave it to her kids they went totally mental. I'll take her some sparkling water instead, just to be on the safe side.

Mum has been on holibobs for a few days but she's still been a star and read through my daily tales for me. She sent me a photo on Messenger with the caption, 'Is this Precious the Shih Tzu?' I thought that she had been bored and had done some random Google images searching. It actually transpired that she had hidden behind SDK's body to surreptitiously take a picture of a real dog they had seen that was dressed in a pink tutu, crop top and had a pink bow in its hair. It was the crop top that freaked me out. Crop tops (as well as flesh coloured leggings) should really be made illegal and this applies to animals and humans alike. I think I should raise one of those government petitions. I think that you only need 1,000 people to start one off. I know at least a

1,000 people that think that flesh coloured leggings should be banned.

I then told Mum that if someone had spotted her taking the picture she would probably be labelled as some dog-ophile (a paedophile for dogs). I don't think she will be allowed in Suffolk again. I told her to make the most of the remaining part of her holibobs, just in case she was now on some 'Police list'.

On a final note for today, my furry psycho is back to normal. I did panic a bit this morning when she struggled to eat her Dentistix. Mr H said, "Her pain relief is probably wearing off, so her teeth are probably hurting her a bit today."

By the time that we were back from the christening though she was bouncing around as normal, chasing her tail and barking at the horses at the fence. She is grinning again too. (I know that this sounds stupid – but Bonnie and Lucy are both very smiley dogs and when Bonnie didn't smile for nearly two days after her op it made me incredibly sad.) Mr H just thinks I'm a head case. But he married me, so who is the head case really..?

Monday 16th May

Missions for today:

- *Don't give in to Mr H's wistful looks at the digger (Ron the digger man is back today to continue preparing the land for the Alpaca shelter)*
- *Set up the 'garden' office without last week's palaver of nearly falling in the moat*
- *Have witty banter in the pub tonight at sign language practise*
- *Try and keep my sister's spirits up while she is in hospital (thank goodness for mobile phones)*

The first mission is going to be by far and away the hardest one to achieve. I remembered that it was 'digger day' again when I came downstairs all bleary-eyed to hear Mr H chuckling at something on BBC breakfast. I asked him whether Lucy had woken him up early again and he turned around to kiss her on the nose and said, "Oh, it doesn't matter, does it poppet?

You're getting old and can't help it." This was a world apart from yesterday when the 'f' word escaped his lips at least three times when she wanted a wee at 5:30am.

Once again, I momentarily thought about buying him a tractor but I'm not convinced that if I did buy one I would have a happy husband all of the time. His new yellow sit on lawnmower has just this second stopped working and he's gone from happy chuckling toddler splashing in a paddling pool to moody stroppy teenage boy that grunts when you ask him a question, all in the blink of an eye.

My second mission was a piece of piss*. I think it had something to do with the fact that it wasn't windy today. I didn't have to weigh down all my work with rocks (or Casper) and I managed to put up the parasol without doing a Mary Poppins into the apple tree.

* I suspect that this is a local phrase. I have no idea where it comes from though. It makes no sense whatsoever. What would a 'piece' of piss look like? I have enough trouble if I have to wee

into one of those specimen bottles for the doctor and have to try and stop before it goes all over my hand. 'Piss' really isn't something that you can cut into pieces...

Although this did remind me of a few years ago when we had a big BBQ in the paddock in the summer. I had bought a 'party gazebo' from B&Q and had followed the instructions for putting it up (I nearly used the word erection but I knew it would then be followed by some smutty comment and Mum also tuts at my overuse of innuendo. Actually, scratch that. I think she likes it really).

Anyway back to the gazebo...

The following day when we all got up after a heavy night of drinking, it appeared that the party gazebo had decided to jump into the moat at some point in the night. To begin with I think we all wondered whether it had been some drunken party game we had partaken in before we went to bed. It wasn't. The space hoppers in the Farmer's field (and one hanging limp off the barbed wire) told another story though.

With my excellent knowledge of contract law I took photos to show that the stakes and ropes that held it down (well, were supposed to) were all still firmly attached to the ground. The thread that held the straps across the top had all unravelled and that's why it was in the moat.

We spent a lot of the morning fishing poles and gazebo panels out of the moat and I put them in the boot of my car and took the algae soaked gazebo back to B&Q. (I think a few poles sunk to the bottom but that will be some exciting 'Staffordshire Hoard' for the people of the future to find one day. Maybe I should also sink some photos from the BBQ too to put it into context for them. With climate change, the people of the future might not understand the concept of a BBQ. And a lot of my friends are crazy, so I'm sure they would like to see their antics in print.)

I have to give B&Q a gold star for their service. The lady on customer services took one look at the green smelly gazebo and bent poles and said, 'I really need to call the manager about this.' Mark was brilliant as he looked at the photos on my phone and said, 'Looks like a cool party' (I had accidentally scrolled back too many and he had seen the one of our friend giving a pug a French kiss).

He then went back into manager serious mode and said, 'That will be the fault of the factory in China. They haven't sewn the top tabs on properly. I will email our supplier to let them know.' I did hope that I hadn't just lost some poor worker their job. On the plus side though it was so mangled that there was nothing to show who had approved it and the box was at the bottom of the recycling bin underneath a load of bottles and cans and a whole family of wasps.

Mark understood why I hadn't fished it out. I left with a new party gazebo. This one did not end up in the moat. It blew into the Farmer's field instead when hurricane George came to visit. I did not take this one back. Quite clearly the instructions said, 'Do not put up in severe windy conditions.' Even with my excellent knowledge of contract law, I couldn't have stood in front of Mark again with a straight face, nor more importantly a gazebo that this time was covered in horse manure. Although, I think that Mark might have given me another one on the proviso that he got an invite to the next party.

My sister is in for her minor 'procedure' in hospital today. When I woke up, I momentarily forgot that her husband was taking her in and when a calendar reminder popped up to say that she needed taking in at 7am I had momentary heart failure. It was 9am when I woke up. I'm a bad bad sister, I thought. (I've exaggerated a bit I think. It was probably more likely heartburn from eating my toast too quickly.)

I texted her for a lot of the morning and she assured me that I would have had lots of tales for my book from the waiting room. She categorised the other people in the waiting room. There was:

1. Overly-chatty-shares-too-much (OCSTM)

    You probably know the sort... tells you about her relationship with her husband and that she thinks that he's having an affair because she's been having fru-fru problems and hasn't been able to see to his needs for the last six weeks while she's been on the waiting list for her appointment.

Then she goes into intimate details about her medical complaint.

2. Doesn't-know-she-is-born   (DKSIB...   I really tried to get this to spell 'Nob' at the end but I've pondered for at least ten minutes now to no avail. I'm hoping Mum with her cryptic crossword and anagrams ability will be able to come up with something when she does her read through later. And while you're at it Mum can you try and come up with one for numbers one and three as well. It's only her wedding anniversary, so she won't be doing anything else...)

Luckily she was going in for her procedure before my sister, so she didn't have to listen to her for longer than two hours.

Apparently DKSIB knew that her Mum never wanted her. She knew this because her twin sister, at the age of five, got to choose what colour dress she wanted to wear first for their joint birthday party. Her sister got to wear pink whilst she had to suffer the brown dress. Her sister also got to choose which pony she wanted first, at aged 12. 'She chose the white one knowing that was the one that I wanted. And then when we were 17, my sister got to choose which car she wanted first. She got the Fiesta and I got the Kia.'

I think if I had been in the waiting room it would have gone one of two ways. Either I would have taken the line of 'At least you had a dress to wear! I had to wear my sister's hand-me-downs and they always hung off me as she was four years older and about a foot taller. And you had a pony? I was lucky at the age of 14 to be allowed to have a Russian hamster and that was on the proviso that I got an Avon round and paid for it myself. You got given a car at 17?! I got three jobs at 17 so I could finally buy my own clothes and not get teased and need therapy for the rest of my life.'

Alternatively, my evil twin might have reared her ugly head and I might have gone with the one-upmanship. 'Oh that's dreadful. I know exactly what you mean. My sister had Beyoncé play at her 18th birthday party and all I got was Justin Bieber. And I totally get the car thing! When we flew by Concorde to New York for New Year, she got to choose which first class seat she wanted before me and when Daddy bought us a house each, she got the five bed and I was only allowed a four bed.'

3. Stressed-out-and-needy (SOAN)

She would probably have been the one that I felt sorry for. Apparently, she had a really controlling mother-in-law who kept texting her to ask if she was going to be back at dinnertime to fix her son's dinner. According to her mother-in-law, it was her fault that she was in hospital when she should be at home looking after her son.

My sister asked her what she was in for (it seemed to be a random collection of medical issues in the waiting room). She said that her mother-in-law thought that she was in for removal of a wart when in reality she had come in to get sterilised 'You just don't breed from bad stock', she whispered 'and I couldn't bear having a daughter like her.'

She also suffered tinnitus, 'probably from the mother-in-law's incessant chatter', I thought. In the space of five minutes she had texted her daughter-in-law 20 times and none of them were concerns for her welfare. When the doctor popped his head into the room, he told her that she would be in next. Apparently her face fell and she asked if she could be put to the back of the queue.

My sister being in hospital reminded me of when I ruptured my Achilles and Mr H had to drive me to Physio before my leg was strong enough to push down the clutch in the car. It also reminded me of how he secretly likes me travelling the country for work as on more than one occasion he forgot to turn off to the hospital and my,

"Where are you going?" prompted a, "Oh! I forgot. I thought that I was taking you to the train station." He would then look glum for the rest of the journey to the hospital.

One of our neighbours has just this second been down. Like me, she is a fan of Derek Morgan in *Criminal Minds*, Special Agent Seeley Booth in *Bones* and Tony from *NCIS*. She asked me if I had seen *Hawaii 5-0* as she was sure that I would enjoy it. It's not on Freeview and Mr H and I are too tight to pay for Sky, so she has just popped down with the boxset for me to watch.

Amazon Prime also delivered today (two days late though, so they will be getting an email) with my box set of *My Name is Earl, seasons 1-4*. I really need Amazon Prime and home delivery of fish n chips to be made illegal. My patience running out at the age of 41 with the combination of Amazon Prime has done nothing to help my bank balance and online ordering of fish and chips has done nothing for my waist line.

Mr H and I had one of our totally pointless conversations again last night when he said,

"You could just borrow other people's box sets instead of buying them." He really doesn't try to understand the female mind at times. And he has just been forced to eat his words as I have just borrowed a boxset. He gave me one of his 'suspicious narrowing of the eyes' looks, as if to say, 'You spent the entire night defending buying boxsets and now you are borrowing one.' It's good to keep him on his toes with my random ways.

One of my friends on Facebook put as her status today, 'David Beckham was in our workplace.' More importantly she put up some pictures of him looking H.O.T. (You need to say that with your voice going extremely high pitched.)

Another of her friends replied, 'Lucky you – we had Ofsted.' Thankfully, she didn't put any pictures up of the grumpy 60 year old woman that had been in her school. No one wants to see that. DB is on my laminated list. (I'm allowed to call him that. As long as I don't do it within 200 feet of him.) He now has 'full status' on the list. He used to have 'restricted status'. This was back in his younger days before he had speech therapy. He was only allowed on the list for no-strings sex as long as he didn't talk. Now he can talk as much as he likes...

It is my good friend Jade's birthday soon. She's the one that has Professor Noel Fitzpatrick at the top of her laminated list. I said to Mr H that I was going to book us VIP tickets to 'Dogfest' as that way you get a personal Q&A session with him. The only downside is that you have to take a dog and Lucy can't walk far enough (but is an angel in the car) and Bonnie can walk hundreds of miles but barks constantly in the car.

Mr H said, "Take one of the Alpacas, as we'll have them by then." I said, "It's called 'Dogfest' because it's all about dogs." Mr H said, "Still take one of the Alpacas and if he queries why you've taken an Alpaca, act all surprised and say, 'But the guy that sold it to me said it was a 'Great Poodle' - a Great Dane crossed with a Poodle.' You're blonde and dim so he won't be suspicious." I pondered about the viability of this plan for a minute or two and have decided to run the idea past Jade.

Tuesday 17th May

Missions for today:

- *Be an ace sister and spend the day nursing my sister back to health after her operation*
- *Not curse the fact that Lucy was fast asleep when the alarm went off at 6:30am and I had to prod her awake to go outside to the loo*

I have kept my missions simple for today as I really just need to make sure that my sister is fed and watered and alive when her husband gets back from work. It's the same motto I live by for any house plants. Although maybe that's a bad analogy. I have never successfully stopped a house plant from dying. But I'm not as worried about my sister, it normally takes me two weeks to kill a house plant and I'm only going to be with her for 24 hours.

I headed off to my sister's at 7:30am so that I could be with her whilst her husband was at work. To be fair men make rubbish nurses. If I relied on Mr H to nurse me back to health then I would likely die in a cholera infested pit.

When I had norovirus Mr H disappeared 'shopping' in the afternoon and didn't come back for four hours. Conveniently his phone had stopped working so that I couldn't get in touch with him and tell him that I had ruined yet another pair of pyjamas and he would need to buy extra thick rubber gloves to remove them from the ensuite floor. I actually ruined seven pairs in total in four days. I also needed to buy new ski boots after they were also ruined by my projectile vomit. Mr H couldn't understand what they were doing on the floor of the ensuite. I told him that it was down to his untidiness and not the fact that I wanted a new pair and had put them there.

Norovirus was hideous. I was convinced that the devil had inhabited my body and was expressing his anger through every orifice that I had. Amazingly Mr H never went down with it and we concluded that a dodgy oyster was to blame. According to the NHS website norovirus is present in 75% of oysters. This is another of those important things that you should really be taught in school. Trigonometry has never helped me in life – well apart from when I had norovirus and was trying to work out the angle to vomit down the toilet and not the wall - but it didn't work, so it really was an unnecessary part of the curriculum and if I had known about oysters containing norovirus then I wouldn't have needed trigonometry anyway as I wouldn't have been projectile vomiting. I must write to that Mike Hunt about this, or is it Jeremy Gove?

Anyway... back to my sister.

I have to say that I am an excellent carer. I Googled 'duties of a competent nurse' and made sure that I followed the practice standards of the College of Registered Nurses of British Columbia (They had a nice website). Having a read of their standards they seemed to take their duties seriously. Their rules are:

1. Nurses must provide their clients with safe, competent and ethical care.

I realised that my sister was my client, so I drew up a contract at 8am and made her sign it. It had the usual disclaimers in it, such as, 'I will not be held liable for injury or death howsoever caused... etc etc'. Having done this, I felt ready to attend to her needs.

2. Nurses do not abandon their clients.

I made her a hot water bottle, peppermint tea, put a fruit bowl by the side of her bed and put her painkillers in reach (her husband had placed them in an unsafe high place out of her reach). I also made sure that we chatted (it's important to attend to someone's emotional needs according to the website) and when she complimented me on my sandals, we Googled 'Earth Spirit' and she had successfully ordered three new pairs of shoes by 9am.

3. Nurses may withdraw from care provision or refuse to provide care if they believe that providing care would place them or their clients at an unacceptable risk.

This happened when one of her kittens managed to get into the bedroom. I swear that it is a ninja in disguise. It was swinging off the curtains at one point before leaping to the bed before landing next to the soup that I had brought her for lunch. Unfortunately, its tail dipped into the bowl and as it ran from the room a trail of beef vegetable soup could be seen on the duvet cover. It looked like my sister had had an accident and hadn't made it to the toilet on time.

4. Nurses do not provide care that is outside the scope of their expertise except in an emergency.

My sister didn't look very happy when I said that I needed to check her 'obs' (apparently this is slang for observation) and produced a rectal thermometer. I don't know why she was bothered, I've seen her drunk on the loo plenty of times and helped her wipe before...

5. Nurses recognise that informed, capable clients have the right to be independent, live at risk and direct their own care.

Apparently, she didn't enjoy the Mensa test that I gave her in order to assess her levels of capability.

In all seriousness, we had a really fun day together. I took my work there and produced a seminar entitled 'Coping with the unexpected at work.' Today's events helped a lot in writing it.

We did think that hospitals are a bit rubbish at telling you what you really need to know after having an op though. The leaflet talked about eating healthy and doing gentle exercise. What it really needed to tell you was:

1. How much farting you would do to release the humongous amount of gas that needed to escape from your body due to them blowing you up with it in order to operate.

2. It should give you advice on how to wipe your bum after going to the loo when you can't twist your body. (I did offer to get the fish slice from the kitchen and wrap some toilet paper around it for her.)

3. It should also provide you with a week's supply of wet wipes and dry hair shampoo, instead of helpfully telling you not to get your dressing wet in the shower.

My sister has two kittens and I had forgotten how much hard work they are. They were as manic and hyperactive as two year olds on caffeine for most of the day before they dropped in an exhausted heap around 4pm. (This lasted for about 45 minutes before it started all over again.)

One of them did the biggest, smelliest poo in their litter tray and I swear that it was the size of one of Bonnie's. Even my sister said that her cat has done poos bigger than a human being. I did make a mental note to check the *Guinness Book of Records* when I got back home just in case she might be able to make some money from her elephant-poo sized cat.

The other kitten took a liking to my furry pom-pom. I had taken my work bag and it is still attached to it. This pom-pom must have some weird mystical powers as it seems to attract dogs and cats. I'm convinced that one day I will be walking down the street and some pied-piper for animals episode will happen whereby I will turn around to see dogs, cats, squirrels and raccoons* following me.

* I'm not sure that raccoons actually live in this country but they really should. They're such cute creatures. I quite fancy getting one. I must check whether it will happily live with the Alpacas.

Wednesday 18th May

Missions for today:

- *Try to stop Bonnie from biting the vet*
- *Don't kill my sister - as I'm back there today*

Bonnie was back at the vets today, so that he could check her dental work. Given that I was seeing a hot vet, then I made the effort to put on some make-up. I also didn't want to bump into Brandy and Precious without looking half decent. Normally putting on make-up isn't that much of a difficult task. It initially involves slapping on thick, expensive, foundation so that I look like I've been airbrushed when I take a selfie and put it up on Facebook.

This morning, however, didn't quite go to plan. I had finished my old foundation yesterday and being the super organised person that I am I had a new one ready and waiting to be opened. If ever I run out of foundation it is worse than an international incident. It happened once in 2003 and Mr H remembers it well. He will periodically ask me if I have a spare one as he has said that he can't go through that ever again.

I took my new foundation out of its box and went to squirt some onto my finger. Unfortunately, nothing came out. I tried again but nothing. I then realised that there was a little foil top on the end of it that needed to be removed. Unfortunately, once again, my knowledge of Physics let me down. As I picked off the foil, the foundation squirted out like a long thin worm and landed down the side of my face and in my hair.

Who knew that foundation in hair was such a nightmare to get out? My newly blonde (well - ginger) hair now had a streak of 'warm English rose' down one side of it that wasn't going to come out. 'Great.' I thought. 'It would happen on the day that I'm off to the vets and I'm bound to bump into Brandy.' Luckily though, she wasn't there today.

It seemed to be 'Portuguese waterdog' day today in the vets. This was the first time that I have ever seen one of these dogs and in the 20 minutes that I was in the waiting room, I actually saw three. They all belonged to different owners as well. I knew that this was the breed as I asked one of the owners what her curly haired dog was.

I told her that her dog looked like me before my hair has been straightened. I then retracted the statement and said, "Actually, your dog's curls look much better than my natural hair." She seemed pleased with the compliment. Her dog was called 'Romeo'. I didn't think that was a very Portuguese name but then again the only name that I could come up with was Cristiano, after Cristiano Ronaldo the footballer. At least, I think he comes from Portugal...

Bonnie embarrassed me by barking at the other dogs in there. I suspect that she was saying, 'Stay close to your owners, guys. Last week I was left here and they gave me some medicine that made me very sleepy. When I woke up I was missing some teeth. I think they're selling them on the black market. If a nurse sticks a thermometer up your bum then run for the hills!' (Bonnie gets her expressive, exaggerative language from me.)

Henry inspected Bonnie's mouth. When I had tried to look in her mouth the day before she had snarled and bared her teeth and I quickly retracted before I lost some fingers. I have my sign language exam in a few weeks. It would be just my luck to be missing some fingers.

However, she was a little angel for him and even rolled on her back to let him tickle her tummy. I swear that dogs are like children at times. I have one friend that has three children and they are evil little b*****ds at home (her words - not mine. 'I should have stopped at none'. Again, her words, not mine) but apparently are absolute angels at school. That was like my family when I was a child.

I was an awesome sister again today as I didn't want to leave my sister on her own, whilst her husband was at work, so I went back to play nursey. I did think that if this went on then I really should order a proper nurses uniform from Amazon. Mr H seemed to perk up when I said this. I still thought that there would be little chance of me killing her. As I said yesterday, it takes two weeks for me to kill a house plant. But if she's not better in 13 days then she's on her own.

Her tongue was all bruised and swollen yesterday, which was from the tube that they put down her throat and her husband had bought her sorbet the night before, which had gone down well. I offered to pick some more up on the way over.

I only went into the supermarket for flowers, sorbet and trashy mags* but came out with ten donuts, a fresh bloomer loaf and poo spray for the toilet (Mr H has been eating too much wheat) as well. I also bought some crisps that were 'Chardonnay white wine vinegar' flavour. I really am an advertiser's dream...

* To clarify, these 'trashy' mags are not of the nudey-rudey variety but of the 'pointless tattle about celebrities' variety. They are obligatory reading for anyone laid up in bed.

The reason why I came out with ten fresh donuts is because I gave into their clever marketing scheme. They put them right by the door and when you wandered in the glorious smell of fresh baked dough made your tummy growl. I wasn't the only one that had succumbed to them. There were only four of us in there and three of us had two bags of donuts in our shopping baskets.

The only guy that didn't was about 30 stone in weight and I think that he had already eaten his ten donuts whilst wandering around the store and that's why there weren't any in his basket.

I concluded this by the amount of sugar around his mouth, on his top and the splodge of jam that was working its way down his jeans. I didn't stop to tell him. It's hard to have the 'you've got jam on your crotch' conversation with a stranger and I didn't want him to think that this was some weird chat up line.

When I was paying for my goods, the cashier asked me if I wanted a 'flower bag' for my flowers. 'It's free.' she said. Being the inherently tight person that I am, I decided to accept her kind offer. I didn't really need one as my sister lives about a one minutes' drive away but I like to get one over on the government.

'Ha!' I thought. 'Didn't think about flower bags in your carrier bag tax did you now?' I have decided that the next time that I go shopping to Sainsbo's, I'm going to ask them for ten flower bags to put my shopping in. I am such a frickin' genius at times.

Back at my sister's house we had a look through the trashy mags and noticed a four page spread on Cheryl Tweedy-Cole-Versini-Focaccia-Ciabatta or whatever her name is. We noticed that the four page spread actually said very little when you thought about it afterwards (a bit like my book really...) The only thing it really said was that she was dating Liam Payne from One Direction. We got momentarily excited by this because Liam Payne comes from Bushbury which is six minutes' drive round the corner from Mr H and me. We did think that we should monitor his twitter feed to find out when he is going to take Cheryl home to meet his mum. We can go and lie in wait. I've not had a selfie with a celebrity in a while and I'm starting to get withdrawal symptoms (and I don't have an injunction for either of them...yet).

My sister said, "Whereabouts in Bushbury do they live?" I said, "I don't know - they probably own the whole area, by now, what with his millions and all. I mean it's got an Aldi, a Co-op and a crematorium, so it's quite an attractive investment I would think."

We also did some Googling to find out how long my sister might be off work. When hospitals discharge you they don't really tell you how long your recovery will be or what to expect.

I think my sister could have done with a heads up about the fluorescent yellow gunge that she was coughing up from her throat. I could have done with one too. It nearly put me off my second donut seeing her hack it up. I found some forums online of people that had had the same op and it was comical seeing the type of people and comments on there.

One woman said, 'I've never been the same again. I took 13 weeks off work and had to go back part time and am now thinking of taking more time off.' We decided to put her in the category of 'never worked a day in her life welcher'. There were some positive people on there and for some it started to look like a competition.

'Fitnessfreak87' said, 'I was back in work the next day. I just worked through the pain and got on with it and was back at the gym doing press ups by day three.' Unfortunately, we didn't see any more posts from her so suspected that she was probably dead after rupturing her wounds from going back to work and the gym too soon.

We had to stop reading the forums as they were making us chuckle too much and it was hurting my sister's stitches. I did not relish having to call an ambulance to explain to them that she had ruptured her wounds through laughing at all the crazy people in the world.

I did start to panic that maybe today would be the day that I killed her. I stopped the frivolity and went back into stern matron mode. I don't think she liked this as much but in my mum's words from when we were kids, 'I don't care if you don't like it - it's good for you.'

Before her husband left for work, he said, "I really hope that she does a poo today. I would much rather that you wiped her bottom than I." Unfortunately, for him she hadn't done one by the time that I left. But I did give him helpful advice about using the fish slice covered in loo paper. I just hope that he remembers to clean it before using it to stir risotto.

I was convinced that her kittens were plotting to kill me today. They were eerily quiet. I was working at the dining room table and turned around to pick up some documents from the floor and as I turned back her ninja kitten was sitting on my laptop and staring at me. I don't like to let kittens get the upper hand, otherwise you will wake up at 3am feeling like you're suffocating as they sleep on your face. So we had a staring competition. Obviously, I won. OK - I think I cheated by moving my hand down to wiggle my furry pom-pom and he immediately gave up to pounce* on the pom-pom but, nevertheless, I won.

* That's not all that he did to the pom-pom. He started humping it at one point. I think I might have to get rid of it (the pom-pom, not the kitten. I don't think that my sister would be happy if I got rid of one of her kittens. She nearly killed me when I buried her Pippa doll in the garden, when I was five years old, so I dread to think how she would react if I took her kitten.

Just to clarify, I would never bury a kitten in the garden. I would at least choose somewhere she couldn't find it*).

So far, a dog and a kitten have both humped the pom-pom, another dog has aggressively barked at it and I narrowly missed a third dog from cocking its leg up on it.

* Note for thickies: obviously this is a joke.

When I got home, I gave Mr H a big hug and a kiss and said, "I've really missed you the last few days. It feels like I haven't seen you for ages." I have realised though that this is the way to put up with his man nonsense the rest of the time. Maybe I need one of those second homes like MPs have? I wonder if I can get a council house. I'm sure when I explain what living with Mr H is like, then I will go straight to the top of the list.

I went out for a curry with Little Wren tonight. We went to our usual place, *The King's Repose*, where the head waiter guy loves us. He said that Jade had been in a few weeks ago with her husband and he had asked her where we were. Jade had told him that we couldn't make it. I told him that Jade was a big fat liar and I would have to have words with her as she hadn't invited us at all! The head waiter said, "You look like you've lost weight. You look really good." Sadly he was talking to Little Wren and not me. I think when he looked at me he managed not to blurt out, 'Flip me! You haven't lost weight though have you?'

My hair definitely has started turning quite ginger but Little Wren said that she won't tell Bobby. I'm back at the hairdressers next week anyway, so the blonde will be back.

Thursday 19th May

Missions for today:

- *Don't miss the train for London by over-sleeping (I've been up early a few days in a row now and this is a big possibility, what with me not being a morning person and all)*
- *Have a fabulous catch up with my work wife*

I had to go to London today to see some new clients about providing them with training for their new recruits on 'confidence building' and basic skills for presenting. I was only going to be in meetings for the morning so would have the afternoon off to catch up on some 'me' time.

There are a lot of birthdays coming up so I thought I might go shopping for cards and presents. This did make me think as to why a lot of people had birthdays at this time of the year. I came to the conclusion that this would mean that they were conceived in the last two weeks in August, which was probably holiday time when Britain used to have a nice summer and husbands and wives forgot that they hated each other for a while. I also suspected that alcohol played a big part.

Mr H dropped me off at Wolves train station. I was too tight to pay the £9 parking fee and wanted to have some cocktails with my work wife. *Heart FM* was on the radio and they were asking what strange thing was on a lot of British people's lists for taking on holiday abroad. Mr H and I both said 'tea-bags' at exactly the same time but the guesses from people phoning in were rubbish. Who takes cheese on holiday abroad or board games? Talk about random...

The fence should be up by the end of today. The fencing guys arrived at 7am and were working away when we left. I can tell that I'm middle aged now as the thought of the fence being finished made me feel quite aroused.*

* Maybe I am exaggerating a bit. (We all know I'm not.)

Mr H was wide awake at 5am. He says it was because he didn't want to oversleep for dropping me off. I think it was the excitement at the digger, tractor and fence post putter-inner-plunging machine that was coming. He was mortified that he had to be in work all day and wouldn't get to drool over them all day.

My train was a connecting one, so initially I had to suffer London Midland between Wolves and B'ham New Street before getting the luxury of Virgin to London. I really must Google the Chief Exec of London Midland. I bet he's nothing compared to Sir Richard's looks and charisma and that's why his train company sucks.

First class London Midland was rubbish. The small carriage was rammed and I had to ask a grumpy woman to move her bags so that I could sit down. She sighed and spent ages doing it. It's amazing that I have no patience for most things but can smile all happily at someone forever and a day waiting for them to move their bags. I think this is because it seems to annoy them more than me. This is my evil twin surfacing again. I should have words with her really. But at times, I totally adore her. This is one of those times.

A guy in the carriage was on the phone and said rather loudly, "Now, Pete, this is highly confidential and hasn't been released yet, so you need to keep it under your hat." At that point the whole carriage went silent whilst everyone was intrigued at this highly confidential conversation.

Turned out it was mega boring and was just to do with someone called 'Jack' in their office that had complained to HR about someone called 'Wendy' that had been making inappropriate, sexual advances, towards Jack. The way that Jack was being described though, you would have thought that he would have been grateful for the attention. He sounded a right nob.

Of course I'm joking. I do not condone sexual harassment in any way, shape or form – unless of course any of the celebrities on my laminated list want to harass me, that is (then I condone it in every way, shape or form).

Someone was breaking wind in the carriage. Being first class you would have hoped that the smell would have been of a better calibre. It wasn't. But then I remembered, this was London Midland first class...

At B'ham I relaxed when I was seated on my Virgin train and enjoyed the eggs benedict breakfast on the journey. It told you on the menu that there were 752 calories in it. The full English only had 500. I decided that today I would turn off MFP. It was going to explode with the cocktail calories later anyway, so I may as well blow them in style.

London totally surprised me today. Normally the people here are miserable and look like they want to end their lives. A lot of people were quite cheery today. A guy let me get on the bus ahead of him and didn't even tut when my Oyster card didn't work and I was issued with an emergency ticket.

I succeeded in my second mission and had a fabulous catch-up with my work wife. We put the world to rights. If anything happens to Mr H, then I might have to ask her to move in. We really do get on well together and I suspect that I won't be picking her dirty undies off the floor each morning, or have to remind her to trim her nose hair.

On the way back from London I stopped to chat to Jason, the Big Issue seller. He remembered that I wasn't supposed to be down until next week. He's got a good memory. He also said that he was thinking of moving further North as I said how much nicer it was. He is one of the nicest people that I have met on the streets in London.

The train back was rammed and people were jockeying for seats. A guy wandering through the carriage had to momentarily sit in a seat to let another guy past who was trying to walk through the carriage the other way. I do wonder why they don't make train aisles wider and two-way. The train-rage that I have encountered over the years is a ridiculous amount.

These incidents are often caused by people with rucksacks on their backs. Their rucksacks will swing into other people's heads (of people that are already seated and therefore lower down) and I once nearly got concussion from a laptop. That would be a really embarrassing way to die. I want to at least go out in some dramatic altruistic way. Maybe saving a child from a burning building or if that's unrealistic falling under a bus because I'm chasing a celebrity but definitely not 'death by laptop.'

Anyway, back to the guy that momentarily sat in a seat to get out of the other chap's way...

He leant over the table to the girl opposite and said, "Hi. I'm Marius. You're looking good today." He then winked at her and as the other guy walking along the aisle had gone, Marius disappeared off. We all chuckled and the girl he had winked at said, "Well that was a bit like speed dating." Unfortunately, for her she got evicted from her seat a short time later by a guy wearing a tuxedo-kilt get-up and his wife who was wearing a Jacques Vert type ensemble with a massive hat. The girl disappeared off down the carriage. We all suspected that she went to find Marius...

I surreptitiously took a picture of the guy wearing the kilt and asked my Scottish friends on Facebook whether he was likely to be wearing anything underneath the kilt. My non-Scottish friends told me to ask him but I thought that was rude. Instead I decided that when he went to get up to go to the toilet then I would pretend to drop something on the floor and look up his kilt. That sounded a much less intrusive plan. (Although I decided that I wouldn't take a photo on my phone, that would be one step too far.)

I got momentarily distracted as the first class announcement came on the tannoy that they were a bit short staffed so were going to start serving alcohol straight away rather than wait until Milton Keynes. I swear that I saw at least three people do fist pumps* and the word 'Yes' escaped from the lips from around half of the carriage. This also meant that the trolley came back round for the second time just before the train got into Wolves. I was offered more wine and I said, "I'm getting off shortly, I don't think I've got time, thanks." The VT girl said, "Oh, of course you can. It's wine – you can neck it." She was right. I don't know what I was thinking... Maybe I'm coming down with a bug.

* I still call it a fist bump. But I've changed it because I don't want to look dim.

I chatted to the guy in the tuxedo-kilt and his wife and it turned out that they had been to a Buckingham Palace garden party that day. I asked if they had met any celebrities as Mr H and I got the opportunity to go to one ten years ago and met Baby & Ginger Spice, Brian May, Rod Stewart, Philip Schofield and a host of others. Unfortunately this was in the days before decent mobile phone cameras so we only have the memories in our mind.

They said that there weren't many celebrities there. He said, "The Health Secretary guy was there and the Education Minister. Unfortunately, when they were presented to the Queen, the crowd boo-ed."

I chuckled at this. Mike Hunt and Jeremy Gove (I can't stop turning their names around – I think it's a disease) at the same event and unpopular. I had visions of people dressed up in flash clothes throwing small sandwiches with the crusts cut off at them and the two of them hiding in some bush to wait until everyone had gone home.

I also asked the Scottish kilted-up guy whether he was wearing something under his kilt. He replied, "There's only two other people that will know that. One of them is my wife and the other is another Scottish man." 'Really?' I thought. 'He shares a lot. I don't think that I would talk about some weird threesome to a random stranger that I've only just met. Maybe that's just the Scottish way?'

Friday 20th May

Missions for today:

- *Research 'how to find a publisher' and send off my letter and extracts from the book*
- *Go outside lots and get irrationally excited at the new fence*

I can tell that I'm middle aged. The fence was finished yesterday (they worked like Trojans and it was all done in 12 hours) and every time that Mr H put a picture up on Facebook for me to look at while I was in London, I did get overexcited. I think the people on the train on the way back thought that I was ogling over some nudey-rudey pics rather than a fence. If I was then it would definitely be of my favourite rugby player, Morgan Parra.

I don't think that I have actually told you that he is number one on my laminated list. He is often the captain of the French rugby team and plays scrum half most of the time. He is around 14 years younger than me but as Mr H is around the same amount of years but in the other direction (i.e. he's nearly 14 years older than me) then it is prudent that as Mr H advances in years then I have a younger model to take over.

I did go out and did get irrationally excited at the new fence today. The land feels like it's properly ours now and we are ever closer to George, Chester and Cyril's arrivals. Mr H was in work today, so as he was leaving I did my normal wifely duties of asking him, "Have you got everything?" In usual husband fashion he replied, "Yes." "So, you don't need your phone today then?" as I turned my head and nodded to his phone charging in the lounge. I am still thinking of putting a clause in my will to provide a carer for him. I'm amazed that he is still alive when I come back from being in London for more than a day.

This publishing lark is crazy. Most publishers won't accept unsolicited manuscripts and you have to find an agent. I have tested the water by emailing three of them with my book extracts and we will see. I have been thinking that maybe

I should just self-publish. It seems a lot of hoops to jump through to get published and remember that my patience ran out aged 41. Pity I didn't write my books two years ago really...

Today should really be named 'random' Friday. The following incidents all happened:

1. I swallowed a fly.

   Mr H came back from work at lunchtime and we went for a walk along the new fence. As we were walking back I was yabbering away to him and a massive fly* flew into my mouth and to the back of my throat. There was nothing that I could do but swallow it as I was choking on it. I refuse to phone up the doctors again this week. I will have to wait at least three months before contacting them again. 'Chicken gate' is still too fresh and they are going to think that I really am a crazy loon if I phone to tell them that I swallowed a fly and am worried about it having babies in my tummy and flies coming out of every orifice they can. One day I'm sure that I will wake up in a strait jacket and to be totally honest, I won't be surprised.

* I'm hoping that it was only a fly. It was really quite big. Not as big as a squirrel but maybe it was some flying beetle type thing? Obviously it wasn't a squirrel. That would have been ridiculous. I know that squirrels are furry and this creature definitely didn't have fur.

2. An old man was standing in a bus stop without his shirt on and appeared to be having a wash.

This was at 8:15pm in Walsall on the way back from sign language. It was chucking it down with rain and he was washing himself underneath the bus shelter. I did think that he could just stand in the rain and that would be an easier way to get clean but we didn't stop the car to tell him. People don't like it when you point out obvious things to them and I wasn't wearing my stab vest.

3. Local news reported a suspicious package being discovered and a controlled explosion carried out on it.

   I suspect that this was the package sent by Bobby. It still hasn't come. I'm hoping that they didn't look at the address on the front before they blew it up. I really don't want drones flying over the garden when I decide to sunbathe in the nude.*

   * I don't actually do this anymore. Not since I went on 'aerial view' on Google Earth and realised that you can see everything. No one wants to see my tinnitus. (Autocrapet fail – obviously spell checker thought I didn't want to write 'tiny tits.')

Saturday 21st May

Missions for today:

- *Go and visit my sister and check that she is still alive. I only messaged her yesterday and that could have been her husband hacking into her account replying to me*
- *Go out for Jade's birthday and remember to wear my 'drinking shoes'*

I woke up this morning to find that my garden parasol had died. This is where Mr H and I had another of our totally pointless conversations. He also did it before I had had my two morning lattes. After 25 years, he really should have learned by now. I went to rescue the parasol from the apple tree and decided that as it was broken in four different places then it needed to go in the bin.

Mr H spent five minutes telling me that I obviously hadn't tied it down properly. He has clearly forgotten the greenhouse blowing into the Farmer's field or our big marquee nearly taking off and blowing into the Farmer's field (I must remember to add in this tale), both of which were his fault. He then spent another five minutes saying that it could probably be repaired and that I did not need to buy a new one. In true husband and wife fashion, I shall totally ignore him and buy another one and I shall put the old one in the bin just before the bin men come so that he can't try and mend it.

Whilst I was sitting drinking my morning lattes, both dogs were licking the floor tiles in the lounge. I did wonder whether they were trying to tell me that my housekeeping skills were not up to scratch but when I looked down I could see a bit of a chip stuck in between the tiles.

We had been naughty and had some fish and chips on the way back from sign language last night. I must have dropped one of my chips. This is really not like me. First I refuse alcohol on the train and now I had dropped a chip. I'll take my temperature later just in case I have a fever. (I still have the rectal thermometer from using it on my sister this week. I'll make sure that I give it a good clean first though. I'm not stupid. Mr H's electric toothbrush will make a perfect cleaning implement.)

I went to see my sister and it was also her birthday today. I went to the shops before going so that she would have a birthday cake. I also bought more donuts. I don't think that I am ever going to be able to get out of there without succumbing to them. I also bought some more Chardonnay crisps.

There was a woman in the queue in front of me who said, "Having a party?" as she saw the cake, donuts, crisps and a load of chocolate bars* on the conveyor belt. I was dying to reply with, 'No – just that time of the month' and do some overly exaggerative rubbing of the tummy. But I didn't.

* Mr H had once again ignored me writing 'chocolate bars' on the shopping list, so today I have had to take matters into my own hands. I obviously can't rely on him to attend to my needs.

She was on crutches with her ankle in plaster, so I decided to tell the truth. (I don't know why this makes a difference. I feel that lying to the disabled is wrong. Whereas, able bodied people are fair game. This is totally crazy logic and some weird form of positive discrimination. I sometimes do wonder about why my mind works the way it does. I blame the time that I ruptured my Achilles. My emotions were up and down like a yo-yo when my leg was in plaster and I wasn't very good at coping with humour, so I think that all people with limbs in plaster must react the same. I also blame my genetics – it's bound to come from Mum's side of the family... She won't be happy when she reads this...)

I also asked her how she had done her injury. Turns out she had been cleaning and had slipped on the bathroom concrete tiles. "If I was a dirty b*****d then I wouldn't have injured myself" she blurted out. Me and the cashier both nodded at this and I thought about the one time that Mr H slipped on the newly mopped kitchen floor and banged his head. I bet there are some comical statistics from A+E about cleaning related injuries. I made a mental note to Google this at some point...

My sister was alive and well and is looking much better. She bought me some beautiful flowers as a thank you for looking after her. Her instructions to her husband were, 'Buy some classy ones. Don't get her naff carnations.' He did well. And she is right – I can't stand carnations.

We went out for dinner with Jade, as it was also her birthday (more drunken August bank holiday sex on the part of her parents methinks...) Unfortunately we had a balsamic vinegar and oil moment when it fell from a great height and oozed all over mine and Aimee's dresses and more importantly over my phone.

Luckily my £1.99 case took the brunt of it and use of a wet wipe later it was back to being as good as new*. Mr H (extremely hypocritically) said, "Well, you shouldn't have your phone on the table at dinner, it's rude." Later on he was asking Cortina a question and taking selfies. I was going to point out his hypocrisy but I have decided to log it and leave it until a later time. A woman knows that she needs to store up these things for future use.

* I think some oil has leaked into the speaker as when I get a text notification, the noise sounds like a dalek farting. It's comical so I don't mind. As long as the oil doesn't decide to ooze out while I have my phone to my ear and people wonder what the goopey stuff running down my neck is, then all is well.

Bonnie liked the fact that 'Balsamic vinegar oil gate' had happened as she was happily stuck to my side licking my dress when we got home. I'm hoping that's what she was licking and it wasn't something of the poo variety that had stuck there when I tripped up walking down the drive home.

I was annoyed at my fall as I had specifically put on my drinking shoes. These are flat so that I don't have an embarrassing 'falling over in the road' incident. Obviously they didn't work and I now need to go out and buy some new 'drinking shoes.'

Mr H (once again totally pointlessly) said, "Just don't drink. Then you won't need to buy some new shoes." He doesn't understand that he is the main reason as to why I drink. So it is totally his fault that I need 'drinking shoes'. And every woman knows that you need a variety of colours. D'uh! It's Physics. Everyone knows that pink and green don't go together. It's why the sky is blue and the grass is green. Science doesn't lie. Mr H always narrows his eyes in these arguments. He doesn't like it when I turn his precious Physics against him. I, on the other hand, love to turn his precious Physics against him.

We did discuss politics over dinner. We shouldn't have. It nearly caused an argument. I thought that I might need to Google funny videos of kittens doing silly things to diffuse the situation when Aimee talked about how she nearly unfriended Mr H on Facebook because of all of his posts about Brexit. In my opinion, Facebook should be purely social. There is no place for politics on there. Cats with their heads in toast, funny e-cards and texts from dog are on the other hand totally appropriate uses for it.

We did have a chat about some funny fake twitter posts that had gone up there though. I particularly like the one that is supposedly David Cameron tweeting, 'I am confident that Britain has the means to resist a nuclear attack from North Korea' with the response, 'Dave mate – we weren't prepared for snow in winter.' Apparently another Twitter user had tweeted about 'Shania law' and how all the Muslims should go back to Islam where they came from. Someone had replied, 'Islam isn't a country and Shania is a country singer.'

Tonight was a really funny night. Aimee ordered cherry Bakewell tart for her dessert but it arrived with a noticeable gap on the top of it where a cherry had once been. We asked the waitress where the cherry was and she said that she would go and get one for her. I'm sure that I then saw the waitress on her hands and knees further up the restaurant looking under a table. I hypothesised that there was a cherry on it when it had come out of the kitchen but that it had decided to detach on route to our table and rolled onto the floor. I warned Aimee to check it for hairs when it arrived.

The waitress obviously couldn't find it though as she didn't come back for half an hour and when she did she apologised that she had 'forgotten' and brought a bowl of strawberries and raspberries as compensation. Poor Aimee didn't get to eat much of them as everyone else round the table tucked into them.

When I got home Bobby put a post up on Facebook showing how he first came up with the '#tractor4graham' saying. I did respond with, 'Someone clearly has too much time on their hands.' He insisted that he didn't do the research and got his friends at GCHQ to look back and see. I know for a fact that this is totally made up. Bobby doesn't have any friends.

I changed the bedding today and momentarily panicked when Mr H put a picture of the unmade bed up on Facebook. I thought that he had finally spotted the new pillow. Turned out that he was only worried that I would forget that it wasn't re-made and had visions of us coming back from Jade's birthday meal and having to fight with putting on a new duvet cover at 1am.

He's not the best at putting the duvet cover on when sober and wrestles enough with it as it is. I really don't understand this. He really is selectively good with Physics. With both of us having had a drink or two we might have got ourselves tangled up in it and trapped. Death by duvet cover would be really embarrassing, although we might be the only ones that did it, so at least our families would have a funny story to tell the next generations. It would also be embarrassing having to call out the fire brigade to come and release us, if it didn't actually kill us. I know what you're thinking… but when a horse got stuck in a hedge the fireman that came out were either old, had massive beer bellies or were female. So it really wasn't worth doing it just to call them out.

Sunday 23rd May

Missions for today:

- *Have a day with absolutely no missions whatsoever*

It is really important in life to have days where you do not draw up a jobs list and just relax and take the day as it comes, doing what you fancy doing at any particular moment in time. It started out well as I ate two donuts for breakfast with my lattes.

It then went downhill when I was tucking into the second donut whilst simultaneously counting my blessings and thinking how great life was. Mr H walked into the lounge and immediately turned over the telly. This did not go down well with me.

1. I was watching *Diagnosis Murder* and it was getting to a crucial bit in the story

and let's face it, who doesn't need a bit of Dick Van Dyke in their lives.

2. Mr H turned over to Andrew Marr on BBC1 who was having some boring discussion about politics and Brexit (and he is no Dick Van Dyke in my book).

3. I dribbled jam down my dressing gown as I turned to glare at Mr H for ruining my morning, and...

4. As I was giving him the evil eye he cheerily piped up, "I think one of the dogs has poo-ed on the rug in the hall, so you'll need to clean it up. I picked the main bit up and it's in a poo bag by the front door but I think you'll need to wash the rug." (There was a lot of 'you' in his sentence, I noticed.)

So my lovely relaxing, 'don't do anything that you don't want to do', day was not off to the best start. I finished my donut and decided to wash the rug whilst I was still in my pjs. I thought that this was the sensible thing to do because last time I set up the electric carpet shampoo machine, I hadn't correctly tightened the stopper and as soon as I turned the machine on foamy liquid shot out from it and soaked my slippers.

Having learned from that episode, I also cleverly removed my slippers this time. Unfortunately for me I removed them too soon and I trod in the rest of the poo that Mr H hadn't seen (or had seen and left because it wasn't in a firm mound) as I walked through the hall. By this point Mr H had done a disappearing act. So all in the space of three minutes he had ruined my TV programme, my dressing gown and my feet*.

* Quite clearly the chain of events were all down to him.

At this point I did think about feeding the raw pork joint to the dogs that I had got out of the freezer last night for Mr H's dinner and thought that he could have fish fingers instead. Of course I'm kidding. But that's only because I didn't want to give anything to the dogs that might upset their tummies further and upon checking the freezer I saw that we were out of fish fingers.

I decided to wash all of the rugs downstairs. This was a mistake as when I went to empty the dirty water out into the sink I nearly retched from the disgusting colour and bits that were floating in it. I did wonder whether to bottle it in case I ever needed to poison Mr H in the future. I'm pretty sure that there was Ebola, bird flu and TB floating in there, along with some questionable insecty-looking creatures. (Obviously I'm exaggerating. I'd only need a syringe full, not a whole bottle, I'm sure.)

We went out for a wander around the new field in the afternoon and both dogs decided to find some fox poo and roll around in it. I thought that this was karma for the poo incident this morning caused by Mr H and said to him, "I washed the rugs this morning, you can clean the fox poo off the dogs. Marriage is all about sharing." He hates it when I quote from 'The Perfect Marriage' book. (He doesn't need to know that there actually isn't such a book and I make up sayings when it suits me.) He didn't look best pleased.

But that will teach him for turning off Dick Van Dyke, I thought.

Mum said that she had never smelled fox poo (I told her about the incident on Messenger). I helpfully offered to bring Bonnie over and let her wash it out of her fur. Strangely, at that point she went silent for the next two hours.

I actually thought that she and Mr H must be related as that's exactly what he does if I ask him to do something that he doesn't want to do. But then that would make me and Mr H related and the thought of that made me grimace and feel sick more than when I trod in the poo with my bare foot this morning.

I forgave Mr H for his morning man nonsense and went to cook the pork joint for evening dinner. (I did this because he left me alone for the rest of the afternoon with Derek Morgan in *Criminal Minds* whilst he worked on getting the base down for the Alpaca shed.) Remembering what had happened last time when I tried to open the packaging on the last pork joint (the pork blood squirting down the onesie that seems to have resulted in me not having seen that courier since), I made sure that it didn't happen again. However, once again my knowledge of Physics let me down. I cut into the packaging away from my body so that it wouldn't squirt onto me. However, I forgot that it would simply squirt in the opposite direction and this time it landed all over Casper who was sitting on the kitchen table washing himself.

He initially gave me a 'I will kill you' look but as his nose started to wrinkle and sniff the air and he realised that the sticky stuff on him was a tasty treat, he seemed to forgive me. I put him on the kitchen floor so that he didn't do a 'dog-like' shake and fling blood all over the kitchen but I forgot that the dogs would also be able to smell the tasty treat. Lucy ran after him trying to lick him. I once again got the 'I will kill you at some point' look from Casper as he was furiously running away with Lucy right behind him. The one positive thing to take from this episode was that Lucy's legs looked really good while she was running after him.

The packaging on the pork joint said it was 242g in weight. I Googled 'How long do you roast pork for?' and it said 25 minutes at 190° and then 35 minutes per lb minus the original 25 minutes. Now I think we all know that I'm not great at maths. So I got out my calculator and worked out that 242g was about half a lb so it would need 25 minutes and then I would need around 18 minutes but I needed to take off the original 25 minutes. I concluded that it would be done in -7 minutes. I pondered this for a while and thought 'that really can't be right...' So, I weighed the pork joint and it turned out that it actually weighed 2lb 8oz. 'Strange', I thought. But I worked out how long it needed and put it in the oven.

As it was cooking it was starting to go a really nice brown crispy colour on the outside. 'Funny,' I thought. 'It didn't look like that when I cooked the last pork joint'. But I put it out of my head.

As I was dishing up Mr H went to cut the pork and said, "This looks surprisingly like beef." Turns out that it was. I had forgotten that when I had been shopping, the butcher department had accidentally stuck the pork chop sticker onto my beef, so they stuck the beef sticker onto my pork chop.

Mr H gave me his 'You really are dim, but I love you' look. (It melts my heart when he does this.) So we tucked into a lovely beef dinner with pork gravy and apple sauce. Luckily the beef had cooked ok using the pork instructions. I'm not sure that I deserve the wife of the year award after this. But Mr H prefers beef anyway, so he was happy.

Whilst we were eating our dinner we put *Britain's Got Talent* on TV. It's the live semi-finals this week. I was actually really disappointed with the show. Mr H doesn't like me watching it. "You always moan that there are too many singers and everyone in the world knows that you hate dancers, I really don't know why you watch it."

Obviously he has forgotten that Dec is on my laminated list and every time I look at Simon Cowell, I think 'His lips touched both of my cheeks...' I did chuckle at one point during the show when I mis-heard one of the names of one of the acts. Apparently they were called 'Spartan's resurrection' and not 'Spartacus's erection.' I did think that they might have got more votes if they had been named the latter though...

After all the acts had been on I turned over as *Ghost* was starting on More4. Mr H said, "There's no point starting to watch that as you'll want to watch the BGT results in half an hour." I said, "No − I'll see on Facebook who went through. I'd much rather watch Patrick Swayze."

Mr H said, "You are a hypocrite. You hate watching dancing yet you love watching Patrick Swayze dance." As usual, he was talking total nonsense. Patrick Swayze doesn't dance in *Ghost*, everyone knows that. But yes of course I do love to watch *Dirty Dancing*. A hot guy dancing is not the same as twenty 12 year old girls from Wales doing ballroom dancing. D'uh...

Trying to make up for pork/beef gate I went to get Mr H a fake Magnum from the freezer. Just to clarify, I don't mean that I have Tom Selleck in the freezer. I mean one of those Supermarket own brand cheapy rip-offs of the real thing. I'm too tight to buy the real ones.

Unfortunately for me I missed the most important bit of *Ghost* trying to be a fab wife. It was the bit where he got shot. In all honesty though it's probably a good thing. I cry at that scene (and so does Mr H. The fake Magnum seemed to cheer him back up though).

Monday 23rd May

Missions for today:

- *Try not to swallow, sniff, or suck up any more insects through any orifice whatsoever*
- *Try not to panic that I have two flies and a spider living inside me (and do not go on Google to see whether it might be true and if so what could happen) [This was a last minute addition – see below.]*

I think that the local bugs around here have taken offence to me. Today I was wandering back from taking the dogs for a walk and as I breathed in some insect shot up my nose and down my throat. Jeepers! What's the chances of two insects being swallowed by me in the space of three days? I then started to wonder that maybe the fly that I swallowed on Friday was Mrs Fly and maybe this was her husband looking for her. Now I really am worried about having baby flies hatch inside me.

I think I might need to Google whether this is possible or not. What made the day even freakier was a spider dropped from the ceiling whilst I was brushing my teeth and landed in my hair. I put my hand up to see what was causing my scalp to itch and there was Mr Spider crawling around.

This conspiracy by the insects around me is starting to freak me out. And I am now beginning to become the lady in the song of 'There once was a woman who swallowed a fly...' I didn't sing it all as I started to get uneasy when she swallowed a cat. I suspect that the spider was after Mr and Mrs Fly and I'm now going to shut the bedroom door at night because I really don't want Casper to try and launch himself down my throat as well.

Mr H laughed at me when I told him why I was shutting the bedroom door. But then he seemed to go quiet when I said, "I suppose I am being a bit melodramatic. I mean there's no way that Casper would fit in my mouth. It's not that big."

I spent most of the day trying to dodge spiders and other insects. It did unsettle me when I went to the toilet in the upstairs bathroom though. When I had positioned myself on the loo, I looked up to see a big daddy long legs type spider happily weaving his web in the window recess. I did my business, flushed the toilet and when I glanced back up, he was gone.

This did not fill me with confidence and I immediately started to feel a fluttering 'down there'. I wondered whether it was purely psychological or whether Mr Spider had decided to try and find Mr and Mrs Fly through some other orifice. I tried to relax and say to myself that the spider had probably disappeared off due to the awful smell of what I had just done. (I did have spicy curry the other night and I think it had finally decided to make its way out.)

On the plus side, if Mr Spider had decided to take a peek inside me, then I think he would soon make his way out. The curry was really spicy and I think I was also emitting the smell of spices through my sweat and other orifices.

I don't think Casper has forgiven me for the beef blood incident from yesterday. He spent the entire day trying to kill both Mr H and I. Cats are incredibly clever. They will wrap themselves around your legs and feet while you are trying to walk and I nearly broke my wrist once falling over him. Luckily for me, I landed in the washing basket which broke my fall.

When Casper tried to trip Mr H up, a few swear words escaped from his mouth (Mr H's not Casper's. He's not that clever a cat). I chuckled as it was a really funny cartoon comedy slip and I said to Mr H, "Well. Remember there is a pack order in this house and Casper is jockeying for your position." Mr H replied with, "I'm below the dogs in the pecking order?" "Yes. But you are above Casper." ('Just'. I thought.) He really does say some stupid things at times.

There was a massive commotion on the moat today. Two grey geese tried to move their home here. The 19 white resident geese were having none of it and were honking and trying to scare them off. I did chuckle as this morning there had been a piece on the news about Brexit and how the 'Out' campaign was being labelled as xenophobic and wanted to 'close the borders.' As I was watching the geese, I thought, 'Really, these animals are no different to the human race.' The white geese successfully shooed the grey geese off and order was once again restored. Immigration really is a universal topic. Of course if the grey geese had have been from the EU then I think the white geese would have had to have accepted them. 'They must have been Russian', I pondered...

I decided that I needed to take my mind off worrying that I now had two flies and a spider living inside me (probably the spider would be living out some real life Pacman game working his way through my colon and intestines to seek out Mr and Mrs Fly). So I decided to Google A+E cleaning accidents (remember this was from my visit to the Supermarket on Saturday when I chatted with the woman on crutches who had broken her ankle cleaning her bathroom floor).

It's amazing what 'open government' and 'freedom of information' has done for us. I scrolled through some documents about A+E statistics trying to see what cleaning accidents had happened last year. Unfortunately, they probably came under the category of 'other', so I couldn't laugh at what people had done. (To clarify. I only laugh because I am the most accident prone person around and I can empathise* with other people that are likely to encounter the same accidents as me.)

* take the piss out of

What I did find interesting though was the following:

1. Monday is the busiest day in A+E. Let's face it. Who wants to go to A+E on the weekend and interrupt their drunken partying? You may as well wait until you're supposed to be back in work on a Monday and then go. That was my hypothesis for the large number of visitors. Really there should just be a category of 'people who hate their jobs and would rather sit in A+E for four hours instead' in their statistics.

2. Friday was the least busiest day for A+E. Again, I thought this logical. If you've just finished work for the week then you really don't want to spend your weekend in hospital contracting MRSA. The 20-24 age group were most likely to attend A+E. I suspected that alcohol played a big part here or the fact that they still played sport at that age (or combined the two and played sport whilst drunk... I know that 'Drunk Twister Darts' is a particularly funny game).

3. The people of Northern Ireland had the highest rates of attendance at A+E. This really did not surprise me. I have a lot of relatives there and they are all complete nutters. They're the sort of people that will play 'chicken' with tractors that are racing around a field and they have a game of 'try and outrun the bull in the field.' The latter game is notorious for causing injuries (or death), especially as my relatives all like to drink as well. My Grandad on my Dad's side was Irish. It's

probably where I get my accident-prone-ness from. He came over here in the 40s I think. Dad says that he came here for work. I personally think that he was evading the police...

4. Those of working age were less likely to attend A+E. Probably because high blood pressure from work killed them and they went straight to the mortuary bypassing A+E entirely. I did get momentarily excited when I saw that injuries from birds was one of the common causes of accidents. Turned out it said 'ophthalmological' and not 'ornithological'. The birds in our garden are evil so-and-so's, so I could believe that they caused injuries. As soon as the birds hear me get the seed tin out of the Utility they're swopping on me. I better not swallow a bird that's looking for Mr Spider...

We went to practise sign language in the pub tonight and on the way back there was a group of lads around the age of 20 cycling along the road. It was getting dark and they were all wearing dark clothing, none of them had helmets on and they were doing wheelies down the middle of the road.

I really should have stopped and told them about my Googling and the statistics for Monday being the busiest day in A+E and their age group being the most likely to attend. I didn't though. Natural selection would probably kick in at some point and they would be straight off to the morgue and by-pass A+E. It would help the statistics I thought. Of course I'm kidding! I didn't think this. I was too tired and it's only just dawned on me now...

<u>Tuesday 24th May</u>

Missions for today:

- *Get rid of the ginger at the hairdressers*
- *Con Mr H that I am off to London for work tonight*

My second mission sounds mean but Mr H and I have been working together at home for too long and I need a break from him. I'm pretty sure that he thinks the same too (as in he probably needs a break from himself as well). I am obviously totally adorable whereas he is totally annoying, so he is bound to miss me. He will definitely miss me not being there to cook for him. He thinks that I am going for work.

My training got cancelled and I could have re-arranged my train ticket and hotel but when Mr H said, "Is this pink top yours - the one on the floor right next to the washing basket? It doesn't take much to put it in the basket you know," I was honestly speechless. I've been picking up his dirty undies for 27 days in a row now (yes I counted - I will need to use it against him at some point) and the one time that I missed the basket when playing 'netball hoody', World War III breaks out.

It was at this moment that I thought, 'Screw him. I'll go and have a nice trip to London and have some 'me' time.' It's important to have 'me' time. Living with Mr H is mostly 'him' time and I think I need to re-dress the balance.

My first mission looked like being a failure at 9am though. My hairdresser was sick. When they saw my lip tremble and heard me whisper, "But I really need some pampering. Mr H is driving me crazy at the moment", they sprang into action and looked at re-arranging clients*.

* I always love how the hairdressers call their customers 'clients'. It sounds dead posh. I also loved the fact that my new hairdresser couldn't remember my name so resorted to calling me 'chick', 'sweets', 'babe', 'doll' and when she ran out of names she just started all over again.

I have been going to the same hairdressers for a long time now and they are all familiar with man nonsense and Mr H with his own personal brand of man logic. So all was well. By 9:05am I was stationed with a latte and a trashy mag and had my hair full of bleach by 9:25am. I immediately relaxed.

The music in the hairdressers wasn't working so we had to resort to what they used to do in the 80s. We had to talk. Some clients (mostly the younger generation) could not grasp this phenomenon and buried their heads in their phones and spent most of the time trying to avoid eye contact with everyone else in there. Those with an iPhone had to resort to chewing their nails after two hours though when their batteries ran out.

I embraced the chatting. I knew it would give me good fodder for my book. One of the clients in there was talking about her husband. She said, "He owes me forever. My body is wrecked because of the child that I gave him." Another client said, "Well, I think that you look fantastic." "You should see me naked. It's not a pretty sight."

I haven't had children but I was pretty sure that she still looked better than me, fully clothed or naked. Remember, I don't go to the gym. But then she was at least 20 years younger than me and obviously didn't comfort eat like me. Just as I was pondering this, I dropped my ginger nut biscuit in my latte. I immediately went on MFP and deducted 30 calories. I would need those calories on the train later when the alcohol trolley came round.

The hairdressers were discussing a possible work trip out to Alton Towers. One of the nail technicians said, "Oh no! I don't want to go there. I might lose a leg." One of the hairdressers said, "I wouldn't be bothered if I was you. You'd get two million pounds in compensation and you only sit down all day doing nails, so you'd still be able to work. In fact, I wonder whether it might be worth losing one deliberately."

It went silent and I honestly think that a number of people were pondering the idea. I'm not sure that they had totally thought through the concept though. They didn't seem to know how they would chop off a limb but make it look like an accident.

One of the hairdressers said, "I've come to the conclusion that the majority of my conversations consist of sex, food and poo." I hoped that she didn't mean all at once. I then unfortunately couldn't get rid of the image in my mind of her doing a poo on the loo, whilst some hot guy came in to ravish her whilst holding a chicken kebab. This did remind me of the one time that I interrupted a couple having sex in a toilet in a pub. I was horrified. Neither of them washed their hands when they came out and I definitely heard one of them clinging to the sanitary disposal bin while doing the dirty deed. I could hear the lid keep flapping up and down. Goodness knows what germs they passed on when they went back to join their family.

When I came back from the toilets and told Mr H the story about the toilet shaggers, he asked me to point them out. I said that I hadn't actually seen their faces as they had been in the cubicle next to me. Mr H suddenly pointed and whispered, "Is that them over there?" I was about to ask him how he knew but as I turned to look I saw that there was a sanitary towel stuck to the back of the guy's shoe. That wasn't the most distressing bit of the story though. The girl he was with was picking peanuts out of the dish on the bar with hands that I knew had been clinging to the disposal unit. I made a mental note never to eat from communal food again...

I've digressed. Back to the hairdressers...

My ginger was fighting the blonde but it meant that I spent four hours in the hairdressers instead of two. They also do a lovely head massage on you when they wash your hair. One of my friends said that she nearly had an orgasm when she went to a Toni & Guy hairdressers and they did it to her. I like to think that she was joking. I like to think so...

When I got back from the hairdressers, all suitably relaxed (obviously from the head massage), Mr H surprised me by telling me how nice my hair looked and that he had bought me a present. 'What's he done?' I thought. He never likes it when I change my hair colour. He will always screw up his face and say, "I preferred how they did it last time."

I got momentarily excited at the box from Amazon but apparently upset him when I didn't look happy at what was inside. It was a pair of gardening shears. "These are nice and sharp! You will be able to cut back the hedges really easily with them." I pondered trying them out on a part of his anatomy but I dismissed the idea as I needed him to drop me at the station later. I'll do it on Friday when I'm back.

I kissed Mr H as he dropped me off at the station. He said, "I hope that work goes well." Not wanting to lie, I said, "I'm sure London will be fine." I was pleased with my politician style answer. I was also pleased when I made it into the first class lounge five minutes before it closed and managed to fleece it of a latte, a can of Pepsi, some chocolate and crisps. I also got to look at the visitor's book and had to chuckle. Every comment was along the lines of 'No cereal at breakfast. No croissants in the fridge. There was nothing to eat at lunchtime.' I was tempted to write, 'Loved the cheese platter and the Bucks

Fizz was very refreshing. Didn't have time for the foot massage but will try it next time.' Obviously I didn't. The guy came to turf me out as it was shutting. I'll do it next time.

I got irrationally excited on the train when I saw that Virgin Trains had a new addition to the alcohol trolley. They now serve Mojitos. Round of applause for Sir Richard. He really is on my wave length and I think I need to meet him. Maybe he is really my Dad - I've got his curly hair and sparkly eyes and remember that I am really a princess. I must remember to ask Mum whether she has met* him before...

* shagged

When I arrived in London, Jason the big issue seller was outside Euston. I stopped to chat to him and give him some money. He remembered that I was down. He is really thoughtful. He said that business was a bit slow as there was a new person not far from him down the road, which was slowing his trade. I promised that I would give them evils as I walked past. Obviously I didn't - they weren't there and had probably sold all of their mags.

As I was walking down the road a car kept crawling slowly following me. I kept looking at it over my shoulder and hoped that my new ash blonde hairdo didn't make me look like a prostitute. Although, I would be a weird type of prostitute, I thought, dragging a work case with a furry pom-pom on it.

I then wondered whether the furry pom-pom was some sign in London that you used if you were a prostitute. A modern day version of the red light. I really need to get rid of this pom-pom, I thought. Luckily though, the kerb crawler was actually looking to pick up a friend and I carried on my way with my pom-pom bobbing behind me.

Wednesday 25th May

Missions for today:

- *Remember to keep up the pretence that I am away working in London*
- *Don't go on Facebook too much (see first mission)*

I didn't sleep well in the hotel last night. You might think it was guilt at being away and pretending that it was work related. It definitely wasn't. I should have felt guilty... I should have but I really didn't.

I woke up with a headache which I put down to sleeping in a room at the back of the hotel. I had to decide between a room on the front but smaller and with no bath, or a room on the back with two beds and a bath. I chose the latter, as let's face it girls, contrary to what we tell men, size does really matter.

I was, however, regretting my choice when the bottle banks were being emptied at 3am and woke me up.

I also dropped my headache tablet down the side of the bed and being the responsible hotel person that I am, I didn't want a child in the future to consume it and get ill. Did I say child? Sorry, I meant dog...

As I was drinking my morning cup of tea (this was a temporary fix until I went to Costa on the way to the shops - I mean work) I found a hair in it. If I had have been at home then I would have sworn that Mr H had put it there, along with some 'eye of newt' in his bid to poison me without anyone knowing.

I held up the hair alongside my own and realised that in all probability it would be mine. To be on the safe side, I sealed it in a clear plastic bag* and will get my friend in forensics to test it for my DNA. She's not that busy at the moment and doesn't mind doing me favours. She once tested some dog poo that had been left at the top of our drive, so that I could determine the breed and work out which one of our neighbours Mr H had upset.

* It was a shower cap. I don't carry around forensic bags. I simply don't have any more room in my handbag for anything else.

Mr H nearly sprained his wrist lifting my handbag out of the car last night when he dropped me off at the train station and exclaimed, "What on earth have you got in there?"

Luckily he didn't look inside to see the ten pairs of his manky undies that I was taking to London to dispose of. The wheelie bin isn't being collected until a week on Monday and I didn't want to chance putting them in there. To be fair they weren't the cause of the heavy bag. It was mostly my snacks that caused the weight.

Well, once my train terminated at Leighton Buzzard at 11pm and I was panicking more about missing my milk and cookies* before bedtime than getting mugged. Leighton Buzzard sounds really posh. It doesn't sound like somewhere where muggers live. I didn't want to run the risk again that I would be stuck somewhere without food.

* Obviously I'm joking. It's not milk and cookies but beer and pork scratchings.

I don't think that I chose the right footwear for my shopping* trip today. Carol on BBC breakfast said that it was going to be heavy rain and thunder today. I always believe her. She has such a soft dreamy Scottish accent, how can anyone not believe her? Due to the weight of the handbag, I really couldn't carry a range of footwear as well. My motto is 'a girl needs to eat but she can always walk bare foot.' As I wrote that, I've just had flashbacks to my barefoot dog poo incident on Sunday. But, no. I still think I would eat over having an extra choice of footwear.

*if Mr H is reading this, then that should say 'work'

As I was making my way to Costa for my morning latte, I heard a shriek behind me. A woman walking her Chihuahua had accidentally let it slip its collar and the Chihuahua had ambled into the road to sniff some roadkill. Initially I thought that she was being attacked by a rat and I took my umbrella out ready to whack it for her, until I heard her call, "My Angel has run into the road."

Back in rural Staffordshire roadkill tends to be a pheasant, a badger or occasionally a mangy-fox. In London it is more likely to be a rabid-pigeon, a drunken student or a kebab. Angel the Chihuahua was sniffing the roadkill just as a lorry came careering down the road. Luckily it went right over the little dog and he/she didn't join the pigeon in animal heaven. With a name like 'Angel' it would have been highly ironic. As the lorry shot past it was emblazoned on the side 'Looking out for vulnerable road users in London' with pictures of cyclists. Obviously, it did not care to look out for vulnerable Chihuahuas...

As well as my choice of footwear letting me down today, my attire also let me down. I was wearing a skirt and had forgotten to pack my fake spray tan, so that my white pasty legs complete with chicken bites were on show for the world to see. London is full of bonkers-dressed people though. I had already walked past a guy wearing a keyboard around his neck (with no top on - it looked like the keyboard was chaffing his nipples), whilst eating breadsticks out of a cardboard packet. After realising that no one was staring at me, I shrugged it off and continued on my way.

Unfortunately, I hadn't noticed until I was 500 metres down the road that I had trodden in some toilet roll at some point and it was dragging behind my sandals. Thankfully, it was my clean loo roll from the hotel from the looks of things and not some that a tramp had already wiped his bottom on. 'Be grateful for small mercies,' I thought.

As I got side-tracked by a '70% off' sale sign in French Connection, I stopped and looked down at my bag with the furry pom-pom on it. (I had had to bring my work bag to keep up the pretence for Mr H and thought that I might need to fill it with shopping goodies on my day out around London.) A small child was playing with it. His mother said, "Oh! I am so sorry. He really likes balls." I didn't correct her that it was a pom-pom (why do people find this so hard? It's a pom-pom people, not a ball!) I also didn't like to tell her that when her child was rubbing his face against it, that at least one dog had tried to hump it, one cat had tried to hump it and another dog had cocked his leg up against it. The timing just felt all wrong...

I happily wandered round the shops today and remembered to strategically post on Facebook. Mr H texted me to ask if my day was going well. I didn't reply for an hour and a half and said, 'Oh - it's not too bad. I'm doing some group work with adults working in the retail sector about 'how to get ahead in work.'' Mr H replied to say, 'Tell them to lie!' I wondered whether he had rumbled me. As I was tucking into my lunch in Covent Garden I looked up to see whether there was any CCTV. It would be just my luck that Mr H was somehow spying on me.

Covent Garden was bonkers. A woman pulled up to the table next to me with a pram and smiled at me. I knew that I would have to give into social pressure and abide by the rule that anyone with a pram means that you have to lean over and say something like, 'Aw. What a gorgeous baby.' I smiled back and leaned over and just about managed to avoid saying, 'Flip me! What the heck is that?'

It wasn't a baby - or if it was - then it must have been grown in some laboratory. I didn't say anything and just stood there like a fool, totally mesmerized. She said, 'It's a ....' I didn't catch the name but apparently it was a breed of dog. I spent the entire night Google-imaging to try and find out what it was but to no avail. I'm now thinking that maybe it was actually some type of monkey and that she had rescued it from some research facility. She was a very interesting* lady.

* That was a polite way of putting it.

I was exhausted from my day of shopping and I did remember at least to bin Mr H's manky underpants. I put them in a bin in the toilet in John Lewis. They clean their toilets regularly so I felt safe that they would soon be in landfill heaven. I had nearly managed to palm them off on a tramp that was making his way along Oxford Street. I had stopped to give him some money and asked whether he wanted clothes.

He said that underpants were always useful, in his line of work, but when he saw them he said, "Actually, I'm ok for now. I've recently been given a lot." He shuffled off. I made a mental note to tell Mr H this story at some point in the future to emphasise that even a tramp did not want his manky underpants. I went into Primarni and picked him up some more (Mr H that is - I didn't see the tramp again).

Back at the hotel, I looked out of the window thinking, 'I really wish I had picked the small room on the front' and this was reinforced all the more as I noticed an old ugly naked guy pouring what looked like scotch into a glass in one of the rooms opposite.

What is it with men wandering around naked for all the world to see? No one wants to see 60 year old droopy dingle-dangles. I quickly ducked down when I thought that he had seen me. I then crawled across the floor of the hotel room until I was sure that I was out of his view before I stood up.

As I turned on the TV, some news reporter was talking about 7.1m people who would be missing out on the Brexit vote in June because they had 'disappeared' from the electoral register. I pondered this and came to the conclusion that it was women like me that had removed their husbands. I just posted Mr H's postal vote in the doggy poo bin on the Cannock Road, whereas they obviously went one better and took them off the list when the confirmation paper came round, asking who, in the household, was eligible to vote.

I had successfully stopped stressing about the flies and spider that were wriggling inside me. Well, I had until *Britain's Got Talent* came on telly and Dec said, "I've got butterflies in my tummy for tonight's show." It did make me wonder whether he was giving me some secret message that he had received my 32 tweets today. I've heard rumours that married life doesn't suit him...

Thursday 26th May

Missions for today:

- *Enjoy my last day in London and remember to pretend to Mr H that I'm working still*

Lying is not good for the soul. I discovered this when Mr H sent me a text to say that his Mum and Dad were coming over and meeting one of his cousins at our house. Mr H wasn't actually going to be there but he told them to make themselves at home.

I immediately started stressing. Mr H will have been in the house on his own for around 36 hours. Goodness knows what devastation will have fallen on it. I had visions of his mum going round the house picking up his dirty undies and his porn (obviously I'm on about his tractor mags) and removing the chilli grinder (as she will think it's a vibrator) and putting it out of sight in the pantry.

I know that she's his mum so she will have dealt with his dirty nappies as a baby and his accidents as a toddler and then normal teenage smelly-and-other-boy-tissue-down-the-back-of-the-bed issues but he's nearly 55 now. Also, I don't want her to think that this is how I keep the house.

I texted back, 'Well make sure that you tidy up before they come.' He replied with, 'Oh. I'm already at work and they're on their way over.' I had to stop myself from dropping her a text to apologise in advance for the state of the house. Was it wrong that I started to pray that one of the dogs would have a vomiting episode which might keep them all from wanting to go in the house?

I like to think that I am quite a rational person. But I don't think I'm alone with these thoughts. A few of my friends have said that their biggest fear, if they died young, was who would keep their house clean in their absence. I'm not quite that bad. Mr H is quite forgetful and I'm more concerned as to whether he will remember to feed the pets or take them to the vets for their booster injections. I bet Brandy will pounce on him like a Cougar on a gazelle though. She looks exactly the type. And he will be vulnerable.

Maybe I will have to put a clause in my will that says that if he gets it on with her then he gets none of my riches. (To be fair I don't have any but it would be just my luck to find that my books sell well when I'm dead and Mr H ends up being minted as a result.) All the good composers and painters were only famous when they died. And I have a feeling that Shakespeare was poo-pooed and rejected by a lot of publishers in his lifetime...

I decided that stressing over the state of the house wasn't going to do anyone any good, so I went to The Ritz to have a champagne cocktail (and do some celebrity spotting) to settle me down. There was a sign up in their cocktail bar which said 'waiting staff wanted'. I thought, 'Oh that's good – I won't have to tip them very well as they're bound to be short staffed and hassled, so they won't be very attentive.' I like to see the positives in every situation.

There was a couple in there that I thought were probably work colleagues. She was a nine but he was only a three*. She was flirting just enough so that he would pick up the tab and he was obviously thinking that she was going to sleep with him later. I gave him a sympathetic, 'It's never going to happen' look. His look in return was, 'Look at me with the hot blonde.' I did think about following him when he went to the toilet to tell him that he shouldn't waste his time, or money. I knew that she was only using him as after he had got up to go to the loo she took a phone call.

* I had to explain this to mum. People are judged out of ten for their 'hotness'. Mum said that she thought that was what I meant but had hoped the answer was spicier than that(!) I didn't ask her what she thought it meant...

I, obviously, could only hear her side of the conversation but it was clear that she did this a lot with men to get them to buy her lunch, dinner and drinks. I felt bad for womankind everywhere. At least when she tripped down the steps to leave and flashed her Bridget Jones's knickers did I get a small sense of satisfaction. So little Miss Perfect wasn't so perfect after all (and I'm sure I glimpsed a bit of cellulite). Unfortunately, this seemed to excite the man that she was with all the more.

Probably it reminded him of his mother, who I concluded, lived with him. He was probably looking for a girl that his mother would approve of and who was just like her. I shuddered as they left the bar...

Friday 27th May

Mission for today:

- *Hide all of my shopping from London, so that Mr H doesn't realise that I wasn't working the last two days*

I only have one mission and the main problem will be to integrate Mr H's new underpants in with his old ones without him knowing. This mission is very delicate and likely to involve a lot of thought and strategy. I might need to draw up some sort of flowchart on the computer to work out all the possibilities of Mr H thwarting my plan. He has been in work this morning, which has made it easier.

Phase 1 – make them look old

I initially cut off all of the tags from the new pants that I had bought from Primarni. I put some of his old ones in our neighbour's bin so that Mr H wouldn't find them. I then took the new pants and stretched them out, trod on them on the floor and wiped them round the rim of the bath.

I concluded that they no longer looked new and could phase them gradually into the drawers containing his current ones.

Having successfully completed Phase 1 it was time for a latte and chocolate biscuit before embarking on the next phase.

Phase 2 – integrate them into his current supply

This phase involved me slowly integrating the new underpants into Mr H's current supply. This involved very careful thought and planning. If I put all of the underpants in his drawer at once, then he would spot that they were new. If I put in too few pairs then he would notice that the number had dropped considerably and I would be rumbled.

I put three pairs into the drawer (carefully hiding them amongst others that were already in there). I put two pairs in the washing basket. For each of these pairs I pulled them over a pair of his inside-out jeans that were in the basket so it would look like he had already worn them and had removed both underpants and jeans at the same time and thrown both into the washing basket in one go.

This accounted for five out of the ten pairs I had bought. I pushed two pairs under the bed and later when Mr H came back I would exclaim, "What's that peeking out from the bed?" and let him find one of them. I would then say, "No wonder it looked like you were missing underpants. I bet there's probably more under there." I would then ferret around and pull out another pair.

You are probably thinking that he would spot that they were new pairs. With these, I made sure that I scrunched them up and rubbed a spider's web on them (from the corner of the chicken shed), so it looked like they had lived under the bed for a while. I would also exclaim, "Well – the last time that I cleaned under there was about three months ago – no wonder they look so manky. Here, let me put them in the wash." I would then take them off him before he could look more closely at them.

Phase 3 – the double bluff

I shall say to him, "Some of your underwear is looking really old – do you think that we should buy some new ones?" When he says, "No – they're fine – they'll last another month." I shall spend three minutes arguing that he really needs some new ones (I will have to keep the pretence up) before shrugging with, "Whatever! You're the one that wears them" and then flounce off in a huff.

I had three pairs left over and I hid them in the bottom of my wardrobe. Next week after the dust has settled and I'm convinced that he doesn't know that I have bought him new underwear, I shall integrate these. I will pretend to find two out of a suitcase, exclaiming, "These seemed to be still in there from holiday. I'll put them in the wash, just in case they're dirty." The final pair I shall hang on the washing line when he's not looking.

I congratulated myself on my successful mission and went to have a bath. This did not go as smoothly. I used my new strawberry shower gel and was happily washing myself when I did a massive sneeze and then felt some of the real strawberry lumps get sucked up my fru-fru as I breathed back in.

Ordinarily I wouldn't have panicked too much about this but given that I am convinced that two flies and a spider are living inside me then I really don't want to feed them and encourage them to stay. I did then chastise myself for being such an idiot. Let's face it – I haven't seen the flies or spider since it happened so I'm sure they must be dead by now from not being able to breathe. I'll keep an eye out when I go to the toilet and see if they come out in my poo. I might save my poo when I do go and send it to my friend in forensics. She will be able to tell me quite quickly if it contains insects.

As I was getting out of the bath the phone rang. I often don't bother to answer the phone but given that I have put the feelers out to publishers and agents for the book, I didn't want to chance missing a call. I quickly wrapped a towel around me (just in case the government now has some secret way of seeing you down the phone line). Obviously it wasn't anyone so exciting and this was the conversation that then followed:

"Hello? Is that Mrs Hughes?"

"Yes – who is this?"

"Before you hang up Mrs Hughes, this isn't a sales call. I'm calling from Weatherboard..." (I think that's what he said) "...cavity wall insulation and it's a marketing call."

"Oh great! So you're phoning to give me some money are you?"

"Ermmmmmmm.... no."

"Oh – it's just that you said that you weren't selling anything, so I assumed that you were phoning to give me something?"

"Errrmmmm.... no."

"Oh – so why are you phoning?"

"Erm... I'm phoning to find out if you have cavity wall insulation?"

"My house doesn't have any cavities."

"Erm… ok…. so how's that then?"

"Well – I'm guessing you're the expert, so you should really know. But about that money you're phoning to give me."

"Erm…. I'm not phoning to give you money."

"Well – that's not very good marketing is it? You're not marketing yourself very well."

Can hear rustling of paper as these responses are clearly not in his script

"So – have you any plans for the weekend?"

"Sorry, Mrs Hughes – why are you asking me about that?"

"Oh! I thought that you were phoning me to ask me some questions and it's only polite to ask you some questions in return."

"I think I'm going to need to speak to a manager and call you back later."

"That's nice – we can chat about what you fancy doing over the bank hols. I don't get to see many people, so it would be nice to have a chat."

Phone goes dead

The moral of this story was that he really should have known better than to mess with a 42 year old woman (naked and dripping from the bath) whose patience ran out a year ago.

We also subscribe to the telephone preference scheme so shouldn't be getting unsolicited calls. I'm thinking that he probably won't phone back...

Saturday 28th May

Missions for today:

- *Vacuum out the cars (I have put this off for too long now)*
- *Go up the ladders to cut the wisteria back before it ruins our solar panels*
- *Have a fabulous time at Miranda and Matt's anniversary party tonight*

I woke up this morning and once again determined that it was good for the sake of the human race that I did not decide to have children. I did not hear Lucy bark at 5am and I am convinced that if I had a baby then I simply would not wake up to hear it crying. Mum is also a good sleeper (remember that I get it from her). I do wonder whether she didn't use to wake up when I cried as a baby, either…

Apparently, I was talking fluently by the age of two (and was doing my own washing and ironing by the age of ten). I wonder whether I learned to talk early so that I could say to other adults,

"Help me please! Please adopt me and pamper me." You already know that I used to routinely tell everyone I met that I was adopted. I really don't know why I did this. Maybe it is because of never having enough loo rolls in the house?

We have been doing a lot of work outside today in the garden. It's a miracle that it's not been pissing it down really. It is a bank holiday weekend and normally that means the weather is crap. Dad has been over helping us in the spare room too.

I spent a lot of the morning collecting logs to put in the house. When Mr H does it, the job involves lots of swearing, as the dogs always get in his way when he has an arm full of logs. He generally bashes his elbow on the door handle (at least twice – he doesn't learn from the first time) and then cries like a baby (and swears some more).

He also doesn't vacuum up the bits that he's dropped afterwards, so when he takes his socks off (because they are soaked through from being in his wellies all day), he treads on a splinter and cries like a baby again. Ok, maybe I am exaggerating a little... (we all know that I'm not).

I decided that I would have a perfectly easy time of bringing the logs in. I did not swear once. The dogs did not get in my way as I cleverly opened both of the porch doors, made a ramp out of some ply board and simply wheeled the barrow straight into the lounge to deposit all of the logs by the wood burner.

This also meant that I did not drop bits everywhere as I did not have to carry my logs through the front door, down the hall and finally into the lounge. Mr H obviously did not like the fact that my method was so much better than his (and more importantly did not involve any crying), so he had to criticise my stacking of the logs.

"Don't stack them back to front. You need to stack them front to back otherwise they are likely to fall when we pull one off the top and it will be easier to use up all of the space." Once again I had to sigh. He had only just been in the kitchen making some custard as we were having a homemade apple pie for lunch (which his mum had brought over) and he had missed the saucepan when pouring in the milk and spilled custard powder all over the worktop. I do wonder where this selective attention to detail comes from...

I thought that I did an excellent job bringing in the logs and was congratulating myself as I went to put the wheelbarrow away.

Unfortunately, pride comes before a fall and as I went round the corner of the path I didn't notice that the gate was shut and ploughed right into it. I now have two small 'circle wheel' imprints on my thighs where the handles of the wheelbarrow dug into them (the plastic protector that sits on the end of the handles degraded years ago and Mr H is too tight to let me buy a new wheelbarrow).

When I took my jeans off it looked like I had a case of ring worm on both thighs. At least they are high enough to be hidden by any shorts that I might wear. And there is little chance of me being seen in a swimming costume (ever), so no one will see them.

I might tell Mr H that it's ring worm, if he continues to annoy me. I will tell him that it's highly contagious (or is it infectious?) and that he will need to sleep downstairs on the settee in case he catches it. Once the circles have faded I can always ram my thighs into the wheelbarrow handles again if ever I need an excuse to keep him away from me. Of course, I'm kidding! I'll just use red pen to draw them on next time– it hurt when the metal from the handles cut into me.

We also trimmed the wisteria back today as it has been working its way up the roof and attaching itself to the solar panels. Mr H was in charge of holding the ladder while I went up with the secateurs.

He hates heights and can only just about stand on the coffee table to change a light bulb in the lounge. Of course I'm joking. He can't even do that. It's a good job he's not a tall man. As well as outside 'poo picking', I also have 'ladder jobs' on my job list in our household. His job was to hold the ladder so that I didn't fall off.

I did think that if he was trying to kill me then this might be his opportunity. But Miranda, Matt and Carrie wandered past as I was up the ladder and called out to us, so I think they thwarted his plan. As I was nearly at the top of the ladder, I trapped my fingers between the ladder and the top of the porch. A swear word escaped my lips (obviously I don't cry at small things like Mr H does) and Mr H said, "Are you ok? What's up?" I said that I had trapped my fingers as the ladder moved and I asked him whether he was holding it properly. He swore that he was. The picture I saw on Facebook 30 minutes later told a different story.

He had taken a picture of me up the ladder (my bum looked ginormous) and had put 'cutting back the wisteria #whatcanpossiblygowrong.' If I had have died then he would have felt really guilty. He obviously wasn't holding onto the bottom of the ladder when I trapped my fingers.

I decided not to row with him while I was at the top of the ladder, just in case he did try and pull it away from under me. I don't think that the wisteria would have taken my weight and I'm pretty sure I would have splatted on the floor. I didn't want to die just yet. We had a party to go to tonight and I had bought a new dress. It would be such a waste.

We stopped for a break with Dad in the afternoon and sat in the sunshine. We discussed Brexit and Dad spent about ten minutes telling us that he didn't think the EU worked and that he was worried about Turkey joining and the money situation.

So when I said to him, "Oh – so you're voting out then are you?" He said, "No – I'll vote to remain. All of these things probably won't happen for maybe 20 years so they won't affect me in my lifetime." "Thanks, Dad – so you're not bothered about them affecting us then?" "Oh yes – of course I worry about you and the future." "So – you're going to vote 'out' then?" "No – I'll still vote remain." I definitely do not get my logic from Dad… You're probably thinking what a hypocrite I am. I've already mentioned that I don't do politics (although I will vote, even if it's just to cancel out Mr H) but in all honesty whilst Dad was talking about Brexit I was fixated on something else. I had noticed that my fat-ball stealer has been at it again. This time the wire contraption that holds the fat balls was empty and half way across the garden. I think I might set up a webcam to find out who/what it is.

Whilst we were taking a break we chatted about a friend that had had an accident in the last few days and chuckled as we could see how easily it was that rumours got started. I had texted Mr H to say that they fell over on a walk. Unfortunately though autocrapet had changed it to say 'wall'. So Mr H thought they had fallen down a wall. Dad thought it was a different friend as he had two friends with the same name and my step-mum had misheard the story and thought that they had had a brawl.

I hope that the government has better safeguards in place in case we ever have to go to war. Imagine David Cameron getting a text from the head of the defence saying, 'Dave mate –

Simon needs to hit the red button.' He might start off some nuclear attack, if 'Simon' is code word for pushing the button to start a war. It would be embarrassing to admit that we went to war over the Head of Defence watching the final of *Britain's Got Talent* and thinking that Simon Cowell should 'buzz' one of the Acts.

Sunday 29th May

Missions for today:

- *Remember to tell you about my other missions yesterday*
- *Go and check that my sister is still alive*

I forgot to tell you yesterday that my mission to vacuum out the cars was partially successful. (Sorry for being slack but I had to abandon writing as Mr H's Mum and Dad arrived for Miranda and Matt's party so I shut down the computer to go and have a dance.)

The vacuum cleaner has been playing up and not sucking up properly. (I really want to write about some rude double entendre here but I'm trying to be good and limit my innuendo.)

In all honesty, I really hate it (the vacuum that is – I love innuendo) and wish that I had never defected from Dyson. James – if you're reading this then I would love a new Animal Dyson, if you fancy sending me one for free. I promise to remain faithful and true in the future. Mr H won't buy me a new one as he says that I have to wait until this one breaks. If it has some mysterious accident the day after the warranty runs out, then I won't be surprised. I can imagine Mr H coming home to see a burned out vacuum cleaner on the front lawn and exclaiming, "How on earth did that happen?" I shall have to plan my vacuum cleaner demise carefully.

I will start posting on mumsnet under pseudonyms and talk about how I can smell burning when I use my cleaner. Those mums look totally bored in life so I'm sure they will latch onto my drama, especially if I talk about my six children and how I only want to keep them safe blah blah blah.

I will let mumsnet take its course and then over a period of a few months (just before the warranty is up) I will gradually feed to Mr H that there has been a lot of talk of this particular brand of vacuum cleaner spontaneously combusting just after two years.

I will Google some part names and wow him with things like 'apparently some say it's due to the inadequate metal housing of the electric motor and how it attaches to the intake port. This causes a reaction with the fan, which makes it overheat and set on fire. You're good at Physics – I don't know what this means – but you will.'

Mr H knows that I am totally dim and don't have the intelligence to make something like this up and loves it when I make him look like a genius (men – they're so shallow). I will show him the posts on mumsnet and start to convince him that there really is something wrong with it.

Every time that I use the vacuum cleaner I will sigh. Mr H will do the obligatory, "What's up?" and I will tell him that it's making a funny noise and I'm sure it smells of *slight* burning. This will sow the seeds in his mind.

Just after the warranty has expired I will take the vacuum cleaner onto the front garden, pour cooking oil over it and set it on fire. Obviously being the responsible adult that I am I will make sure that the pets are inside and nothing flammable is within distance of it. (Not like when we did Chemistry aged 13 and I set my friend's fringe on fire with a Bunsen burner. Well, it was the 80s – big hairdos were all the rage.)

When Mr H gets back from work I will say, "The important thing is that I'm ok" as we both stare at the burned out vacuum cleaner. He will look at the charred remains of the vacuum cleaner (probably cry that I didn't die along with it) but I will get my new vacuum cleaner.

I think that I should have been a spy or something. My stealth and cunning is pretty good... Of course I wouldn't need to go to these lengths if 'man logic' didn't exist. Mr H will buy new tools (and especially electronic ones or those powered by petrol) at the drop of a hat but I have to make do with a wheelbarrow that injures me and a vacuum cleaner that I hate.

If I happen to find out that the warranty is for more than two years then I'm going to throw it in the moat and pretend that it accidentally rolled there when I was vacuuming the lawn. (I've got friends on Facebook that do this. Yes – I really have.)

Back to vacuuming out the cars...

Mr H determined that the filter was clogged. "When did you last clean it out?" "I've not cleaned it since we bought it." "Well, that might be why it's not working then." After creating the biggest dust cloud in the world the filter was a bit cleaner and I managed to vacuum my car out. I told Mr H that his could wait until another time. He sulked but I ignored him. He needs to learn that he can't always get his own way.

My final mission was also a success. We had a fab time at Matt and Miranda's party and I was the designated driver because I had a headache and didn't fancy having a drink. This meant that Mr H had three pints (the most I think he has ever had in one night) and we were on the dance floor all night. It always makes me chuckle that because I love dancing and will generally be the first and last on a dance floor most people think that I must be totally pissed.

They will then be dumbfounded when I tell them that I've been on diet coke all night (well Pepsi Max in this case – but it's basically the same) and that I'm driving Mr H. I really don't need to get drunk to get on the dance floor. In fact, it's preferable that I'm not – otherwise I tend to end up on the floor (the actual floor, generally spread eagled in a heap, obviously I was already on the dance floor) because I really can't dance in anything other than totally flat shoes.

My new ash blonde hair caused a stir as a few people that we haven't seen since the end of last year thought that Mr H and I had split up and that he had brought a new woman to the party. I overhead one of them in the loos saying, 'She's got nicer hair than Jo but she's a bit chubbier'. I made a mental note that I really should take dieting a bit more seriously. I pondered this as I was tucking into my second helping on the buffet. For those of them that came up to me and said, 'Blimey! We didn't think it was you – your hair is so different.' I told them that that it highly unlikely that Mr H would have another woman (ok I actually laughed hysterically) and said that no other woman would put up with his man nonsense ways.

My sister is alive and well, thankfully. Her husband loved me all the more as I brought with me some custard donuts (his favourite). She is looking much better and doesn't walk like the hunchback of Notre Dame anymore. She was also looking a bit tanned* from sitting in the garden.

* This really means red – we are English Rose in complexion (or in my case tanned vampire).

We chatted about our usual important topics of conversation – poo-ing, weird dreams about toilets and the influence that Grandad on my Mum's side had on our lives. I'm going to spend a day with her next week and will take some work. She has good Wi-Fi.

On the way back I called into Essington Fruit Farm as I decided that I was going to be an excellent wife and make Mr H a roast lamb dinner. The usual butcher was there and waved hello but he was serving another couple.

Another butcher (the one I saw last time) came to serve me and remembered me. I pointed to the leg of lamb and said, "Is there a lot of meat on that leg, as I don't want it to be all bone." He replied, "Oh there's plenty of meat on my bone." After we had both finished chuckling he said, "That will do a family of eight." The other butcher called over, "So – yes. That will do for you and your husband." He is a star – he knows how Mr H and I like our meat. I love shopping there – I didn't see Donald and Olive or the lady who drugs her husband but it was a successful visit.

I also didn't have a 'pork blood squirting down the front of my clothes' incident and as I was cooking the lamb tonight I knew what meat I would be serving. My cheeky friends on Facebook commented, 'Are you sure that's lamb?' when I put a picture up.

Monday 30th May – bank hols

Mission for today:

- *Drool over Patrick Swayze on the big screen at the drive-in cinema*

No one really needs more missions than the one above in a day. We had booked tickets to watch *Dirty Dancing* on the outside cinema screen in Telford (and by 'we' I mean me, Miranda, Carrie and Samantha. Can you tell that they chose their pseudonyms?) We packed appropriate snacks. They entailed Prosecco, Rosé wine and damson vodka. We also took crisps, popcorn and sweets. Obviously, I turned MFP off today. It's very judgemental when I log food and drink like this.

It will say, 'Do you realise that there's 10g of sugar in this?' or, 'You have hit your maximum goal for fat today.' I don't need it to tell me. Obviously, I know. It's why the food and drink that I log tastes so delicious. Log celery and MFP loves you. But celery tastes like crunchy urine (just to be clear I haven't actually tasted urine, I just suspect that it tastes exactly like celery).

We were off to the cinema at 3pm, so I spent the morning catching up on 'home admin'. Well, that's what I told Mr H but in all fairness 'internet shopping' does fit under this category and given that he spent a fortune on the credit card last month with his lawnmower and chainsaw then I decided it was my time to spend this month.

I got sucked in with a sale on *Marisota* that was advertising some garden furniture. I think that I have a fetish for it (garden furniture that is – not Marisota. I'm not a 13 year old boy sneaking a look at women models wearing underwear).

We have lots of it and I love to have chairs and tables in lots of different spots in the garden. Mr H will sigh when he sees them arrive but the garden bench on the front is falling to pieces and even he said that it isn't economical to repair it. I will have to twist the conversation to make it sound like I've done him a favour by sorting out the new replacements.

Mum sent me a message on Messenger to say that she was having a mammogram tomorrow afternoon. I think that when you hit a certain age they test your tits for cancer. (I don't think they call it a 'tit test' but they really should. Autocrapet wanted to change 'mammogram' to 'mammoth grans'.)

She said that she thought it was unnecessary as hers were so tiddly that surely they could just see whether she had any problems without struggling to put them under a machine.

Apparently it's harder to do the 'tit test' with tiddly tits. I replied to mum and autocrapet changed 'tiddly' to fiddly. I do wonder what 'fiddly tits' would be like. Would they randomly move without you knowing and point in different directions when you tried to take a selfie?

In all seriousness though, go and get your tits tested people. You never know when the big 'C' is going to strike (or when the NHS might no longer be free). I told Mum that when I talked of being a princess and adopted in the book that I was obviously only joking. Let's face it, I definitely get my tiddly tits from her side of the family. Pity its Dad's double chin and Mum's tiddly tits and it's not the other way round… damn you genetics - you and your humour really love to tease me.

I've had to give Mr H a bit of a wide berth today. Lucy woke him up at 5am and he tried my suggestion of, 'Just ignore her when she barks as she often just wakes herself up barking and she will go back to sleep.' Apparently, after half an hour, he decided that my advice was hooey. Luckily, I, once again, totally slept through her barking and Mr H got up to let her out.

He has also been complaining of man flu today. I could tell that he was gearing up for it this morning when he did exaggerated sniffing and coughing (all of which I ignored) until he sighed over dramatically and put his hand to his head and I had to ask the obligatory, "Are you not feeling well?" question. He wouldn't listen to me when I suggested that it could be hay fever due to the cutting back of the conifers without wearing a face mask. He also wouldn't listen when I told him to take some Lemsip. I didn't bother to try and help again. I was wasting my breath. I decided that the best cause of action for both of us was for me to stay out of his way. This was a win-win as I wouldn't have to listen to him moan and he couldn't accuse me of not being sympathetic when he did moan.

Last night we watched the last of Marcella that we hadn't yet seen. Anna Friel gets it on with Jamie Bamber so I'm thinking that there probably is little chance of her taking Mr H off my hands and Jamie Bamber rescuing me. I wished we hadn't watched it now.

The outside cinema was fabulous (once we finally found it). We had a totally hilarious time. On the way there in the car, Samantha pointed out the new school that was being built at the end of her road and said, "There's the new BRJ catholic school." We quizzed her on what the BRJ stood for as we assumed it was the initials of the name of the local minister for schools in the area but it turned out that it wasn't. It stood for 'Bloody Rubber Johnnies' given that it was a Catholic school. We chuckled at this but given that the uniform was some disgusting yukky brown and yellow colour, with skirts that grazed your ankles, then they really didn't need to worry about the kids having sex. We were pretty sure that the uniform was the only contraception they would need.

They really had thought about everything at the outdoor cinema. McDonald's employees came round to each car with an iPad taking orders for food and then different employees would come and deliver the food.

Samantha says that Telford has one of the highest obesity rates in the whole of the UK. It was easy to see why. When the Maccie Dees employees came to our car and saw our stock of alcohol and snacks they said, "Flipping heck – doesn't look like you girls need anything." They were right, we could have set up our own stall and supplied the rest of the people in their cars watching the film.

A guy with 'fire warden' across the back of his jacket came round half way through the film to collect rubbish. "Have you got anything for my sack?" he asked us. After we had finished laughing (I blame the alcohol) we put our empty Prosecco bottle, rosé wine bottle and damson vodka bottle into his sack. He exclaimed, "Well you lot win the award for drinking the most and filling up my sack." He looked quizzically at us as we laughed again.

Luckily for us Carrie doesn't drink so the three of us enjoyed Patrick Swayze all the more with a bit of liquor inside us. Samantha had a bit of a dropsy moment when her rosé wine sloshed on the leather on the back seat but being the organised person that I am I had brought wet wipes with me. (This was for two reasons. One – for spillages on the back seat and Two – I had no idea what the toilet facilities would be like.)

There were a lot of open top cars in front of us and the two people in one of them had moved to the back seat of their car and had gotten a duvet out of the boot to snuggle under. We kept surreptitiously watching them as we thought that they might get a little frisky* when Johnny and Baby got it on.

* I haven't used the exact terminology that Carrie said. She said, "Well, it's a bit public for them to actually shag in the carpark but he might cheekily slip her the finger." (Mum — please note that it wasn't me that said this. Oh no, it most definitely wasn't. I can't actually put in print what I said...)

There was a massive lamp post in the way of the screen and before the film started a guy from Signal radio (who were sponsoring the event) came round with his camera to chat to us beforehand. He said, "You've got a good position in your car here." "Yes – apart from that massive erection over there" I said, pointing to the lamp post.

Without a blink of an eye he said, "It's not that big really. I've seen bigger." He promised to pop back later as he wanted to video us watching the film. He was a total liar though and didn't. We think he was probably making some soft porn film and was too busy filming the people under duvets in their open top cars...

Just before the film was about to end the screen went all funny. It was just after Johnny had said, "Nobody puts Baby in the corner."

Everyone in the car park started pipping their horns and I thought that a fight might have broken out if they hadn't got it mended. The end is one of the best bits of the film. Luckily though all was well as they re-set the Wi-Fi and the film continued. Samantha said, "Just like a typical man really – doesn't finish off as it's getting to the end."

Tonight was totally double entendre night and it was totally ace. We will definitely go to another one, although we might need a new designated driver as I think Carrie might not take us again due to the rosé wine spillage on the leather of her rear seats...

Mr H was still moaning about his man flu when I got back. I didn't bother to ask whether he had taken any medicine. I knew what the answer would be and it would be a waste of my breath. Although if we had have had a totally pointless five minute conversation about it then on the plus side I could have logged it as an activity on MFP. 'Five minutes talking' burns off three calories after all...

Tuesday 31st May

Mission for today:

- *Hope the day gets better… it didn't start out well (see below)*

The way that the day started, I didn't bother to have more than one mission (and really should have just gone back to bed and woken up tomorrow instead). They say that things come in threes. Today, mine came in around eights…

1. I looked in the mirror and saw a big hair sprouting from my cheek, which I removed with tweezers (I think this must have been my 'Samson with the long hair secret power' though because after I pulled it out everything went wrong for the rest of the morning. I'm sure the next chain of events are all to do with me removing my facial hair. Although if God had intended that I have a beard then I'm sure he would have grown more than one measly hair.)

2. I tripped down the stairs (luckily I didn't break anything or land on Lucy lying asleep at the bottom of the stairs). If she had have bitten me then it wouldn't have been her fault. As she is deaf then having someone of my weight land on top of her whilst she was asleep would probably have made her think that she was being attacked by a bear. It is immaterial that there are no bears in England – Lucy doesn't know that. She didn't go to school.

3. I had a headache start to come on and as I went to take a Nurofen out of the medicine container in the pantry, it bounced out of my hand and I thought that it had landed on the floor. I spent five minutes on my hands and knees trying to find it because I didn't want the dogs to eat it. After finally giving up, I stood up and the tablet bounced out of my pyjama top and rolled under the bottom shelf. (Our friend Bobby

commented on this, when I put it up on Facebook, and said, 'I loved the bit where your pyjamas didn't conceal your bottom shelf. But I've never heard it called that before'. If you then read 'bottom shelf' as fru-fru then it makes the rest of the story even more funny.)

I then spent another five minutes on my hands and knees trying to poke it out from underneath the shelf. I had to use a fish slice to reach it and also pulled out what looked like a dead mouse. I jumped up, screamed and banged my head on the shelf above. This did not help my headache. I was doubly annoyed when I realised that it wasn't a dead mouse at all but a decayed peach.

I reached up to get another headache tablet for the now really throbbing pain in my head. I didn't want to chance this one bouncing out of my hand so I stood on my small steps to reach into the medicine container. Unfortunately, I didn't position myself centrally and twisted my ankle as I slipped off the side of the steps. I grabbed onto the shelf to stop myself from falling and managed to poke my right eye with a tube of tomato puree that was sitting on the shelf and a jar of Dolmio fell from the shelf above and also bounced off my head. I did think about taking a whole packet of headache pills as my ankle was now throbbing and my head (and eye) felt like it was going to explode.

I didn't want to see what was going to happen next though, so decided to give up on the headache tablets and glug some damson gin* instead to dull the pain. I hoped that I hadn't suffered concussion. I did not want to go to A+E and have the receptionist laugh at my tale of how I had knocked myself out with tomato puree and white lasagne sauce.

* Mr H had decanted the damson gin and damson vodka yesterday. He obviously had a premonition about what was going to happen to me this morning and knew that I would need it.

4. I tried to set up my office in the garden and spent 20 minutes hunting for the extension lead before texting Mr H to ask if he had seen it. His reply was, "Oh yes – I borrowed it. It's in the log cabin." I needed two laptops today to prepare a presentation and neither one of them would stay connected to the Wi-Fi. One of the power leads wouldn't work and when I wiggled it I nearly got an electric shock as it made a fizzing noise and a blue spark shot out from it. 'Great!' I thought. 'Firstly, I nearly kill myself with a jar of Dolmio and now I was going to die from electrocution. It was not turning out to be a good morning.

5. I went to get the post out of the post box and did the sort of thing that I tell Mr H

off about doing. In my defence I think I still had concussion from the Dolmio jar, so wasn't thinking clearly. Instead of going to get the key to the post box I decided to put my arm in and pull out the post through the flap. We have one of those boxes that sits on a wall, so I was on our neighbour's drive while I was doing this.

I had forgotten that I wasn't as skinny as I used to be and got my arm stuck trying to pull the parcel out that was in there. I wriggled around for five minutes (OK – it was probably 30 seconds but it felt longer) panicking that I was stuck and would have to be rescued by the fire brigade. I wouldn't normally stress about this but I wasn't out of my dressing gown yet and hadn't straightened my hair or put any make up on (and I probably smelled of damson gin as well).

I did not want to be seen like this or read the headline in the local *Express & Star* -

'Drunk woman wedged in post box is released by firefighters.' It would make it sound like I had crawled into one of the big red pillar boxes on the Cannock Road. This was all the incentive I needed and luckily a few sharp pulls (and minus a bit of skin) I was released from the box.

6. Bonnie had rolled in fox poo and stunk to high heaven. This made my already pounding head feel even worse. I didn't have the energy to clean her and thought it could wait until Mr H was back from work. She didn't smell of fox poo last night so it was obviously his fault that she had rolled in it this morning. He takes them for their morning walk.

7. Mr H still has his man flu so I knew that by lunchtime when he was back from work he was going to be coughing/sneezing and generally annoying me. The thought of this was even worse than my banging head, my

throbbing eye, my twisted ankle and my painful skin on my arm...

8. About 20 minutes after I had set up the outside office, dark clouds descended and it started to rain. I then had visions of being electrocuted again whilst trying to rapidly bring in my laptops and other electronic equipment. I think my Facebook friends put a curse on me as I had put a picture up on Facebook of my outside office in the sun and they had all moaned how it was raining near them.

9. One of my computers decided to shut itself down as a box popped up saying, 'I.T. is updating some of your security licence settings'. It didn't give me chance to save my work and just shut the computer down and re-started it. I lost two hours of work.

I think this day is destined to try and kill me. 'On this day' popped up on Facebook and it reminded me that a year ago today I had:

250

- sliced my finger on the shears while gardening
- uncovered an ants' nest
- trapped my finger in the green wheelie bin and
- got stung on the face by nettles

I have now put a calendar reminder into my phone so that on this day next year I am going to stay in bed and have a duvet day watching a box set.

I shouldn't be so negative though (I have to give myself a talking to every now and then because there are lots of people much worse off in life) and I need to focus on the positive. (Otherwise, I am definitely not getting out of bed tomorrow...)

There were a few good things that happened today:

1. I received a cheque in the post for £3.73. Years ago I had taken out an extended warranty and if you didn't claim on it then you got all of your money back. I

have never taken out one of these policies since given this company went into liquidation and I did not get back my money. The company went into liquidation in 2003 and the liquidators were just writing to me to tell me that I was getting a 'modest payment that was a very good result.' I'm not sure they share the same definition as me on 'very good result' and I am tempted to send it back to them with a print out from the Oxford English dictionary showing the words 'good' and 'result'. Obviously, I'm joking, the £3.73 can go into Mr H's tractor fund. I'm such a generous wife...

2. My Amazon subscribe and save order is due to be despatched and as we are down to our last nine loo rolls, this has come as a welcome relief. I panic if there are fewer than three rolls in each toilet in the house. 45 loo rolls will be descending on us in the next few days. We are also saving 15% (although the system said, 'You don't save this on

nappies.' I don't know why it said that. We have no babies and Mr H isn't quite at the age of needing old man nappies.) I won't put the 15% savings into Mr H's tractor fund. I've been generous enough with the £3.73 cheque. After all, he wasn't expecting this – he only thinks he is getting the money from the sales of these books.

OK... obviously I lied as I can only think of two positive things that happened today and not 'a few'. I am hoping that a new month tomorrow will bring new good fortune. I also won't tweezer my random cheek or chin hair in the future, just in case it does have mystical special powers...

Mr H went to bed early tonight because his man flu was annoying me – I mean - him. I went to bed at midnight (as he was annoying me) and being the considerate wife that I am, I didn't put the light on and felt my way around the bedroom in the dark trying to find my pjs. Unfortunately, my plan didn't work. I did find the pjs ok but as I was trying to step into the pj bottoms, my right foot got caught in the cuff of them and I hopped on the spot twice before tipping sideways and crashing into Mr H who was asleep in the bed.

Just like Lucy, I think that he thought that he was being attacked by a bear and jumped up with a start. (Really, there is no excuse for him thinking that it was a bear. He did go to school, so should know that there aren't any bears in Wolverhampton.)

He then proceeded to moan that I had 'deliberately woken him up'. Believe me, he would know if I had done it deliberately and given his constant moaning at the moment, then it's a dead cert that I wasn't going to wake him up. He obviously didn't know about the sleeping tablet that I had put in his drink earlier. I nearly had to put another one in his drink what with all of his moaning. Luckily though he dropped back off to sleep quite quickly.

Tuesday 1st June

Missions for today:

- *Try and go out for the day as Mr H is at home all day and I fear that I might kill him*
- *Be an excellent Occupational Therapist to my sister, by trying to integrate her back into the outside world (well…. Cannock)*

Lucy barked at 7am this morning. She obviously knew that Mr H had man flu and was being considerate to me, as I was the one to get up to let her out. I was an excellent wife as I made him a coffee and then proceeded to complete all of his morning jobs. Bonnie still stank of fox poo but I didn't have time to wash her so just sprayed her with the equivalent of doggy deodorant* to reduce the smell.

* It wasn't actually doggy deodorant but some fake rip off Britney Spears perfume that someone had bought me back from a car boot

sale once. It made me smell of cat piss when I put it on but it seemed to agree with Bonnie. She smelled of fresh lavender. I made a mental note to tell car boot sellers this if I ever saw them selling perfume again.

I really don't know why he moans so much and makes out how hard his jobs are. Within the space of 40 minutes I had made him breakfast, emptied the dishwasher, taken the dogs out for a walk and fed them, fed the chickens and the ducks, fed the cat, topped up the bird seed in the feeders hanging in the trees, collected in the post and made my own toast and latte. This takes him about an hour and a half on a good day.

I hoped that today wasn't going to be like yesterday. I didn't really enjoy the concussion and near electrocution, if I'm honest. I actually thought that today was going to be an awesome day when I had an email from the National Lottery, saying that they had news about my Euro millions ticket. I allowed myself all of one minute to dream that I had won it big and nearly messaged my work wife to say that the skiing chalet might be a go-er (and I thought that I could hire a nurse to put up with Mr H's man flu) but in reality I knew that I wouldn't have won it big. I was right. £3.10 would just about get me a Starbucks latte.

My sister has been decomposing in her sick pit for a while now since her op, so I have taken it upon myself to act as her occupational therapist and re-integrate her into the world. I knew that if she could face a shopping centre in half term then she would be well on the way to recovery.

I also said to her that if she found it too difficult then I would crack the window on the car open while I went shopping, so that she didn't boil to death waiting for me to return. (I assume humans can die in hot cars too, although they don't seem to do adverts or posters for them. They do lots about dogs dying in hot cars, so maybe humans don't. Either that or no one gives a s**t if people die in a hot car*.) I congratulated myself on being such a good sister.

* This has reminded me of the uproar on social media this week about the gorilla that got shot

and killed because some toddler climbed (or was thrown?) into its cage in America. From reading all of the comments on Facebook and Twitter, people really do hate other people. Hardly anyone was on the side of the child or its parents. Everyone mourned the loss of the gorilla.

Just like when I was being her nurse, I thought it prudent to Google the duties of a competent occupational therapist. I didn't want her to sue me if she died whilst in my care. 'Although if she did die then she couldn't sue me, so really it would be better that I killed her, rather than just injure her', I pondered...

Google was most helpful as it said that the common duties of an occupational therapist comprised the following:

1. Undertake patient assessment of communication skills

    I concluded that she had no problem with communication skills when she texted me to say that one of her kittens had had diarrhoea and had jumped on her lap and smeared it across her top.

This had resulted in her changing her top (which was a good job as I had just vacuumed out and cleaned my car) and she had banished the kittens to the front room. She had also had a telephone conversation with Dad about his blood pressure. Her communication skills were fine.

2. Plan and provide appropriate activities

I drew up a schedule of our morning's activities and brought my clipboard with me to assess her progress and grade her on the completion of each of the activities. 12pm – leave in car for Cannock Orbital. 12:15pm – park in TK Maxx car park. 12:45pm depart TK Maxx and head to Boots. 1:15pm walk from Boots to M&S food hall.

I felt that the activities would help with her rehabilitation. TK Maxx would involve me picking out some summer sandals for her. This would test her ability to bend down and touch her toes.

Boots would test her cognitive skills as we were going to order a mug for Dad for Father's Day with pictures from our day out to Birmingham City football club on there. She would need to crop and place the photos appropriately.

The M&S food hall would test a variety of responses. Dodging pensioners would test her coordination, carrying a basket would test her muscle response and using the self-service till would test her mental acumen.

3. Give advice and arrange support with family members

When I dropped her off back home, still alive (but totally exhausted), I said to her husband, "Tag – you're it" and promptly left. Of course, I'm kidding! I went through my findings from the clipboard with him first and told him that I was a bit disappointed with her results from the 'speed test' I had given her. This had consisted of me giving her a list of four items to find in Boots and I stood by the door with a stop watch to see how long it took her. She wasn't thrilled when I made her do it three times to see what her PB (Personal Best) was out of the three attempts.

4. Plan further treatment

Next time I will enhance the range of activities by adding lunch into the mix. She seemed to perk up when I said this to her.

The M&S food hall visit was comical. A member of staff saw me wandering aimlessly around and said, "Can I help you Madam, what is it you're looking for?" I said, "You won't be able to help me find what I'm looking for." "Oh – I'm sure I will." "I'm looking for my sister, as I've lost her." "Oh – I'm sure I can probably help identify her." I chuckled and then had a conversation with him where we played 'spot the sister.'

He picked three other women out, none of which were her. When I saw her come round the corner of the bread aisle, I said to him, "There she is!" He said, "OK – She's nearly six foot and you're what about five foot something? She has curly hair and yours is straight? Your faces are totally different. Are you sure that you're sisters?" I nearly told him that I was a Princess and adopted but I think you can only get away with saying that when you're five years old.

There was a woman in her 30s wearing a 'Build a Bear' bear in a rucksack on her back in M&S. I thought that she was probably carrying it for her child but as she went to leave with no child to be seen, then I came to the conclusion that it was hers. Cannock is very much like Wolverhampton, full of totally bonkers people.

Using the photo machine, in Boots, to design a mug for Dad, was fun. You hook your phone up to the computer and then you can choose photos from it to put on various gifts like mugs, bags, tea towels, canvass pictures for your loves ones in prison etc.

We chose a mug for Dad and picked out some pictures from our day out from taking him to Birmingham City football club. My sister said, "Good job you haven't got any 'private' photos on your phone" as all of my photos popped up on the big screen for all to see.

I do not have nudey rudey pics on my phone (well apart from a naked one of my favourite rugby player Morgan Parra, from a calendar photoshoot), so how very dare she. (Obviously I don't keep them on my phone – how stupid would that be...)

A nosy elderly female customer wandering by said, "Awwww what cute animal pictures. What are those tall sheep-looking things?" I told her that they were Alpacas and hoped that she would go on her way but she didn't. "You like your food and drink don't you love?" she said. It is true. I do take a lot of pictures of food and drink. I think it comes from being a child where you ate what you were given and there was nothing else to graze on if you were hungry.

"Oh my! He's a fittie – who's he?" she said when she saw the naked picture of Morgan Parra. "He reminds me of my George – well obviously not now – because he's dead an' all – but when he was in his 20s he was a real looker and well endowed – down there you know."

We knew where 'down there' was. But just in case we didn't, she decided to point. She then continued, "And then when he was in his 80s they were down to there." She gestured to her knees and then wandered off chuckling to herself. This is something else that they should warn you about in school, when you're growing up. I think I'm going to be traumatised if Mr H's dingle-dangles droop to his knees when he's old.

As we were going to leave, a sales assistant noticed that there was a picture in the collection point of the photo booth and asked us if it was ours. It was a picture of a child with a dog. We both said simultaneously, "Oh no – we don't have kids – that's not ours. Cute dog though." Of course I'm joking. I actually said, "Bleurk! Good grief no – can't stand ankle biters. It's definitely not mine."

Mum messaged me today to say that she had had an awful dream with me and Mr H in it. He was unfaithful to me and I was upset and she was therefore upset because I was. I replied to say, 'He's got man flu, so it's unlikely another woman would take a second look at him at the moment.' I think that I put her mind at rest...

Thursday 2nd June

Missions for today:

- *Catch up on work*
- *Go and get my nails done and don't cry when I ask my nail technician to make them 'boring'. (I need to do this for my sign language exam that's coming up.)*

I totally failed in my first mission but I blame the delivery of my new garden furniture at 9:10am (It's important to be precise). In all honesty I blame Lucy the most. She woke me up at 3am, after I had only gone to bed at midnight. She then woke me up again at 6am and then the courier with my garden furniture woke me up again at 9am when he phoned to say that his satnav was trying to send him the wrong way. As Mr H is still man-flu-ed up, then being the excellent wife that I am, I got up to let Lucy out at 3am and then again at 6am*.

* He better be over his man flu later though. There's no way that I'm doing it again tonight.

I've been grumpier than the comments that people have been putting up on Facebook this week about the death of the Gorilla because of the child that climbed into its pen. And man – have they been unhappy.

I think this is what my friends that have babies and toddlers go through on a daily basis. (Just to clarify, not throwing their children into gorilla enclosures, I mean the getting up at stupid o'clock.) I don't know how they don't go doo-lally and end up in some mental institution (or *Wetherspoons* every night) as I was a head case having only had sporadic sleep for one night.

There is no way that I could do it on a regular basis. I'm thinking that if I didn't live with Mr H then I would either put a dog door in, so that Lucy could let herself out when she needed to go to the loo in the night, or I would simply adapt Casper's kennel and sleep outside every night with her.

We went camping lots as kids, so I've floated on water on an air bed before. I can do it again. I'm pretty resilient. (I will have to put the extension lead into the kennel though as I can't live without my electric blanket.)

Due to the lack of sleep, I decided to postpone work until later on in the day. I struggled to remember my age and who all the characters were in *Frasier* this morning while I was sipping my latte and watching TV. This did not bode well for preparing some presentations (which were ironically entitled 'How to remember vast amounts of information in five easy steps'). Instead, I decided to start assembling my garden furniture.

I groaned when I saw a massive pack of assorted nuts, bolts, plastic thingy-me-jigs and Alan* keys. I really need to find this guy Alan who invented this key and shove one in a place where the sun doesn't shine. I only ever succeed in bruising my hand when trying to turn the key and it does nothing for my new year's resolution of reducing my unnecessary swearing.

* Apparently, it's not spelt like that. It's spelled 'Allen'. All I can think of is that 'Alan' didn't want his real name associated with the invention in

case an angry mob of furniture assemblers ever got hold of him and decided to screw parts of him...

I bet he designed the key on the last day in his job before he retired. I bet he wanders round Ikea laughing his head off at his invention.

Although, if I were him, I wouldn't point out to customers that it was me that invented it. I don't know anyone that thinks it's a useful tool and he wasn't likely to get congratulatory slaps on the back. (He would get slaps but not of the congratulatory variety.)

I tell a lie though – I did find a use for one once. It was when I dropped an ear ring down the sink plug hole and it was just the right size to hook it back out. Luckily there was a load of gunky hair also stuck down the plug hole. I don't think the Alan key would have got the ear-ring out without the assistance of that.

The furniture was a nightmare to put together. The instructions were just three pictures. One of the items on one of the pictures had the wrong letter allocated to it. Being the genius that I am though, I did spot this (only because the chair would have had the head rest at the foot of it though - although it did look like a comfy addition, so I pondered about removing the headrest from Mr H's chair and putting it at the base of mine.) Of course I didn't though – it didn't actually fit in the end.

I was like a dog with a bone (or as they say in Wolverhampton, I was like a fat chick when the take aways were selling £1 kebabs). I was determined to finish putting this furniture together without Mr H's help. Two and a half hours later and I had to admit defeat. I needed the brute strength of a man to hold one end of the stools down so that I could turn the useless Alan key to tighten the bolt. Mr H was back at lunchtime and helped me to finish off putting it together.

His man flu must be worse than I thought though as he didn't ridicule me or check that I had put it together properly or sigh with a, 'You really should leave these jobs to me' look on his face. I actually started to worry about him at this point. He also didn't moan or say, 'What have you bought now?' I might need to book him into the doctors...

The furniture was finally finished, apart from two small parts that were broken, so I now need to email Marisota to get replacements for them. I didn't worry about the assorted screws, bolts and plastic thingy-me-jigs left over in the packet. I'm sure they always put far too many in there.

This experience has taught me a worthwhile lesson – never ever buy unassembled garden furniture again. It really wasn't worth losing three hours of my life to...

I did go and get my nails done and the conversations in the nail salon were very tame today. One of the girls in there was pregnant but as it was her 6th child she wasn't going to bother going to the doctors until around the five month mark as 'it would just be a waste of time.'

I always remember people saying to me, "Oh you're the youngest of three children are you? I bet your parents just let you get on with things and weren't so paranoid like they were with the first one."

I'm not sure if it's some child law that the more children you have the less you care. I don't think the youngest is destined to die at a young age because the parents 'forget' to be safety conscious.

Although thinking about it, my brother and sister never got hit on the head with a stone that someone threw at them when they were five. They never broke a bone in their foot from doing a hand spring on their bed at seven. They never cut their stomach when shuffling along a sewer pipe and toppling off sideways, hanging from the barbed wire at nine. They never broke their wrist and got concussion playing netball at thirteen.

Just to digress slightly... It always makes me chuckle that our team came from Chasetown High School and we were the under 14s team. Some teacher in their wisdom had called us the 'Chasetown Unders Netball Team'. How on earth did no one spot at the time what it spelled if you just looked at the first letter of each word?

In all honesty I would like to meet the teacher that came up with the name, as she sounds a legend. I doubt it was the lesbian gym instructor who stared at you in the showers... oh? wait...

Back to the story...

Maybe there is some truth in it after all... Although it wasn't always me that got injured. My sister got a black eye once when my brother head butted her while they were playing balloon football and has a hole in her foot where he threw a dart at her.

We had a conversation in the nail salon about how times have changed. When I was growing up, if you were naughty (obviously I was the perfect angel) then you were sent to your room as a punishment. Back then my room consisted of old furniture and a few books and board games. I had no TV, no smart phone, no IPad. I was lucky to have a bed. Nowadays, you can't send kids to their rooms if they're naughty because that's where they want to be. The woman with five kids said that she sends hers outside instead, if they're naughty. Apparently they hate that.

I also remember mum saying things like, "If you're naughty, then I will send you to your Nan's." This was if we were really bad. Nan's house smelled of wee and she watched black and white films on her portable telly. You knew that you'd been naughty if you were threatened with the wee-house.

Again, the woman with five kids said that she couldn't use this as a punishment. Her kid's Nan (ie her mom) was only 35 and took the kids to Bentley Bridge to go bowling and Nando's. She had to threaten the kids with not being allowed to see their Nan as punishment.

Back in my day, if mum had really had enough of us she would say, "Wait until your Dad gets home." Dads were strict back in the day and you did not want your mum tattling on you to your Dad.

Again the mum of five said that you couldn't do that these days. Her kids had three different Dads. One – their biological Dad, two – their current step Dad and three –according to two of her kids that were waiting for her to finish having her nails done - Uncle Pete, who only seemed to come around when neither of their other Dads were around and helped Mummy with DIY in the bedroom. Either way, the Dads spoiled the kids to get one-up-man-ship on the other Dads.

I have had to have really boring nails as my sign language exam is coming up and there need to be no distractions with the signs that I make (and it is videoed – that reminds me I must book into the hairdressers if I'm going to be on video and I might need a new dress). The colour I chose was 'wild mink'. You know that they wanted to call it 'mink' because 'dull non-descript beige' simply wouldn't sell and they obviously added the 'wild' to the front of it to try and entice people into thinking it was a 'hot' colour. It's really not.

Tonight has been a sad night. My *Actifry* which has been faithfully serving me for six and a half years now has died. I will mourn it until my new one comes tomorrow thanks to Amazon Prime –

well it will be Friday – Friday is definitely chips night. My Actifry allows me to eat guilt-free chips, as it only uses a tea spoon of oil. I don't know why I don't lose weight – it really is a healthy way to cook.

Mr H just chuckled as he read over my shoulder what I've just written and said, "It's not the chips that keep the weight on, it's all the lattes..." I can tell that he is getting better. As soon as his sarcasm comes back then all is well in his world. He is definitely getting up for Lucy in the night...

Friday 3rd June

Missions for today:

- *Go and walk George, Chester and Cyril on their halters (and help with their shearing)*
- *Try not to kill a certain member of my family (you'll see where this is going in a bit)*

Last night after Mr H went to bed early, to try and get rid of his man flu, I caught him in the act in bed doing something he shouldn't have been. No – it's not what you're thinking, you rudey people. It was worse than that.

He was eating my box of Thornton's chocolates. As I wandered in he was mid-mouth with one of them and he stopped like a rabbit caught in headlights (or teenage boy caught watching porn) with the chocolate wedged between his lips. If he had been sensible then he would have swallowed it and pretended that nothing was happening but being a man he couldn't multitask. He was also trying to turn the TV over with the remote control at the same time, after all.

The look on his face was priceless. It was the same guilty look he had when I caught him looking at Tractor's Monthly on his computer, the other week. I concluded that maybe his man flu was totally put on to make me get up for Lucy in the night. I think he knew that he had been rumbled because when Lucy barked to go out at 6am, he got up straight away. There was no way that I was getting up after this.

I was watching *Frasier* whilst in my pjs and eating my morning toast and it was the episode where he has a butler. I watched it thinking, 'I really could do with a butler'. It would be fab to have your every whim attended to.

No more picking Mr H's dirty undies off the floor. No more cooking. No more fishing gunky hair from down the plug hole in the bathroom. If I ever win the lottery then I think a butler will be my first investment. This would also stop Mr H's eternal moaning.

I made him a packed lunch today and all he did was moan about that the fact that there was a squashed spider at the bottom of the sandwich container. Honestly! Men! At least it was dead and wasn't one of those poisonous black widow ones. I think they bite the heads of men off after mating with them – so he really should be more grateful. If I had a butler then he could make Mr H's lunch instead.

Today was a really fun day. I was supposed to be working but when I got a text from our Alpaca sellers to say that they were shearing today and did I want to come and walk the boys on their halters and help with shearing then it took me all of two seconds to decide to ditch work and go and have some Alpaca love. Mr H was in work but I texted him to see if he wanted to come in his lunch break.

In typically annoying fashion, when Mr H was walking the Alpacas on their leads they behaved impeccably for him. When I led William (the one we were originally going to have with George) he bounced around like I was taking him to the vets to be put down, whereas all of the Alpacas Mr H led walked beautifully.

Mr H gloated and said, "Obviously they recognise my strong male aura and know that there is no point in challenging me." Personally, I thought I saw a look of, 'He's not worth messing with as he is so low down the pack order' on their faces. I think they saw me as a challenge (either that or it's mating season. I did feel a head come over my shoulder at one point. I'd not been told what to do if an Alpaca tries to mate you – I was just glad I was wearing thick jeans. I've never been taken from behind by an Alpaca).

Before I went to see the Alpacas I had a very stressful phone conversation with a member of my family. We will call him 'Grandad'. (He's not really my 'Grandad' and the reason that I know this is that both of my Grandads are dead.) I think that you will all relate to this conversation and understand how I very nearly glugged a load of damson gin after having it.

GD "Hi Jo – I need to go to the hospital. Your sister said that you might be able to take me as you're working from home. She tried to book me an appointment online yesterday but as she couldn't get in touch with you, she didn't book it."

Me "OK Grandad. Yes I can take you. Have you got the piece of paper there that says how I book it?"

GD "Well... let me see..." *proceeds to read out entire letter*

Me "OK – Grandad. I've got it. Let me grab my mobile and I'll do it now." *Goes to get mobile*

Me "OK – I've got my phone – read out the web address for me."

GD "Is that the one that begins with the three w's?"

Me "Yes – that's the one – read it out exactly as it is."

GD "It says www.nhs.co.uk"

Me "Is that all it says?"

GD "Yes."

Me "OK – that's only taking me to a home page. There must be more on it that takes me to an appointment page."

GD "Oh? Do you mean the bit at the end that has one of those signs – it's a slash I think - and then says referrals?"

Me "Yes – that's the one. OK, I'm on the page. I now need an ID number. It will be on the letter."

GD "Well, it's an appointment for me. And I need to go to Walsall. You see I've been suffering from..." *I cut him off before I had to stop myself from gagging at some old person ailment that I really didn't want to know about*

Me "I don't need any of that. I need the 16 digit code that is broken up into four lots of four."

GD "Four lots of four? Four lots of four? Four lots of four?" (He has number Tourette's, quite clearly.)

Me *Desperately trying to remain calm and not wander into the kitchen to grab some alcohol.* "Yes – is there a 16 digit code?"

GD "Oh? Do you mean the 16 numbers that seem to be broken up into fours?"

Me *through clenched teeth* "Yes – that would be the ones."

[I have just messaged my sister to say that I am typing up the story of booking the appointment and have realised that it is strangely therapeutic to put it down on paper. I really must do this more often… to clarify – I mean write down irritating situations - not message my sister – we message each other all the time and that's not stressful.]

Me "OK – now it needs a password – now – this is really important. Passwords need to be in their actual format. For example, this means if there are any letters in capitals then I need to know."

GD "OK – the password is… 'fuck this s**t'. (OK – obviously my Tourette's is back. The password clearly wasn't this – but in all honesty it is what I typed in the box three times in a row after five failed attempts.) ...the password is 'spicey things'."

Me "OK – Are there any capital letters, or is it all little letters?"

GD "I'm not sure..."

Me "What do you mean – you're not sure. You should be able to tell if any of the letters are capitals. If they are going to use capital letters it would normally be at the start of a word. So is there a capital 'S' and is there a capital 'T'?"

GD "Well... it's definitely a little 't'. I think it's a capital 's'... but it's really hard to tell."

Me "Nope – that's not worked. Are you sure there are capital letters?"

GD "Well... the two words are separate and it says to make sure that you put them in separately... I'm not sure."

Me "Sorry? Did you say that the two words need to have a space between them?"

GD "Yes – didn't I say that?"

Me "No – you didn't – ok I'll try that. No – still not working."

GD "Well – it looks like capital letters… In fact – I think that the first word is all in capital letters."

Me *Losing the will to live and contemplating slitting my wrists* (OK – I'm kidding. I was contemplating going over and slitting his wrists) "OK – so the first word is all capitals, then there is a space and then the second word is all little letters."

GD "Yes – that's what it looks like."

Me "No – that's not worked either."

GD "Well – your sister got in yesterday. I don't know why you're having so much trouble."

Me *About to explode and say, 'Because she could read off the password and she's not a f***wit and knows what capital letters and little letters look like'. I also wanted to say, 'Is this hospital appointment really necessary? Will you actually die without it?' Obviously I didn't*

"Let me try it again with all little letters. No – ok – it's locked me out because of three failed attempts."

GD "What does that mean?"

Me "It means that you're going to have to do things the old fashioned way. You're going to have to phone them."

GD "Oh – so how do I do that?"

Me "Is there a phone number on the letter? If there is then phone them up and ask when they have appointments."

GD "But how will I know if you can take me?"

Me "Ask them for a range of dates – maybe three or four and say that you will phone them back within the next five minutes. The appointments aren't likely to have gone that quickly."

GD "Oh – you'd be surprised! These appointments are like gold dust. They're probably all getting booked up as we speak."

Me "Well get off the phone from me and phone them up!"

GD "Can you phone them?"

Me "NO!!!! THEY WON'T SPEAK TO ME AS I DON'T HAVE YOUR CONSENT. PHONE THEM NOW AND ASK THEM FOR SOME DATES. I DON'T CARE HOW MANY – JUST PHONE THEM NOW AND ASK!" *I felt the need for shouty capital letters at this point to reflect the tone of my voice*

GD "Oh ok – I'll call you back in a minute."

I go and phone my sister in the meantime to vent off my anger. She helpfully tells me that she could remember the password and it was all lower case with a space in the middle. We both realise how appalling the education system must have been years ago if someone of advancing age cannot tell the difference between capital letters and little letters and whether there is a space in between two words. Phone rings so I tell her goodbye and I'll speak in a bit.

GD "I've sorted it. Turns out that they still had the same appointment your sister tried to book yesterday, so I've booked that."

Me "That's great Grandad – but I'm on the other line and need to go."

Phones my sister back and says, 'It's no wonder that I drink' and then I go and get a drink.

Sadly, I expect that this type of conversation is quite common in a lot of households. At least when I'm old, I will be able to book appointments through the internet and generally survive in life as I can do online supermarket shopping, order home delivery of take aways online and can play candy crush and the lottery on my phone too. There's not much more I will need in life. Even writing this tale has made me feel the need to reach for the Sauvignon Blanc...

After the Alpaca shearing, being the good wife that I am, I went up to Mr H's room at 5pm and said, "Do you want your dinner yet?" As he was pausing to answer me, I wrinkled my nose and said, "Can you smell sick? That's a disgusting smell. Where on earth is it coming from?" Mr H said, "I can't smell anything with this cold." As I looked down there was what looked like dog poo on his carpet – but it couldn't have been, as Bonnie was shut in my office while we were out and Lucy can't get up the stairs. I concluded that it must be Casper's poo.

It smelled the most disgusting smell in the world and I couldn't believe that Mr H couldn't smell it. I went and got a doggy poo bag – as poo – whether indoors or outdoors - is on my job list – and scooped it up. I also went and got the Vanish carpet mousse to clean the carpet. 'At least he is a cat with taste', I thought. He goes to the toilet on the old manky carpet in Mr H's office and not the nice wooden floorboards in the new spare rooms.

I like to think that Casper thought this through but I suspect he probably just thought, 'Oh no – I'm shut in. Either I go downstairs and poo where the dog might eat me, or I just do it right here and now and the dog won't eat me.' I wished that he had gone downstairs and done it. Not because I wished that Lucy would have eaten him but she definitely would have eaten his poo and then I wouldn't have had to have cleaned it up...

Saturday 4th June

Mission for today:

- *Catch up on work for missing it yesterday*

I only have one mission today. I need to finish my presentation on 'How to remember vast amounts of information in five easy steps'. Ironically, when I woke up, Mr H said to me, "What are your plans for today then?" I told him that I needed to catch up on work and had a presentation to write. "Oh? What's that on then?" He said, feigning interest. "It's on… it's on… Oh – it will come to me," I replied. This did not bode well, I thought, afterwards.

Actually though, I think that personal struggles always help you more when you are trying to help others. It will be a funny story to tell my attendees when I hold a seminar on it. Since I hit 40, I think my brain has begun to deteriorate (either that or it's the alcohol).

Talking of alcohol…

My work was successful and I rewarded myself with a large glass of Sauvignon Blanc in the garden. We had two friends pop in who are borrowing my wheelchair (from when I ruptured my Achilles) and they brought with them a bottle of chilled Sauvignon Blanc as well. I love it when friends call in and I love them even more when they bring Scooby* snacks.

* Just in case this is a local phrase, I'll explain. It means treats. It comes from the cartoon Scooby Doo. Obviously I don't give dogs Sauvignon Blanc. I'm not that stupid. I mean, why would I waste alcohol on them?

Back to our friends and a fabulous afternoon catching up. Our friends are older than us and proof that you can still have a wicked sense of humour and take the piss out of life, no matter how old you are.

A lot of old people are bitter, twisted and miserable in life. I have told Mr H that if he gets like that (it's genetic on his grandparents' side, so there is a chance) then I shall immediately put him in a home. Of course, I'm joking – I'm not shelling out for one of those. I think it costs around £448 (it's important to be precise) a week to put someone in a home. Instead I will commit a crime, frame him for it and he can go to prison instead.

My friend who works in forensics will happily let me send her some of his hair and DNA to plant at the scene of a crime. Luckily, Featherstone prison is only round the corner from us, so I will be able to visit him but not have to put up with his man nonsense on a daily basis. It will also cost us nothing for him to be there. It's one of those win-win situations. I hear they have Sky Sports in the new block as well. I'm too tight to allow him to have that here. I'm sure he will love it there.

I don't know why but the topic of conversation got onto 'checking your prostate'. Mr H assured them that his PSA is checked every year and that he's currently waiting for an appointment for the specialist because it is 0.1 above the maximum level that the GP is allowed. The specialist's maximum level under government guidelines is slightly higher, so if his PSA continues like this he is going to be back and forth to the hospital like a yo-yo (why they don't have the same maximum limit, goodness only knows).

But it gets him out of my hair for a bit, so I don't really mind. He told our friends that the doctor said that aggravating factors for prostate cancer are 'sex, cycling and infection.' I then had visions of someone having sex in a muck heap having just cycled there. Our friend said, 'Well there is a position in the karma* sutra called the 'bicycle', you know.' I made a mental note to Google it later – just out of curiosity mind. (I bet you're Googling it now, aren't you?) I also wasn't sure whether to be horrified that someone in their mid-70s was talking about the karma sutra or whether I should applaud them. It beats moaning about the 'youth of today' or constantly telling everyone about your medical problems.

* I know that this is probably not how it's spelled – but I wouldn't know. I don't have a copy of the illustrated edition from 1993 in my bedroom. I mean - I wouldn't put it there just in case Mr H's

mum was over cleaning and happened upon it. She's still traumatised by the chilli grinder in the kitchen.

I cooked us chicken and chips for tea tonight. I was going to do chicken and salad because we've both been eating too much lately (and our afternoon of Sauvignon Blanc progressed to damson gin as well...) but I decided that I couldn't bear the 'screwed up face that's about to cry' look when I told Mr H he wasn't having chips, so I did make chips. (This is what I told him but I actually wanted to try out the new Actifry anyway.)

I didn't bother reading the instructions for the new Actifry. It is exactly the same as the one that went to Actifry heaven (well – apart from the fact that this one works). When Mr H queried that the chips had a bit of a funny taste to them, I went to look out the instructions.

Apparently, I should have washed the plastic out first to 'avoid contaminating the food.' I'm pretty sure that he won't die from eating them but if he did then I think that it would at least be classed as an accident for life insurance purposes. I like to look on the bright side of things.

We were both shattered from the day's events. I like to think it was because we both worked today but in all likelihood it was the two bottles of Sauvignon Blanc and damson gin that did it.

We decided to spend the night watching telly. I let Mr H take charge of the remote control (I was too tired to fight it from his clasp) and we watched NCIS all night. At least five times Mr H finished off one of the sentences from the characters in the show and said, "I could have written this." He couldn't. His English is appalling. He will write one whole page of A4 and there will be one full stop (usually in the wrong place) and no commas at all. Given that I wanted a quiet night though, I simply said, "I'm sure you could..." (whilst crossing my fingers behind my back. That still works as an adult. It doesn't just apply to children.)

I was tired by around 10pm, so decided to go to bed early. I thought it strange that Mr H with his man flu hadn't already decided to go. He's been in bed for around 9pm most of the week. I then realised why when I got upstairs. I had changed the bedding this morning and had let the bed 'breathe'. (I have no idea why I do this – I'm not sure all the dead skin cells and general grime is going to magically evaporate into the air. But I suspect that I'm not the only person that does this either. Yes – you! I bet you do too.)

Anyway, back to the bedding...

I suspect that Mr H had not long been to the bathroom and had spotted that the bed hadn't been re-made and as this is one of his least favourite tasks, I suspect he was waiting for me to go to bed first so that I could re-make the bed. I groaned when I saw the un-made bed. The fresh bedding is currently in the ottoman in the spare bedroom which now has loads of foam board on top of it that Mr H is using in the restoration of the bedroom. This means that I have to only use the bedding that I washed last time to put back on the bed (which is usually still in the ironing basket) as I can't get to any new bedding. Luckily I had done the ironing last week.

You probably won't remember because it was such a boring non-event that it won't have featured in the book.

As Mr H has had his man flu then he has borrowed one of my pillows (as he is using three) and I have a new one from the spares that we have. This caused a problem though with putting fresh bedding on. We were short of a pillow case. I told him that in all likelihood there was another pillow case knocking around in the bottom of the ironing basket and he could use an un-ironed one. I didn't offer to iron it – I had freshly ironed ones on my side and he has gone out in an un-ironed t-shirt and jeans before to the pub, so I didn't think he would get all prissy about this.

He didn't and found one in the bottom of the basket. As I saw him pick up the pillow that didn't have a case on it, I realised that it was the one that I had swapped for his favourite one. I had a momentary panic and tried to distract him with 'The Karen Carpenter' story that was coming on telly, just in case he noticed. I needn't have worried though as he never even flinched. I'm now thinking that a lot of his behaviour is totally psychological and made up in his head. He hasn't noticed the new underpants that I've integrated. But that has reminded me that I need to get the other two out of the bottom of my wardrobe soon.

As we were settling down to go to sleep, Mr H went to get a glass of water from the ensuite. When he came back I said to him, "Have you just weed in that?" It was all cloudy and a very strange colour. He insisted that he hadn't but when I went to top my glass up, the water was perfectly clear and was not yellow. I think I might need to keep an eye on him. I wonder if he has been sucking too many lockets. There's a warning on the side of the packet to say something like, 'Don't eat more than three packets in a day.' I think he's been swallowing them like candy so they've probably messed with his head.

Sunday 5th June

Missions for today:

- *Integrate Mr H's final two pairs of undies (and hide the four new pairs of sandals I bought)*
- *Go out for dinner with a friend*

I like to achieve a balance of missions in my life.

One of them is quite clearly a tricky mission requiring stealth, cunning and meticulous execution and the other is just plain fun and frolics.

Our friend is down to see us and is staying overnight with us for two days. As we still don't have the spare rooms finished then he is sleeping with the dogs in the lounge. I haven't warned him about Lucy's night time exploits – I think he will get the gist that she wants to go out when she barks in his ear, licks his face and if that doesn't work to wake him up then she will likely let out a really smelly fart. In typical fickle

Border collie fashion though, she didn't want a wee in the night and slept like a baby.

The first mission was partially successful. I got out the two pairs of remaining man pants from the bottom of my wardrobe. Sadly they didn't smell quite right and I had to think whether I had rubbed these in anything offensive before putting them in there. I concluded that I hadn't and as I sniffed them again I realised that Casper must have weed on them when he was shut in the other night. He must really hate Mr H as he avoided weeing on anything of mine and if you remember he had pooed on the carpet in Mr H's office as well.

It's his own fault (Mr H's – not Casper's). I've told him that cats are cunning sneaky little devils and they don't forget anything. Mr H had accidentally trod on Casper as he was sunbathing by the back door a month ago (to clarify - Casper was sunbathing – I don't allow Mr H time off from chores for that) and I think this was Casper's revenge. Cats are worse than women for enacting revenge. I thought that women could hold a grudge but given that for every year of Casper's life it's really around seven of ours then I worked out (with the help of a calculator of course) that Casper had held his grudge for about six months. Even I don't hold grudges for that long. I would do, but my memory isn't so great these days and I simply forget. I really should log my grudges in my phone as a reminder.

Back to the man pants...

As they smelled of wee, I said to Mr H, "I've just found two pairs of your undies underneath the cases from when we went on holiday. I think they must have fallen out when I unpacked. Unfortunately I think that Casper has weed on them, so I'm going to put them straight in the wash. I really think you should consider getting some new ones. If Casper is weeing on them, then I think he is trying to tell you that they're manky and need changing."

Mr H replied, "I'll think about it." We all know that he won't and I will have to bring up the conversation again in a month just to keep up the ruse. I think I'll put a diary reminder in my phone for this as I'm starting to lose track on the lies.

I also needed to hide the four new pairs of sandals that I had bought. In my defence, it would have been a crime not to buy them as each pair was only seven Starbuck's lattes. (Ironically I was actually consuming a Starbuck's latte when I bought them.)

I thought about my strategy for integrating the man pants and whether I could apply the same principles to my sandals. But I really did not want Casper to wee on them and I didn't want to wipe them around the rim of the bath. It was Lucy's fault (see Monday 9th May) as to why I needed to buy them in the first place but Mr H doesn't do proper logic.

I thought about driving over them with the car to 'rough them up' a bit so he wouldn't know that they were new but they were really pretty and I didn't want tyre marks across them. I then pondered about dunking them in the moat for a second but I didn't want them stinking of algae and turning green. I was running out of ideas to make them look old, that wouldn't actually make them look old. You can see my dilemma?

I came to the conclusion that honesty was the best policy, so I hid one pair in the bottom of my wardrobe and another under the pile of my jeans in the cupboard in the bedroom. I put one pair in full view on the middle of the shoe rack (going for the 'it's too obvious to be noticed' double bluff) and decided to wear the other pair tonight when we went out with our friend. If Mr H saw them when our friend was here then he probably wouldn't say anything for fear of looking like a cheapskate.

Mum sent me a message today, as she's on holiday (again). The retired really do have the life of riley. She said that there was a three year old boy playing with his toy tractor on the beach and she was dying to take a video of him playing with it and post it to Mr H's timeline on Facebook. She didn't though.

Not because of some loyalty to Mr H and not wanting to wind him up about me not letting him have a tractor because she loves to wind him up about it. I think it's because she didn't want the parents to think that she was some paedo who went around videoing kids on the beach. I'm glad that she didn't do it as well. I have no money for bail at the moment, with having just paid out for the Alpaca's shelter and fencing.

Whilst I was trawling through Facebook this morning, I spotted a post by *BBC Breakfast* about new 'emojis' being released and they were asking the general public as to what new ones they would like to have. I don't normally comment on posts like this because no matter what you say you will always end up offending someone. I am pretty sure that there are people that sit on Facebook all day long moaning about everything just for the sake of moaning – they are known, to me, as the 'professionally offended'*.

* Well – that's the polite term for it. I actually prefer Jason Manford's name for them of 'cockwombles'.

I decided though that this was a bit of fun and couldn't possibly result in upsetting anyone. I commented that I would like an 'Alpaca' emoji as we were getting three in a few weeks and I was fed up with using 'goat' emojis. I scrolled through some of the comments on there and after posting my comment I did think about deleting it! O.M.G. – how on earth can such an inoffensive topic become so emotive with people?

One woman was ranting about the guy that had been talking on *BBC Breakfast* about emojis and how he was wrong about them and that she was 'screaming at the TV' when he 'clearly didn't know what he was talking about'.

Someone commented on my post to say, 'Beautiful wild creatures should not be contained like this.' I did think it a bit strange and decided not to respond as I didn't want to unleash the beast in them (oh the irony...) but then the same person put another comment and said, 'Woops – sorry – wrote this on the wrong thread, I was trying to put it on the one about the gorillas being kept in zoos.' I also decided not to respond to this and have now made a mental note not to comment on anything public again. I really should have known better...

Even though I knew that we were going out for dinner tonight, my inner evil fat twin did not appear to know (or was likely in denial). She made me cook her a burger for lunch (with grated cheese on it). The grated cheese was from the M&S when I went the other day with my sister and it was in some weird shaped packaging that insisted that if I followed the three step guide to opening it, then the cheese packaging would be 'easy self-closing' and would keep the cheese 'deliciously fresh' for at least a week.

Having read step one three times (and not having understood it once) I didn't bother to move on to step two or three. I simply took a pair of scissors and sliced across the top of the plastic and then re-sealed it with a freezer bag clip. The cheese was quite expensive - I expect I paid more for the elaborately designed re-sealable feature, which I actually didn't use. I also suspect that a man designed the feature.

If I had have followed the three steps then I think it would have taken me the best part of three minutes to re-seal the cheese. This was not 'easy self-closing' in my book. It made me not want to buy cheese again from there. I did think about tweeting M&S to tell them to invest more in the actual food itself because I ultimately don't eat the packaging. I didn't though because a bit of the plastic ended up in my burger and when I swallowed it, I didn't want to look like a liar when I contacted them.

Today I emailed eight more agents with extracts from my book, to see if anyone is bonkers enough to think that my book might sell. I suspect that I will end up down the self-publishing route as I'm not sure anyone 'gets' my humour. Even Mr H (who being my husband has to indulge me – it's in the 'Perfect Marriage' book – well, that's what I tell him) doesn't really 'get' me and he's been with me for 25 years.

This afternoon, I wrapped a few birthday presents up. Remember that this time of year is popular for having babies because it would have been drunken bank holiday August sex that resulted in these births.

I really should add something else into the introduction – the fact that I cannot wrap a present up without it looking like a three year old did it. It's times like this that I do wish that I have children because I could at least say to people, 'Little Zebedee wrapped that up especially for you – didn't he do well?' I don't think that I would have named my child Zebedee but it was the first name that popped into my head while I was writing that sentence.

If I had had children then I would not have given them some awful names that would have resulted in them being bullied in school or needing therapy for the rest of their lives. I actually know someone who called their child 'Gaybor' and someone else that called their new arrival 'Valerie Gina' (you just know that 'Va-Gina' is going to have one hell of a ride in school - erm - so to speak...) A friend of mine years ago was so worried about giving her future children awful names that she called her cats the names instead to get it out of her system. Her cats were

'Norman', 'Derek' and 'Ronald.' (Apologies if any Normans, Dereks or Ronalds are reading this book...) I asked her once why she didn't just give all of her cats and all of her future children nice names. She pondered for a while before saying "I don't know." And people say that I'm bonkers.

I think I've digressed again. Never mind... I think I had finished on that topic.

We had a fabulous night out with our friend. We went to the Hundred House near to Shifnal and the food (and wine) was amazing. We couldn't eat all of the food and the chips were absolutely ginormous so I put two of them in a doggy poo bag to take home for Lucy and Bonnie. The only part of the night that distressed me was going to the toilet before we left. You know that I have weird toilet issues.

These toilets were of the kind where the hole is in the middle and sunk into what looks like a big worktop. I always think it is incredibly unhygienic as there is too much surface for it to be free of bacteria and I end up crouching and not touching anything with my hands (which often results in the inevitable splashing of pee-pee on the 'work top').

I never know how you are supposed to go. My sister totally gets this. When I put the picture up on Facebook, she said, 'Are you supposed to stand on the side bits?' I don't know why but the concept traumatises me. One of my other friends said (in response to my 'work top' comment), 'It's OK – I don't think anyone is suggesting that you chop your veggies on it.' I wasn't sure whether this was a euphemism. Knowing the friend that said it then it probably was. I think that this friend will buy my book, she's as bonkers as me...

Monday 6th June

Missions for today:

- *Take my sister to the doctors to check that she is still alive and well**

* I know that she is alive but I think the doctors want to check how she is doing following her op.

Obviously after last night's toilet incident, I dreamed of toilets. I'm sure one of these days, when my bladder valve slackens, I am going to wet the bed. I bet Mr H can't wait for that day to come.

I did lots of work in the morning so that I could go and pick my sister up and take her to the doctors. I grabbed my clipboard before I left as I thought that the doctor would be interested in my sister's responses to the various assessments that I had carried out on her when I took her out last Wednesday.

I thought that I would need to be brutally honest with the doctor and say that I didn't think that

312

her response time to picking the four items in Boots quite met the required standard of someone out of hospital for just over two weeks but I decided that I would discuss this on my own with the doctor as I didn't want to upset my sister's mental state of mind.

According to the occupational therapy guidelines, it is important to keep the patient upbeat and happy. With this in mind I promised her that I would take her out for Costa later in the week and treat her to a Nando's when she was feeling up to it. I congratulated myself on how well I was looking after her mental health.

Before I left to go and pick up my sister, I noticed that Bonnie was circling my handbag and making a 'growling' noise. Initially I wondered whether there was a mouse in there but it was the type of 'happy growl' that she makes when she knows that one of her toys has gone under the settee or if she is standing by her treat container trying to get you to give her a Dentistix. I looked into my handbag and saw a full doggy poo bag.

Momentarily, I forgot that I had put two chips in there from last night's dinner and thought, 'When did I decide to put a bag of poo in my handbag? How drunk was I last night? And did I actually take the dogs out for dinner?' I even pondered as to whether it was my own poo at one point. Had I not been able to go down the toilet that was embedded into the work surface? I realised how stupid that was though. My own poo would never have fit in just one doggy poo bag. So I dismissed that idea.

When it finally came to me that it wasn't poo in my handbag but chips, I realised why it was Bonnie's happy growl. She knew that there was a tasty treat to be had. The chips didn't look quite as nice as they had done last night but Bonnie and Lucy were extremely grateful for them and gulped them down after breakfast.

Being the good sister that I am, I was early to pick up my sister for her doctor's appointment. Mr H had forgotten that he had a meeting a lunchtime so I had to take his car because he was in mine. I prefer to be in mine as it is smaller and therefore I can fit it into parking spaces more easily. Don't think that I'm one of those typical rubbish women drivers though. I'm much better than Mr H. I don't get road rage. I don't race off other cars. I look much better behind the wheel of a car than him and can fix my lipstick whilst changing gear*.

* Obviously this is a joke. Mr H's car is automatic. There are no gears to change.

His car is so wide and long though that it is hard to park in tight spaces. Also my sister's doctors is in a really rough area and my car is 14 years old and no one would waste their time bothering to steal it whereas Mr H's car is only a few years old and quite posh.

I know this because I only know how to use about three of the paddles on the steering wheel. My steering wheel only has lights and indicator stalks on it. I don't care much about cars so have happily had the same car for donkey's years, whereas Mr H is a typical man and needs a flash car and needs to swap it regularly (and 'regularly' is not the same definition he gives to how often he cleans the house). I think it's to do with what they teach young boys in school. Something to do with self-worth and the size of your car being dis-proportionate to something... I forget what it is now...

Anyway, back to the doctors...

As it is in a rough area and I was in Mr H's car (he would literally kill me if anything happened to his precious car whilst it was in my care) then I told my sister that I would wait in the car while she went in to see the doctors. Cars in this area are normally on bricks within five minutes, the VIN number has been scratched off within eight minutes and the car has been re-sprayed within a further 13 minutes and booked on a one-way trip to Eastern Europe.

It's amazing how efficient car thieves can be. They would really excel if they applied themselves and actually got jobs working in the logistics industry or maybe they could work for HM Customs at the ports trying to stop car thieves - oh? Wait...

She thought that she would be in and out in around five minutes. 35 minutes later and she came out. I nearly boiled to death in this time. Even with the windows wide open (but obviously the doors locked) and the air con blasting* (Mr H will also kill me for this. He is so tight when it comes to putting the a/c on. I put it on in winter and wear six layers just to annoy him) I was still roasting.

* It turns out that the air con wasn't actually on. I forgot that the engine needed to be running for the air con to work. The blowers were just blowing boiling hot air at my face. No wonder I also needed the windows open.

Luckily my presence seemed to put off any would-be-thieves. (If Mr H had been driving then I think he would have been on the doctor's doorstep with a concussion and his car half way to Ukraine** by the time that he woke up.)

** I put 'The' in front of the word 'Ukraine' and Mum nearly had a seizure when she saw it. Apparently, it does not have 'The' in front of it. But as I didn't do Geography GCSE then I can get away with being dim and ignorant and bow to her superior knowledge.

I actually think that they should have a 'The' in front of it. If I was a country then I would definitely be 'The Jo' – it makes you look more important, I think. After all we always say 'The Queen', 'The Royal family', 'The toilet' – oh….

I dropped my sister off home before driving back. Unluckily for me it was school chucking out time as I made the ten minute journey home. I've already said that not having children allows me to ridicule those that do but I actually think that those of my friends with kids would have been embarrassed by some of the parents at the local primary school.

There were at least 30 cars parked all the way along the road near to the school. I couldn't get past and had to wait for some of them to put their kids in the car and move off. The car that I was following drove all of 400 metres round the corner and then pulled into a drive of a house. Her drive was actually closer to the school than where she had had to park. I shook my head in despair and wondered what on earth the world is coming to.

I moan about Mr H and his man logic but I'm now thinking that 'parent logic' is such a thing and not a good thing at that. If any of my parent friends start to exhibit these traits then I will have to give them a good shake. Obviously the same goes for me – if I start to exhibit some weird traits then I hope they will tell me. (I think we all know that that ship has passed...)

Tuesday 7th June

Missions for today:

- *I'm too tired to have any missions today*

The reason why I'm too tired to have any missions is because our friend has stayed over the last two nights and has been up at 6:50am to go water skiing.

You know that I'm not a morning person and having to get up at this (unearthly) time to make them a bacon and sausage sandwich and a cup of tea has nearly killed me. But being the good hostess with the most-ess that I am, then I have sucked it up and got on with it.

They aren't staying overnight tonight though so I am definitely not setting the alarm tomorrow and will have a lie in. Lucy, ironically also slept through the night last night so I think I am going to recreate the illusion of someone being in the lounge, just in case this is why she is settled at night and doesn't bark to go out for a wee.

I'm going to make a person figure out of pillows and duvets and put it in a sleeping bag on a camp bed on the floor in the lounge. Just in case she susses that it's not a real person, then I will also dress it in some of Mr H's clothes that are currently in the washing basket so that it has a bit of B.O. to it and I'll pull out some of Mr H's hair and spread it on the pillow (this will be the trickiest bit of the process. I might have to do it when he's fallen asleep on the settee during *The Mysteries of Laura* tonight).

I would pull some of my own hair out but given that it has been dyed so many times then I really don't think it will smell real anymore and Lucy is, after all, Mr H's dog.

If this works tonight then I'm going to carry on doing it. (Either that or I'm going to be frank with Mr H and tell him that Lucy is his dog and he needs to man-up and take responsibility and sleep in the lounge from now on.) You might think that I'm mean but Bonnie is my dog and Lucy is his. If it was Bonnie being unsettled in the night then Mr H would most definitely remind me (a lot) that she is my dog. I'm just being consistent.

The weather forecast is that from 2pm today for the next nine days it is going to rain and there will be thunderstorms. I am not best pleased to hear this. I love working from home for most of the summer because it enables me to get a tan* through working outside. The rain is not going to help me tan.

* I never really tan on my legs. My arms go a beautiful brown colour, whereas my legs will only ever go 'white with a hint of rose'. I know that this is the colour because I took a picture of my legs on Instagram once and sent it to B&Q's colour-match paint department to ask if they could match it and this is what they came up with.

The guy who replied to me said, 'It's basically a white colour with a smidgeon of pink in it, but you can barely see the pink, so basically it is cheaper to just buy some white paint and be done with it.'

Because of the rain and thunderstorms forecast then I have had to strategically work out my working from home schedule. I spent all of today in the sun with my hard copy print outs and when the rain descends then I will be able to type them up on the computer (inside in my office) into my presentations and handouts for my attendees.

One of the presentations was entitled 'How to be flexible at work' and this has given me a prime example to use. I don't know which parent I get my flexibility from. I think probably it's Richard (Sir Richard of Virgin Trains). I do hope that people reading this book have a sense of humour. I will not be pleased if Mum says to me, "Some random woman in the street came up to me today and called me a hussy." I think the world has gone a bit potty lately. It seems that no one understand humour these days. I also get my humour from my Dad (which one...?)

In typical 'crap weather predictions' fashion, the free APP on my iPhone had not got the weather report right (funny that...) and the predicted thunder and rain never materialised. But this was handy as I was just getting to the part of my presentation entitled 'What happens when work doesn't go to plan?', so once again I had a real life example to use.

Mum sent me a message from holibobs (I think she hates me and is rubbing it in) about a couple she had observed in M&S. Apparently they were a sweet old couple buying lunch in the café and the server told him that the sandwich was gluten free. He and his wife didn't understand what that meant so they swapped the sandwich for something else. Mum said they were a really sweet, naïve couple.

I said, 'So were the Schumacher's in Dirty Dancing, and they were wanted in about 13 different states for theft of people's wallets, check you've still got your purse.' She responded, 'Ha-ha. You are funny.' But I didn't hear from her for another four hours. I expect that she was down the police station filing the report on them.

Someone on Facebook today posted one of those e-card type things which said, 'It's the little things in life that count.' As I was reading it I saw the 93 year old farmer and his wife wandering past to go and have a beer in their garden. It really did make me feel a warm glow inside. (Either that or it was the damson gin that I went and got after seeing him with a beer. But either way the little things really do count. The homemade damson gin is small and delicious.)

In all seriousness though, the e-card was right. Mr H was back at lunchtime and we had a lovely chat about life and happiness. Admittedly, I think that I did most of the talking and he said, "Uh-huh, you're so right, yep – totally agree" while he looked like he was watching a funny video on YouTube on his phone but nothing was going to darken my mood today.

I texted my sister to check that she was still alive today. Thankfully she is.

Wednesday 8th June

Missions for today:

- *Successfully go to the vets without anyone getting bitten*
- *Try and discourage Ron the digger man from egging* Mr H on that he needs a tractor*

* I'm pretty sure that to 'egg someone on' is a universal phrase. But on the off chance that it isn't, it means to encourage them or urge them to do something. I have no idea where it comes from. I have visions of throwing eggs at someone. We used to egg and flour each other on the last day of school but that wasn't very encouraging.

Especially when we egged Sophie who was allergic to them and her face puffed up like a big ball and she had to go to hospital. To be clear, we didn't know that she was allergic to them and neither did she. As it was the last day of school we never saw her again but on a positive note I've caught up with her on Facebook since and discovered that this actually started off her acting career.

Apparently, whilst her face was all red and swollen, she got chosen to do an advert for one of those medicines that contain antihistamine and since then she has been snapped up for other adverts too. So maybe getting an 'egging' is good luck after all and it is where the phrase comes from.

Anyway... back to today.

Ron the digger man was back today to finish off laying the scalpings for the Alpaca shed. I, once again, knew that it was 'digger day' as I woke up to hear Mr H doing sing-along-karaoke to Madonna's *Vogue* on the radio.

I lay in bed and could picture him dancing around the kitchen as well. I just hoped that he was dressed. I was starting to picture the serial killer guy in *Silence of the Lambs* at this point. He's the one that kills women to make a female skin costume to wear. There is a really creepy bit where he dances around naked and hides his thing between his legs. I really have no idea why that picture came into my mind but I didn't want to chance interrupting 'naked karaoke time'. I therefore decided to wait until the song had finished before getting up.

I forgot to tell you about last night. With all the 'Brexit' stories at the moment and the imminent vote, ITV were doing one of those Cameron v Farage programs. I had taken my contact lenses out when Mr H was scrolling through the telly guide and I said, "Oo – is there a boxing match on? I wonder whether that's worth watching?" Mr H looked over to me and sighed and said, "It's not a boxing match. It's a debate between David Cameron and Nigel Farage about Brexit." To be honest, I think they would have got more viewers if DC and NF had actually had a fight. If DC won then I think his popularity would increase tenfold. He so looks like the kid that got sand kicked in his face in school.

I started to ponder about what songs they would come out to in their silky robes if they were having a boxing match with each other. I think that Nigel would have chosen something by 'Foreigner' and Dave would have likely picked

'March of the pigs'. (OK...I confess. I have just Googled 'what songs have 'pig' in the title?') I should feel guilty about this... I should...

I didn't want to watch the debate. You know that I don't do politics. (Although I will be voting. If a woman goes to the drastic extreme measure of throwing herself in front of a horse to give us – the superior sex – the right to vote, then I'm not going to let her down.) I won't actually need to post Mr H's vote in the doggy poo bin on the Cannock Road, this time though. Amazingly, we won't be cancelling each other out.

Anyway... I've digressed... back to the telly...

I wanted to watch *The Mysteries of Laura* but as Mr H wasn't letting go of the remote control, then we watched the debate instead. I noticed that a few of my friends on Facebook were watching it too. I went to put a post up about the debate (I don't know why I went to do this as talking politics on Facebook is a no-no and I was breaking one of my rules about keeping things social) but autocrapet kicked in and actually made the post funny. When I went to write

'Farage' it changed it to 'Garage' and when I went to write 'Cameron' it changed it to 'Camp moron'.

I'm not sure that I would have giggled this much watching *The Mysteries of Laura* as Jake isn't well, so I forgave Mr H for his boring choice of telly. I was chuckling even more when DC came on. I can't get it out of my head that he looks like a chubby Chandler Bing (from the show *Friends*).

I also chuckled when someone on Facebook commented, 'Well, if we Brexit then London hotels will have to stop serving continental breakfasts.' I love to see when people have their priorities right. I am hoping that it was a joke...

Talking about politics reminded me of one of my journeys to London over ten years ago. The train had broken down at Leighton Buzzard and the train itself was full of politicians and journalists etc who had been attending the Conservative conference in Birmingham. Pete Waterman was on the train but it was before the days of decent phones, so I didn't get a selfie with him.

I had to share a cab into London with four other people. A couple of them were politicians and the other two were from some political newspapers/magazines. Obviously not doing politics, I had no idea who any of them were.

We all introduced each other in the cab except for one guy who said, "Well. I don't think I need to introduce myself. You probably know who I am?" Apparently my answer of, "Oh – were you the conductor that stamped my train ticket?" did not seem to please him (although it really pleased my inner evil twin). To this day, I still have no idea who he was. He also has no idea who I am, as I certainly did not give my real name to them.

The conversation in the cab was so boring and I was regretting my choice of fellow passengers. I really should have shared the cab with the mother (who was popping pills) with the three children under the age of five that were screaming. I think it would have been a more pleasurable journey.

My cab-buddies were blathering about how we should all pull together as a community and we all had a part to play. I think their part was being rich and lauding it over us commoners. One of them asked where I came from. I told them Wolverhampton (mainly to annoy Mr H when I re-told him the story but also to see what their reaction was).

One of them said, "Oh – yah. Terribly mis-guided youngsters live there. It's such a shame as all they need is someone to show them how to behave. For example, if they drop litter, they don't know it's wrong. It's up to people like us to tap them on the shoulder and say 'I say there young fellow. Did you realise that you've just dropped that litter. You really should pick it up.'"

In my head, my evil inner twin was repeating the word 'nob' over and over again. What came out of my mouth was, "If you actually said that to someone, then you are likely to end up in hospital with a stab wound." His reply was "Pish-tosh! This is exactly the sort of silliness that stops people from showing other reprobates the error of their ways. You won't get stabbed. How overly dramatic! The young fellow would simply turn around and say, 'Golly-gosh! I didn't realise that dropping litter was wrong. Thank you for showing me the error of my ways." I did suggest to him that he came up to try out his theory. I would visit him in hospital, mainly to say, 'I told you so.'

One of the other politicians in the cab was a woman. She said, "And don't get me started on all of these women who want these silly tax credits so that they can bring up their children. I work full time and have three children and I can manage." I asked where her children were (it was past 10pm at this point). She said, "Well my husband will have got in about half an hour ago but before then the live-in nanny would have been looking after them."

I would love to say that I have embellished this conversation. I would love to say that I have...

Whilst I was being forced to watch the NF/DC debate, talk turned to the Australian 'points' system to decide if people would be allowed to work in the country. I was getting bored with the program so started to make up my own 'points' system for allowing people to visit me and come in the house. This is what I came up with:

	Number of points
Bring me alcohol	3
Bring me chardonnay crisps	2
Bring treats for the dogs	2
Bring me fruit	-2
Visit while you have flu or another contagious disease	-10
Talk about politics	-10
Talk about hilarious drunken stories	3
Take my washing and ironing away	50
Bring Mr H a tractor	500

I decided that provided that you had five points then you would be allowed to enter. We really should just employ a similar system in the UK for allowing people in. Bring a bottle and some snacks and you're welcome. (As long as you don't have Ebola.)

The trip to the vets was successful. Brandy and Precious weren't there (and thankfully the mother and son from a previous time's visit weren't there either) but I think Brandy's twin sister was (or it could have been her mother that had had a lot of 'work'). I pondered this as her face had the same expression on it the entire time that she was sitting there. When the receptionist asked her three different questions about her dog* her eyebrows did not move once and her mouth looked like she had been stung by a wasp and was temporarily paralysed.

* I think it was a dog. It was hard to tell as she carried it everywhere and you couldn't see its face due to the amount of fur. In fact, it could have been one of those big Russian furry hats as I never actually saw the dog move.

Unfortunately, the owner (who I originally thought had said to the receptionist that her name was 'Tequila' - turned out it was Delia) mis-took my quizzical look at her as one of bonding across the waiting room.

She said, "Oh – isn't your dog so pretty" as she looked at Bonnie. At this point, Bonnie let out a burp. Tequila – I mean – Delia tried to wrinkle up her nose to show her disgust but she still had the same expression on her face. I took the opportunity to turn to Bonnie and say, "Oh no – is that caviar and lobster playing havoc with your constitution again? Don't worry, you can have oysters tonight."

Delia was making constant coo-ing noises to her furry hat and at one point she said, "Aren't you just a perfect little fru-fru." I, just about, managed to stifle a giggle (OK – I lied. I didn't stifle it at all). I was then thinking, 'No! She hasn't just called it that. I've mis-heard.' But then she said it again and I chuckled again. Delia got called into the vets at this point and (if her face could have moved) she would have given me a quizzical look at my weird outburst.

Henry, the vet, managed to check Bonnie's teeth and there were no biting incidents. (To clarify – I mean that Bonnie didn't bite the vet. Obviously, I did not bite the vet. He didn't like it the last time I did it, so I haven't done it since.)

Bonnie has now been signed off. When Henry told Bonnie that she didn't have to come back she jumped up him and licked his face. He said, "Oh look at that. Kisses for me. I do like kisses". (He is a liar. He didn't seem to like it when I did it.)

Lucy slept like a log again last night, so I now have to go through the palaver of pretending that someone is sleeping in the lounge to keep this 'sleeping through the night' routine. Last night, I took a glass of water to the pretend guest, I called 'goodnight' through the door and left the dining room light on so that the pretend guest could get up and see their way to the loo. It is a mad routine to go through but a lot of my friends have to do crazy things to get their kids to go to sleep at night. One of them has to put milk and cookies in their child's wardrobe to feed the monster, so that the monster doesn't eat the child. Another of them has to sleep on the child's floor until it goes to sleep. I'm not going to do crazy s**t like this. Lucy is Mr H's dog – he'll have to do it.

Thursday 9th June

Missions for today:

- *Have a productive day working*
- *Have a fun night out tonight with Little Wren*

The free APP on the iPhone that predicts the weather is really rubbish. It has predicted rain and thunderstorms for the last two days and the next seven days. Apart from one shower last night about 8pm and a bit of thunder and no rain whatsoever today, I'm not trusting its predictions for the next week. No wonder it's free.

I'm going to have to start to watch *BBC Breakfast* again to see what the lovely Carol has to say. She gets paid so I suspect that she tries harder to be more accurate than the APP. She could lose her job if she didn't do it well. I've tried to delete the weather APP from my phone but Apple won't let me, so it really has no incentive to be accurate at all. I could do with freeing up some storage as well. I also tried to delete the unnecessary 'stocks' APP. I have no spare cash so really have no use for this APP. Again, Apple has decided that this is a necessary app in my life. It's not.

As the weather APP failed to predict the nice weather, I headed outside at lunchtime to work in the garden. I took one of the spare pillows, as now that I'm 42 I find that my back aches much more than it used to and it helps to prop me upright on the garden chairs. (I need this because I once fell asleep whilst working and slipped off the chair and onto the grass. I woke up when Bonnie was licking my face and to hear Miranda calling out, "Drinking in the day again?") The pillow would help to keep me upright in the chair.

Mr H saw me taking the pillow outside and exclaimed, "Is that my favourite pillow? Have you taken that from my side of the bed?" My evil inner twin really wanted to tell him that his pillow was probably sitting under a load of dirty nappies in Cannock landfill site but the sensible part of my brain said, 'He still has man flu. He won't be able to deal with it.' I listened to the sensible-Jo and simply said, "Of course it's not. It's one of the spare ones we keep for guests when they stay over. I know how you can't sleep without that pillow." Mr H said, "Phew! Yes. You know how I have to have that pillow on the top when I sleep. I don't know what I would do without it." (I tried to stifle a smirk whilst he stood for a minute gazing pensively.)

I walked off and I swear that Bonnie raised her eyes at me as if to say, 'What a doo-fus.' I had to agree with her. Work went surprisingly well today and as a bonus my arms have tanned quite nicely. My legs are still basically 'white with a hint of rose' but you can't have everything in life.

I emailed yesterday's tales to Mum and she asked me what breed the dog actually was that was in the vets with Delia. I had to be honest and say, 'I actually have no idea. It could have been a rabbit for all I know. I never saw its face and it didn't move. I wonder whether Delia had tried out Botox on it before she gave it to herself.' I didn't like the thought of this. Animal testing it just wrong. I was very much up for 'Delia testing' though.

I also forgot to tell you about the Basset Hounds that were in the vets yesterday. They were called 'Ant and Dec'. They were quite similar to the actual comedy duo as Ant always stood on the left and Dec on the right.

Dec also got a little frisky with the courier that came to drop off a parcel. He was licking the guy's leg as he stood there. The courier looked like he was wearing trousers. His owner became very embarrassed when she saw it and said, "Oh! I am so sorry. Dec appears to be licking your leg, it's a good job that you're wearing trousers. It would likely have tickled otherwise."

The courier replied, "I'm wearing shorts but I didn't feel it, so don't worry." The waiting room went quiet at this point as we all looked up and stared at his legs. They were so thick with hair that it looked like he was wearing black trousers. At this point Dec started to make a hacking noise and hacked up a massive chunk of black hair. Suddenly Delia's Botox wasn't the most interesting thing in the waiting room (although her expression, once again, did not change).

Speaking of dogs, my good friend Jade had to have her fourteen year old dog put down today. Henry the vet came out to their house to do it. Normally I find humour in most situations but I find absolutely no humour in this. When she put the post up on Facebook, I shed some tears for Mr P and looked across at Lucy lying on the grass. Her legs really aren't great at the moment and I think I'm in the 'denial' phase of pretending that she is fine. She will be approximately sixteen in October, so she is already living on borrowed time.

I messaged Jade to see whether she needed some hugs as I was working from home so could pop over to see her. She thanked me but said that she needed some alone time. I know that when Lucy goes to doggy heaven then I am going to be an absolute mental head case. I love my pets more than some people that I know. I went upstairs to have a hug from Mr H and even he didn't make some jokey comment about annoying him with my demands for hugs. When it counts, he is a star and knows exactly what I need. I made a mental note to stop taking the piss out of him so much. (It didn't last long, to be fair.)

I tried to forget about pets getting old and feeling sad, so went to have a quick look at Facebook to see if there were any cheery stories. Facebook had sent me a message about the *tractor4graham* page and said, 'Your tales about urine is performing better than 90% of the posts on your page.' I did chuckle at this and even more so, because as I was reading it Lucy went and did a wee on the garden.

I scrolled through the page and thought it interesting that posts covering 'urine', 'toilets' and 'sex' were performing the best, whereas the posts about politics were performing the least well. 'That just about sums it up', I thought.

Everyone likes a tale about an orifice, except when it's drivel coming out of the orifice of an annoying politician. I made a mental note to spend more time in public toilets, so that I can bring you more tales about urine. I just hope that loitering in toilets doesn't get me into trouble.

Staffordshire Police are always posting pictures of 'wanted' people caught on CCTV on Facebook. I don't want to see my own face staring back at me one day. (Although, when I do take a day out to spend in some toilets then I will definitely put on my good make-up. If I do end up caught on CCTV, then I don't want to look like a serial killer.)

Mr H was sitting at his computer for a lot of the afternoon as he had ordered the wrong filter (for the horrible vacuum cleaner that I hate) and was trying to find the right one on the internet.

He swears that he ordered the right one for our model but he quite clearly ordered part number sixty and the filter says that it is part number ninety-six. He is now going to have to send it back and get the right one. He wouldn't admit that he had made a mistake. I blame his man flu. He gets very defensive when he has it, as his tolerance is low and his mind isn't as sharp. Somehow it was my fault that he ordered the wrong one. Given that I had absolutely nothing to do with ordering it and hate the vacuum cleaner and want to set fire to it, then I think he's got a cheek blaming me.

When he was trying to print off the return address label from Royal Mail's website the screen froze and then some nudey-rudey pictures of a woman popped up. I knew that the website had been hacked as he didn't have his 'liar face' on when it did it. When I went up later, his 'liar face' was back but that's because I could see that he was watching a tractor on eBay. I reminded him that he wasn't allowed to have a tractor until my book(s) sell(s).

Tonight we went out with Little Wren and Alan for a meal at Ego in Cannock. I had received an email today offering me 25% off their al-a-carte menu. Being the inherently tight person that I am, I was well pleased with this. It would give me more money for cocktails. I could tell that Mr H's man flu was annoying him (it was definitely annoying me) as he said, "You can drive tonight." I reminded him of the rule that says that if we go out with my friends then I'm allowed to drink and if we go out with his friends - then we haven't bothered to sort out a rule for this - as he doesn't have any friends and the situation has therefore not yet arisen*. After he was starting to annoy me with this nonsense then I was definitely going to need that 25% off for more alcohol.

* Obviously I am joking. Mr H has one friend. He's been friends with Brett since Primary School but Brett has a gland problem and is thirty stone and can't get out of bed and has been stuck there since he left school at sixteen. I think he's Mr H's friend because he can't actually get away from him.

I knew that Mr H's grumps were still there when we got back from our meal out and he immediately put on *Question Time* on the telly. All I said was, "Oh no – not Question Time..." and he immediately turned over to 5USA and left the room. He went to watch it in bed so I took the opportunity to write my book. (I've had a few cocktails tonight so I am going to have to do a careful spell check tomorrow). Hopefully by the time I am finished *Question Time* will be over and he will be snoring fast asleep in bed. I'm hoping that he gets over this man flu soon. I would like to say that it's for his benefit that I'm saying this but in all honesty it's for mine. I don't want to put up with it any longer.

Tomorrow I am once again re-integrating my sister to the world (well – we're going to go to Bentley Bridge in Wolverhampton and possibly Nando's if she can cope with it). Because it might be a long day out for her then I am going to make sure that I am prepared for what might happen.

1. I have packed some Tena Ladies. Laura Ashley have a 50% sale at the moment and she* might get over-excited at their cushions.

    * I

2. I have packed plenty of wet wipes and alcohol gel. She's been at home for too long and her immune system might not be able to cope with Costa's toilets. They are basically the only toilets in the shops there, so there is a chance that they might not be very clean. Also, as she isn't walking very well she is likely to need to hold onto railings etc as she walks. Goodness knows what she might pick up from them and I've just cleaned my car out remember.

3. This also reminded me to put my latex gloves in. She is a bit unsteady on her feet and if I need to catch her when she falls then I don't want to grab onto a hand that has three different lots of people's wee on it and probably some cocaine (this is Wolverhampton after all). I would wear winter gloves but they'll be far too warm and I really don't want to look silly.

4. I have packed my whistle. As she is walking a bit hunched over at the moment then she will be harder to spot in the shops when I lose her. She is nearly six foot and I'm only five foot four. Normally I only have to look up and see her head bobbing along one of the aisles to work out where she is. I can use the whistle to call her.

(I'll have to run through some basic commands with her first. One long blow will mean 'stop where you are.' Two blows will mean 'go to the end of the aisle you're in' and three rapid blows will mean 'meet me at the tills.')

You might wonder as to why I won't just phone her. But remember, part of her rehabilitation is to check her cognitive skills. She will need to distinguish between the three different whistle types and react in an appropriate fashion.

5. I have packed some sherbet lemons. You might think that these are for her to keep her energy levels up. They will actually be to throw in the air in Sports Direct if we need to get any kids out of her way quickly. Their aisles are really narrow* and I don't want her rupturing her wounds because some small child has head-butted her in the fru-fru and she's keeled over on the floor. (As she is tall most children come up to this height. If they ever run into me then I tend to get it in the tits. Well – I would if I had any...)

* After mum did her read through she said, "Oh yes! When we went to Sports Direct it was really dark. I think 'Father Christmas' (the new name for the guy that owns it) has been saving money on electricity to pay his staff minimum wage instead."

(There has been controversy in the news this week about staff who work for Sports Direct giving birth in the loos in the warehouse and having pay docked for having to go through airport security screening before being allowed into the warehouse to work. Given the trouble that I had going through security for my flight to Belfast, I don't think that I will ever go and work for them. I couldn't cope with only being able to consume 100ml of liquid over an eight hour period).

6. I'll put my body protector in. (I leant my stab vest to my friend who is going on a hen weekend and is dressing up as a

Policewoman.) This is just in case we pop to Aldi. They very kindly sent me a £10 voucher for the broken plate in the picnic hamper. I might need to leave her in the car if I decide to go in there. I only have one body protector and being so much shorter than her, if she wore it, it would sit on her shoulders like something that the Gladiator's used to wear. (To clarify, I don't mean the female Gladiators from the TV program, like Jet and Scorpion, but the Gladiators that fought lions donkey's years ago – or was it Christians that they fought? I need to Google this...)

It's now half past midnight. *Question Time* will have finished and I'm hoping that Mr H is snoring like a baby, cuddled up to his special pillow that he can't sleep without...

Goodnight tractor-ites and spare a thought for Jade tonight x

Friday 10th June

Missions for today:

- *Bring my sister back alive from our trip out to Bentley Bridge*
- *Have funny witty banter at sign language tonight*

You will notice that I didn't say that I needed to bring my sister back from our day out unscathed and in one piece. This is because Wolverhampton is full of bonkers people and anything can happen.

Once when I was shopping in B&M a guy stole a load of Duracell batteries and as he was running out the door he nearly took out an old lady. Unluckily for him he chose the wrong old lady to run past because at the precise moment that he was trying to make it to the door, she turned around and accidentally* tripped him up with her walking stick. He ended up spread eagled on the floor before another customer landed on top of him to hold him down before the police turned up.

* When she turned to look at me, I swear that she winked. Old people here don't take or put up with any s**t.

I remember that another customer tutted and shook his head at the offender. I thought that he was doing this because he didn't condone what he did but as he looked down at the batteries strewn across the floor he said, "Flip me mate. You've just got smoke alarm batteries there. You really should have stolen AA, they're much more useful."

I had a £10 voucher from TK Maxx to use and decided to treat myself to some gardening gloves. Last time that I was in the nail salon, my beauty therapist noticed a bit of 'green' near my little finger and had to use her tweezers to pull out a thorn. I didn't want this to happen again. I love having my nails done and I don't want them to think that I have questionable hygiene with my hands. I got irrationally over-excited as I saw that they were selling Laura Ashley gardening gloves. There is a Laura Ashley just over the road from TK Maxx (which was to be our second visit of the day) but I suspected that they were cheaper here and I had my voucher. I got sucked in by their marketing (I really am an advertiser's dream). The gloves' colour was 'Erin Chalk Pink' and the leather had 'cotton with a strengthened cuff'. They really were beautiful.

As we wandered over to Laura Ashley we were just about to go in the door when we overheard a woman chatting to her friend, "I'm thinking of buying a present for my friend. She really likes gardening, so they might have some nice lanterns in here."

My sister and I looked at each other and I said, "TK Maxx are selling Laura Ashley gardening gloves. They're really nice and a really good price too." She thanked us and promptly turned around to head to TK Maxx. I like to help others to save money. I did feel a bit guilty though as I had headed off a potential customer but in my defence I did buy some beautiful vases from Laura Ashley as presents and a cake slice (well there was a 50% off sale and TK Maxx didn't sell them...)

We also wandered to Peacocks and I saw a lovely top (which I didn't need but wanted) and as it was only five Starbucks' lattes, I decided to buy it. After I had made my purchase they gave me a £5 off voucher for my next visit. My next visit turned out to be five minutes later. While I had been making my purchase, my sister was in the changing rooms trying on trousers. She didn't want to but I made her go in there to test her physical therapy. If she could successfully bend down to take her own shoes off and negotiate taking off trousers and putting on new ones in the tiny dressing room that didn't give you enough space (and no seat to sit on) then I knew that she was on the mend.

I also timed her to chart her progress. When I was paying for my top and the alarm on my phone went off, the sales assistant said, "Is that alarm important?" I sighed and said, "She should be out by now. I'm going to have to do this all over again in Next, now." She looked puzzled but simply said, "Do you want a 5p carrier bag?"

Being the inherently tight person that I am, I make sure that I carry around at least two bags for life. I must have saved at least enough for two Starbucks' lattes over the course of our shopping trip. When my sister finally came out of the changing room and asked what her time was, she knew from the look on my face that she hadn't met the required standard. We bought her trousers (with the £5 off voucher) and headed to Next. She was quicker in their changing rooms but they are much more roomy and have a lovely chair to sit on.

We went to Nando's for lunch and I have to say that the one at Bentley Bridge is fab. The staff are really friendly and will give you a booth, even if there is only two of you. They have a new dressing called Pomegranate dressing. My sister tried it but when she offered it to me, I said, "It really looks like one of those cranberry juice Innocent smoothies and not something that you should be putting on your food." It also had questionable looking pips in it that I really didn't want to come out in my wee later on (or worse still turn around after I've wiped to see that my wee was a bright red colour) and get freaked out.

I would end up taking a sample to the doctors on the off chance that I had some weird infection but would be embarrassed when I phoned for the results three days later to be told that it was a urine/pomegranate mix.

My sister was getting a little tired so when I popped to Sainsbo's I let her stay in the car. I cracked the windows for her because if I left the air con on and the windows up then I didn't want some shopper breaking open the window if they thought that I had left her locked in a hot car.

I did think afterwards that this was unlikely to happen. In Wolverhampton they would be more likely to video it and put it up on Facebook with a caption of - 'Shocking. Sister left to die in hot car' and then wander off. They wouldn't actually do anything about it (but would get thousands of 'likes' and 'shares' on Facebook).

I whizzed around Sainsbo's and didn't see the old guy that had followed me on previous occasions. Today though, love was definitely in the air. I passed one couple holding hands. They were in their 40s and looked totally in love. They caught me looking at them and I had to pretend to wave at a person behind them, so it didn't look like I was staring at them. Unluckily for me, the person behind them saw me do it and waved back. They then started towards me and looked like they were going to stop me to chat.

I had no idea who they were and didn't want to have the 'where do I know you from?' conversation, so did the only thing that I could in the situation and pretended that my phone was ringing and put it to my ear and said, "O.M.G. Really? No – I'll be straight there." I then quickly gestured 'sorry' at the person and scuttled off. I hid in the 'health food' aisle. No one in Wolverhampton goes down this aisle and after a few minutes I concluded that I was safe and continued shopping.

They weren't the only loved-up couple in there. A couple in their 70's were joking with each other and she squeezed his bum cheeks at one point in the cheese aisle. I did not make the same mistake again and quickly looked away when I saw her do it. Unfortunately, this backfired as she said, "Oh look, Albert. We're embarrassing that young girl over there." I scuttled off again (but was secretly pleased that she called me 'young.')

I then saw a third couple hugging each other in the queue for the tills. I wondered if there was some drug coming through the air con system, as I had never seen so much love in the store. Most of the time I encounter couples arguing about whether to buy the small, medium or large sized box of cornflakes. Large is obviously the most economical per kg but if the box doesn't fit on your shelf at home and has to go on its side then you will lose a lot when you don't close it up properly, so it will actually work out worse value for money. This was the exact argument I heard a couple* having once, in there.

* OK. I confess. The couple were Mr H and I.

I wasn't as loved up as everyone else in there (I was obviously immune to the drug) and nearly had heart failure when I went to get my Vanish carpet mousse. It was £6 (two Starbucks' lattes). I nearly put it back but the smell of Casper's poo on Mr H's office carpet came flooding back to me and although that didn't really bother me because I rarely went into his office, Lucy has vomited on the downstairs rugs before and that does affect me.

Instead, I chastised myself and said, 'Don't be so tight.' I just put back Mr H's gluten free pasta, gluten free lasagne sheets, gluten free fruit bread and gluten free chocolate brownies, to pay for it. At least if Mr H had bottie issues then I had my Vanish mousse to clean it up. To be clear though, I am pretty sure that it was Casper's poo on his carpet and Mr H hadn't pooed on the carpet himself.

I did notice that there were no aggressive OAPs shopping in Sainsbo's today and the 'Stressed Out Mummy' that had been in there on a previous visit wasn't in today. In fact, all of the children were really quiet and the mums all looked really chilled out. I'm now thinking of tweeting Sainsbo's to ask if there was some placating drug being pumped through the air con. (I could do with some for Mr H, as he is still moaning about his man flu.)

I popped to the Fruit Farm before dropping my sister off and when the younger butcher saw me approach his counter, he said, "Oh no! Here comes trouble." I said, "Well, it's double trouble today. This is my sister." He did the 'flip me! You don't look anything like each other' look and then said, "I bet she's not as naughty as you." I think he said that because she is nearly six foot and thought that she might take him out*.

* Locally this means punch someone's lights out and doesn't actually mean that you are going to take them out for a meal.

Olive and Donald weren't there and neither was the lady that keeps her husband permanently drunk. I told him that his sausages looked a bit small today and after we had both finished laughing he asked me what other meat I wanted of his today. My sister rolled her eyes (she has to pretend to be embarrassed by my actions, it's older sister law. Really though she loves it.)

I bought some scratchings for Jade and will take them round to her tomorrow to cheer her up.

They won't stop the hurt from losing a pet but they will help a bit.

When I was driving home after dropping my sister off alive (mission one complete) I saw a guy, who was walking his dog, doing a wee in the hedge. Unfortunately for him, he:

1. Thought that no one was watching (I was and my naughty evil inner twin did think about waving to him)

2. Didn't time it right as the heavens opened just as he started and this was the time that his little dog* decided to try and get out of the rain and stood underneath his stream.

* This is not a euphemism. It was some white Westie looking dog. After it had got caught in his urine, it was definitely no longer white. I could imagine the conversation with his wife when he got back home after walking the dog. He would have to pretend that it had rolled in some cooking oil that someone had fly tipped.

This reminded me that Bonnie has rolled in fox poo again and I'm going to have to wash her tomorrow. I really don't understand why fox poo smells so bad and doesn't wash out easily. The foxes around here seem to eat only chickens and rabbits.

I have eaten chicken (and I think I ate rabbit once) but my poo doesn't smell that bad. To be fair I haven't ever rubbed it in Bonnie's fur to compare it but I don't need to use the 'poo spray' in the loo so I'm pretty sure that it doesn't smell as bad as fox poo.

Sign Language was its usual hilarious night tonight.

We played a game where one person in the group has a card with a picture on it and the rest of the group have to ask questions, in sign language, to guess what the picture on the card is.

Mr H's group nearly had a fight as the picture on the card was some French fries in a box and he wouldn't accept 'chips' as the right answer. A discussion of 'All French fries are chips but not all chips are French fries,' then ensued.

My group had similar trouble. I had a picture of some lollies that were rainbow coloured. Unfortunately, one of the group mistook the finger spelling of 'snacks' for 'snakes' and asked whether the picture was a chameleon lizard. I did become a bit concerned about her eating habits at this point. I thought that she was a vegetarian but maybe I had misheard her and that she didn't eat meat but only reptiles. I'm sure I saw our teacher banging her head against the wall at the end of the night (like she does most weeks).

Saturday 11th June

Missions for today:

- *Try and whip #tractor4graham into shape*
- *Look at getting a cover sorted for it*
- *Go and blub like a girl at the cinema tonight (obviously this applies to Mr H. He's a softy when it comes to a sad film)*
- *Wash fox poo off Bonnie*

I was shocked when I woke up this morning as Mr H came into the lounge to eat his breakfast with me. Normally, he will eat in the kitchen because he is all boring and wants to watch the news at the same time.

I always eat in the lounge, so that I can watch *Frasier* (if it's on) or *My Name is Earl* (if Frasier isn't on) because I really don't like to watch the news. It is so depressing. I am so glad that I ignored Mr H and bought the *My Name is Earl* boxset. It is totally genius writing and given that

I'm not a morning person, it really helps to cheer me up in the morning.

I mistakenly thought that Mr H wanted to spend some time with me and thought, 'Awww... how sweet. He's not so bad after all.' I knew this wasn't the case when the unmistakable smell of burning started coming from the kitchen. When I went to put my plate in the dishwasher and make another latte, I had to waft my hands through the smoke to see my way to the latte machine. He had burned his toast in the grill. I did think about coming back later but the thought of delaying my second morning coffee was far worse than the thought of dying from smoke inhalation.

I forgot to say that Lucy woke me up at 1:30am to go out for a wee. Mr H was snoring and didn't even wake up when I bounced up and down on the bed twice and pulled his pillow from under him. I gave up (after silently mouthing a few swear words at him) and begrudgingly got up to let her out. It's funny that her legs don't work very well during the day but when she has the scent of a fox in the early hours of the morning, she can run like a gazelle.

She went missing at one point and I stepped outside to see if she was lying on the lawn watching the world go by. I had no slippers or shoes on my feet and nearly screamed when I trod on something slimy. I was just praying that it wasn't wet dog poo (it had been raining) and was slightly relieved to see the squashed slug when I lifted my foot up (although it was pretty sticky and stuck to the duvet cover when I climbed back into bed).

I don't think that the slug was best pleased as the weight of me had killed him outright. Lucy came up to me at this point (which I was grateful for. You try and chase a deaf dog around the garden at 1:30am with no shoes on your feet) and the look on her face was, 'Mummy – why have you just killed that slug?'

I ushered her in the house. I am starting to think that we might need to hire a person to sleep in the lounge every night or maybe the homeless guy in Wolverhampton that wears Mr H's old shiny green shirt would like to sleep there...

I was out of bed by 9am but only because someone woke me up phoning to book a caravan pitch. They didn't seem best pleased when I told them that we had closed the site down last December and they said, "Well – where am I going to go now? I've been a good customer of yours. I stayed two nights with you in 2013, after all." At 9am, I was lost for words...

The postman knocked the door at 10am and in my usual 'I'm not a morning person' fashion, I was still in my dressing gown. He gave me a sympathetic look as he handed me my parcel from Boots and said, "Are things ok at the moment then?" I replied with, "Well, apart from weird phone calls at 9am waking me up, things are fine." He walked away saying, "Look after yourself." I think he does think that I have some awful incurable disease as he never sees me dressed and unfortunately without make-up on I do look pretty pale first thing in the morning. The package from Boots was quite large as well.

I suspect he thought that it contained loads of drugs to treat whatever illness I had.

What it did contain was my Estée Lauder night cream and foamer/cleanser/toner (it's a three-in-one miracle in a pump action bottle. I really am an advertiser's dream).

Now I know what you're thinking. I am inherently tight so why on earth do I spend money on Estée Lauder and not just go to Poundland for my night cream and use Carex hand wash on my face. I have weighed up the pros and cons and when I use my Estée Lauder products (and make-up) then I do look much better on photos and in the flesh. When I use Poundland products then I look at least 13 years older. I'm not bothered with looking younger, I just don't want to look older than I am. Otherwise, I have to have the inevitable 'Mr H ages me' conversation with people that I meet.

Usually, I wait until there is an offer on whereby I buy two products and Estée Lauder give me a load of other crap, which I don't really need, for free. The freebies usually consist of the following:

1. A free make-up bag (that I will never use)...
2. A free coral lipstick (that doesn't suit my complexion and in all honesty doesn't suit anyone's)...
3. A mini mascara that lasts one application, and...
4. A voucher for a free consultation to try and sell me £250 worth of other products that the lady doing my make-over will insist that I simply can't live without and especially someone with 'my pores'.

There was no such offer though but as we are off to Ascot next week and I need to look my best, I really needed to get my cream and foamer. Also, Boots were offering me £7 worth of points if I bought them and that would get me a tub of popcorn in the cinema tonight.

This reminds me of when you meet people for the first time and they ask you to guess their age.

Why is it always the people that look much older than they are, are the ones that ask you the question? When we were skiing once, we met a woman who asked us to guess her age. Being the genius that I am, I thought that I would guess her real age and then subtract seven years so that I would compliment her.

Unfortunately, this back-fired and I should have deducted 13 years for the extra six years that sunbeds and cigarettes add on. It turned out that she was only 53. I genuinely thought she was about 65. She took the huff when I guessed her age as 58.

I have since learned from this encounter. I no longer guess people's ages, weight, income or anything else with a number in it, especially if they ask you to guess the number of previous lovers they've had. (I have no idea why someone would want me to guess that. But it has happened on more than one occasion now. Admittedly those occasions involved drink - but still.)

People are just so touchy. I have a friend that works for the civil service and when I introduced them to another friend of mine the, "Oh – you work for the civil service do you? You work on 'the bins'" did not go down well. I don't know why they were so insulted, our bin men are young, fit and tanned (unlike the firemen they send if someone reports a horse stuck in a hedge. I think they must send the reserve firemen for non-fire emergencies).

Anyway. I have digressed... back to today...

Bonnie still stank of fox poo this morning, so I decided that my first job of the day would be to wash her in the wet-room. I remember my very first tale in *#tractor4graham* about trying to wash wee off Casper and getting more wet than him and thinking that I should just wash him naked (me, not him).

Bonnie isn't as agile as Casper though and I thought it unlikely that she would be clinging to the sink with me trying to prise her back. I knew that I could use the headlock technique on her (that I had been developing in case Mr H had needed eye injections) to hold her in place. I needn't have worried though as she was an absolute angel and let me wash her without wriggling around. (I must admit that this started to perturb me a bit as I wasn't expecting it.) Having been so successful in this mission, I thought that the rest of the day was going to go well and surprisingly it was a good day (apart from nearly* killing Mr H – see below).

* To clarify. I don't mean that I wished that I had killed Mr H (although like when the National Lottery emails me to say that I have won something (usually £2.60), I did allow myself two minutes to dream about what I would spend the life insurance on).

I spent a lot of time whipping *#tractor4graham* into shape and another day spent on it tomorrow and it should nearly be ready to go. I'm going to have to pause writing at this point as I need to put on my make up to go out to the cinema. I toyed with not bothering (as it's dark in there) but we're going for dinner first with Jill and if I don't put make-up on then I will definitely bump into lots of people that I know.

Just before I went to pack up my computer, Mr H tripped up over the mouse*. (The computer was resting on the pouffe on the lounge floor and he hadn't noticed the mouse trailing on the floor.) He did an exaggerated footballer's dive and exclaimed, "Are you trying to kill me? Can't you pick things up instead of leaving them lying around?"

* Obviously I mean the mouse to my computer. We don't have a pet mouse running around. That would be silly, especially since we have a cat that eats mice.

I looked around the lounge to see empty chocolate wrappers lying on the settee, Mr H's work strewn across the coffee table (and spilling on the floor) and his slippers lying near the lounge door. I counted, all-in-all, three trip hazards of his, plus loads of his crap lying across various settees and surfaces.

He said, "Don't bother answering me then" as he wandered off. Honestly. Man logic. I, on one isolated occasion, leave one trip hazard and World War III nearly breaks out but his numerous infractions did not count at all... Good job we were off to the cinema, I could gesture swear words in sign language at him in the dark and he wouldn't be able to see them.

We left for Star City in Birmingham (or 'Stab City' as the locals call it) to go to dinner with Jill and watch *You Before Me* at the cinema. Jill had warned us that it was going to be a tearjerker (the film, not dinner), so I made sure that I had plenty of tissues in my bag. (Mr H blubs like a girl at the cinema.) "Why did Hooch have to die?!" is still ringing in my ears from a previous visit. I had to make sure that *You Before Me* did not have a dog die in it. Otherwise, I wouldn't be able to take him.

When I was Googling the film, to also see if it was age appropriate for him, I noticed that it was a 12A and contained 'moderate sexual references and references to suicide.' I pondered as to what that meant and concluded that it probably meant that only the missionary position would be shown and because there wasn't a dog in it then I wasn't so concerned about the suicide references. I checked the BBFC website to see if there was anything else that I needed to be concerned about and they said that there might be moderate language such as 'bitch' and 'twat'. This didn't concern me. 'Bitch' is a friendly term in Wolverhampton and is used every day and I have called Mr H the 't' word before. (I feel bad about this but in my defence he will have deserved it.)

We all went to the loo before the film. Once you hit 40 you don't seem to have as much control over your bladder, so it is wise to go before the film (especially if like me you proceed to drink a litre of diet coke in there because it was only 10p more than the small one. You need to free up space in your bladder for this). As I wandered into the ladies I did my usual careful choosing of my cubicle.

1. Cubicle One – I never go in this one out of principle. Being closest to the door it is likely to get used by the last minuters (be they of the puking, weeing or have the uncontrollable trots variety). This cubicle is likely to be the least clean.

2. Cubicle Two – This cubicle did not have toilet paper. I always check before finalising my choice of cubicle. You do not want to be caught with your pants down, doing the business, to find that there is no paper.

3. Cubicle Three – Had a big floating poo in the toilet. I dismissed this one immediately and moved onto the next one.

4. Cubicle Four – Had no toilet seat. Why would someone steal a toilet seat? Or maybe this was for women that brought their own seats with them, so they wouldn't have to hover their fru-fru over the ones already there? I actually, in hindsight applauded the idea of this. But even my handbag isn't big enough to carry my own toilet seat around in.

5. Cubicle Five was my cubicle of choice. There was plenty of loo roll, there was a clean seat. There was nothing floating in

the bowl to distress me and was at the far end, so the lazy would probably not bother to walk that far. Satisfied with my choice of cubicle, I could now get down to business. It's a shame that by this time the film had started... (Ok I'm kidding. I only missed the adverts.)

The cinema was funny as they only let us in about three minutes before the film started as they were 'meticulously cleaning it'. They didn't actually use the word meticulous. In fact what they said was, "You need to wait outside, someone has stuck chewing gum to two of the seats and we've sent Jake to go and get something to scrape it off."

When Jake returned it looked like he had got one of those scoops from the pick-n-mix. I seriously hoped that it wasn't, or if it was then he didn't just return the scoop to the pick-n-mix afterwards without thoroughly cleaning it. When I saw him wipe it down the sides of his trousers, I guessed he probably wouldn't. I made a mental note not to buy pick-n-mix again.

The film was a tear jerker (I think Mr H cried the most – probably having flash backs to *Turner & Hooch*) but on the plus side the lead guy looked just like Jamie Bamber (who is on my laminated list remember), so that was welcome eye candy. Mr H was also pleased because one of the actresses was one of the hot lesbians from *Emmerdale* that he quite liked.

We thought it comical that the cinema were very fastidious* about the cleanliness in the cinema itself but when we went to use the ladies loos after the film, the same big poo was still in the third toilet on the right and the half-drunk bottle of Coke was still on the side that we had seen two and a half hours earlier. It was a good job they didn't have one of those 'I just cleaned these toilets' sheet up with someone's name and the time next to it, as I would have written next to their name, 'Where exactly did you clean them?'

* I can occasionally use fancy words

Jill hasn't seen me since I have gone blonde and says that she loves it – it's definitely not ginger –

and she said that I look loads younger. Jill has always been one of my favourite friends. Because of the comment I forgave her when she let it slip that England had scored a goal against Russia. (The Euro-something-or-others are on at the moment.)

Mr H and I were going to watch it when we got back in. Being the genius that I am, I turned off the radio on the way home and instructed Mr H not to check Facebook or Messenger or texts in case he saw the result. He also said that he might watch a bit of the Wales game.

We managed to turn on the TV and start the recording without catching the end of the match but Mr H insisted on watching the build-up to the match. The first thing that happened was Ian Wright talking about how Wales had beaten someone (you can tell I pay attention to football, as I don't know who they were playing) so Mr H wasn't best pleased. I had warned him to go straight to the match and now he was paying the penalty (get it?) for not listening to me.

I used to love watching football. But I can't stand the diving, the rolling around pretending to be injured and the disrespect for the ref, these days. I much prefer rugby now. They are real athletes who don't dive or pretend to be injured and will continue to play with a broken neck and their leg looking like it's about to drop off. Footballers are more like celebrities than sportsmen and cry if their hair gets messed up by another player. If I want to watch a load of celebrities crying then I will simply watch *I'm a Celebrity – Get Me Out of Here!*

It's half-time in the football match and it's 0-0. I've been writing my book while Mr H has been watching the first half. Apparently, it's not been very exciting. As a few of my friends have said on Facebook today 'England will be leaving Europe before June 23rd'...

Sunday 12th June

Missions for today:

- *Try and integrate the new de-caf tea bags into the normal ones without Mr H knowing*
- *Go through the fridge and pantry and throw away 'expired' products*

It's forecast to piss it down today so I have decided to have 'indoor' missions. The day didn't get off to a happy start in the Hughes's household as while I was watching *My Name is Earl*, Mr H came into the lounge, grabbed the remote and turned the telly over to some boring Brexit debate, without asking.

This is the second time that he has done this in the last couple of weeks (I will have to scroll back and check exactly when he did it because I think I documented it in this book. I have realised how useful this book has become as a record of all of Mr H's misdemeanours. If I try to bring him up on this behaviour he will say, "No I didn't do that, you're making it up. Come on! When exactly did I do it?" I now will be able to tell him exactly when. I suspect he will still deny that it happened...)

I am not alone with this behaviour. I mentioned it to a number of my friends and out of nine of them, apparently eight of their husbands do exactly the same. The ninth friend said that her and her husband aren't actually speaking at the moment and he's living in the spare room while they sort out some issues and she didn't want to talk about his behaviour. (I took this to mean that he also did this and I suspect that him coming in and turning over the telly, is one of those 'issues' that they are sorting out.)

To show Mr H the error of his ways, I thought that I would play him at his own game. We were in the kitchen and Mr H went to wash his hands at the sink. I immediately stood next to him and pulled the tap towards me, so that he was standing there with soapy hands but no water. He gave me a look and said, "Can't you see me standing here?" I replied, "Oh sorry – didn't notice you were wanting to wash your hands.

You really need to make it more obvious." I wandered off hearing him mumble, "Women! Flippin' fruit loops."

When he went to go outside, I quickly walked to the door and we got sandwiched as I tried to get out of the door in front of him. He said, "Didn't you see me trying to go out the door?" I replied, "Oh? Were you – sorry hadn't noticed."

The best one came when he went to go to the toilet and just as he was opening his fly to take a leak, I stood right next to him. He said, "What on earth are you doing?" I said, "I'm just waiting for you to finish and then I'll go. Carry on, I don't mind waiting. It's only polite after all." He zipped his fly up and mumbled, "I can't go now. You may as well."

I'm going to see if my subliminal messages have got through to him. Men are complicated creatures. There's no point in me telling him what he did as he will (pretend to) listen, (pretend to) process the information, decide that he is in the right and carry on regardless. Advertisers use subliminal messages to get their message across. Maybe I will edit into some of the programs that we've recorded a picture of me holding the remote control and have this flick on for a millisecond every minute or so. I obviously dismissed this idea as going too far. I have no idea how to edit a program like that.

My first mission of the day was a bit like when I had to integrate Mr H's new man pants in with his old supply (although I won't rub the tea bags around the rim of the bath). I've noticed that Mr H has been a bit hyper lately. Initially I put it down to the numerous times that Ron the Digger man has been here but I'm starting to think that caffeine is to blame.

Because of this I unilaterally decided to buy some de-caf PG Tips. I did not decide to hold a referendum on the matter as I knew that Mr H would be voting to 'remain' with the old PG Tips, whereas I was definitely going for 'leave'. Mr H has been drinking PG Tips all of his life. When we got together he didn't bother to ask me what brand of tea I liked, as it was clear that we would be having PG Tips.

I was going to distribute the new tea bags evenly into the tea caddy with the caffeinated ones and gradually mix them in with the rest that were in the pantry but unfortunately the gods conspired against me. We only had one tea bag left in the caddy and none in the container in the pantry. I decided to take the bold approach. I filled the caddy with the new tea bags and put the rest in the container in the pantry and hid the cardboard box in our neighbour's recycling, so that Mr H wouldn't see it.

I also went and told our neighbours I had done this because they see everything (with their secret webcams that I'm sure are up). Luckily, the Farmer's wife said, "I totally understand. I had to do that with milk once. The shop was out of full fat so I had to mix a bit of the semi skimmed in with the remaining full fat milk in the fridge every day, so that my husband wouldn't notice." I suspect a lot of this skulduggery happens in houses across the country (by very clever wives, I might add).

As luck would have it, Mr H hasn't noticed at all. I have though. He fell asleep on the settee for three hours this afternoon, so I think the lack of caffeine is having an effect. I really enjoyed those three hours and looked forward to more of them over the coming days… It also makes me smile as remember he can't sleep without his favourite pillow (you know – the one that's in Cannock Landfill site).

As it was still pissing it down with rain, while Mr H was sleeping, I decided to go and have a root through the fridge and pantry for 'expired products.' Time really does fly. I removed some English mustard that expired in 2012. (I gave it the sniff test first but there was a weird layer of liquid sitting on top of it that I didn't want to chance. It looked a bit like that culture that grew when some famous guy (I'm thinking Louis Pasteur?) discovered some important medicine (I'm thinking it begins with 'P'…but it's not Paracetamol. Penicillin! I knew it would come to me.) This went in the bin.

There were some weird looking green lentil type things in a jar in the fridge that had no label. I didn't even bother to unscrew the lid to see what they actually were (and whether they were naturally green or had turned that colour over time and in all honesty whether they were a food product). They went straight in the bin.

The Christmas pudding that says 'Best before July 2014' is still sitting on the shelf though in the pantry. It's full of alcohol and therefore is probably safe to eat. Another factor in deciding to leave it there is that I don't eat Christmas pudding. So I'm going to let Mr H chance it with this. It will be character-building if it turns out to be bad. He needs to understand the horrors of norovirus so he can be more empathic when I have it again.

Before the football came on, Mr H decided to catch up on the Soaps. I totally blame his mum for this. She watches every single soap opera and will even record them all when they go on holiday and watch them all to catch up when they get back. I can't stand the soaps. The same thing happens in all of them.

1. There are at least five murders in the space of three years and someone will end up in prison (with The Sun

newspaper demanding their release and starting a government petition).

2. There will be a lesbian love triangle, which will end in one of the murders in point 1.

3. There will be three weddings that don't actually happen because the bride is having a secret affair with the brother (or mother) of the groom (or if it's *Emmerdale*, one of the sheep)

4. At least once a year a car will be driven into a canal/river/bingo hall and someone will be on life support for three months following it (whilst the actor/actress disappears off to appear in either *Strictly Come Dancing* or *I'm a Celebrity*)

Unfortunately, Mr H gets really involved and will shout at the screen. Today was no exception with Emmerdale. "That's right! Drive her straight back into the arms of drugs... See! You've gone and done it. I could have written this." As I have mentioned on numerous occasions now, he couldn't have written it because his English is appalling. I had to bite my lip from shouting at him, "It's not real - you muppet!"

Luckily the football came on so he turned over. I'm not keen on football at all these days, as I've already mentioned, but I was less keen on watching Mr H shout at a fictitious program with such vigour, so I was actually relieved when he turned over.

He really can be weird at times. I was pleased to see it was Germany playing in the football, as my favourite 'name' player ever was on the pitch and scored a goal. I defy anyone to say 'Bastian Schweinsteiger' in an evil-Gestapo-James-Bond-villain type voice and not get excited. Maybe I also can be weird at times... It's a good job we're married to each other really.

Monday 13th June

Missions for today:

- *Play hooky* from work and meet my friend Rachel in Birmingham*
- *Wish happy birthday to Mr H's mum*

* I have no idea where this phrase comes from. I went to ask Siri but she unfortunately misheard me and said, 'Where does the craze praying hooker come from?'

The first web address to come up was 'hookersforjesus.net.' I didn't want to click on it (but you know I did). I couldn't work out whether it was Christians trying to help people get off the game or whether it was an organisation trying to promote the 'oldest profession in the world'. Apparently they sell 'Hookers for Jesus' t-shirts and iPhone cases.

I did think about ordering one just out of curiosity. I didn't though. By the time I got to check out, I noticed that they didn't ship to the UK.

I have swapped my work days around and have taken today off to do fun things. The day didn't start off well when Mr H and I had one of our totally pointless conversations.

Remember that Lucy isn't sleeping well and we have been going through a palaver of pretending that we have a guest staying in the lounge in order that she will sleep through the night. Mr H was moaning when I got up that I had left the lounge door open last night and that is why Lucy woke him up at 7:30am barking. I reminded him that he had left the lounge door open the previous night and that she also had barked at 7:30am. "Well – that's because I forgot. You shouldn't have forgotten." "Yes that's right…you're allowed to forget but I'm not." He just looked at me with a, "So what's your point?" look. Man logic strikes again.

I was just happy that she also didn't bark at 1:30am and that I therefore did not have to chase a deaf dog around the garden in my pjs and then have to scrape any slugs off my bare feet before getting back into bed.

Mr H dropped me off at Wolves train station this morning and we ended up running late because an old guy in the station car park couldn't decide where to park so just decided to sit in his car in the way of everyone.

Constant bipping from the guy in the car in front of us (which was directly behind the old guy) had no effect whatsoever. I got out the car and Mr H reversed to turn around and head back the way we had come in and by-pass the old guy.

I did think about hanging around for a bit just in case a fight broke out between the old guy and the car driver behind him and I might need to run* over to the British Transport Police to summon help. When I saw the queue for tickets though, I decided to leave them to sort it out themselves.

* I say 'run' but with my ruptured Achilles from a few years' ago, it would be more of a lollop.

I decided that I couldn't bear to go standard class on the train and was certain that I would get £3.80 in drinks and snacks from the first class lounge and/or the train to make the extra cost worthwhile. I made it to the first class lounge and got a latte, banana and a bottle of sparkling water.

I was going to write in the visitor book about enjoying the fruit platter and massage but there was another couple in there watching me. (I think they were first class lounge 'virgins' because they didn't take any coffee or food until they saw me do it.) I'll write in the book when there is no one else in the lounge (and will turn my back away from the CCTV as I do it).

The Cross Country train went from the same platform as the first class lounge, so I didn't have to do my usual rushing for the train when it is re-platformed at the last minute. The first class train manager let me board without seeing my ticket but he stopped the lady behind me (who didn't actually have a first class ticket). I told you that Estée Lauder make-up is worth it. If I had have been wearing my Poundland make-up then he would have asked to see my ticket, for sure.

He also gave me two pieces of cake for breakfast and called me darling three times. (I suspected he wasn't long divorced as his shirt was creased and he had gone overboard on the aftershave. He also lost interest when he spotted my wedding ring and moved on to a younger girl further down the carriage.) But after my pointless conversation with Mr H, this morning, my day was starting to get better. Just as the train doors were closing I heard a thump and looked out of the window to see a guy bounce off the train and land on his bum on the platform.

The platform staff just shook their heads at him but the reaction of a child nearby was priceless. "Mummy! Why did that man try and run through the door when it was shut? Is he one of those fucktards that you talk about to Aunty Gill?" 'Mummy' looked highly embarrassed and said, "That's not the word that Mummy used, darling. I said... I said... 'retard'!" I'm not sure that made things much better as the platform staff were now shaking their heads at her.

The guy on the floor on the platform tried to get up in an graceful way to at least rescue a bit of dignity. Unfortunately, for him, it had been raining so the platform was wet. He did a comedy slip and ended up back on his bum. I shouldn't have laughed... I really shouldn't have (and I shouldn't have busily written some notes in my phone to remind me to put this tale in my book).

As I was getting off the train at New Street, a Virgin Trains staff member was departing and said goodbye to Dan the Cross Country train manager. "Blimey!" I said. "I'm surprised you allow the competition on here." Dan said, "Oh don't worry – this foreigner will be banned if Brexit happens." And then he laughed and laughed. I didn't get it. Were Virgin going to emigrate if we left the EU? I had a momentary panic as thoughts of going to London Euston on London Midland sent shivers down my spine. I started thinking that I might have to give up work and send Mr H out to work full time instead.

Shopping with Rachel and her gorgeous baby girl was a fun day. You forget how much you rely on lifts in shops when you have a pushchair though (I also wasn't very good at manoeuvring the pushchair. It did a wheelie on one side twice but luckily I wasn't in charge of the pushchair whilst the baby was in it).

There was a 'scary' lift in JD Sports. You have to keep your hand on the button otherwise it randomly stops (and often won't start again and you end up stuck between floors). Also it's just a platform that moves up and down the lift shaft. Rachel and I both looked up to the ceiling as it was closing in and thought the same thing at the same time, 'What if it didn't stop and kept going. Would we be squished?' Again, I didn't want to die like this (I'm still going for rescuing a child from a burning building) but luckily the lift did stop before we hit the ceiling.

It's another good reason as to why I don't have children, (not being able to push a pushchair is one reason) but secondly I'm not really a fan of lifts and the people we encountered today quite clearly did not know 'lift etiquette'. As we were trying to get out, they were trying to push past us to get in. I concluded they must be visitors from London who were used to getting the tube every day and had no manners. Locals know lift etiquette and aren't rude.

I did conclude at the end of the day that shopping with a baby was very similar to shopping with a man.

1. They would be happy at the start of the day but start to lose interest as the day went on, especially if you tried to go into changing rooms to try anything on. As soon as you were in the changing rooms with your hand half way into a new dress they would start to cry. (Mr H exhibits this exact behaviour when I try on new clothes.)

2. They would need the toilet at the most inconvenient times. Rachel's baby is obviously in nappies which made it easier to pretend for at least ten minutes that neither of us could smell the disgusting poo* that she had just done (the baby – not Rachel), whilst we finished our Frappuccino's.

* Just like when my sister's kitten did a massive elephant sized poo that stank to high heaven, Rachel's baby's poo was

just the same. I was mesmerised as to how much came out of such a little person and the colour of it was really strange. I momentarily forgot what was happening though as she was changing her and I went to get a doggy poo bag out of my handbag. Rachel said, "What are you doing?" "Oh sorry – forgot it wasn't one of the dogs." Her baby at least giggled at me – she loves me because I am bonkers.

It did make me think that 'Man-nappies' might be a worthwhile investment for a future shopping trip with Mr H. Mr H has the bladder of a gnat and is forever sloping off to go to the toilet (at least I think it's that – maybe it's just because he's had enough of shopping... hmmm...) Maybe I will raise the idea of them with him and see if he miraculously doesn't go for a wee more than four times on our next trip.

3. Babies cry and tell you when they want feeding and they have to be fed at that exact moment otherwise the crying starts to sound like you're torturing them and you start to get looks from people close by. Men (just like being in charge of the remote control) will dictate when you stop for lunch. It doesn't matter if the next shop you need to go into is next door to the one that you are currently in and on the way to where you are going to have lunch. You will have to walk ten minutes to get lunch bypassing it and come back to it afterwards (or often not at all, as it's home time).

At one point during the day we were in Debenhams and they had a big cushion department. (I don't mean they only had one massive cushion in there, I mean they had lots of cushions.) As I was out with a friend and an impressionable baby (apparently the first three years are the most important in shaping our lives), I did not re-arrange the cushions that had letters on them to spell a rude word. (If I had been on my own then I would have. And I'm sure the store deliberately puts an 'N', 'U', 'C' and 'T' together on one row just to see how many people do it. To be fair, I would if I worked there.)

The train journey back was fun. As we were pulling into Wolverhampton the train manager came over the tannoy to say:

"We're just arriving into Wolverhampton, so please make sure that you have all of your belongings and people* with you when you depart the train. We're pulling into platform one, which is on the left hand side – no wait – Gwenda has just told me that we're actually coming in on platform two. No wait! It is platform one, I was right the first time. Oh – looks like it is platform two after all. I think I'll shut up now as quite clearly it sounds like I have no idea what I'm doing."

Neither did Gwenda apparently (whoever she was)? We came in on platform one. The number of people that were on the wrong side of the train wondering why when they pressed the 'open doors' button nothing was happening, was highly amusing.

* Telling you to have all of your 'people' with you is a new addition to the announcement. I'm not sure that anyone would deliberately leave their children or granny on the train, so is this announcement really necessary? I could understand a group of friends accidentally leaving a drunk friend on the train but given it was only 3:30 in the afternoon I don't think that was a likely possibility ('although we were in Wolverhampton', I pondered...)

It was obvious that there was no platform on that side and if the doors opened they would fall onto the tracks. It was a pity that the train manager (or Gwenda) didn't accidentally open the doors on the wrong side, it would look like lemmings all running off a cliff edge (or natural selection as most people would call it). I should feel bad for writing that as it's rude... I should feel bad...

Although, thinking about it, maybe my friend with the three devil children has left hers on the train before and that is why the announcement is now there… (Although I'm not convinced that just because they announce it, it means that you're going to follow it. I now have visions of lots of children in 'left luggage' at Wolverhampton. I wonder if when people come to claim them they choose a different one to take away, maybe on the off chance that it isn't as bad as the current one they have? If it was my friend with the devil children, then I can imagine that she would opt to claim the bright pink suitcase instead of one of her children.)

Mr H was waiting for me in the car park and I asked him how his day had been. Apparently our neighbour had brought our blue bin back for us (it was bin day and the bins all go in the farmyard) but unfortunately she had managed to ram it next to the black bin so that the gate wouldn't open. Mr H had had to scale the wall to check the post box for post. I thought it best that we didn't tell her – as she had tried to do a nice thing.

Later on though she grabbed me for a chat and said, "I thought I saw a burglar trying to get into your garden earlier. He was scaling your front wall. I went to get our shot gun but they had gone by the time that I came out." I told her what had happened and she said, "Well it's a good job I didn't shoot him in the bum then!" Even though I joke about claiming on the life insurance, Mr H still hasn't finished the groundwork for the Alpaca shed, so I need him alive for a while. (Although I now know what to do if he starts to annoy me too much...)

I also got news from Mummykins today that her 'tit test' came back all clear. (Again, I don't think that they called it 'Tit results' but they really should. 'Mammogram' just makes me think of woolly mammoths combined with women so they have droopy boobs with hairy nipples... I don't know why I think this...)

It was Mr H's mum's 79th birthday today, so his parents popped over for a quick cuppa and a chat. The Farmer's wife saw her and when I told her that it was Mr H's mum's birthday and that it would be the big 8-0 next year she said, "Well – of course – that's if you make it that far." She is a cheery soul at times. I said that we would have a big party (we'll have one even if she doesn't make it... I, at least, like to look on the bright side of life).

We practised sign language for nearly three hours tonight as our exam is on Friday. I told my teacher that 'shopping for dead dogs' was going to come into the conversation at some point (all the signs are very similar). She replied, "As long as you aren't dogging in the shops then that's fine." She has a wicked sense of humour. It's a good job with me and Mr H in the class really...

Tuesday 14th June

Mission for today:

- *Get out of bed*

You might think that this was an easy-peesy mission but unfortunately I woke up with a massive banging headache. I don't think I've had one in a while so maybe Mr H has been too tired to crush my head in a vice while I've been sleeping but is back on it again? There is also another possibility that the vice he ordered turned out to be faulty and his replacement has only just arrived.

I would like to say that Mr H was a really good nurse today... I would like to say that he was. No – I'm being mean. He did whip into action first thing and bring me my headache pills, toast and latte and a wet hanky for me to put on my head. He is well trained in the 'practical' side of 'operation migraine'. He also repeated the task at lunchtime when he was back from work.

The only nursing skill that he was lacking was 'empathy'. But I think this is universally a 'man thing'. He didn't actually ask me how I was and was a bit of a grump monster today, if I'm honest. He was obviously having a 'Graham day' – this is so named if everything goes wrong.

He was at work in the morning so me and my headache were alone together. The dogs were good nurses as they didn't bark when they heard the postman or the farm dogs running around. Their empathic skills are excellent. (If only I could train them to bring me drinks and food then they would be an all-round help and I could let Mr H go.) Obviously this is a joke. I won't let Mr H go – the dogs couldn't drive me to hospital if I needed it.

When Mr H got back from work he huffed and puffed around the house as everything he touched went wrong. He made rissoles for dinner with the left over beef and the mincer wouldn't work, so when he went to get the food processor off the shelf he managed to knock over a tub containing red lentils which spilled all over the floor. I could hear his swear words from the bedroom, which is above the kitchen, along with trying to stop Bonnie from eating the lentils. Apparently, it was my fault that he knocked the lentils over (even though I was upstairs and in a different room) because the plug for the mixer was on a different shelf to the mixer itself and that's what knocked the lentils over.

The kitchen looked like a family of immigrants had moved in and Mr H was cooking for 13 of us rather than just two. The kitchen also filled with smoke as the rissoles were cooking. The smoke and the swearing was doing nothing for my headache. He also seemed to have wrestled with a bag of flour at some point. Bonnie had a load of it on her back for most of the night.

I had had a conversation with one of my friends on Facebook about how men also have a 'time of the month'. Now that this is in writing, I will see if the grump monster rears its ugly head again in three to four weeks' time. (I do actually feel bad now that I'm reading this back. I blame my migraine. Most men are totally clueless as to how to deal with a woman's illness. Mr H isn't totally clueless, so I really should count my blessings.)

I had awful dreams while I was in bed today. I dreamed that Bonnie had a big lump on her back and when I woke up I nearly phoned the vets to book her in. It felt so real.

I had a chat on Messenger with Jade who said that she often had bad dreams involving her husband and would then be annoyed with him for the rest of the day. I'm glad it's not only me that has these types of dreams. I once didn't speak to Mr H for three hours after he was nasty to me in a dream. Mr H thinks that this is totally irrational behaviour. I've had this conversation with at least three other friends before and they agree that it's fine to be mad with your husband for something that he did in a dream.

At one point during the afternoon we had terrible thunder and lightning. Lucy is so deaf now that it doesn't bother her. She used to run around barking crazily at it and we used to have to pin her to the floor to stop her from shaking. Bonnie hates it but will lie under my desk in the office and zone it out. (It's the same technique I use when Mr H is watching politics on telly and trying to talk to me at the same time.) Mr H came in to see if I needed anything else (gold star for practical help) and I asked him if Bonnie was ok. He said that she was fine and under my desk. At this point a massive clap of thunder happened and Bonnie shot upstairs and jumped on the bed. Mr H looked at her as if to say, 'That's right – make me look like a liar.' Bonnie looked back as if to say, 'I don't care – I'm scared.' She settled down at the side of the bed until the thunder had gone.

When I finally woke up at 5:47pm (it's important to be precise) I had had a message from Jade. I replied to it and used the emoji with the clenched teeth. Apparently though, the emojis have been upgraded and they are now 3D and the clenched teeth one doesn't look the same. On my phone (because I haven't bothered to download the latest update to Messenger) it shows clenched teeth and you would use it if you were talking about something like having to pick up dirty undies off the floor. Jade has downloaded the latest update and if I send a 'clenched teeth' emoji it arrives with her as a 3D grin. It now makes it look like you are happy about what you've written and not annoyed. It has totally changed the context of the conversation.

Now this is something that they should have had a referendum about. I will have sent one thing but it will have been received as something else. Never mind Brexit – this is exactly the sort of thing that will cause World War III. We also pondered whether Messenger was also changing the actual words that we were writing. I went to write, 'I love you' but what if Jade actually received, 'Yo bitch – I want to fight you' instead? It would totally change the meaning of the sentence and cause offence. Jade thinks a few of her friends have gone quiet lately and it's probably because of the new emojis. "No wonder a few people have deleted me – they probably thought I was being sarcastic."

Now these are important conversations, not like the totally pointless ones that me and Mr H have. We both decided that the new 3D emoji's were horrible and I'm not going to update Messenger until it stops working. We finished our conversation with Jade saying, 'Yo bitch – I want to fight you.' I replied, 'I love you too.'

After having a cold wet hanky on my head for most of the day, I looked in the mirror tonight and nearly had heart failure. I looked like Keith Lemon. I usually look like Bev Callard but tonight I had gone one stage further and turned into a man. I thought about taking a picture in case I do ever decide to become a serial killer as this would be a perfect picture for the news to put up. The alternative, I pondered was to send it to Estée Lauder so they could use it as one of their 'before' pictures and then they could have one of my professional make-up photoshoot ones as the 'after' picture. I obviously didn't do this. After taking the photo I realised that no one should ever see it.

We have been practising our sign language again tonight (luckily my head had subsided by about 7pm). Unfortunately, Jayne tried to say that she liked to read biographies in her spare time but she spelled it wrong and the first five letters spelled 'bigot'. The sentence ended up being 'I like reading bigot books at the weekend.' With my 'dogging' and her 'bigot' we are sure to pass the exam on Friday…

Wednesday 15th June

Missions for today:

- *Pop and see Jade (and remember to take the pork scratchings)*
- *Practise for sign language exam, on Friday*

Thankfully the horrendous banging headache had done one and I only had remnants of my head feeling like it had been crushed in a vice (or the brain tumour that Bobby keeps insisting that I have). Lucy barked to go out at 2:30am. I actually think that she was barking at the dishwasher* and didn't really want to go out because when I came downstairs she made no effort to go outside and just kept staring at the kitchen door.

* Mr H and I are inherently tight so we put electrical items on in the middle of the night as our electricity costs us less between 2am-5am (or something like that). I don't do daft things like set the alarm for 2am to straighten my hair

but I did toy with it given that I had had to get up for Lucy anyway. I also pondered about printing out *#tractor4graham* as I need to do a final proof. I didn't though. I didn't have the energy to turn my computer and printer on and I knew that my printer was low on ink.

As my hair still resembled Keith Lemon's and I was off to see Jade today (and as she was already sad with the passing of Mr P, I couldn't disturb her further with my crazy hair), then I washed my hair and straightened it. As I was in the shower, I saw a spider scuttle across the ceiling above me. Remembering 'spider up the fru-fru' gate, I panicked and went to swat it away. I lost my footing* and ended up doing a 'snow angel' pose up against the clear shower cubicle door. I bounced back off it and just about managed to stay upright.

* I thought about tweeting Dunelm about their rubber bath mat and its poor adhesion but decided against it as I really didn't want to explain what had happened and I definitely was not going to take a photo to show them.

As I looked at my squashed body imprint on the clear glass, I was once again reminded of the need to diet properly. My belly looked ginormous and the silhouette looked like a telly tubby looking back at me. Crucially though, I lost track of the spider. I hurriedly finished my shower and got dressed.

I changed the bedding today. Given that I had lain in bed all day yesterday, I felt the need for fresh bedding. As I went to put my pillow cases in the wash, I noticed that one of them had a massive rip in the back of it. I concluded that must have happened when I had the bad dream about Bonnie and having a lump on her back.

Mr H saw me throw it in the bin and said, "What are you doing? That can be mended, surely?" I gave him 'the look' and knew that we were about to have one of our totally pointless conversations. Pillowcases cost one Starbucks' latte (at the most) and I was not going to get the sewing machine out to try and mend the hole. I ignored him and continued to put it in the bin.

"It's a good job that I'm not the wasteful one in this house. Take my pillows. I've had them for years and years now and there's nothing wrong with them at all." He gestured to them on the bed.

"I'll remember that rule when your lawnmower breaks or your strimmer breaks or your car breaks. We will just keep mending them with the sewing machine too," I countered.

"There's no need to be sarcastic," he said. I felt that there was every need to be sarcastic...

Although my head wasn't feeling as bad as it did yesterday, it nearly went back to a full on migraine when one of my friends posted on my Facebook timeline that *The Mysteries of Laura* had been cancelled after season two. So not only had Shemar left *Criminal Minds*, now one of my other favourite shows (and more importantly eye-candy in the way of Jake) was being axed.

I decided to do 'gentle' things today to not upset my head, so cleaned the bathroom and the ensuite. I had to clean the bathroom. Every time I went to sit on the toilet, all I could focus on was the squashed imprint of my body on the clear glass of the shower cubicle. It looked like when a bird flies into a patio door (without the concussion, thankfully) but a much fatter bird (one the size of a bear).

As I went to clean the ensuite I noticed that Mr H had done one of his 'party tricks'. It's not really a party trick but if I come up with fun names for his annoying habits then they don't seem to stress me out as much.

This 'party trick' was where he had obviously pulled off the last bit of loo roll but couldn't be bothered to remove the old tube (as it's a complicated procedure to unscrew the wooden cylinder that goes through the middle of the roll, put the new roll on and re-screw it back together), so he had put back one single sheet of the old roll and draped it over the cardboard tube.

Given that he is much better at Physics than me then you would have thought that he would be an ace 'new loo roll putter-on-er'. I suppose I should be grateful that he didn't use the last piece first to wipe and then put it back (I suspect it crossed his mind)... I sighed and put a new roll on.

I'm thinking of removing all the spare loo rolls from the three toilets in the house and leaving one sheet on each of the rolls on the holders. I'll do it when I'm out for the day and see what happens when he is caught mid-poo and hasn't got enough loo roll to use. It's a bit like the remote control – I think I need to use subliminal ways to get the message home.

As we were going to bed tonight, Mr H put the telly on. I knew we were going to be in for some boring Brexit program. It's all that's on at the moment and in all honesty I am totally bored with it now. Both sides should be ashamed of themselves for how they have conducted themselves and the bullying/scare mongering and abusive way that they have acted towards each other. I can't wait until the vote is over and I no longer have to watch these programs before going to sleep. I'm thinking of voting to leave the UK...

There was some weird looking guy on the program and I said to Mr H, "Who's that?" He kind of looked a bit like Penfold from Danger Mouse, as his glasses were too big for his face. Mr H said, "That's' Michael Gove." "I think you mean Mike Hunt", I chuckled. Just as it left my mouth, I thought, 'I'm going to have to be really careful when I make stuff up as it seems to turn into reality.' Mr H gave me one of those 'I think her migraine has addled her brain' looks.

I went to see Jade today and gave her the pork scratchings from the Fruit Farm that I had bought for her. They can't make up for losing a pet but comfort food is always better than eating a salad when you're miserable. This has reminded me of a sign outside a pub that I saw once. It said, "No good story started with 'I ate a salad'." It's true though. You're not going to wake up with a tattoo and married in Vegas by eating a salad. Drinking tequila, however, might give you an exciting story to tell your grandchildren.

Jade is still doing lots of reviewing for Amazon and I asked her whether there was a merkin in one of the boxes that arrived while I was there. I noticed that she answered, "Not in one of these boxes" and then I swear that she winked at me. I must remember to ask her next time if they're itchy. I also wonder whether they are like hair extensions? If you buy decent hair extensions, then they are really nice and silky but if you buy the cheap ones then they are wiry and stick out in all directions when they start to encounter extremes of temperature.

I then started imagining what would happen if you bought a cheap fru-fru wig and you got a bit hot 'down there'? Would it start to expand and stick out? You could end up looking like you had a hedgehog wriggling around in your pants. This definitely made me decide that if I ever needed a fru-fru wig then I would not be tight and would buy a decent one. Given that my hair looks like Keith Lemon's when wet then I really don't want to look 'down there' and have visions of his private parts (without the dangly bit of course...)

Thursday 16th June

Missions for today:

- *Do EU vote (should I stay or should I go now?)*
- *Get nails done (in a flat boring colour because of sign language exam)*

I did my postal vote first thing as Mr H was heading up to the Post Office before work. I think the sneaky devil has been peaking a read of my book, while I've not been looking.

I deduced this when he said, "Do I need to put your vote in the doggy poo bin on the Cannock Road?" before winking at me. I told him that surprisingly, this time, we weren't cancelling each other out. I'm not sure whether he thought that I was lying, so just on the off chance I swapped our envelopes around in his bag.

If he put mine in the doggy poo bin then it would actually be his. And if some government office is collecting statistics on who votes and who doesn't (and on the off chance they pass legislation to disallow votes to the lazy) then it will look like he can't be bothered and I will have a perfect record. Occasionally, I do have glimpses of genius.

England and Wales were playing in the football today and I got to see the first half before heading to get my nails done. Being English but having a Welsh surname meant that I wasn't too bothered about who was going to win (remember that I am a rugby girl now). But if it had have been England and Wales in the rugby then I would have reverted to my maiden name. In all honesty, that doesn't really work as that is Irish…but if we go by my biological father than I think 'Branson' is probably an English name…

Apparently most school children were sitting their Physics GCSE exam today. Someone put on Facebook, 'So England playing Wales will be the reason that no children get a GCSE in Physics today.' I didn't think that that would be the reason. Like me, they probably just didn't understand any of it. They probably also had some mad professor of a teacher that looked like Einstein who wore patches on the elbows of their jacket and sandals with socks and simply couldn't bring the subject to life.

Whilst the football was on, I decided to turn the sound off and practise my lip reading skills for my sign language exam tomorrow night. It was going well to begin with when the camera focussed on Joe Hart in the tunnel and I definitely understood his 'get that f***ing ball!' but it went a bit awry when the game had started and the camera focused on the Welsh manager.

I'm pretty sure that, 'Get the fluffing wall up, pass it to the rich as we need to bore a hole' wasn't what he said. I momentarily thought that I was watching the Great Escape when they dig a tunnel and try to escape when playing a football match. There was no point trying to lip read what Rooney said. All I got was, 'I day-dee-dor-ir-ged-it.' Without the sound he looked like a baby learning to talk for the first time.

In the nail salon one of the customers had the game on her phone, so we could keep up with the score. I had to have boring coloured nails with no gems or patterns on them because of my sign language exam tomorrow.

Dazzling your teacher with your nails so she can't see your finger spelling is not a sure fire way to pass your exam. As we were off to Ascot on Saturday, then I went for a flat pale green colour to match my dress. I haven't actually tried on the dress since I last wore it, which was August, and it has been washed since then (even though it said 'dry clean' only, I like to frolic with washing labels telling me what I can and can't do and I'm too tight to pay £7 to get it dry cleaned when the washing machine (and Mr H) will do it for free), so I'm hoping that it still fits.

As I was leaving the nail salon, I booked in for my next appointment and noticed that some customers had 'FB' written next to their names. I thought, 'I bet they're the awkward ones and it is code for 'F***ing B***h'. Turns out it meant 'Facebook' and that's where they had booked their appointment from (that's what the salon says... I'm still not convinced). As I was leaving England scored a goal in the dying minutes of injury time and all of the cars on the Cannock

Road pipped their horns as they had won. One car driver (who obviously wasn't following the football) mistook this for anger directed at them and revved up their engine and zoomed in close to the car in front and started flashing their lights at them. Road rage over a football match – got to love Wolverhampton.

Mr H has lost the keys to the container. Every week he loses one set of keys or another. I really need someone to invent some sort of GPS device to attach to keys. I'm going to start adding up the time that I spend hunting for his keys for him, as I'm sure over the course of my life I will have lost around one year doing it.

According to some website that I happened upon, you spend 1.1 years of your life cleaning, spend 2.5 years cooking and 1.5 years of your life in the bathroom. I think we need to skew these statistics for Mr H. Given that he has the bladder control of a gnat and also has bottie issues if he eats too much wheat, then I think that he probably spends three years of his life in the toilet. I can deduct the 1.5 years needed for this from his 2.5 years cooking, as I do most of that in this house. I'm sure that he will also spend around one year looking for keys that he has lost (or tools) and I can deduct that from the 1.1 years you spend cleaning, as I do most of that in this house.

Back to his keys though...

He told me that they weren't hanging up where they were supposed to be and had I seen them. I decided that I ought to look for them as he only does a 'man look'* and never finds anything doing it that way.

* A 'man look' is where a man pulls a drawer open for a millisecond, scans the stuff in the drawer and closes it again announcing that what he wants isn't in there.

A 'woman look' means opening the drawer, carefully moving the items around the drawer until she finds what the man was looking for and then closes the drawer. There really should be special lessons in school for men on how to look properly for items that you've lost. They could replace cross country as most men I know, know how to run (especially when they have an angry wife behind them). I mean! Who needs lessons in how to run?

I (stupidly) thought that Mr H had at least looked for the container keys when he said that he couldn't find them so I started looking in places that I assumed they could be. I spent 40 pointless minutes looking for them in the cars, the shed, the washing basket and his coat pockets.

When I went upstairs to ask him if he wanted a drink, I saw his fleece on the back of his chair and found the keys in one of the pockets. I said, "I thought you couldn't find them – they were here all the time." "Oh! I hadn't actually started looking for them yet, so I hadn't checked in there."

I am going to deduct my 40 minutes today of 'looking for Mr H's s**t' from the 14 days of our life that we are supposed to spend kissing. Looking for his crap does make me want to kiss him less, so it seems the right category to remove it from. (I didn't want to remove it from the 'Eight years of our lives spent shopping' category, as looking for his crap makes me need to shop all the more.)

When Mr H got back after work, he said, "Did you record the football for me?" "No – you told me it was on but you didn't say you wanted it recording." "Oh – thanks Honey. I didn't think that I needed to spell out such important things." He really needs to spell out everything as trying to understand the male mind is like rocket science. (Although I'm thinking that rocket science might actually be easier. If there is logic to it then I'm sure I could learn it. Men do not have any logic at all in their brains.)

We were good students and practised our sign language again tonight for two and a half hours but all of us were a bit woolly headed and didn't do as well as normal. We blamed it on the chips, as we had been to the chip shop as a treat and the chips made us sign badly. I've made a mental note not to eat chips before going into any of my exams.

After Mum read yesterday's tales, she asked me which tellytubby I was. I like to see that she focuses on the most important things in life...

Friday 17th June

Missions for today:

- *Don't have a panic attack in sign language exam*
- *Get sorted for Ascot and drop Lucy off at Dad's*

I had a lot to do today. I didn't really want to be rushing around but it did at least take my mind off my exam tonight.

Our pet food delivery was due today and Mr H was in work. I asked him whether it would be coming to the house. (If it is the big lorry then we meet him in the layby as he got stuck on the paddock once turning round and had to be pulled off by the tractor. The driver won't come down again, unless he is in the small van, as he was really embarrassed the last time it happened. We have, since then, had hard core put down but he doesn't believe us and isn't taking any chances.)

Unfortunately, if I have to go and meet him in the layby then it looks like we are doing something of the nudey-rudey variety.

The layby is known as 'Prostitutes layby' as this is where the truckers stop at night and the prostitute from Wolverhampton goes to provide them with a service (or services). When we first moved in there were two prostitutes but after a few weeks they went down to one and we have only seen the one since then for the last few years.

She is really small and thin and from behind she looks about 14 years old. The first time that I saw her we were in the car driving past and I said to Mr H, "Oh no! There's child exploitation going on here. I need to call the police." Thankfully, before I did that I turned in my seat to look at her from the front. She is actually in her 50s.

You might wonder why I am telling you this. It occurred to me that meeting a lorry driver in the layby might make me look like a prostitute. Because of this, if I have to go there then I deliberately try and wear non-prostitute looking clothes. Not being a prostitute though, I wasn't really sure what they wore. I have watched a number of *Law & Order SVUs* and *Criminal Minds* but thought it prudent to look at some Google images of prostitutes (just in case British ones did not dress like their American counterparts). I didn't want to look silly after all.

When the lorry driver saw me arrive in an outfit that looked like I had wandered out of a Jane Austin novel, I think he thought that I was de-ranged. But I didn't want any of my friends to be passing and wonder what I was doing in a lorry in the layby (everyone here knows what goes on in this layby). I was pleased that I did dress like this though as one of my friends wrote on my Facebook wall later that day, 'Saw you on my way to Cannock. Enjoy your fancy dress party.'

Lucy was off to Dad's for a couple of nights as we needed to leave for Ascot at 7am and wouldn't be back until 10:30pm. Bonnie was staying at home as Mum is still on holiday (again... the life of riley of the retired) and Aunty Jade was coming over to Bonnie and Casper sit. The journey to and from Dad's provided me with some interesting tales. I knew it would be an interesting journey when five minutes from the house there was a car smashed into a lamp post. Luckily no one was injured but the lamp post was leaning at a 90 degree angle and looked like it was about to topple over at any point. Amazingly, in the space of an hour and a half the lamp post had been chopped off at the middle and made safe. I've never seen such quick work (but when someone told me that it was *Eon* that came out and not the Council then I wasn't surprised).

It was really warm in the car so I had the air con blasting on its lowest setting, At one point I thought that I had wet myself though as I felt a warming sensation under my bottom. 'Oh no!' I thought. 'It's started happening.' You hear such awful things about 'the change'. Turns out that due to the 350 dials and buttons in Mr H's car, I had turned the wrong one on and instead of turning up the fan to the highest setting, I had turned the seat warmer on instead. I was relieved...

I dropped Lucy off at Dad's and had a five minute totally pointless conversation with him (I think he has been taking lessons off Mr H.) I asked him if he wanted me to leave Lucy's dog ramp with him in case he needed to put her in the car.

He said that he didn't as he wasn't going to take her anywhere because of her bad legs. I said, "But just in case you need to take her to the vets, wouldn't it be a good idea to leave it?" "Why would I need to take her to the vets?" "Well, she is old, just in case of an emergency and something happens." "Have you booked her in then?" "No Dad. I tell you what, I'll leave the ramp here anyway but if she is ill then you can phone me on my mobile and I will call the vets out to your house." I quickly left as I needed to get to the M&S food hall to buy our picnic for Ascot for tomorrow.

M&S wasn't as bonkers as usual. All of the customers seemed quite normal. To be fair, I was thinking of wandering round for another hour as I was disappointed not to have any exciting tales to tell. But I didn't. I didn't want to get an ASBO and be banned from going there if I looked like a suspicious person caught on their CCTV (their fresh bread is lovely).

I was also on a tight timescale so thought that I would just have to not write about this in my book. Luckily though the gods were on my side. As I was putting my trolley back a woman was trying to get her £1 coin back out of the slot.

She said, "Oh thank goodness! I've been here a few minutes and I can't get it out." "Is it stuck?" I asked. "No – I've got my nails on so I can't ruin them by pulling at it. I've been bouncing the trolley up and down in the hope that it would fall out. Have you got your nails on?" "I have – but mine are gel, so don't worry I will be able to pull it out for you," I said. I pulled out her £1 coin and she thanked me immensely before eyeing up my gel nails in a jealous fashion.

Looking at her in her D&G shoes with her Coco Chanel handbag, I initially thought, 'You live in Cannock?' and then thought she might have just left the £1 coin and been done with it. She was obviously very rich and it wouldn't have mattered to her. But then she climbed into a battered beat up old Fiesta that looked about 40 years old, so maybe she needed the money for a new car fund…

I had been to the M&S to get our picnic for tomorrow as we suspected that Ascot would be a rip-off for food and drink. We were allowed to take in a bottle of champagne each and soft drinks (as long as they were sealed). By the time I had chosen all of our party food bits n pieces, the bill came to £63. I did ponder that maybe we should have just eaten at Ascot.

As I was driving home I saw the 'No car cruising in Cannock – High Court injunction in force' road sign. This always makes me chuckle. You aren't allowed to cruise in your car but if you drive to a spot on the Chase, not far from Stan Collymore's house then you can happily partake in a bit of dogging. They don't have a High Court injunction against that.

I got back to find Casper eating his way through the rest of the trifle that Mr H had left on the side and not eaten for his lunch and thought, 'Well – Jade is looking after him tomorrow, if he has diarrhoea then it won't be my problem.'

Obviously, I did not really think this. I told Jade that if either Bonnie or Casper had bottie issues then not to worry, just shut the door to whichever room it was in and I would sort it on Sunday. Casper went one better than bottie issues though (see tomorrow's tales).

We both think that our sign language exam went ok. I didn't mix up 'dogs' with 'dogging' and Mr H did not mix up 'prostitutes' with 'hallelujah' (as he has done on a couple of occasions before), so fingers crossed for our results. The exam is videoed and is assessed by an external assessor, so Mr H's offering to carry our teacher's bag was all in vain.

As Lucy is at Dad's tonight then we are both hoping for a good night's sleep with no interupptions.*

* Why did I tempt fate?

Saturday 18th June

Mission for today:

- *Have an amazing day out at Ascot*

I only have one mission for today but it's an important one. Mr H and I have never been to Royal Ascot and the Queen is going to be there today (I hope she hasn't read the Facebook post on the *tractor4graham* page and isn't annoyed with me about the comment about male prostitutes seeing to her needs). I love the Royal family and our heritage makes me proud to be British.

With Lucy being at Dad's, I thought we might get a good night's sleep. We needed to be up at 5:45am and as we didn't go to bed until midnight, then I thought we would have a peaceful night. Sadly though, I think all of the stress for our sign language exam last night had made us both a bit 'wired' in our heads (either that or it was the cheese sandwich I ate at 9pm) as we were both wide awake for much of the night. I was wide awake at 4am and didn't drop off to sleep until 5:30, but the alarm woke me up 15 minutes later. (I bet this happens in a lot of your households too.)

We caught the coach at 7:30am after having parked in the train station. I know I moaned about the £9 a day charge last time but it's only £4 on a weekend, so I don't mind the smell of wee for that (and more importantly it meant a shorter walk to get the coach). We had enough food to feed around six of us and as the weather has been very rainy of late, then I put in my nice wellies in case the ground was all muddy. Luckily for us though it didn't rain at all and although it was overcast that meant that we weren't moaning that it was too hot and didn't come back looking like lobsters from sun burn.

The coach made two more pick-ups and I was once again surprised at how many people are up early in the morning and more importantly what crazy things they do at this time of the morning. There were two people in Dudley mowing their lawns at 8am (I bet their neighbours loved them). Mr H didn't seem as surprised as me and said,

"Well, given all the rain, it's probably the only window of opportunity they're going to get." There was no way that I would be up at 8am if that was the only time I could mow the lawn. Mr H mows the lawns in our house – he would have to get up early.

We were choosing which horses we were going to bet on during the coach journey. In typical fashion, I either went for the one whose name I liked the most, or whose colour clothes I liked, or if something in the description about them caught my attention (for example, if it said that they performed well racing at Wolverhampton).

Also in typical fashion this meant that I backed no winners at all. I was annoyed with the first horse that I picked and did think about tweeting the jockey. It came in second on the first race and at 25-1, I would have won over £120 (Mr H told me the amount. We all know I'm rubbish at maths). If only he had tried a little harder than he would have had it. He was in the lead until the last furlong. 'Typical man', I thought, no staying power until the end.

We did chuckle picking our horses though. One of the ladies in our group said, "I like it firm. I don't like it soft." The rest of the women all nodded at this and agreed. It was going to be a good day for innuendo.

You could tell when we were getting closer to Ascot as the houses got bigger and posher and instead of having *Sky* dishes on their houses they had dovecotes. The layby's didn't advertise 'Greasy Lil's caf' either but 'Fresh cherries for sale'. I was glad that I had decided to wear my fascinator. (And as luck would have it, my pale green dress did still fit me. I think washing it must have slackened the seams, as it felt looser and I've not lost weight.)

We stopped for breakfast on the way at a *Beefeater* and one of the customers in there saw me with my posh dress and fascinator and asked where I was going. My evil inner twin tried to rear her head but I stopped her from saying, "Oh. I'm up in Court later and my defence lawyer told me to wear something smart." He was a nice guy, so I told him the truth. I told him that I was related to the Queen and would be sitting in the

Royal Box at Ascot and to look out for me on the telly.

I was panicking that I would spill something down my dress, so I wore a cardy over the top of it for breakfast. This turned out to be a sensible plan as I spilled some of my latte down it and Mr H said, "Why have you got a brown stain on the back of your cardy as well?" That was from the coffee I had on the coach and had placed my cardy over the top of my dress like a bib in case I spilled it. I can be a genius at times.

When we arrived at Ascot there was a tractor parked opposite where the coach parked (which I caught Mr H staring wistfully at). Mr H and I only had a bottle of champagne between us as we got so caught up in the excitement of the Queen being there and had butterflies in our tummies that felt like the bubbles of champagne. Mr H also bet on her horse and won. I think it would have been treason not to. No wonder her horse was the favourite.

Just before Mr H had been to claim his winnings there was a steward's enquiry into the decision.

It didn't last long and the Queen was announced as the winner. I expect someone got beheaded for this act of treason and if the decision had have been overturned then I'm sure the Queen would have texted DC to pass an emergency Act of Parliament declaring her as the winner. When the steward's enquiry was announced a hush descended on the races and you could see everyone look at each other as if to say, 'Who has dared to challenge the Queen?'

When we watched the replay on the big screen you could see how excited the Queen was to have won as I'm sure that I saw her do a fist pump and when her head disappeared from view (as she seemed to put it to her knees) I expect that was when she swore "I've f***in won! Get in you losers!" so that the cameras wouldn't catch her swearing. She doesn't half hold herself with dignity.

I texted Jade to see whether Bonnie was ok and she replied with a photo of a dead squirrel. Apparently, Casper was thrilled that she was there today and had decided to bring her a present. I think she would have been happier if he had gone into someone else's house and stolen some money to bring her but Casper didn't go to school, so he doesn't really understand what human's like so brings what he likes. Thankfully, he hadn't been bitten on the cheek this time in his fight with the squirrel (you might remember my first tale in *#tractor4graham* about his wee-ing and poo-ing in the cat carrier on the way to the vets) so I'm hoping there won't be a repeat performance and a visit to the vets soon. Jade said he only had a small scratch and a bit of pink tinged fur.

If he does need to go back to the vets then I have learned from the previous visit. If there is going to be the chance that he wees and poos in the carrier then I shall be prepared. I will put a sheet of Bounty* in there with him, as according to the adverts one sheet will mop up spilled milk, mud from your child's shoes and broken eggs. Casper's wee and poo would likely be around the same volume.

* I obviously mean the kitchen roll and not the chocolate bar. That would be silly. The chocolate bar would be unlikely to soak up his wee and poo.

445

Although I have now realised that Bounty was renamed as 'Plenty' a few years ago. I wonder whether some thickie tried to sue them when they went to eat it. I can imagine them writing to the manufacturer and saying 'It didn't taste like coconut.'

Luckily Miranda's husband, Matt, was down the farm so he obligingly went and removed the dead squirrel from the utility. It always amazes me how Casper manages to get himself and his prey through the cat flap (he is a bit porky at the moment). Miranda was with us today as it was her friend that had organised the trip.

Royal Ascot was a fab day out. Although I really think they should tell you, on their website, what you really need to know before going. Their website is full of happy smiling people, drinking champagne and eating oysters. In reality by around 3pm it was full of posh, upper class drunk people throwing up everywhere.

Because of this, if any of you decide to go to Ascot, here is my no-nonsense useful guide:

1. Do not (like me) make the mistake of wearing a floor length dress.

    I only spotted one other lady in a floor length dress all day and by the end of the day, I knew why. Rich posh people have lots of money, so can afford to drink the expensive champagne in Ascot. (You are allowed to take in one bottle per person but have to then buy the rest.) By 3pm there were lots of drunk ladies stumbling to the loos and although the cleaners at Ascot worked like Trojans to keep the toilets clean they couldn't keep on top of the puking.

    I struggled to go to the loo in a cubicle that didn't have a door lock, didn't have a hook for your handbag and had questionable looking liquids on the floor. I had to loop my handbag round my neck, tuck it into my shawl and hoist up my dress to also wrap around my mid-riff so that none of it touched the questionable liquid. Luckily I was wearing my £24.99

bargain glittery sandals so decided to chuck them when I got home if they couldn't be cleaned.

I did fail in my mission at one point as the door kept being flung open and my dress dropped to the floor and soaked up something disgusting. Ascot should warn you about this. Wear short dresses. (When I got home I realised that there was some questionable brown mark on my shawl as well. I hope it comes out in the wash...)

2. Take a photo of the coach that you arrive in and its number plate. When you arrive there might only be three coaches in the car park but when you go to leave there are around a hundred. Luckily we hadn't drunk too much champagne (Mr H and I were light weights as we only shared a bottle between us) so knew exactly which one was ours but the number of drunken people that tried to get on our coach

and had no idea where theirs was, was too many to count.

I pondered that Ascot could hire out GPS trackers for men to pop in their pockets or women down their bras (most women had tiny handbags and no pockets) so that the coach drivers could find them at the end of the day.

3. Wear sunglasses all day (even if it's cloudy).

As each person can take in a bottle of champagne you are likely to get poked in the eye by a cork at some point. If you wear sunglasses then you won't risk an eye injury. It was quite comical watching corks whack unsuspecting drunk people on the heads, as they had no clue what had just happened and gazed aimlessly up to the sky for a few seconds afterwards pondering if a seagull had done a big poo on them.

At the end of the day, there was a drunken girl in the loos with grass stains on the buttocks of her dress calling out to her friend 'Shana'. At one point she was crawling on her hands and knees on the floor trying to see under the cubicles to spot her friend's shoes.

Someone asked her what her friend's shoes were like and she replied, "Gold and black spots. They're really pretty." (You need to say this in a slurred voice.) "So are her shoes the same as yours then?" The drunk girl looked down at her shoes and said, "Yes – they're Shana's shoes." "Are you Shana?" The drunk girl thought about this for a second and said, "I don't know…"

Another drunk girl was having a fight with herself at the washbasins. There were mirrors above some of the sinks and the others looked through to the other set of cubicles next door. This girl obviously thought she was looking at a girl at the sink opposite but she was in fact looking at herself in a mirror. "Who are you pointing at? Who do you think you are? You're an ugly-ugly girl. Let's take this outside."

I have come to the conclusion that Ascot has more in common than Wolverhampton than it thinks... drunk girls are exactly the same no matter where you come from and whether you're working class or upper class:

1. You'll still end up throwing up on the grass, with your friend holding your hair back
2. You'll still ruin a nice dress (and possibly some shoes) and
3. You'll still pick a fight with someone*

* In Ascot, it's more likely to be yourself though.

(After I put this tale on the *Tractor4graham* Facebook page, someone commented that this was one of the reasons as to why Ascot had a 'knicker wearing' policy.

To be fair even with all the drunk girls bending over toilets there were no fru-frus on view. I thought the policy quite sensible really. Shame Mr H hadn't known about it. He went Commando for the day...)

Sunday 19th June

Missions for today:

- *Go and pick up Lucy*
- *Finish the final proofing of #tractor4graham*
- *Wish Dad a happy Father's Day on Facebook (even though he won't see it as he doesn't have Facebook)*

It is comical really that we all write 'Happy Father's Day' to our Dads on Facebook and most of them aged 70 or over won't get to see it as they don't do technology. My post was no exception to this rule but I still felt it necessary to do one.

Dad doesn't have Facebook. There are many reasons for this. One of them is that he hasn't yet managed to successfully reply to a text or pick up an answer machine message on his mobile phone. The second reason is that when he sends me or my sister an email from his kindle he immediately phones us up to ask whether we have had it. It's a job to get him to keep his mobile charged and actually take it with him rather than leave it in the kitchen drawer because in his words, 'Why would I need it with me if I'm not expecting a call?' I do love you Dad and I honestly wouldn't change you for the world (it's the same words that I say to Mr H...) but you do suffer Mr H's 'man logic'.

I had to pick up Lucy at 12:30pm as Dad was then off to my sisters for a Father's Day meal. Mr H was heading off to see his Dad for a bit at lunchtime as well. It was Father's Day love all around. I'm wondering whether Casper was a day early with his present and that the squirrel was actually meant for Mr H. He would have appreciated it more than Jade. Our friend Bobby said 'yum' when he saw the picture of the squirrel on Facebook. But he had a recent head injury when he fell off his scaffolding so I'm not sure whether he was joking or not...

Picking up Lucy should have been easy but traffic was murder heading on the A460 due to the two annoying car boots that happen every Sunday (which I had forgotten about) and the 'Sunday drivers'* that clearly were all going to the car boots. I nearly drove into the back of one of them that seemed to have a panic attack when an ambulance came down the road. They didn't know what to do (even though the road is wide and the ambulance could fit between both lanes of traffic) so decided to do an emergency stop which resulted in immediately braking to a halt whilst simultaneously swerving into and hitting the kerb. Luckily Mr H's car has fantastic brakes and also luckily the motorbike behind me had fantastic brakes.

* This is my name for drivers that can't drive in the week in rush hour as it scares them and they would likely have an accident on the first day of driving due to their awful incapabilities and never drive again. They, therefore only drive on a Sunday when they think there is less traffic and it's easier for them (but harder for everyone else on the road).

At least I was in Mr H's car (I'm not sure my car would have stopped in time) but I didn't think he would be best pleased if I returned with a massive dent in the front and had to pretend that I had hit a bear. I know what you're thinking. There are no bears in the UK. And I went to school so should know this. But the circus are in town and the dent would have been too big to claim that any other creature had done it. So I would have told him some elaborate story of how the bear had escaped from the circus and jumped out in front of his car. Unlike Mr H, I don't have a 'liar face' and am very plausible when lying. (I've had to be having lived with Mr H for 25 years.)

I have realised reading this back that I sound very grumpy today. I put it down to post-Ascot comedown and blues (and stupid drivers that shouldn't be on the road – most of which were men as well).

Mr H moaned at me when I got back. (I did now think it would have served him right if the car had have come back with a massive dent in it.) His fuel light had come on when I was leaving. He is really tight when it comes to the price of petrol and I have to fill up with petrol at a petrol station that is on his accredited list. If I don't he nearly has a seizure. I didn't want to run out of diesel when picking up Lucy though so only put in £12.53* at one of his non-accredited stations. I knew he was in work first thing in the morning and decided he would be more annoyed to find no fuel in the car than some that had cost more. I was pleased with this but he wasn't.

* I'm not anal when filling up with fuel and don't have to make it a round £ number like most people (Mr H) do. (In all honesty it's too stressful. If you miss the £10.00 then you have to go to £11.00 and then if you miss that you end up at £12.00 and so on. Because I get bored easily I end up with £109.83 when Mr H's car is totally full with diesel because I've missed every £ along the way.) Of course I'm joking… of course…

Dad said that Lucy slept like a log the two nights that she was with him and categorically stated that the reason why she doesn't wake up in the night is because he gives her a night time walk at 10:30pm. I have just come back from giving her a 10:30pm walk and if she barks at 2am, then I will phone Dad at 2am to tell him. Of course, I'm kidding. I'll message my sister. She is a morning person, so she can phone him while I go back to bed. As predicted Lucy has also been doing disgusting farts today, so I'm not sure what 'treats' she has had in the last two days.

For breakfast, Mr H made me a bacon sandwich. He woke me up by putting it under my nose at 10:40am. I asked him what time he had woken up and he said, "Only about an hour ago at 9:30." Bonnie isn't a morning dog (she's so my dog) so unlike Lucy she's not bothered about going out at the crack of dawn. Mr H said, "I thought I better wake you up, otherwise you might never have woken up." "Cheeky! I was only up an hour after you." As he walked away, I thought, 'Even if he had woken up at 6am then I still would have woken up at 10:40... but my argument fit the timings this morning.'

The rest of today's food of choice consisted of 'Ascot leftovers'. Having spent £63 on our picnic I wasn't going to waste any of it. For lunch I ate olives, chicken tikka bites and an egg sandwich and had two mini meringues. For dinner I had olives, ham, half a scotch egg, three cocktail sausages, some potato salad and a roll.

For pudding I had two French Fancies and five 'Malted chocolate biscuit coated balls' (the M&S version of Maltesers quite clearly – although because they came in a little tub with a handle they were about three times as expensive).

Today I successfully finished my final read through of *#tractor4graham* and just need to put through the corrections and get the cover sorted. Sadly I have only heard back from five agents and none of them want to represent me and the rest haven't replied.

It will be the self-publishing route for me (but on the plus side it will be out quicker). I'm hoping that other people get my warped sense of humour, otherwise I should have spent the time writing doing something else that would have put money into Mr H's tractor fund... but not selling wares down the layby (just to clarify in case you were thinking this). I couldn't do that and make any money. I suspect the 50 year old prostitute killed off her competition when there used to be two of them. She might be the size of a 14 year old girl but I suspect she could kick my ass. So that's really not a viable job option...

After a long day yesterday, Mr H and I decided to have an easy afternoon/evening and watched two films. We each chose a film to watch. We watched *Chalet Girl*, a romantic tale of 'girl next door' that bags 'rich posh boy' with skiing and snowboarding thrown in. This was obviously Mr H's choice (I did check that no dog died in it before we put it on) and as predicted he was close to tears towards the end. He is an old romantic bless him.

After that it was my film of choice. I chose *A Good Day to Die Hard*, an action packed thriller starring Bruce Willis as John McClane. I love it when he says 'Yippee-ki-yay Motherfucker.' (You'll notice that I didn't use *** to blank out the rude bits of the 'Mother' word. This is Bruce Willis after all, it would be illegal not to use the actual phrase.) Mr H didn't cry at this but he has gone to bed early. I think he is emotionally drained from watching *Chalet Girl*.

Monday 20th June

Missions for today:

- *Do a day's work*
- *Put changes through on #tractor4graham*

I didn't really mind working today. It has pissed it down with rain all day long, so I've not wanted to be outside. I could tell when Mr H was back from walking both dogs this morning as the smell of 'eau de chien mouillé'* came wafting through the hall, while I was eating my toast and drinking my latte in the lounge.

* I had to ask Siri 'what is 'wet dog' in French?' I'm hoping that she hasn't lied to me (she's back to treating me with contempt because of the stupid questions I ask her) and that it doesn't say something like 'I love dogging.'

After smelling wet dog for about an hour, I popped to the loo downstairs. It was at this point that Bonnie decided to lick the turtle mat* where the dead squirrel was on Saturday. She then made some sort of hacking noise and nearly threw up. I had made the mistake of not closing the downstairs' loo door whilst I was tinkling so saw all of this. I couldn't get away (or shut the door) as my trousers were around my ankles. I made a mental note not to be so tight again. Because the Vanish carpet mousse** was £6, I had decided to use it sparingly and hadn't used it on the mat where the squirrel had been. Me being a tight arse*** was biting me in the bum.

* I don't know why they call it a turtle mat. I hope that it's not made from real turtles (although 'turtle' is one of my favourite words in sign language). I might Google this and see. (I'm giving Siri a wide berth for a bit until she forgets that I'm dim.)

** I also assume that the Vanish carpet moose isn't made from mooses. (I now need to Google the plural of the word moose…) Today is turning out to be a tiring day…

*** Being a 'tight arse' might be a local saying. It means that you don't spend money and like to hoard it and will participate in other people's rounds in a pub but will mysteriously disappear when it's your turn. I don't really understand where the saying comes from. Do people really keep their money up their bum? That would be extremely unhygienic (and inconvenient if you needed to get it out at the till in Sainsbo's to pay for your shopping).

Dad's fool-proof way of stopping Lucy from barking in the night turned out to be bum-cum* (I don't think it's spelt like this but I'm bored of Googling, so Mum can tell me the proper spelling when she does her read through later). Dad insisted that giving Lucy a walk at 10:30pm was the reason as to why she didn't wake up in the night. Turns out the reason why she didn't wake up in the night was that she actually did but just didn't wake him up with her barking.

We discovered this when Lucy barked at 2:30am and woke Mr H up. Mr H immediately phoned Dad to tell him that he was talking rubbish but no one answered the home phone. I asked Mr H if he phoned Dad's mobile. I then laughed at the idea. It would be turned off and in the kitchen drawer.

* Mum was a star and said, "I think you mean 'Bunkum'." (I prefer my spelling. It's a happy accidental innuendo.)

My work mission was successful but my computer decided to have a paddy at one point and the internet stopped working. It only happened when Mr H was back from work, so I suspect he was hogging the Wi-Fi looking at his tractor porn (he has got very excited that the book is nearly ready to be sold) so I suspect he is hoping it sells and he can start choosing the colour of the tractor that he wants. I don't want to burst his bubble. He's more considerate when he's happy. I might need to make up how well the book is selling to keep him happy. He is much easier to live with when he is happy and doesn't seem to suffer as much from man-nonsense. (I'm now wondering if this is an actual medical condition.)

He was very sexist earlier though but I managed to get my own back. He had put our pasta bake in the oven and when it beeped to say it was done he turned to me and said, "Your microwave oven beeper has just gone off to say that your dinner is ready." I noticed that it was 'mine' because I do most of the cooking in this house. When I heard the washing machine beep to say it was finished I said, "Your washing machine has just beeped to say that it's finished." "My washing machine? My washing machine? I think you'll find that it's 'our' washing machine." (As he said this his voice went really high – a bit like Joe Pasquale.)

I turned around to give him 'the look' but he genuinely had no idea how hypocritical he was being. We then had one of our totally pointless conversations where I had to point out his hypocrisy, while he was trying to defend what he'd said (sometimes he is like a dog with a bone and won't admit when he's wrong).

Unluckily for him I have jaws of steel and won't let go of the bone either. But then I got bored with the argument. He smirked in that 'I've won' kind of a way. He totally hasn't. I'm going to sleep with my headphones in so that when Lucy barks in the night he will have to get up because I won't hear her.

We watched *Pointless* on BBC1 whilst we were eating dinner. My general knowledge is appalling and generally the show makes me look really dim. However, the gods were on my side when I knew five out of the six answers in one of the rounds.

The round was entitled 'Strong Man events'. Even Mr H piped up, "Look Honey! This is your round." I have to confess to you now (and even I don't know why I like it so much) but I love to watch *Britain's Strongest Man* and the *World's Strongest Man*. Mr H said, "Is it because the men remind you of me?" If the men were 5'8'', 11 stone, had no muscles and could be beaten up by a girl then they would be exactly like him. I didn't actually say this out loud though. I just made notes to write it in my book.

England are playing football in a bit so will no doubt play s**t and lose in injury time. We will see if my prophecy comes true.

(It is now football time, so I will be back in a couple of hours wishing I hadn't bothered wasting two hours of my life watching it.)

As predicted I totally wasted two hours of my life watching the football. England didn't lose but it was a boring 0-0 draw. Although, in hindsight, maybe it wasn't time wasted. My constant moaning about footballers and the ridiculous money they get paid, when they can't even kick with both feet, seemed to annoy Mr H throughout the match. Now he knows what it's like to be me putting up with his constant moaning. Although being a man I don't think he will see the parallel and learn from this...

We were four minutes behind real time as Mr H was taking a wee when the match started. Being the good wife that I am, I did pause it. I knew that we would be able to catch up when the first injury happened and both teams spent four minutes complaining to the ref and the injured player rolled around on the floor in agony but was amazingly running like a gazelle within 30 seconds (after the four minutes of complaining).

As predicted, that's exactly what happened and we did catch up.

Two of the Slovakian footballers had hair like punk rockers with stiff looking Mohicans straight down the middle of their heads. This just goes to show that they aren't athletes. Every time either one of them went to head the ball the ball shot off in a weird direction and the looks on their faces was, 'Where the heck did that go? How on earth did that happen?' (Obviously they would have said this in their native language but I'm not trusting Google translate to put it into Slovakian. It will probably lie and make me look silly.)

I turned to Mr H and said, "D'uh! It's Physics." He likes it when I use Physics correctly. He said, "Well done Honey! I think you just used Physics in a correct way with the Croatians' hairstyles." Sadly he did not do a CSE in Geography, as I said, "I think you mean Slovakians'." He reverted to the normal look he reserves for me... contempt...

It's funny how we all become football experts when watching a game. Mr H decided to tweet

Roy to tell him to take Wiltshire* off as he was rubbish. I think Roy must have been checking his twitter feed because two minutes later he substituted him.

* Apparently that isn't his name. I also got a lot of the other names wrong. I thought we had Wiltshire, Dorridge, Carlisle and Clyde playing. I did wonder why Roy picked names of towns and places in the UK but I thought maybe he had done a 'Mike Bassett' in the film *Mike Bassett England Manager*, who had picked players with names of cigarettes (Benson and Hedges). Apparently, the players were Wilshere, Sturridge, Cahill and Clyne. I think my names made it much more interesting. They made me smile more than the football match did...

Tuesday 21st June

Mission for today:

- *Successfully take my sister to the hospital for her check-up*

I only have one mission because it's a really important one and I need to focus. Lucy didn't bark in the middle of the night. I was disappointed as I had worn my headphones for no reason. I bet Mr H knew of my plan and had drugged her. (I drug him occasionally to block out his nonsense, so maybe he has found the sleeping pills.)

I set my alarm so that I would be on time to pick up my sister. I groaned that I hadn't left five minutes earlier or five minutes later as I got caught in the school traffic on the way.

Once again, I had to shake my head and sigh as I followed a woman that had reversed out of her drive (about 500 metres from the school) and then had to wait three minutes whilst she tried to parallel park as close to the school as possible.

I counted that it took her five attempts. You would have thought that she would have learned how to parallel park by now if she has been doing this five days a week since September.

As it was an important day today, I put on the nurse's uniform that I had bought off eBay to deliver my sister safely to hospital for her check-up. She didn't look thrilled when I arrived with a urine* bottle and a wheelchair as well. I wasn't taking any chances though. I hadn't anticipated the reaction that I would get from other members of the public though and on the five minute walk from the car park to the hospital, I had successfully directed a woman to the Physiotherapy department and given the Heimlich manoeuvre to a child choking on a Haribo.

* They didn't have any female bedpans for sale on the internet but I thought it would be a good test of her bending ability. If she could manage to wee into a willy shaped cardboard receptacle then she would be well on her way to being able to go back to work.

Like good citizens we used the alcohol gel on entering the hospital (in all honesty there was a lot of coughing going on and people wandering around with disturbing looking liquids in specimen bottles (one of which tripped over and nearly dropped it), so I wanted to be extra cautious. I did chastise myself for forgetting my face mask (like they wear in the Far East) and thought that next time I should dress like a surgeon (or a dentist), because then I could wear my mask and it wouldn't look out of place.

When we checked in with the receptionist, she asked my sister who her next of kin was. Apparently me piping up, "Why do you want to know this - are you going to kill her?" wasn't the anticipated response. The receptionist looked me up and down with my eBay nurse's uniform and concluded that I had special needs. She replied, "Don't worry sweetheart. We won't let anything happen to her."

Of course I'm kidding about wearing the nurse's uniform. I decided to wear my onesie. After all I had had to get up early and it was either have time to drink two lattes or drink one latte and get dressed. The coffee won...

After my sister had been called through, every time the nurse came out to call through another person she kept looking at me. (She obviously thought that I was there as a patient.) "Are you Betty Duff?" she asked at 10:15am. "Are you Lucy Weekes?" she asked at 10:20am. "Are you Rashi Kaur?" she asked at 10:30am. My inner evil twin was dying to say yes by this point. (I think the nurse was clutching at straws with this last one, truth be told...)

Because being stared at by the nurse was getting uncomfortable, I headed off to Sainsbo's to do some shopping. My sister had texted me to say that they running behind time by 40 minutes. Sainsbo's was really quiet and I got a parking space near the front door and didn't have to put a £1 coin in the trolley because it wasn't attached to the next one and I managed to get all of my shopping done within 15 minutes. I have made a mental note to go on a Tuesday morning again. The only problem with such an efficient, eventless visit, was that I did not encounter any bonkers people to write about in my book.

After I had finished at Sainsbo's my sister texted to say that they were now running 55 minutes late. I decided to pop to Dorothy Perkins to see if they had any handbags in the sale. When we went to Ascot on Saturday my handbag was bulging at the seams and I vowed to buy a bigger one, so that I didn't have to carefully place my lipstick, tampon and perfume in a certain way in order that it would shut. I really didn't want an 'unexpected opening' of the handbag incident to happen where my tampon made a break for it and rolled along the floor. (This has happened to me before and I had to pretend that the tampon bouncing off some guy's shoes was nothing to do with me.)

As luck would have it I was successful. I bought three handbags. One in silver, one in gold and one cream. Not having chosen my dress for next year, I thought it prudent to cover all bases. I knew that Mr H would be thrilled with my logic and my purchases when I got back home. I couldn't wait to tell him.

I got back to the hospital and as I was waiting in the waiting room, I noticed a soft coo-ing noise. As I looked up there was a big fat pigeon looking down at me from the open window above my head. I think that he thought that my onesie was a relative (I did look like a big white bird) as he decided to fly in. Unfortunately he flew to the top of the alcohol gel container. Due to the screaming of the staff on reception he obviously got scared and this released his bowels. Pigeon poo dribbled down the side of the label that said, 'Hygiene is our paramount concern.'

I was relieved that I had already alcohol gelled my hands and decided that I wouldn't on the way out. Whilst I was waiting for my sister (and watching the staff trying to shoo the pigeon out the room), a random woman sat down next to me and decided to talk to me. (She hadn't spotted my 'deliberate staring at my phone to avoid making eye contact' move when I saw her sit on the seat next to me. Or if she had she had totally ignored it.)

Apparently she worked in another department of the hospital and was here to 'collect samples'.

I really didn't want to know what the samples were, so just did the obligatory eyebrow raise in acknowledgment and then tried to busy myself in my phone. She carried on...

Apparently she was a 'sperm tester.'* She said that she didn't like handling the 'warm' samples (oo yuk) and that the pots that they 'did the business in' made excellent travel pots for your face cream. (I really hoped that she meant unused ones and didn't use ones that had already had 'cream' in them.) She also said that a lot of people couldn't handle sperm so in order to see whether you could cope with it on your first day in the job, they put a real eye on your desk, floating in a glass of water.

* I assume she's not a taste tester like my friend Kim, who tests the saltiness of soup for Heinz.

I concluded that it did not matter that Sainsbo's had been quiet today. She was my bonkers person of the day to write about in my tales and really I should have thanked her for it. (I should also really have thanked the pigeon. But I don't know 'pigeon language' and didn't want to make a 'coo' that was the wrong one and end up offending it.)

Wednesday 22nd June

Mission for today:

- *Come back from hospital having been told that I have a simple muscle strain and not to darken their doors again*

You might think that this is a strange mission. Something I have neglected to tell you all week is that I have had a pain in my calf. (The reason that I have neglected to tell you is because it's not interesting and I don't want you thinking that I'm 'one of those people' that constantly moans about their ailments.) It has felt like I have pulled a muscle and generally hurts first thing in the morning but seems to disappear after I have walked on it for a bit.

Today I woke up with a really painful calf and my leg was swollen and I couldn't walk downstairs properly but had to do the 'sideways shuffle'. Mr H was asleep on the settee as both dogs had barked manically at 5am and he thought that we might have a burglar. So at 5am he went outside to see if we had a burglar. I did point out to him that maybe that was the worst thing that he could have done because if it was a burglar then they would likely have bopped him on the head with a hammer and then walked through the open door and stolen my shoes and DVD boxsets.*

* We don't have expensive electronic equipment or antiques or jewels, so I suspect they would have gone for these instead.

Anyway... back to the painful calf...

As Mr H was just about waking up, I said to him, "Do you think my calf looks big and swollen?" He grunted something and I decided that he might need a few more minutes to wake up. To cut a long story short (because I really want to tell you about the bonkers people in A+E) we ended up taking a trip to A+E. A blood clot in my right leg tried to kill me at 25 and 17 years later (after taking its time quite frankly) it was trying again.

Mr H drove me to A+E and dropped me off at the door before going to park the car. Unfortunately, for us, A+E had moved the previous November and I had to hobble the entire length of the hospital to find it. In true government fashion though, no one had bothered to move the signs (or the helicopter pad either). It took me ten minutes to get to A+E and Mr H beat me because as he was parking the car around the other side of the hospital he spied the new signs. I guess that they left the old signs up in the hope that those that didn't really need it would give up on the walk through the hospital (or stop at Greggs half way and forget what they had come for, when they smelled the steak bake cooking).

A+E sent me to the 'Urgent Care Unit'. I think they should have called it the 'Care Unit: Nurses Triage', which is basically what it was but I suspect C.U.N.T as an abbreviation on the signs would be bound to offend someone (no one has a sense of humour these days). I had to wait there for nearly an hour and started to ponder about some of the patients and why they were there. (I also think that 'Urgent Care Unit' was an overly elaborate name. Most of the people in there were eating crisps and chatting on their iPhones and took forever to get up when their names were called. There was nothing urgent about the place.)

There were interesting categories of injuries in there. There were lots of women limping. Either, like me, they had blood clots, or they had kicked their husbands too hard this morning for talking nonsense and had injured themselves in the process. I did notice that it was only women that were limping.

I wondered what Richard Gere was in there for. Sadly it wasn't the actor and I did ponder whether the guy had given his real name. I watch *Law & Order* on TV and criminals with gun-shot wounds don't normally give their real names. Although, I don't think he had a gun-shot wound, it looked like he had a urine infection, as he was carrying around a specimen bottle with a questionable coloured liquid in it. He probably was embarrassed about it and gave a fake name.

Before we went in, Mr H looked down at my jeans and said to me, "Why didn't you wear a skirt? They are going to want to examine your legs." I don't like wearing skirts in hospital. I worry about sitting on a chair and sucking up MRSA through my fru-fru, so sensibly wore a dress over my jeans.

In order to work out when I would be the next person in, I tried to memorise the people that were already sitting down before I arrived. There was Marius the Polish builder (who looked like he had hit himself with a hammer). Now don't think I'm generalising here – that was his name as I ear-wigged on his conversation with the receptionist.

There was Charlie, the hyper-active three year old, whose Mum just looked like she needed a break from him. He was continuously eating from a packet of sweets that made his tongue go a blue colour. (I was dying to tell his mum that maybe that was the cause of his hyper-activity.)

There was Alison, who obviously had some 'female problems' as she leant in close to the receptionist to explain her illness and I couldn't hear what she had to say. The receptionist nodded in a sympathetic fashion and I think I caught the words 'hot flushes' from her.

The final person was Naz and I didn't need to ear wig on his conversation with the receptionist as he was in a wheelchair with a bloody bandage on his leg. (I pondered whether his wife had gone one better and had stabbed him with a knife rather than kicking him.) Once Naz got called in, I knew that I would be next, so unplugged my iPhone from charging at the NHS's expense and got ready to go in.

I explained to the nurse as to why I was there and accidentally nearly showed the world my fru-fru. When I bent over to remove my jeans, I hadn't noticed that there was glass in the door to the room. The nurse was rapidly trying to close the 'modesty curtain' when she saw me undressing, which only succeeded in shutting Mr H off on the other side of the room and I said, "Oh don't worry about my husband, he's seen my bits before." That's when she pointed to the glass in the doors behind me (and Charlie the hyper-active child waving at me).

Due to a cock-up in the NHS's procedures, I ended up back in A+E having to start the whole process off again to get seen by a doctor before I could get a scan on my leg.

The doctor said that he needed to take some bloods and measure my legs. Mr H had to look away at this point. He is squeamish and hates seeing blood taken. As they had to take so much blood they attached a hose pipe contraption to it which filled about four vials. I was quite mesmerised watching my blood spiral around it. (And pondered buying one for when we decant the damson gin into shot glasses. It looked a very efficient contraption.)

Mr H wasn't as squeamish when it came to them measuring my legs. The doctor disappeared and came back with an IKEA tape measure. He also used one of those free IKEA pencils to write down the measurements. I wonder if one of the nurses has to go to IKEA each week to steal tape measures and pencils for the department. (Either that or A+E is now sponsored by IKEA? If so, then I'm looking forward to the 50p meatballs. The sandwich Mr H bought cost £5.49.)

A woman came past the bay wheeling behind her a big suitcase. Initially I thought that maybe she was going on holiday and had tripped and fallen on the floor but then I realised she was just much better prepared than me, given the long waiting times. We were there all day and hadn't brought food or water. She could have housed a fold-up chair in her suitcase for her husband to sit on when she went into a bay to see a doctor, along with a picnic for their lunch. I have made a mental note to be better prepared next time.

The doctor came back to tell me that he was 99% certain that I had a blood clot as the one test has a maximum figure of 0.4 and mine was 4.0. (He said he double checked the level twice.) For some reason though they couldn't do a scan this afternoon and I now have to go back tomorrow to see whether it is a clot. (I'm hoping I will be in the 1%.) In the meantime, I had to have an injection in the tummy to 'stick' the clot. (I was pleased that I am a bit chunky at the moment as it didn't hurt when it went in. Although my rolls of fat did seem to make the needle disappear which made me panic at one point.)

When we got back we saw Matt, the Farmer and the Farmer's wife. She was really sweet as she came to give me a big hug and said, "We're not ready for you to die yet." I wondered if she meant that they were ready for Mr H to die. He had borrowed the tractor yesterday and it had broken down in the field...

Thursday 23rd June

Mission for today:

- *Hope the 1% reason for the blood clot is true*
- *Try not to cry in front of the ultra sound radiographer if it turns out to be a blood clot*

I know you shouldn't but last night I Googled 'other reasons for high D-Dimer in the blood.' There is apparently a 1% chance that I have been bitten by a snake and it's not a blood clot. I'm wondering whether the chicken bites from a few weeks ago might actually cause this reaction. If the ultrasound is negative then I will put forward this suggestion to the doctor.

Mr H was back from work at lunchtime and as my appointment was at 2pm he categorically announced that we wouldn't need to leave until 1:30pm. Luckily, I, (as usual), totally ignored him and we left at 1:15pm. It was a good job that we did as we got held up going round the hospital ring road as the Air Ambulance came into land.

We had the roof down on my car which was good for capturing the landing (and take-off) on video but bad because of the crap that the propellers* chucked down on top of our heads. I was doubly annoyed as I had put on my good make-up and had styled my hair nicely. Now I was going to have to wander in to the hospital looking like I had had a 'quickie' in the bushes outside. (Well, this is Wolverhampton. It happens...)

* Mr H read this snippet on FB and gave me the 'look'. Apparently, I have got the Physics of the situation wrong. The propellers don't throw debris down from the sky, they suck it up from the floor (or something like that. After he went into his fourth minute of explanations, all I heard was 'blah... blah... blah...')

I really wanted to look professional and presentable whilst I had my scan (I had made sure that I was wearing my good knickers too – the ones with the slogan 'smile', just in case I accidentally flashed the world again) and now my plans were being thwarted. The gods were conspiring against me further as it turned out I was at the wrong Radiology department and had to hobble all the way across the hospital to the right one. As the air ambulance had delayed our journey then I was checking in at 1:55pm, with only five minutes to spare before my appointment.

My panting out of breath, sweating and hair covered in debris look was not conveying the image I had been hoping for as I tried to check in. Once again the gods were conspiring against me as it turned out that I should have been in the other Radiology department, where I had just come from. Thankfully, common sense prevailed this time and the lovely receptionist said they would scan me there. (I think looking at my ginormous swollen leg and not wanting to be sued if I collapsed from cardiac arrest trying to hobble back across the hospital was something to do with it.)

The nurse, Gemma, called my name and Mr H went to get out of his chair as well to follow me in. I said to Gemma, "Out? Or In?". "Out", she said and then giggled, "As long as we aren't talking about the voting today?" I shot Mr H one of those, 'Do not use this as an excuse to talk politics' looks but thankfully he was already gazing back up at the telly in the waiting room as Jeremy Kyle was just about to announce some DNA results.

Alan the Radiographer scanned my leg and announced that I had a clot from my thigh to my calf. He physically moved back as he said it as I think he was expecting me to burst into tears and Gemma started moving in closer in case she was needed to comfort (or sedate) me. I surprised them (and myself) by not having a meltdown (for which we were all grateful) and Gemma asked if my husband would be able to push me in a wheelchair back to the C.U.N.T centre (I mean Urgent Care Unit). I said, "You've seen him, what do you think?" She said, "Maybe he's stronger than he looks." We chuckled and at this point Alan relaxed as he knew that I wasn't going to have a meltdown.

When I came out of the door I gestured to Mr H that I had a clot from my thigh to my calf (we like to keep up on our sign language practise) and that we needed to head back to the Urgent Care

Unit for treatment. He only nearly tipped me out the wheelchair twice, although taking the outside route around the hospital meant that we bounced over a rockery at one point. (I think he was trying to pretend that he was pushing a tractor.)

When we arrived at the Urgent Care Unit, their urgency was even more lacking today as they had all gone home and it was shut. The nurse said, "Sorry but you won't get treatment here." Once again (or de ja vu as the French say it – I'll have to delete this bit if we do Brexit) we had to go back to A+E to start the process all over again just so I could get an injection.

I started feeling like Bill Murray in *Groundhog Day* and thought that I would bump into Marius the Polish builder, Charlie the hyper-active three year old and Alison with her 'woman problems'. The receptionist in A+E greeted us with an, "Oh you're back again." I resisted the temptation to say, "We had such a lovely day out yesterday, so thought that we would do it again." I thought she might write something on my notes which resulted in a nurse applying some enema up the bum, so I bit my lip.

After about 40 minutes I was called in to see the nurse (or Grumpy McGrumpy as I have affectionately called her). She took my blood pressure, which was amazingly perfect – but I think I had, by this time, adopted a 'fuck this shit' (sorry but I'm not shoving asterisks in today) attitude and had no energy left to care, so I'm not surprised it was fine. She chastised us as to why we hadn't gone to the Clinic to get the injection and Mr H piped up, "We did and it was shut." I once again bit my lip and didn't say, "Oh - why didn't we think of that. We could have been seen straight away and be sitting at home watching Countdown by now, instead we've decided to wait here for what will probably be three hours, before we see a doctor." Instead, I just smiled.

Grumpy McGrumpy made some notes (none of which thankfully had the word 'rectum' in there) and we were sent back out to wait in the waiting room. Whilst we were sitting there, I had a courtesy text from A+E to ask me to rate my patient experience. I rated it '5' which meant I would not be likely to recommend it to family or friends. They re-texted me to ask why. The gods were on my side this time as I knew I probably had an hour or so to wait to see the doctor. I wrote about my experience. It struggled to send, as I suspect it was probably ten texts long and was probably also premium rate but it was well worth it and killed some more time. My sister texted me in the meantime and warfarin was changed to wolverine by autocrapet. "Will the doctors give you Wolverine?" That also made me chuckle and he would be preferable to take home than warfarin.

A young girl with her arm in plaster came to chat to me. (I had removed the debris from my hair by this point and I think I looked approachable. Either that or seeing my gammy leg, she felt that I wasn't a 'predator' that they warn kids about in school these days.) She asked me what was wrong with me, so I told her I had a poorly leg. She had fallen off the swings and had broken her arm. I wished that had happened to me...

The pain in my leg was getting worse and Mr H said, "You can't have anything until you've seen the doctor." He was right of course, although I did think about wandering outside to passively smoke some of the cannabis that was permeating the air. Of course I didn't. The doctor called me in at this point.

The doctor told me I was too young to be in a wheelchair and have a blood clot. When I said that I had had one 17 years ago, I'm sure he wrote something on my chart about 'consider donating body to medical science.' I did think about asking how much they would pay.

The new £38m A+E centre is really worth its money. The lights in the consultation room kept going off because the movement sensors weren't working properly. Mr H had to keep bobbing up and down in his chair and pretending to swat a fly to keep turning them back on.

Three hours after arriving, I finally had the five second injection I needed, with an appointment to be back tomorrow. They have assured me that this time the clinic will be open. (I'm not convinced. If Brexit happens tonight then I reckon loads of people won't turn up to work... You'll see tales from A+E tomorrow again...)

Friday 24th June

Missions for today:

- *Don't kick (with my good leg) the chief exec of the hospital if my appointment isn't there and I end up back in A+E again*
- *Try and ignore all the politics on Facebook now that the 'Leavers' have won over the 'Remainers' (I'm bored with this s**t now.)*

I knew that I should have bought the pop up tent from Go Outdoors, the other day. It would have been easier and cheaper to camp outside the hospital overnight in readiness for today's appointment. Also, due to the fact that I have been there for the last four days, I've decided to ask them to dedicate a seat in their waiting room to me. People do this at football grounds and benches overlooking the sea to commemorate loved ones, after all. 'Glenn' wasn't happy though when I evicted him from his seat saying, "That's my spot."

Back to the 'Urgent Care Unit' I went. (I've stopped calling it the rude 'C' word as I'm worried that Amazon might sensor my book when it's published, for undesirable language.) Thankfully today did not involve a three hour wait in A+E as they did have my appointment and the clinic was actually open. The DVT clinic was in the Urgent Care place and today they lived up to their name. Due to running late yesterday (because of Mr H's lapse time keeping and the Air Ambulance landing), I made sure that we left with plenty of time today. I went in 40 minutes early for my appointment as well.

Brexit didn't seem to have had an impact on the hospital today, although when I went to the main receptionist and said, "Me again! De ja vu…" she tutted in response. The receptionist for the DVT Clinic gave me a look of, 'Flip me! Are you sure that you're in the right place?' The rest of the patients were men in their 80s.

Dr Batman* was fabulous and we were in there for an hour and a half. We discussed my options and I decided against taking rat poison for life (Mr H looked a bit sad at this, as I think he thought that he could secretly up my dosage whilst I wasn't looking and find me dead on the Utility floor one day, looking like I had been killed by Casper and dragged through the cat flap [which is what he would tell the police].) I have gone for a newer drug called rivaroxaban. (I think that's the correct spelling but in all honesty, I can't be bothered to check.)

* This obviously wasn't his actual name but he had on Batman socks and a Batman belt. I asked him whether it was just a Batman thing or whether he frolicked with other super heroes too. Apparently, he's a frolicker... I'm looking forward to seeing which Superhero he is when I go back in four weeks' time.

We tried to work out why I had had a blood clot but nothing out of the ordinary had happened in my life over the last few weeks. (I did not tell him about the incident of swallowing two flies and the possibility that I had sucked up a spider through my fru-fru. I didn't want him thinking I was a loon. Besides, I had already dismissed this idea because Google had categorically told me that flies and spiders living in the body did not cause blood clots.)

Back to the appointment though...

The upsides to the non-rat poison drug were:

1. Being able to drink alcohol (obviously this is not in hierarchical order. It just so happened that I put this first. And it's also a coincidence that it was the first question that I asked Dr Batman as well)...

2. Not having to have injections in the tummy for ten days (I seriously was stressing about losing a needle in my rolls of flab)...

3. I don't have to wear ugly orthopaedic stockings that make your fru-fru itch and are really hot (luckily we don't have hot summers in Britain. Sweating through orthopaedic stockings is not a good look)...

4. I don't have to have daily blood tests...

5.   I can eat cranberries, spinach and grapefruit (I wasn't thinking that this was going to be an issue as I don't really do fruit and veg much but when a friend pointed out that they could be in cocktails, I realised it was another plus).

There is one downside:

1. If I bang my head whilst snowboarding and get a bleed then I will die (cést la vie – damn it! It's happened again. This Brexit thing is harder than you think...)

Thankfully he also prescribed me some kick-ass painkillers (just below morphine) as the pain when I woke up this morning made me want to squeeze (and bite down on) something really hard. Mr H was grateful that he had been watching the referendum through the night downstairs as he didn't relish being the thing that I squeezed (he doesn't mind biting). He is immensely grateful for the painkillers.

Given that the last two days we have been at the hospital virtually all day, Mr H wasn't taking any chances with the car park today. He turned down a ticket from a woman that had just under two hours left on it and paid £3 to park all day. We were only there one hour and 50 minutes. He moaned all the way home about it. "That's another £3 gone from my tractor fund…" I like to see that he focuses on the most important aspects of life…

Today made me think about the irony of this week. I'm sure Mr H has been trying to kill me for the last few months. Turns out he really didn't need to do any of his elaborate attempts of poisoning, shooting, crushing my head in a vice etc. He could have simply cut off the blood supply in my leg and let nature take its course. Unless he did do this while I was sleeping…?

Whilst we were leaving the hospital Mr H said, "I think we need to start eating better as I need to lose weight off my tummy." I asked him whether he wanted to pick up a roast chicken from Sainsbo's but he replied, "No – let's go to the chip shop." I think we'll start tomorrow. This week has been pretty stressful. When we got back our diet continued to go well as Carrie had bought us a cream cake each. She texted to say, "I have something yummy in the barn for you." I replied, "Is it Johnny Depp?" (He's not actually on my laminated list, so I have no idea why I said that. I blame the clot. This will be my new second failsafe reason to being a bit dim. My first one is 'I'm blonde' and now it will be 'My head's not functioning properly with my clot blocking my blood flow to my brain.')

A+E sent me another text today to ask about my patient experience. I re-sent the one from yesterday, saying that I was willing for them to contact me, if they wanted to improve their processes. I doubt that they will. I don't think that they really want to improve. Although their sign says 'Exceeding Expectations', I think they mean people who have really low ones. Maybe most people's expectation is that if you leave A+E alive, then that's all that matters.

I was a good patient when I got home. I have done what the doctor has told me (although he didn't specifically tell us to go and buy fish n chips – but then again he didn't actually tell us not to either). I have put my new medical alert card in my purse (although with the amount of crap in my handbag, I think I would probably be dead before anyone found it) and read through the material about my medicine and do's and don'ts. Apparently one in 1,000 people get a blood clot each year. The odds of winning on a scratch card is allegedly one in four but I've never won on one. I'm thinking that the lottery probably lies.

Seeing this statistic got me curious as to what people die from each year. (I'm super sparkly today, you'll note.) Apparently, 60,000 people die each year from a blood clot. One in 67,000 people will die from being the occupant of a truck or van each year. One in 16,000 people a year die from 'unknown' poisoning. (I suspect this latter one is husbands/wives doing away with each other.)

I was relieved to see that only one in 22 million people die from igniting their own pyjamas. I've got more chance of winning the lottery as the odds of that are one in 14 million. This cheered me up no end and my sparkle started to return. You might wonder why. But I nearly set fire to my pyjamas once when I was struggling to sleep and lit a lavender candle. If I was going to be that one in 22 million then the chances are I will probably win the lottery too at some point. Sometimes I seem to have man-logic. I blame the clot that's cut off the blood supply to my brain…

Saturday 25th June

Missions for today:

- *Take as many kick ass painkillers as I'm able to stop me screaming, 'Why me? Why me?' as I can't take the pain anymore*
- *Try and get showered and dressed*

I totally failed in my second mission. After it took me ten minutes to drag my gammy leg behind me across the hall, through the kitchen, to the toilet and back again (which resulted in a one hour sleep to get over the trauma), I knew that I would not be showering or getting dressed today.

Even knowing that five visitors were coming over wasn't enough incentive to try. I just sprayed myself with Febreeze, tied my hair back in a bobble and pinched my cheeks a few times to put a bit of colour into them. I stopped short of rubbing some of the charcoal from my burned toast around my eyes, as make shift eye liner (although I did ponder it for a few minutes. I came to the conclusion that that was just plain silly – I didn't have a mirror to hand to see what I was doing).

I asked Mr H whether my leg appeared to have gone down and he got out an IKEA tape measure from his jeans pocket to measure it. I didn't ask where he had got it from but even if he had stolen it from the doctor at the hospital and it's been caught on CCTV, I don't think the doctor is one to talk, as I suspect there is similar footage of him (or his nurse) on IKEA's CCTV.

Sadly, it has not gone down but does look a slightly different shape. (I think that it's been flattened by me lying static in one position through the night, so it's now just squashed the clot out the sides instead. It's a bit like what happens to my tummy when I squeeze into my skinny jeans.)

I was intending to try and limit my intake of the kick ass painkillers but I think Mr H knew that this wasn't going to happen when I momentarily couldn't find them this morning and screamed,

"Where are they? If you've hidden them then I swear you'll regret it." My outburst didn't last long as I saw them on the floor next to the bed and went from irrational psychopath to chilled out happy wife in the space of a few seconds. "Oh! It's fine here they are. Morning Honey – do I get a morning kiss." Mr H looked like a rabbit caught in the headlights and was frozen to the spot for a second unsure of what to do.

Just before going to bed last night, Jade and I chatted on Messenger as she had also been in A+E with her husband as he was experiencing weird symptoms. Turned out it was man flu and he couldn't handle the pain. We did chuckle at men and their rubbish pain thresholds. Mr H will cry if he stubs his toe. I did think it was better that it was me that had the clot. He wouldn't be able to handle the pain at all. Although, I told Jade that if my kick ass painkillers did not work then I would need her to drive to Heath Town to find a guy called 'Snake' and get me some cannabis instead. (Obviously this is fiction – his name isn't Snake.)

This morning, I asked how her husband was doing and she said, 'He's finally re-surfaced from the lip.' She immediately sent another message, saying, 'Loo – not lip!' I liked 'lip' better. Accidental double entendres always make me laugh and I needed something to laugh about. I laughed for a while and then couldn't stop laughing. These painkillers are good...

My sister, Mum, Step-Dad, Step-Son and Step-Daughter-in-law were all over at various points today to cheer me up. My sister won the best visitor award, as she bought me donuts. (This is a hint for anyone else that is intending to visit. My blood clot is really hungry for comfort food at the moment. Do not bring fruit though [unless it's in a cocktail] or it is likely that that my evil inner twin will re-surface.)

My sister relished the role reversal and came in her nurse's uniform. It was much better than the cheap one that I had bought to nurse her. I think hers came from Ann Summers (although it was a little on the short side – but she is nearly six foot, so it's no surprise really). Luckily, because there were a few visitors, she didn't get to use the rectal thermometer on me that she had bought. Instead we used it to spear the donuts to 'fling' them to each other. I'm glad that she didn't try and use the rectal thermometer - having a gammy leg meant I wasn't going to be able to run away from her. I had flashbacks to when we were children and played doctors and nurses (although at least this time she didn't make me lie down in the middle of the road, so that she could patch me up after a car ran over me. Luckily for us* we lived in a quiet cul-de-sac...)

* It was more luck for me really, although I suspect she would have been carted off to some institution if I had have been run over, so maybe it was lucky for both of us.

Thankfully the kick ass painkillers have kept my evil inner twin at bay and I have been quite sparkly today. Just to be on the safe side though, Mr H went out with his son and daughter-in-law and left my sister to be with me until he got back. He was gone most of the day, I don't know why... I've been a really good patient and seeing the rainbow unicorns on the lawn today has been a particular highlight. They are such beautiful creatures. I didn't think they lived in the UK – or maybe it's another consequence of Brexit?

Mum messaged me after she had got back home to say that she had forgotten to tell me that when they arrived, Casper was next door with the Farmer and the Farmer's wife. Apparently Casper isn't tolerating my gammy leg. I'm not fast enough getting to the utility to feed him, so he's taken the huff and gone next door to be fed. The dogs were, at least, loyal (well, until Mum arrived with treats for them and then they abandoned me like a shot as well).

We watched the Wales v Northern Ireland football match and I said to Mr H, "Who are we going for?" He said, "Wales of course!" "Why?" He gave me the look and said, "What's our surname?" I thought it mean that he was testing me while I was ill and I just glared back. Two hours later and the answer came to me…

Sunday 26th June

Mission for today:

- *Try and go and see a new house that my step-son and step-daughter in law are thinking of buying (without collapsing in a heap or crying from the pain)*

When you have a gammy leg, you keep your missions simple. Today, the pain was at a very manageable level (yay for the kick ass painkillers) so I decided to try and go and see a show home. I knew that if I couldn't make it up the stairs then I could sit in the car, across the back seat with my leg raised up. I would just make sure that Mr H left me the keys so I could put the air con on and not die in a hot car. This is on my 'embarrassing ways to die' list, that I really don't want to happen. These are the top five currently on that list (although they do change from time to time depending on recent experiences):

1. Don't die in a hot car (bright red and sweaty really isn't a good look for me)...

2. Don't get blown up in a petrol station after someone uses jump leads to start their car (when I went to the Tesco express after having my tetanus injection, put this one on the list)...

3. Don't die from chicken bites (I will have to get Mr H to pretend that it was some poisonous cobra or an alligator, whilst I was on some exotic safari and not from cleaning out chickens in Wolverhampton)...

4. Don't die getting run over by a cyclist in London (I would have to get Mr H to pretend it was some big juggernaut at least)...

5. Don't die from being tripped up by Casper/Lucy/Bonnie/Mr H (I would have to get Mr H to pretend that I fell off a horse. The hardest thing will be him having to dress me in my jodhpurs and

body protector whilst I'm lying spread eagled on the floor before he calls 999).

You might notice that these are all connected with previous tales in my book. I also don't want to die on the toilet, for obvious reasons and especially if I have done a number two and haven't flushed it yet...

Anyway... back to the show home...

I did feel like the Queen being chauffeured around by Mr H, as I sat with my legs up across the back seat, resting them on two big cushions. Although, If I were the Queen, I don't think she would have cushions from Dunelm, which were covered in dog fur (and had some of my latte that I spilled this morning).

Hers would be made of gold and covered in precious jewels, no doubt. I was jolted back to reality and reminded that I wasn't the Queen at one point, as I don't think her chauffer would have sworn like Mr H did when someone went to cut him up. He also didn't say, "Sorry Ma'am" after he did it but continued to rant about the 'typical idiot* Sunday driver'. My 'pretending I'm a Princess' bubble was once again truly burst.

* He didn't use the word 'idiot'. It definitely began with an 'f'.

I managed to hobble around the show home and luckily the lady showing us round didn't mind when I needed a rest and lay on the master bed with my leg up. I don't think she anticipated me falling promptly to sleep but she did thank me afterwards.

Apparently another couple that she was showing round were so impressed with 'how she treated the disabled' and that 'the houses obviously had excellent feng shui', (when they saw me snoring and drooling a bit), so put in an offer there and then. As we were leaving, I saw her put the cushion that I had drooled on into the black wheelie bin. Such a waste, I thought, she could have just let me keep it. She was probably worried that my blood clot would be contagious through my saliva or something, or maybe she was worried about contracting MRSA from my recent visit to the hospital.

Since having been to hospital, Lucy has slept like a log throughout the night. I'm thinking it is now just an attention seeking act and seeing me hobbling around, she has decided to knock it on the head for a bit. I suspect it won't last long though…

I knew I had done too much this morning when I fell asleep in the afternoon while my sister was talking to me. She's not boring at all – we were having a conversation about toilets and fru-frus at the time and that a nice man in the garden centre had said to her, "Nice verbena you've got there." We think he was referring to the plant in her basket and not the fact that she had flashed him as she had bent down to pick up a plant. (She could have mis-heard him but she didn't think someone would be so bold as to use that 'v' word… and not with her husband standing there as well.)

I did think that falling asleep while someone is talking to you is a bit rude but luckily my sister put it down to the drugs and wrote me a lovely note for when I woke up, saying she hoped I had a nice rest. I wrote on Facebook that I was really grateful for the lovely note and our friend Bobby said, "Wait until you look in the mirror and see the glasses and moustache that she drew on you." I did go to check and was grateful that there was nothing on my face. (Although when I went to have my shower the next day, I did get a shock. I have no idea how she managed to get my trousers down whilst I was asleep. It took me a while to scrub off the permanent marker that she must have used as well.) When I sent her a message, she said, "I was just checking that your verbena was ok."

I messaged Jade to ask how her husband was doing with his man flu. Apparently, it is some sort of gastric virus. She said that she won't come over until she knows that she isn't going to pass it on. I thanked her and said that I'm not bendy enough to cope with norovirus at the moment.

I always love to see that people focus on the most important details in life. When I put the post up on Facebook about spraying myself with Febreeze, most people asked what fragrance it was. 'I hope it was the lavender one' was one comment. (I didn't like to tell them it was the one specifically for getting rid of 'wet dog' odour. It seemed appropriate as I do look like a poodle when my hair is wet.)

'On this day' popped up on Facebook from two years' ago, when me and Mum were playing 'Drawsomething' together. I had drawn a picture of a dog spraying itself with something. The correct answer was perfume but the letters allowed for a ruder word to be spelled. Mum spelled 'F***er' instead. I don't think she banked on me taking a screen shot of what she had written and then broadcasting it to the world. She has obviously since learned from this...

Being ill definitely has its up-sides. I have been receiving lots of flowers, get well messages and now friends are bringing cakes and goodies with them. This is the power of Facebook. I put a post up yesterday about my blood clot wanting comfort food and so far have had donuts, chocolate brownies, cream cakes, trifle and chocolate buttons. No grapes or fruit in sight. Mr H said, "You really need to start eating properly.

These will do you no good whatsoever." He said this whilst tucking into a scone that was sitting on top of a bowl of trifle. When I called him a hypocrite, he said, "I'm not ill. I don't need to watch what I eat." I reminded him of the conversation we had had on Friday when he said that he needed to lose weight from his tummy. He simply said, "I just meant that I needed to exercise more – I had no intentions of eating less." Got to love his man logic.

Mr H wasn't a very good nurse again today. He took the remote control from me (luckily the painkillers are making me very placid at the moment, so I didn't resist) and after he had decided what he wanted to watch he then left the remote on the other settee out of my reach and went to do something upstairs. This man logic totally confuses me. Why turn over and then leave the room?

I started Googling his family tree to see if I can get him evicted from the country when Brexit happens. Maybe I will need to encourage all of my Welsh friends to break free from the UK and he will get deported back to Caernarfon. Bobby lives in Wales, so Mr H can go and live with him.

Mr H's man logic went from bad to worse today. I told him that my tablets have days of the week written on them and there is a 'morning' and an 'evening' pill. I sometimes forget whether I have taken a tablet or not, so I thought this was a really useful thing. Mr H is always forgetting whether he has taken his blood pressure tablets (and more often than not has forgotten to take them). I said to him, "Wouldn't it be a good idea if your tablets had days of the week written on them and a 'morning' and an 'evening' too?" He said, "Oh they do say that. But I always start with Sunday – on a Sunday – and then just work backwards and count how many I've taken to work out whether I have taken the correct days."

"So, you basically take Mondays from the 'Saturday' ones and then Tuesdays from the 'Friday' ones?" But surely that makes it much harder to work out whether you have taken the correct days?" "No – because I just count them backwards." (He was deadly serious about this and I am genuinely flummoxed at the logic of this. I wonder whether it's a 'man thing'. I know they hate being told what to do, so when he sees 'Tuesday', does he say to himself 'I will decide when I take Tuesday's pill and if it's a Thursday then so be it. I'm not having a tablet telling me what to do.') I did think about booking him in for an MRI. This is not normal behaviour…

He also said that the other reason he does this is because if he comes to bed after me then he doesn't need to turn the light on to see the correct day's tablet and just feels up with his hand, in the dark, for the next one. He doesn't have an iPhone, so I asked him whether his cheapo rubbish phone had a torch on it. He got all bristly at this and said, "Yes it does!"

Unfortunately when he went to show me the touch screen wouldn't work. He flounced off in a huff saying something like, "That will teach me for trying to be considerate and not put the light on in the bedroom and wake you up. I won't bother next time." I chuckled for a few hours about this one… these pills really are good…

Monday 27th June

Missions for today:

- *Do some work*
- *Try and 'up the anti*' with presents bought by visitors*

* I don't know where this phrase comes from and I've probably spelled it wrong. (I've just Googled it and apparently it is ante.) 'Upping the ante' means trying to get something better or raise the stakes.

I was successful in my first mission. As advised by Dr Batman, I am to do reduced hours working from home. Today's presentation was ironically entitled 'Getting the most out of your workers' and one of the slides was 'Responding to your employees' individual needs'. I feel that I have enough real life material to use for this. I like to look on the positive side of life. My blood clot would help me in my job.

My sister came to visit again today and said that they have discovered a wasp's nest in their shed.

I'm wondering whether her husband has put it there. I don't think he likes gardening and I suspect he deliberately hung a hollowed-out rugby ball next to the lawnmower so that he could get out of cutting the lawn. I suspected this more as the story went on as he didn't order the wasp killer through Amazon Prime and cheerily announced that it would be five days before the powder would arrive.

We had a wasp's nest two years ago living in one of the dog's chewed out toys in the paddock. I deduced this when I heard a massive buzzing as I went to throw it and got stung three times on the face. I didn't stop to investigate it further at the time. I should add 'Don't die from wasp stings' to my list of embarrassing ways to die.

I warned my sister that he needed to be really careful and suggested that he buy a cheap bee-keeper type outfit to wear whilst doing it, so that he didn't get stung. We went on Amazon to have a look and chuckled at the fancy dress ones they had for sale (these were the cheapest). One of them advertised a black outfit for Hallowe'en that covered you from head to toe.

Unfortunately, it looked just like something a ninja would wear (with only slits for the eyes) and I had visions of him dressed like this, heading to the shed at night with his wasp powder and a torch and some neighbour jumping over the fence to attack him with a baseball bat mistaking him for a burglar.

We thought it might be more prudent to buy the one that was in Union Jack colours. I don't think burglars tend to dress like this, so there's less chance of him being attacked with a baseball bat. (Unless someone mistakes him for a racist 'Brexit-er' and clobbers him anyway (this is a topical political joke – or so I'm told. We all know I don't do politics.))

One again, I fell asleep while my sister was talking to me. I think if I do it a third time, she is going to (quite rightly) take the huff. I woke up when the home phone started ringing and answered a call from Dad, who was checking that I was still alive. We chatted about my medication and he is a bit worried that there is no antidote to what I'm on and I might die from internal bleeding. "It's not like warfarin where they can give you some Special K to make you better." I wasn't sure that Kellogg's cereal could do that but he had just woken me up, so I didn't argue.

We have another sign language exam on Saturday. I am a bit worried about it. I'm not exactly mentally sound at the moment. Apparently, there is a box on the form that asks about 'special considerations.' I won't be offended if our teacher writes 'temporarily mentally deranged.' Because of our imminent exam, we are going to practise every night. Tonight we met early so we could practise before the England v Iceland football match came on.

Jayne brought me two bunches of flowers, some cream scones, a trifle and lots of hugs and Mel brought biscuits and chocolate brownies and hugs. The presents are getting better and better. The more pictures I put on Facebook the better the next presents are. I reckon next week I might get a new telly, a day at a health spa and afternoon tea at Harrods. The competition is really hotting up. Jayne went to put the flowers in the wine cooler, thinking it was a vase, but luckily Mr H spotted before she did. (I like to think it's because he knew that being made of clay it would leak but I think I heard him say, "As soon as she's off these meds she's going to need wine, so we need that ready.")

As predicted, practising sign language was more entertaining and had a better outcome than the football and none of us are paid £200k a week to do it. (Although, to be fair, I wouldn't turn it down if someone wanted to pay me that much.) The normal jokes on Facebook then started about 'England leave Europe twice in one week' and 'Joe Hart couldn't save anything at Iceland' (with a picture of him in front of the food store) etc.

Tuesday 28th June

Mission for today:

- *Try and wean off the strong meds*

Mr H was glad that he was working this morning and asked his Mum and Dad to come over in his absence. (I think he wanted someone else to be here whilst I was weaning off the strong meds. After the 'crazy mental wife' incident on Saturday morning, he wasn't taking any chances.)

I am sleeping well but randomly seem to wake up at 3:38am at the moment. I have no idea why and have done it two days in a row so far. Mr H slept downstairs as Lucy is obviously back to her attention seeking ways and has decided that as I'm not dead and not about to imminently die, then I should be able to cope with her barking in the night. I didn't wake up to hear her but Mr H had to get up twice with her.

The postman knocked the door this morning and as he handed me a bunch of flowers that had arrived he gave me a sympathetic look and said,

"How are things? I must admit, I was a little worried that you had died what with all the flowers arriving for you." I thanked him for his kind words.

The pain meds warn you that they make you constipated. I haven't done a poo for four days now. I wasn't overly concerned as I knew that when I went I would immediately lose quite a bit of weight and when my blood clot finally goes that should shed some more as well. I'm a stone heavier than I normally am, so I'm hoping that is made up of poo and clot.

Just to be on the safe side, I asked Siri, "How many days is it safe to go without doing a poo?" Siri said, "That's an interesting question" and also couldn't say the word 'poo' without a bit of chuckling at the end. You have got to love these programmers. Unfortunately, most websites were concerned with children not going to the toilet or women worried about their wombs dropping out of their fru-frus after giving birth (there were similar worries about doing big sneezes and the same thing happening).

'Mick' from Dudley said, 'I guess after about two weeks or so, go to the hospital for them to stick a big tube up your butt.' He sounded like a sound medical professional to me...

'Dan' from Newcastle said, 'Just eat a boat load of tacos with chilli – that goes right through me.'

I decided to go back to mumsnet. Those mums are bound to have had constipation what with popping out their sprogs and the slackening of their fru-frus and all. I got a bit freaked out when a box popped up, 'Do you want to join our research panel?' 'No – I do not', I thought. Just in case they could track me down, I switched to using Mr H's laptop.

One mum said that she got so constipated that it felt like she was passing a grapefruit every four-five days and a watermelon by the one month mark. I did not like the sound of this one bit. Grapefruit is really sharp, I didn't want a sharp feeling as a poo shoots out my bum. Another mum said that Vaseline around the 'opening' helped her. We haven't got any of that but I wonder whether Mr H's Swarfega might do the trick?

A lot of the mums were keeping a 'poo chart' so they could work out when they went and how long it lasted. 'Flopsy' (I'm sure this wasn't her real name) said that she had to get on the bathroom floor on all fours and just had to clean it all up afterwards. I contemplated doing this and leaving it, as Lucy eats Bonnie's poo and horse manure, so maybe she would eat mine as well? Of course I'm kidding! I wouldn't do that. There isn't enough room for me to get on all fours in the downstairs loo.

I didn't really find an answer to my question, so gave up. I'm pretty sure that it will come eventually. I'm not going to force it. That's how you get piles and I don't want them. One of the mums on mumsnet, 'Muffins', said that it was like having a bunch of grapes hanging out your bum. Everyone says that fruit is good for you, but seeing all of these references was putting me off it for life.

I didn't follow Dan from Newcastle's advice about eating chilli and tacos but decided that I may as well eat for lunch what I really fancied, as I wasn't convinced the choice of food was going to magically make my poo come out.

I asked my blood clot what it wanted to eat and it gestured to the fresh donuts that Mr H's mum had brought over. When I got back into the lounge Casper was sitting on my laptop and the screen said, 'Do you really want to delete all of the selected items?' I screamed at him and he jumped off and thankfully did not click on the 'yes' button. If he had have done then *#tractor4graham* would have been no more. He obviously still hasn't forgiven him for treading on him a few months ago (Mr H treading on Casper – not the other way round) and really must hate him to delete the one thing that could possibly get Mr H his tractor. Cats really are just like men. They live by their own rules.

Tomorrow I am off to the hairdressers, so will be taking my fold up stool and two big cushions to prop my leg up while the bleach is applied to my hair. I did think about postponing my appointment but seeing my dark roots was likely to send me into a pit of depression more than the thought of being on a dangerous drug for the rest of my life and having another clot. I like to get my priorities in order. Besides which, my tales are getting boring with me not going anywhere...

Wednesday 29th June

Missions for today:

- *Manage to go to the hairdressers without having some embarrassing 'passing out' incident*
- *Try and upload #tractor4graham to see how it will look in print*
- *Delete anyone on Facebook who keeps harping on about politics*

Lucy was wide awake at 2am but when she saw me hobbling down the stairs to let her out, she gave me the look of 'Sorry Mummy – I thought Daddy would get up. Don't you worry, I will be out for a quick wee and settle straight back down.' She did and typically was fast asleep snoring when the alarm went off at 7:50am. We don't need to be up early tomorrow so you can bet that she will bark at 5am.

One of my friends on Facebook was moaning about her child waking her up at 6am every morning and how could she stop it. I suggested a sound-proofed room and a sturdy padlock. I had meant it as a joke but I suspect that the eight 'likes' were from stressed out mums who also had children that woke up at unearthly hours. I felt sorry for one of them when she replied to my comment saying, 'What type of padlock do you think is best?' and it obviously was not a joke. From her profile picture, she looked completely knackered (and given that when you take a picture these days on your phone, you can apply a filter effect that gets rid of worry lines, moles, birth marks, children etc, it made me feel even sorrier for her. If that was the best filter effect for her picture then she really was looking rough).

Out of curiosity, I clicked on her profile and she had a couple of photo albums on there. One was entitled 'Me and Danny' and another was 'The triplets'. Now the haggard look made sense. The pictures in the album of her and Danny were obviously before they had had kids. They were:

-    Tanned…
-    Happy…

- Drinking tequila in some exotic country and…
- Posing next to a donkey wearing a sombrero.

I nearly didn't click on the album 'The triplets' as I thought that it might give me nightmares. I can't watch 'One Born Every Minute' for the same reason. Something the size of a small dog should not come out of one's fru-fru.

I did click on the album though. The triplets looked a friggin' nightmare. They were all boys and about three years old with 'Damian' looks in their eyes. The pictures of her and Danny were completely the opposite of the ones before they had had the three boys:

- They only looked tanned because in a lot of the pictures they seemed to have sick, food, poo or something else smeared down their tops…
- They only looked happy when they were waving goodbye to the children when Granny and Gramps took over…

- They were obviously still drinking tequila but this was in a semi-detached house in Bolton, whilst trying to hold a screaming toddler, rather than some exotic country, and...
- They were posing smiling next to a gorilla's cage at the zoo (No? too soon....?)

This lady had not set her privacy settings as scrolling down her page, I noticed some 'get well' and 'good luck' messages to Danny on his forthcoming op. Turned out that the 'op' was to have his dingle-dangles snipped off*, so that they couldn't have any more children.

* I have no idea how a vasectomy works. I suspect that they don't actually cut your smiley and bouncy balls off but just open up the todger and rip out some of the leads. It's what Mr H does to the leads at the back of the telly when the *YouView* box is playing up and he needs to re-set it.

I went to the hairdressers with my fold up stool and two big cushions. They were really fab (the hairdressers – not the cushions). The disabled really do get treated better. (Apart from when I overheard another customer say, 'Who does she think she is over there? The flippin' Queen? Fancy bringing her own cushions so she doesn't have to sit on someone else's bum sweat. She must be from that new estate in Bushbury and thinks she's better than the rest of us.')

As my hair has been dyed so many times now, it really is still a surprise to me and my hairdresser as to what colour it will come out. I have never had blue hair, so we decided to go with 'Ocean Blue' on the fringe and 'Lilac meadows' on the sides. I'm pretty sure those were the same colour choices my sister had when deciding what colour to paint her log cabin.

'Lilac meadows' wasn't playing ball, so the sides remained blonde but Ocean Blue was lovely with different tones working their way through the root to the tip of my fringe. Mr H initially thought I had had it dyed grey (it was raining and I had my hood up when he came to meet me) and breathed a sigh of relief when he saw the blue. I don't think he is ready to see me as an old woman yet.

Whilst I was in the hairdressers, it was chucking it down with rain outside and I saw a girl of around 19 (both in age and weight in stones) running (with her hands full) across the grass on the other side of the road. Unfortunately for her she was carrying a McDonalds's paper bag and the rain had turned it to mush. Her burger and fries flopped out onto the grass in front of her. She went down on her hands and knees scrabbling around to rescue them. Unluckily for her, a large seagull had spied her lunch and swooped down and grabbed the bun off her burger and flew away with it in its mouth before she could scoop it up. Obviously fearful that she might lose some more of her lunch she started stuffing fries and the rest of the burger into her mouth.

The 'three second' rule of food dropped on the floor seemed to be a three minute rule for her. I don't think I have ever seen anything so sad in my life (not since Isis the dog died in Downton Abbey anyway). The seagull came back at one point and I heard her shout, "Go and get your own - your dirty creature". Unfortunately, just as she said this a guy was walking round the corner and thought that she was talking to him. He replied, "I'm not going to steal your food you daft cow – there's no BBQ sauce on it!" Yep… that's the sole reason as to why I would not be eating it as well. You just can't possibly eat fries off the floor unless they have sauce on them. As usual, Wolverhampton, did not fail to disappoint.

When I went to pay the hairdresser, she saw my bright yellow medical 'Alert' card in my purse and asked what it was. I said that it was something to do with telling paramedics that I was on medicine that meant that my blood wouldn't clot and therefore they needed to know before they cut me open and operated.

She said the same thing that I had thought, "Are they really going to think that you are on that medication at your age and ferret around in your handbag to see if you're carrying a card?" "I doubt it", I said, "I think I might need to get one of those fancy bracelets instead." I must remember to Google this when I'm home…

My brother-in-law helped me with getting *#tractor4graham* closer to publication today. It's exciting to see what it might look like in print. We need to come up with a price. Mr H said, "£24.99. That way I'll get my tractor quite quickly." I like to think that he was joking… I like to think he was…

As we were working through the Amazon process, a courier arrived with more 'Get Well' pressies. These were from my work wife. They consisted of a hamper filled with chocolate, alcohol and biscuits. She is an excellent work wife. I took a picture and put them on Facebook suggesting that if anyone else wanted to buy me presents then I really needed a 50" telly, as I already had lots of flowers. I said that I was joking (I don't want people to think I'm getting cheeky) and said that 60" would be better.

I haven't yet deleted anyone on Facebook who keeps harping on about politics and Brexit. I came to the conclusion that I would only be left with one friend and that would be Mum. But then she went and put something up, so I concluded that I would be left with no one and the 'Get well' pressies are getting better and better all the time. Maybe I will leave them for the time being on the off chance I get more presents... *winky face* (I'm not really that shallow...)

Thursday 30th June

Missions for today:

- *Don't cry as it's the end of the second book*
- *Stop dreaming of poos*
- *Try and restrict the number of pointless conversations with Mr H to three at the most*

The reason why I keep dreaming of poos is because ever since I put the post up on the *tractor4graham* Facebook page, friends have been emailing me with suggestions on how to relieve my constipation. Whilst I am grateful for these suggestions, I am now fixated on poo-ing. I have actually managed to do what looked like 30 rabbit droppings. It did occur to me that even though I couldn't get down on all fours in the wet room (due to the size of it – the wet room that is – not my poos), I could actually just get down on all fours on the front garden.

As my poos look like rabbit poos then I could just pretend that we had a wild rabbit visit us and it had done it. I would sow the seeds in Mr H's mind first. I would say, "Did you just see that? I'm sure I just saw a huge rabbit run across the lawn." I would do this while we were practising sign language, as it would catch him off guard. I would also drop it in to the conversation that a giant rabbit had gone missing on the estate close by and that I had seen a post on Facebook asking people to watch out for it.

When Mr H saw my big pile of rabbit poo on the garden, I would then be able to exclaim, "Told you – and you laughed at me saying that I had seen a massive rabbit." I would then try not to gag as Lucy came along to eat it. My plan does have some flaws to it. Squatting on all fours on the front garden could result in a number of people seeing me. I might have to do it at 2am when Lucy barks to go out for a wee. I'm hoping I don't traumatise her. She's not used to me using the garden as a toilet – well except for that one time I came home having had too much to drink and couldn't get to the loo in time.

Today seemed to be a day for totally pointless conversations with Mr H. I have been weaning off the strong painkillers, as my leg is doing really well. But I have realised that coming off them has a downside. I don't find things as funny and I'm less able to cope with Mr H's man-nonsense if I don't have any pain relief inside me. I do wonder whether this is why statistically women take more pain medication than men (and drink more as well). It must be the only ways to block out their nonsense.

Here were the totally pointless conversations we had:

1. Totally pointless conversation number one...

This was a conversation that we have on at least a weekly basis. (It hasn't featured in my books so far but that's because I didn't really want to traumatise all of you with the madness of it.) It is a conversation on 'how to load the dishwasher.' Mr H is a dishwasher Nazi. (I'm now allowed to use

that word because of Brexit – No? Too soon?
Man – you're a harsh bunch.)

He will re-open the dishwasher after I have
loaded it, sigh in an overly exaggerative
fashion and re-load it a different way. Why
he wastes five minutes of his life doing this I
will never know. He then wastes three
minutes of my life telling me where I've gone
wrong. It makes no difference and we will go
through the same palaver time and time
again. If you live with a dishwasher N**I, you
will feel my pain.

"Why do you put the wooden spoons in
there? You know you shouldn't put wood in
a dishwasher? Why do you put my non-stick
pan in there? We've had this conversation
before. Haven't you learned yet? You need
to make sure that the plastic Chinese
containers are stable and the right way
round, otherwise they will flip over and just
hold the dirty water. And then what are you
going to do?"

I assumed that his question was rhetorical but just in case he thought that I wasn't paying attention (which I wasn't – whilst he was ranting there was a spider in a web that had just caught a fly and I was mesmerised watching the spider wrap the fly up in its silk before eating it) I said, "I just leave it in there again for next time. The dishwasher needs to learn that if it doesn't clean things properly the first time, then it needs to try again." He sighed again, started banging plates down on the side and shook his head at me.

He then carried on with some other rant about the cost of electricity, blah, blah, blah. I left him to his re-arranging of the plates and bowls and went to watch telly (and take some more painkillers).

2. Totally pointless conversation number two...

As I have already told you before, Mr H does the washing in our house because it's an easy job and it makes him think that he's contributing to a lot of the inside cleaning duties. I decided to be helpful and got the washing out of the machine to hang it up to dry. (Given my gammy leg at the moment, I thought I was being extra helpful.) I noticed that a lot of the clothes seemed to have a white-ish powder type finish to them.

As I got the last few bits out of the machine, I also pulled out a chewed up tissue. Someone* (not me) had obviously left a tissue in a pocket and it had ruined the load of washing in there. I made the mistake of saying to Mr H, "Did you leave a tissue in one of your pockets, as one has gone through the machine?"

* Someone is Mr H

Never mind the outcry on Facebook from Brexit this last week, I thought he was going to explode. "Well, it's got to be one of yours. I don't use tissues." I could agree with the last part of that sentence. I've seen him pick his nose before and wipe it on his jeans. But having scrupulous hygiene, I only ever use a tissue once and then put it in the bin, so I did not agree with the first part of the sentence. Knowing that it really didn't matter where the tissue had come from, I just shrugged and said, "Well – never mind. It's happened." Mr H then spent another five pointless minutes counting the hankies in the washing basket to show that he had used one a day and it wasn't his tissue. He then went through all of the pockets of his clothes that had gone in the wash to check that there was no tissue debris, to prove it wasn't him. Once again, I got bored and wandered off to watch some telly...

3. Totally pointless conversation number three...

I can't now remember what our third pointless conversation was about. To be honest, I was a bit tired with it all and fell asleep on the settee for two hours. It seems that my blood clot needed a rest from all of the drama. I woke up dribbling out the side of my mouth. I really need to stop this. I'm turning into an old person.

Oh! I've remembered what it was. We were going to bed and Mr H was wriggling his bum whilst getting under the covers. "Are you ok?" I asked, thinking, 'I hope it's only piles and not something contagious.' I've had enough medical issues for the time being. He brought his hand out from under the covers and said, "So – what have you been eating in bed?" It looked like a stalk from a grape. "Well – it's obviously not me – we all know I don't eat fruit," I said. We then had another three minute totally pointless conversation where he was trying to prove that it was nothing to do with him. I think he's been watching too much *Law & Order*. Calling it 'Exhibit B' was not a normal reaction to finding it.

I did start wishing that Lucy would bark to go out for a wee so I could escape his man nonsense (and also I was feeling the need to do my rabbit poos...)

Tonight we were good students again and practised our sign language, as our exam is in two days. I'm a bit concerned that this blood clot has made me a bit woolly headed and instead of asking our teacher, "What hobbies do you enjoy in the evening?" I will end up asking, "Do you like sex in the evening?" It is a filmed five minute conversation and goes off to an external assessor. I'm not sure whether there is a criteria on the marking guide of 'decency' for the content of the conversation.

As me, Jayne and Mel were laughing our heads off, Mr H went all serious on us and said, "If you're not going to take it seriously, I don't think you should be practising." In the next breath he then said, "Oh no! I forgot Wales were playing in the football tomorrow night – I'll have to leave sign language class early to catch it." Us three girls just stared at him with a 'What a hypocrite' look on our faces. He looked back and said, "What? Why are you all looking at me like that?"

Our sign language catch ups are always totally hilarious. As we were finishing we put the telly on and there was some programme or other about talking about Brexit (apparently it was the 'News' – I don't watch it – so how would I know?) Jayne said, "I'm glad Fromage isn't standing for Prime Minister." Mr H said, "I think you mean Farage?" We then chuckled and said, "Well with a name like Fromage he's going to be expelled from the country when Brexit happens." Deaf people have a sign name – so we decided that Farage's would have to be the sign for 'cheese'. Shame visually it looks like someone is giving someone else a blow job...We all decided that that conversation should totally have been on *Gogglebox.*

To make matters even more funny – we turned over the telly and realised that Portugal and Poland were playing in the Euros. Just as we turned over a streaker ran across the pitch followed by about ten officials and was rugby tackled to the ground. Initially we didn't think it was a streaker, but when we re-wound the telly, we could see that he was only wearing a t-shirt.

You couldn't really see anything as his t-shirt covered his dingle-dangles. I then said, "Well you know what streakers do beforehand... they shave 'down there' so that their thing looks loads longer." "Who told you that?" said Mr H. I had no idea but Jayne saved the day by saying, "Is that why bald men have bigger heads?"

Jayne then told us the story of when she 'accidentally' went to see a stripper and got pulled up on stage by him. She had been in a pub and had heard music coming from one of the rooms at the back and a private function was taking place. Her and a few friends had wandered in and a stripper had come on stage. She said that apparently her friend said that they attach 'it' to a vacuum cleaner to make it longer, as his was really long.

We then had a discussion along the lines of men and women coming home from a night out saying, "Get the Dyson out love", I'm in the mood! "What if you got it stuck? Imagine if you had to go to A+E to get it removed?" I said. Jayne said that her friend was a nurse in A+E and had seen it all. Women who were attached to chairs, men who had it stuck in vacuum cleaner hoses – the lot. "At least if A+E was busy, then she would have somewhere to sit," I said. We really shouldn't have started looking at the videos for the sign for 'vacuum'. Our conversations in our exam really need to be sensible.

I think Mr H was a bit worn out from all of the pointless conversations today, as he fell asleep during his favourite programme. I lost to 'Rock, Paper, Scissors, Lizard, Spock' (we need to start playing something else – I always lose at it) and we had to watch *Question Time*. He's never fallen asleep during it before. I snuck off to bed and put on Law & Order instead but when Mr H woke up, he promptly came upstairs, turned over the telly saying, "You've got the wrong side on." I should have been annoyed but I was in the middle of a conversation with one of my friends on Facebook. We are considering lesbianism and she said that she would have to be the butch one. I said that she couldn't be the butch one as she had massive boobs whereas I had tiddly tits.

She said that she wished that she had tiddly tits as they always got in the way. It's a good job I don't have them. I would have to fling one over each shoulder if I was gardening to get them out the way and I would probably set fire to them leaning over the hob. I should be grateful for this aspect of my genetics from Mum's side of the family and not Dad's...

So Tractor-ites...

- We have come to the end of another book and another two months of totally pointless conversations between Mr H and I (which I suspect also take place in a lot of households across the UK)...

- Life in the Hughes' household has had a bit of a blip with my blood clot and the delay in the Alpaca stable means that George, Chester and Cyril haven't arrived yet either...

- Mr H is still oblivious to the new pillow and is also oblivious to the new underpants and annoyingly is still oblivious to the hogging of the remote control (which I also suspect is a common occurrence in other households)...

- I hope that you have enjoyed this second book and that I have made you chuckle and as a result that Mr H's tractor fund will continue to grow...

- I also hope that James (Dyson) will sympathise with my plight and send me a new Dyson Animal vacuum cleaner (I prefer the upright ones, James), so that I can set fire to my other vacuum cleaner...

- As I'm writing this, July and August have actually happened (and tales have been written) and unfortunately life has taken even more twists and turns in our household (and sadly not of the good variety) which you will read about in the next book...

- Remember to follow the Facebook page *tractor4graham* for cheeky snippets from the forthcoming books and please encourage all of your friends to download the kindle version (it nets more royalties for Mr H) than the paperback. Just kidding – buy them both, so that when you're on holiday, people can see the book that you're reading ;)

Seriously, a big thank you for buying this book (I can't take his moaning for much longer...)

ACKNOWLEDGEMENTS

Big thanks again to all the encouragement to write these tales, from friends and family.

Two special mahoosive thanks to:

Angela Buckley for being my first time through reader again (and once again - any mistakes are totally her fault...)

Nick White who has (again) been a proof reader and (again) made excellent suggestions to make the first draft much better. "It couldn't get much worse," I hear ringing in my ears from Robin Wiggs...

Printed in Great Britain
by Amazon

84836503R10318